DRAGONWATCH

ALSO BY BRANDON MULL

DRAGONWATCH

BRANDON MULL

ILLUSTRATED BY
BRANDON DORMAN

SHADOW
MOUNTAIN

Library of Congress Cataloging-in-Publication Data

Names: Mull, Brandon, 1974– author.
Title: Dragonwatch / Brandon Mull.
Description: Salt Lake City, Utah : Shadow Mountain, [2017] | First in a
    sequel series to Fablehaven. | Summary: Because Dragonwatch, an ancient
    group of wizards, enchantresses, and dragon slayers, is crumbling, an
    uprising of dragons threatens to destroy the magical preserves as well as
    overrun the nonmagical world.
Identifiers: LCCN 2016043181 | ISBN 9781629722566 (hardbound : alk.
    paper)
Subjects: | CYAC: Magic—Fiction. | Dragons—Fiction.
Classification: LCC PZ7.M9112 Dr 2017 | DDC [Fic]—dc23 LC record
    available at https://lccn.loc.gov/2016043181

Printed in the United States of America
LSC Communications, Crawfordsville, IN

10   9   8   7   6   5   4   3   2

For my partners in dragon tag:
Sadie, Chase, Rose, and Calvin

Contents

CONTENTS

From the Journal of Stan Sorenson

Could this be the end?

Will I be counted among the last of the caretakers? Could this long-standing trust dissolve during my watch?

I have loved Fablehaven since I first beheld the wonders disguised here. Most in the modern world cannot guess at the splendors concealed on these enchanted refuges, where creatures of legend hunt and frolic. More than fifty years have passed since Fablehaven won my heart.

But it comes with a price.

How far am I willing to go to fulfill my duty? To protect the magical sanctuaries of the world? I made peace with sacrificing my own life long ago. But what about the lives of others? What about my family?

I have longed to share the marvels of Fablehaven with those I love most. But knowledge of those miracles means exposure to the dangers as well. Magical creatures can dazzle. They can also kill. For me, the wonder outweighs the threat. But what right do I have to make that decision for another?

I never forced anyone to discover what is really happening at Fablehaven. Certainly not my grandchildren. But I let their curiosity lead them to the truth. After drinking the milk from Viola, the magical milch cow, Kendra and Seth could recognize that the butterflies here were actually fairies, the goats were satyrs, and the horses were centaurs. That first time is so incredible. And it never becomes ordinary.

I could have prevented it. But I allowed Fablehaven to unfold for them.

Inevitably, it took hold of them. As it always does.

And peril followed.

Kendra and Seth know my real reason for living at Fablehaven. As caretaker, I serve the inhabitants of this preserve and protect the outside world from them. I am fed by experiences that stretch the definition of reality. I behold spectacles known by none except those with access to these extraordinary sanctuaries.

My grandchildren appreciate the responsibility of protecting these refuges. They have shown willingness to sacrifice as well.

I thought we had survived the worst of it. We were pushed to our limits. Our lives were in jeopardy. Loved ones died. Kendra and Seth were almost lost, but in the end, they tipped the scales to save us all.

But now they may be needed again.

I believe I can protect them. But I have wrongly believed that before.

Once again, frankly, I don't know what to do. My responsibility is plain. But how far am I willing to go? How much am I able to risk?

Is it fair to give them a choice?

Is it even a choice, when I know what they will choose?

CHAPTER ONE

Eavesdropping

Kendra Sorenson jogged through the warm mist, damp gravel crunching underfoot, wondering if the moisture in the air was falling enough to be called rain. Sprinkles, maybe. She glanced up at the gray blur of the sky beyond the treetops, then over at a trio of fairies, each surrounded by a hazy halo of light. Nothing pattered against the hood of her windbreaker, but it was wet, as were the leafy branches on either side of the long driveway.

This was the murkiest morning of the summer, at least since Kendra had started jogging. The fifteen-year-old typically got up just before sunrise and ran around the perimeter of the big yard three times. Each lap included running up the driveway to the gate and back. Any larger route would either take her beyond the boundaries of Fablehaven, exposing her to threats from outside the preserve, or else make her vulnerable to some of the dangers held back by the magic protecting the yard. Roaming the woods of the sanctuary was not a safe proposition.

There had been no sunrise to watch today. The grayness had simply grown brighter as she followed her standard path, soles slipping on the wet grass.

The gate came into view up ahead, closed as usual—wrought-iron topped with fleurs-de-lis, the only potential opening in the fence that enclosed the entire preserve. Kendra always touched the gate before turning around.

As she approached the black bars and reached out a hand, Kendra paused. She heard a motor approaching, and tires mashing gravel.

That was highly unusual.

The gate to Fablehaven was well back from the main road. A distracter spell helped motorists ignore the nondescript turnoff, and you didn't have to travel far along the driveway before finding several emphatic signs warning away trespassers.

People did not come to Fablehaven by accident.

And when visitors were expected, it was big news. Grandpa or Grandma Sorenson inevitably brought it up ahead of time. Often the gate was left open for the arrival.

So who was approaching?

Who might come to Fablehaven unannounced?

An old friend? A spy? An enemy?

Or somebody really lost and fairly illiterate.

In case the visitor was an enemy, Kendra hurried off the driveway, withdrawing into the trees and crouching behind some shrubs. Leaving the driveway reduced her protection from magical threats, but trouble seldom happened this close to a protected area. The chance to hide seemed worth the small risk.

Before long, a white sedan pulled into view and parked just outside the gate. A cowled figure emerged from the vehicle.

Kendra had a hood herself. The weather called for covering your head. But the hooded brown robe of the stranger looked to have come from a bygone era. It deliberately concealed the face in deep shadow. This was no lost tourist. It might not even be human. This had to be somebody who knew about preserves for magical creatures.

Was the stranger going to try to break in? The gate wasn't visible from the house, but parking on the driveway didn't seem very subtle.

Then Kendra heard crunchy footsteps on the gravel from the direction of the house. She remained frozen as Grandpa Sorenson strode into view, wearing a jacket and a baseball cap. She held her breath as he walked up to the gate. It didn't open.

"You want to talk?" Grandpa called through the bars to the robed figure.

"Briefly, yes," the figure replied in a raspy voice.

As Captain of the Knights of the Dawn, the organization that policed the magical preserves of the world, Grandpa met from time to time with various individuals who provided information. Those exchanges often happened in his office. Apparently he also sometimes met informants at the gate.

Kendra felt guilty for eavesdropping, but it seemed more awkward to announce herself at this point. She hunkered lower behind the shrubs.

"The situation continues to deteriorate," the cowled figure warned. "They will most likely be needed. The boy should settle his affair with the Sisters."

"I understand he has the better part of a year to meet their terms," Grandpa said.

"Owing the Sisters is no small concern," the figure insisted. "Who knows where he might end up over the coming months? What if circumstances prevent him from paying his debt? Why not seize the moment? For how long do you want the sword in his possession? It is powerful, but is it safe? That weapon has a history of corrupting those who wield it."

"I hear you," Grandpa said. "I'll consider advising him. Any word from Soaring Cliffs?"

"No good tidings," the figure responded, taking a step back. "I should depart. We'll be in touch."

"Thank our mutual friend," Grandpa said.

"Thank him by taking the necessary action, Stan Sorenson," the figure warned. "This could quickly become a bigger mess than the previous crisis. Prepare while you have time."

Grandpa glanced down the driveway back toward the house.

"Expecting someone?" the figure asked.

"My granddaughter is out for her morning run," Stan said.

"I must away," the figure said, retreating to his car.

Grandpa started back to the house without a wave.

The engine started, and the vehicle rolled forward and back to make a multipoint turn. By the time the sedan passed out of sight, Kendra could no longer hear her grandfather.

She waited in silence until the sound of the car faded to nothing.

What had she just heard? They had to be talking about her younger brother, Seth. Kendra knew that he had made a deal with some witches to find the legendary sword Vasilis. But why was some shady outsider taking an interest? And what big problem was brewing? Whose help was needed? It sounded like the trouble could involve her and her brother.

Kendra crept back to the road and looked down it carefully. Grandpa was no longer in sight; he had probably entered the house. She jogged back to the yard, then did part of another lap before quitting and going inside.

She found Grandpa Sorenson in his study.

"Good morning, Kendra," he said.

"Good morning," she replied, watching him. He seemed relaxed.

"Strange weather today," Grandpa observed.

"Gray and soggy. Did we have a visitor?"

Grandpa scrunched his eyebrows. "Why would you think that?"

Kendra weighed how much to say. "I noticed you walking down the driveway."

Grandpa smiled. "Just checking the gate. I do that when I get restless."

"Okay," Kendra said. She didn't want to press him. "See you later."

She walked from the room. It wasn't like Grandpa to lie. Part of his job both as a caretaker of Fablehaven and as Captain of the Knights involved keeping secrets. She had no doubt that Grandpa would lie to protect a secret he thought might be harmful to others.

It bothered Kendra to know part of a story that probably involved her and her brother. Should she tell Grandpa she had seen the stranger? Should she relate what she had heard? Should she demand to know the identity of the mysterious figure? Should she ask why she and her brother might be needed?

Her instincts warned her that further probing would yield little fruit. Whatever the details might be, Grandpa wasn't ready to share. And he was a professional at keeping secrets.

Should she talk to Seth about it? Kendra doubted whether her brother could keep this quiet, especially since it involved him directly and there was more to find out. For now it might be best to worry and wonder on her own. Whatever secrets Grandpa and this stranger knew, one thing seemed clear—serious trouble was coming.

CHAPTER TWO

A Promise Kept

Seth crept deeper underground, flashlight in hand. Pale roots corkscrewed from the glistening muck of the curved ceiling. Some caves had a rich, earthy smell, full of gritty minerals. This was not one of them. Things were rotting down here. Bugs were breeding and slime was spreading. The uneven floor of the tunnel squelched beneath every step.

The wraith beside him did little to cheer the atmosphere. Not quite alive and not quite dead, it strode silently, disturbingly still even when in motion, the darkest shape in the shadowy tunnel, radiating coldness and an unnerving aura of fear. Some would have stood immobilized in the presence of the wraith, horrified, speechless, struggling to breathe. And the wraith might have crept up to them and temporarily relieved its own iciness by draining their warmth.

But ever since Seth had become a shadow charmer, not only could he endure the presence of the undead, he could even communicate with some of them. The surest way to survive the company of a wraith was to strike a bargain. Seth had pledged to free this wraith from the dungeon below Fablehaven and deliver it to new owners in exchange for the wraith obeying and protecting him until the transfer was complete.

A few months prior, in order to learn the location of the storied sword Vasilis, Seth had promised to bring the Singing Sisters the sword and a wraith. He had also agreed to fulfill one additional assignment of their choice. If he failed to keep the arrangement, an enchanted knife was ready to hunt him down and kill him. So he had selected the most companionable wraith he could find and set off on a road trip to Missouri with Grandpa Sorenson and the satyrs Newel and Doren. Even with the wraith being transported in a trailer behind their vehicle, its chilly presence had kept the other passengers on edge.

On his only previous visit to the Sisters, Seth had entered through a door in a high bluff. This time, the Sentinel who guarded access to this narrow island in the Mississippi River had informed him that return visitors should enter through a low tunnel on the other side. Neither Grandpa nor the satyrs had been allowed to join him. Since arriving on the island and finding the muddy cave, Seth and the wraith had met no living creatures.

Vasilis dangled from a sword belt Seth had slung over one shoulder. Seth was reluctant to part with the legendary Sword of Light and Darkness. He technically had a full year to return the blade after striking the deal that let him find it, and the time was not yet up. But the weapon had served its purpose, helping him and Kendra hold off the demons who had emerged from Zzyzx. Bracken the unicorn had suggested Seth settle his debt with the Sisters early rather than waiting until the last minute—in case something prevented him from fulfilling his promise. Grandpa had agreed and encouraged him to get it over with.

Normally Seth adhered to a fairly rigid policy of procrastination, but the threat of a knife pursuing him across the globe intent on ending his life helped persuade him otherwise. That and the boring months since the demonic apocalypse had been averted. With his Grandpa and Grandma Sorenson running Fablehaven alongside his Grandpa and Grandma Larsen, life had been woefully uneventful. A road trip had sounded like a welcome relief.

Giving up the wraith was no problem. Early on the drive, the shadowy form had earned the nickname Whiner. But Seth was going to miss the sword. As souvenirs went, a magic weapon was hard to beat.

The tunnel ended at a corroded door. When Seth knocked, it produced little sound. Though scarred on the surface, the wood was thick.

"You're almost home," Seth told the wraith.

Icy words reached his mind in reply. *There can be no home for me. Only unrest.*

"I felt a little like that in the car," Seth replied, trying to keep the conversation light. "Hard to get comfy. My rear kept going numb." The undead tended to dwell on emptiness and yearning. Get them started and it sometimes became hard to shut off. Especially this guy. "Think I knocked loud enough?" He gave the door a couple of kicks.

It swung open to reveal a warty face with bulging yellow eyes. "Who dares rap upon this portal?"

"Good question," Seth said. "You really should wash it."

The river troll blinked in confusion. "This is a domain of perils untold."

"I've been told," Seth said. "I came here before. The Sisters know me."

Leaning forward, the tall troll squinted at him. "Yes, the boy. I suppose you have a right to pass this way. You're not expected for some time."

"I'm early," Seth said. "I brought what they wanted." He touched the hilt of the sword and gestured at the wraith.

The troll took a step back as his gaze shifted to the wraith. "I see. Very well. Since you are returning to fulfill an assignment, you enter by invitation."

Seth glanced at the wraith. "I think you'll like him," he whispered to the troll while stepping across the threshold. "Great roommate. One of the guys."

Long feet flapping against the ground, the troll led them along a corridor that looked like a pale gray throat. The troll periodically glanced back at the wraith, clearly unsettled. Apparently even other monsters didn't love the idea of having their life leeched from them.

The corridor sloped down before opening into a damp chamber cratered with puddles. Huge white maggots stretched and flexed grotesquely, pale flesh rippling, one in each little pool. Several short trolls with puffy builds and oversized heads scuttled away at the approach of Seth and the wraith.

Around one of the puddles, three women stood in a ring. They had no hands. Instead, their wrists were fused together to form a conjoined circle. Seth recalled that the tall, skinny one was Berna. The flabby one with the droopy flesh on her arms was Wilna. The shortest, Orna, had acted nicest on his previous visit. The sisters shifted to better see him. Wilna had to look over her shoulder.

"Seth Sorenson," Berna greeted. "You return well before we expected you."

"Can't you see the future?" Seth asked, trying not to breathe too deeply. The chamber smelled sweet and rotten, like a decaying mix of mushy fruit.

"We don't peer down every avenue," Orna said. "Ruins the suspense."

"We could have sent the covenant knife after you," Wilna said. "You weren't supposed to reveal our arrangement to anyone."

"It wasn't my fault," Seth complained. "Bracken read my mind. He's a unicorn. I didn't tell him."

"She knows that," Orna said. "Otherwise you would already be dead. And such a shame! You're starting out on a path much like the one walked by your great-great-granduncle."

"I have a long way to go before I can compare myself to Patton Burgess," Seth said.

"Don't be so hasty to dismiss the comparison," Orna warned in gentle tones. "It's why I like you."

"We voted two to one against sending the knife," Berna said. "Orna vouched for you because you intrigue her. I joined her because I sense you could be useful."

"Our private agreement leaked to outsiders," Wilna complained with a scowl. "We were within our rights to slay the boy."

"And then we would have no sword and no wraith," Berna said. "That wraith could come in handy."

"The boy still owes us a favor," Orna added. "And don't forget Nagi Luna."

"You heard about that?" Seth asked. He had killed two ancient demons with Vasilis—Nagi Luna and Graulas.

"Why would we need to hear of it?" Wilna snapped. "We can behold such events at our leisure."

"Are you . . . angry?" Seth asked.

The three sisters cackled and swayed, wrists creaking.

"Because Nagi Luna mentored dozens of witches?" Orna asked through her giggles.

"Well, yeah," Seth said. "I guess you heard about Gorgrog, too?"

The witches laughed harder.

"What witch with any right to the title would have failed to note the fall of the Demon King?" Berna asked.

Seth felt confused by the merriment. "Don't witches get their power from demons?"

"That is more or less true," Orna said, using her shoulder to rub away mirthful tears. "But the power comes at a price." She raised her arms, which lifted the connected arms of her sisters. "The demons are our sponsors but seldom our friends. Fear and respect are not the same as love. The fall of a high demon can be . . . delicious."

"To see the king brought low by a child . . ." Berna said.

"An amusing day for one and all," Wilna concluded.

Seth couldn't take credit for slaying the Demon King. His sister, Kendra, had done it. "You're glad the demons were imprisoned after their escape?" Seth verified.

"Oh, my, on the whole, yes," Orna said. "Imagine all the groveling and bootlicking we would have to do with so many powerful demon lords on the prowl."

"It would have shaken things up," Berna said. "No doubt about it."

"We could have found ways to turn an age of demonic rule to our advantage," Wilna asserted stiffly.

"It would have been complicated," Orna said.

"It's always complicated," Wilna replied. "Now we have the dragons to worry about."

"But they have less direct interest in us," Berna said.

"Dragons?" Seth asked.

"No free predictions," Wilna said.

"Did I ask for a prediction?" Seth asked.

"Your future is entwined with the rise of the great wyrms," Orna said.

Berna jerked Orna to one side. "Stop blabbing!"

"Don't pull me!" Orna griped, yanking Berna hard enough to make her stumble.

"You saw my future?" Seth asked.

"We observe many futures," Wilna said. "Not all come to pass."

"Are you going to send me on a mission involving dragons?" Seth wondered.

Wilna narrowed her eyes suspiciously. "You sound hopeful."

Seth shrugged. "I missed some of the dragon stuff at Wyrmroost. I was stuck in a knapsack. The dragons looked really cool at Zzyzx."

"Told you," Orna said. "Patton all over again."

"We have not yet settled on your task," Berna said.

"Are you sure?" Seth checked. "I wouldn't mind getting it over with."

"Why the hurry to repay us?" Wilna asked.

"Things have been kind of dull around Fablehaven," Seth said. "And it doesn't seem like a good idea to owe favors to witches."

"Dullness won't be a problem for long," Orna said.

"Hush," Wilna ordered.

"Why?" Seth asked.

"Turbulent times await us all," Wilna stated.

"You brought the sword," Berna said. "And the wraith appears serviceable."

"It's great," Seth assured them. "Hungry. Cold. Lonely. Everything you could want in an undead servant."

Empty, the wraith thought at them.

"And empty," Seth agreed. "Thirsty, too. Fun at parties."

"You'll serve us?" Wilna asked the wraith.

Seth sensed the answer in his mind. *The boy brought me as a gift. I will serve.*

"It would appear Seth Sorenson has paid back two of his three promises," Berna said.

"I'm happy to do the third now," Seth reminded them. "I get to use the sword for it, right?"

"Leave the wraith and the sword," Wilna said. "We'll contact you when the time comes for your task."

"When will that be?" Seth asked.

"When it suits us," Wilna replied. "Good day."

"Do you want my e-mail address?" Seth asked.

"We have ways to reach you," Berna assured him.

Seth unshouldered the sword and set it down. He turned to the wraith. "Behave for the witches. Thanks for volunteering."

So very cold, the wraith expressed. *No peace. No rest.*

"I'll miss you too," Seth said. "It was a blast." He turned to the witches. "Anything else?"

"Not unless you care to strike a new bargain," Orna suggested hopefully.

"Not today," Seth said. "Especially since I still owe you a service."

"Our business is concluded for now," Wilna said. "Begone."

"Or linger uninvited," Berna suggested sneakily.

"I'll go," Seth said, moving toward the way he had entered. "If you forget to ask for a favor, I'll forgive you."

The three sisters cackled.

"Don't fret about that," Orna said.

"We always collect on our debts," Berna said.

"Our dealings are far from complete, Seth Sorenson," Wilna said. "We spared you from the covenant knife. Kindly repay the courtesy by staying alive."

"What's coming?" Seth asked, still moving away.

Wilna grew grave. "No hints. Knowledge comes at a price."

"Maybe a little hint?" Orna asked.

"No," Berna insisted.

"I have my own mouth and my own mind," Orna fumed. "We already gave it away." She gazed intently at Seth. "A storm is coming. A storm of dragons."

"Orna!" Berna and Wilna cried in dismay.

"You won't have to wait long," Orna promised.

"Good, I guess," Seth replied. "I've never liked waiting."

CHAPTER THREE

The Fairy Realm

A pair of oars propelled the rowboat toward the tiny island, stirring up miniature whirlpools with each powerful stroke. Twelve graceful pavilions surrounded the modest lake, connected by whitewashed boardwalks. Beyond the pavilions, satyrs wrestled on green fields encompassed by hedge walls.

Kendra knew that most at Fablehaven feared the Fairy Queen's shrine. The typical trespasser would be immediately turned to dandelion fluff. It had happened before.

But today was more exciting than scary. Bracken sat opposite her in the rowboat, manning the oars, eyes on her as he guided the craft. Though she knew he was a unicorn, Kendra had never seen him in his horse shape. Bracken had become trapped in human form after surrendering his third and final horn to create an artifact that helped lock the demon prison. All Kendra had ever seen was a teenage boy who looked a couple of years older than her. His silver-blond hair, boyishly handsome features, flawless skin, and penetrating eyes hinted at his true identity—son of the Fairy Queen, a young man of astonishing power and purity.

And she suspected he might have romantic feelings for her. But despite her best efforts to crack his shell, he kept his distance. She was still hoping for a first kiss!

"Are you sure this is all right?" Kendra asked as the prow of the boat slid against the muddy bank of the island.

He flashed a reassuring smile. "I told you my mother granted permission. That is the definition of 'all right' in the fairy realm."

"No humans have ever been there?" Kendra asked.

"Never," Bracken said. "You're setting a new precedent. Mother kept it closed off to the outside world, especially after Gorgrog captured Father."

Kendra shivered at the mention of the Demon King. She could still picture him, titanic in size, a vast tangle of contorted antlers sprouting from his bullish head. Chains had dangled from his wide belt, allowing him to drag around his most prized victims, including the Fairy King. After Kendra had killed the Demon King with Vasilis, the Fairy King had been rescued.

"How is your father?" Kendra asked.

Bracken lowered his eyes. "Not much has changed since we found him. His body is whole, but he keeps to himself and hardly speaks. Others still have to feed him, though at times he will wander on his own."

"I'm so sorry," Kendra said.

Bracken brightened. "It's not your fault. Kendra, you saved him. Most of us figured he was dead. I wish we had known! I would have mounted a rescue. Mother warned me his recovery would take time. After all, he was dragged around inside Zzyzx for centuries, chained to the Demon King. It's a miracle he survived."

"I can't imagine how horrible that would have been," Kendra said, trying not to picture it.

"We're lucky to have him back." Bracken vaulted gracefully from the rowboat and Kendra followed, unable to avoid noticing how clumsy and slow her efforts seemed compared to his effortless coordination. Watching her with eyes that made her feel like the only real thing in the universe, Bracken took her hand.

Three female heads popped up out of the pond not far from the island, and three eager smiles gleamed.

"Hi, Bracken," one of the naiads called in a flirty sing-song.

"Pretty day," another remarked coyly.

"Care for a swim?" the third offered.

Kendra frowned. Normally naiads only welcomed men into their waters so they could drown them. But Bracken was different. Part of his superstar status among magical creatures meant naiads actually wanted his affection. Normally the aquatic maidens would have harassed the rowboat, but the crossing had been tranquil. Kendra had even seen Bracken carelessly throw off his shirt and swim with the naiads before, never experiencing any trouble.

"Hi, Chiatra!" Bracken said. "Good to see you, Zolie! Hey, Ulline."

Kendra watched the naiads blush as their names were spoken.

"Sorry, I can't swim right now," Bracken went on. "I'm taking Kendra to the fairy realm."

Three sets of glaring eyes fixed on Kendra.

"Did you need somebody to sweep up the place?" Chiatra teased.

"Is she going to be sacrificed?" Zolie wondered.

"It's part of our job to forbid the unworthy," Ulline said.

"Be nice, ladies," Bracken said. "Your orders come from my mother. You know Kendra is coming with permission, as my guest."

Ulline and Zolie rolled their eyes and disappeared beneath the water. Chiatra looked Kendra up and down with naked disgust. "I don't get it," she said before vanishing below the gently rippling surface.

"Your fan club doesn't approve," Kendra said. The naiads all had lovely faces. Kendra knew any of them would belong to Bracken in a heartbeat if he showed any interest.

"Don't waste any thought on them. They're silly and harmless."

"Unless they drown me."

Bracken furrowed his brow. "I'll talk to Mother. We ought to forbid that."

He led the way to where a spring bubbled up out of the ground. A two-inch statue of a fairy stood nearby atop a small pedestal. A silver bowl rested close at hand as well.

It had been some time since Kendra had visited the Fairy Queen's shrine.

"How do we cross over?" Kendra asked.

"Simple," Bracken said, but he suddenly seemed hesitant.

"What?" Kendra asked.

His posture slumped a little. "There has been a lot of buildup to this. I don't want you to be disappointed."

"Why would I be disappointed?"

Bracken grimaced. "The splendor of the old fairy realm was unreal. We sacrificed all that to create a new prison for the demons. Zzyzx was a mess when Mother and the others claimed it and began to transform it. This new home is still developing."

"It makes me sad to think of the demons wrecking your old realm."

"It's what got them inside," Bracken said. "In all their millennia of evil, none of them even saw the fairy realm. The chance to go there and spoil it was too hard to resist. Especially when the alternative was to fight dragons. Before they knew it, our old home became their new prison."

"And their prison became your new home," Kendra said.

"It was available," Bracken said. "Like our previous realm, the prison was a pocket dimension tied to your reality. The demons left the way open, and we were free to move in. There was lots of space. We've put in loads of work. Don't forget, Zzyzx held many of the most powerful demons in the world for thousands of years. It wasn't just a mess—it was horrifying. Nobody can purify like unicorns. And beautifying is what fairies do. But plenty of work remains."

"Can I help?" Kendra asked.

"Who knows?" Bracken replied. "Your fairykind status makes you a powerful source of magical energy."

"I'd love to be your battery," Kendra said. "I can't wait to see your home."

"I'll show you a lot," Bracken said. "Mother won't let anyone inside the palace yet. She refuses to accept anything short of perfection there."

"Maybe I can drop by again," Kendra said.

"Once we set the precedent of you visiting, I expect Mother will keep having you back. It is very difficult to get to know my mother. I'm only beginning to understand her myself. But when you killed Gorgrog, you made a friend for life."

"I hope so," Kendra said. "The Fairy Queen has always been good to me."

"She doesn't grant fairykind status to many," Bracken said. "Mother liked you even before you freed her husband. After the battle at Zzyzx, I don't think she has more respect for any human."

Kendra thought about the barrage of fairy kisses that had made her fairykind. Since that day she had understood the languages of the fairy folk and didn't need special food or drink to see the magical creatures at Fablehaven or elsewhere. She could energize magical items, see in the dark, speak several languages, and who knew what else? Her abilities were still emerging. How would the Fairy Queen feel if someday her only son proclaimed his love for a human girl? Would Kendra's fairykind status make her more acceptable?

"Do you think we'll see your mom?" Kendra asked.

"She spends a lot of time in the palace with Father," Bracken said. "If we run across her, she'll probably be in horse shape. She likes to go for runs in that form."

Kendra had been surprised to learn that the queen of the fairies was actually a unicorn. Unlike Bracken, she still had her third horn, so she could take horse shape whenever she pleased. She could also appear as a beautiful woman.

"Ready?" Bracken asked.

"What do I do?" Kendra asked.

A rippling glare of whiteness accompanied a disorienting sensation. Kendra recalled a similar feeling when she stood in the shallows on a beach while the water pulled away. As the seawater withdrew all around her, she had seemed to be in motion while standing still. She felt that same way now.

When the whiteness dissipated, Kendra stood in a blossoming field. The cloudless sky was a golden orange with streaks of red and yellow. Peculiar flowers thrived in all directions, flaunting colors more luminous and bright than any Kendra had ever seen. The blossoms were of such diverse shape and size that Kendra wondered whether they were tropical or if perhaps they existed only here.

Bracken's apprehension had led Kendra to envision a charred landscape with clusters of flowers beginning to grow and shoots of young grass coming up. She certainly had not expected flawless gardens stretching across rolling countryside to the limits of sight.

"It's beautiful," Kendra gushed.

"It's a start," Bracken said. "A big improvement from before. Come this way."

He escorted Kendra to a broad, shallow stream where shimmering water tumbled down a series of rocky shelves. Several fairies waded in the silvery flow. All were taller than Kendra, built with the lithe athleticism of ballerinas, with bright, extravagant wings and lovely young faces.

"Big fairies," Kendra said. "Like the warriors at Zzyzx."

"Fairies tend to be full-sized here," Bracken said.

"Would the tiny fairies at Fablehaven grow if they visited?" Kendra asked.

"Most would, but Mother wouldn't trust the majority with such power," Bracken said. "Fairies can be so foolish."

"I heard that," said an extremely fit fairy with striking red hair and glittering green eyes. She fluttered over and landed before Bracken, legs wet to the shins.

"The fairies here are exceptions to that rule," Bracken explained smoothly. "Tinori, meet Kendra."

"Hello," Kendra said, trying not to feel intimidated as she looked up at a face that belonged on a fashion magazine cover. Thanks to her fairykind status, Kendra knew that fairies were supposed to obey her. But she wasn't sure if that applied to these larger ones.

"I remember you," Tinori said with a broad smile. "You killed Gorgrog."

"Yes," Kendra said, grateful to have some notoriety. "You must have been at the battle."

"I lost most of my left wing," Tinori said, spreading her elaborate wings wide. Both looked perfect to Kendra, with colors like stained glass backlit by sunlight. "It's been healed, of course."

"They're so pretty," Kendra said.

"You," Tinori said, bopping her on the nose with a fingertip, "know the way to a fairy's heart." She gave a squinty, self-satisfied smile and flitted away, her wings allowing her to turn gentle skips into soaring leaps.

"She's a little jealous," Bracken whispered. "You're so radiant."

Kendra glanced at her hands. They looked normal to her. Ever since she had become fairykind, certain magical creatures would comment on her radiance. Kendra had never really perceived it.

"At least she spoke to me," Kendra said. None of the other fairies had glanced her way.

"Tinori has more confidence than most," Bracken said. "You know how fairies get. This is their special realm. You're the first human to come here. You killed the Demon King. You shine brighter than any of them. It's a sure recipe for envy."

The tiny fairies back at Fablehaven had been generally nicer to Kendra since she became fairykind. She supposed their sizes were so different that it was easier for them not to view her as competition.

"This way," Bracken said, leading Kendra toward a bridge composed of smooth, rounded stones in several shades of blue.

She passed a fragrant flower the size of a barrel and a

shrub twinkling with numberless glittery petals. The perfume in the air was almost rich enough to taste.

"Seems like you're already finished," Kendra said.

"This area is more polished than some," Bracken said. "But the land needs more shape and character. Some big trees would add a lot—ancient groves, or forests in their prime. And we have very few structures. We can do grass and flowers quickly."

"It's a paradise," Kendra said.

Bracken winked. "Trust me, it'll be more impressive in years to come."

As they crossed the bridge, a pair of astrids landed in front of them, brawny men with golden, feathery wings. Removing gilded helmets crafted to resemble the heads of owls, they bowed low.

"You look familiar," Kendra said to one of them.

"I'm Denwin," he replied. "This is Peredor. We were both at the battle of Zzyzx."

"Prince Bracken," Peredor said, "Jubaya has announced that she will confer with us."

"Now?" Bracken asked. "I'm giving Kendra a tour."

"I believe that is why we got the offer," Peredor said. "Jubaya expressed interest in conversing with her."

"Absolutely not," Bracken said.

"Who is Jubaya?" Kendra asked.

"A demon," Bracken grumbled.

"You still have demons here?"

"Not all of the demons exited Zzyzx with the horde,"

Bracken explained. "We've purged most who remained, but a few have proven tough to root out."

"You can't get rid of her?" Kendra asked.

"She's hiding in a sludge pit," Bracken said. "There is ancient magic there, deep and dark. Plus her touch corrupts. Unicorns have temporarily purified the top layer of sludge, but the pool becomes tainted again immediately."

"This opportunity could bring her to the surface," Peredor said.

"Out of the question," Bracken replied. "The risk is too great."

"How can I help?" Kendra asked, a little offended that nobody was checking her opinion.

"Chiefly as bait, so to speak," Denwin said. "The demon requested you by name."

"That doesn't sound too bad," Kendra said. After all, she had defeated the Demon King and faced his fierce army. Here she would be surrounded by allies. What could Jubaya do? "How dangerous is she?"

"We have a dozen of our best warriors in place," Peredor said. "We could get another dozen there. I'm confident we could protect you. And maybe capture her."

Bracken frowned. "What about Mizelle?"

"She's on her way," Peredor said.

"Who is Mizelle?" Kendra asked.

"One of my sisters," Bracken said. "She leads the warrior fairies."

Kendra laid a hand on Bracken's arm. "If this would give you a chance to catch the demon . . . "

"She's cornered," Bracken said. "That's never a safe scenario. A desperate demon could get vicious. I'd rather seal up the sludge pit, leave her there until the end of time."

"Begging your pardon," Denwin said, "but can you imagine your mother leaving such an impurity in her realm, sealed up or not?"

"You're right," Bracken said, folding his arms.

"Let me do it," Kendra urged. "I'll be careful."

"I don't like it."

"You have plenty of people to protect me. This could be a chance to get rid of some trouble. Let me do this. I insist."

Bracken sighed. "From what I understand, Jubaya isn't much of a fighter. But she'll undoubtedly play mind games."

"I'll play them right back," Kendra said, feeling brave. "I've been on much riskier adventures than this."

Bracken shook his head. "Don't be so sure. Jubaya wants access to you for a reason. She sees an opportunity."

"I'll keep my guard up," Kendra said. "So will you. It's an opportunity for us, too."

"Very well," Bracken relented. "But at the first sign of trouble . . ."

"You'll bail me out," Kendra finished.

"Shall we transport you?" Denwin asked eagerly.

"Probably for the best," Bracken said.

Peredor scooped Kendra into his strong arms, cradling her, and sprang into the air, powerful wings turning the leap into flight. Looking down at the receding bridge and stream, Kendra saw Bracken rising as well, dangling from Denwin's ankles, using the astrid like a hang glider.

The higher they rose, the more blooming fields and winding streams Kendra could see. Zzyzx had apparently been a very large place, and so was the new fairy realm. In the distance, Kendra could see other astrids heading their way, light glinting off golden feathers and armor.

From her loftier vantage point, Kendra also noticed some parts of Zzyzx the fairies had not yet reclaimed. Off to one side, a row of harsh, fanglike rocks interrupted a series of low, green hills. Sickly fumes steamed from a dark chasm that cut across an idyllic garden like a wound. And up ahead churned a bubbling pond of oily sludge.

Peredor swooped down and landed in tall grass within view of the roiling pond. He set Kendra on her feet as Bracken landed beside them. The reek of the pond overpowered the aroma of the nearby flowers with a foul stench like molten tar and sulfur.

"The fairy realm is huge," Kendra said.

"It's big," Bracken agreed. "Even up high we couldn't see more than a fraction of it. But the sky here does not extend to outer space like it does on Earth. Our atmosphere eventually fades away. And if you go too far in any direction, the ground dwindles to nothing as well."

"Can you fall off the edge?" Kendra asked.

"It would take great effort and powerful magic," Bracken said. "As you get to the edge, you ordinarily get turned around and head back toward the center. Same if you fly too high—you start heading down when you thought you were going up."

"Strange," Kendra said.

"This is not actually a world—just a pocket dimension attached to your world."

I would speak with the girl!

The words hit Kenda's mind like a shout, though her physical ears detected nothing.

Perhaps a conversation can be arranged, Bracken thought back calmly.

You wish to capture me. I will not let that occur. But I may strike a bargain.

We're listening, Jubaya, Bracken answered.

Withdraw your troops from my pool, Jubaya expressed. *If you let me speak to the girl alone, I vow to cause her no harm, and at the end of our conversation, I will surrender myself, if you pledge to transport me to the new demon prison.*

You would exchange your freedom for private words with Kendra? Bracken replied.

Do you call this freedom? Jubaya challenged. *I intend to trade imprisonment among enemies for imprisonment among my kind!*

Why now? Bracken pressed. *You could have asked for such a transfer months ago.*

I have my reasons, Jubaya answered. *And you have my terms.*

"Can she lie?" Kendra asked Bracken.

"Certainly," he said quietly. "But demons tend to keep their formal vows. All magical creatures do. Our natures allow certain oaths and promises to bind us. It is partly how preserves like Fablehaven were founded and how rules were established."

"Then I'll do it," Kendra said.

"Jubaya promised to cause you no harm," Bracken said. "Agreements to confer during a truce are difficult to break. But she might tell you things that could lead you to harm."

"This solves your problem," Kendra said. "It gets her out of here. And who knows? Maybe I'll learn something useful."

"Or something hurtful," Bracken said. "I've been shielding my half of our conversation from her mind. Because you're fairykind, your mind is already protected. Jubaya can only see the thoughts you deliberately project to her. Go ahead and accept if you must."

When should we talk? Kendra thought at the demon.

Immediately, Jubaya replied. *Have the warriors back away. Send Kendra to my pool with your first horn. She will need it for us to interact properly.*

Very well, Bracken responded, then turned to Kendra. He pulled a straight, spiral horn from a leather sheath at his waist and handed it to Kendra. Pearly white and silky smooth, the horn was the length of a dagger. Unicorns shed their first horn after childhood and the second toward the end of adolescence. Both retain magical properties, including the power to purify anything they touch. To certain beings, that purification could be deadly. Kendra had used this very horn to slay a venomous dragon.

"I'm shielding our conversation again," Bracken said. "I was going to give you this anyhow as a precaution. Perhaps she anticipated me. Or she might have a trick up her sleeve."

"I'll be careful," Kendra said.

Bracken gave a nod. "Very well. We'll be close by if you need us."

CHAPTER FOUR

Jubaya Speaks

Astrids and warrior fairies withdrew from the turbulent sludgepool as Kendra walked toward it, the horn clutched tightly in her hand. She stopped a couple of steps from the edge of the roiling pond. The surface became still. Slowly a shape arose from the muck, dripping black filth. It looked to Kendra like the charred head of a praying mantis.

"Hello, child," said a slithery voice that matched the words she had heard in her mind.

"Hello," Kendra replied, unsure what else to say. She did her best not to stare in horror. Judging by the dimensions of the head, Jubaya was probably two or three times her size.

"I am Jubaya," the demon said. "Tell me your name, child."

"Kendra."

"Your full name."

"Kendra Marie Sorenson."

"You are the one who slew Gorgrog the Vile, King of Demons."

"Yes," Kendra admitted, her grip tight on the horn. She wondered if Jubaya might lunge at her to get revenge.

"Relax, child," Jubaya soothed in greasy tones. "I pledged not to harm you, and I am bound by my word. It is you who could harm me. Contact with that horn would send me to the endless night."

"I'm not going to attack you," Kendra said. "How did you know I killed the Demon King?"

"Such an act leaves an unmistakable residue for those with senses to perceive it." A six-fingered hand emerged from the sludge, the grimy fingers extremely long. "Would you take my hand?"

Kendra recoiled. "I'd rather not."

The elongated fingers rippled. "Please, Kendra, I must get a sense of you. The horn will protect you from my touch. It is why I asked you to bring it."

"Can't we just talk?"

"There are other ways to communicate besides speech. Just take my hand for a moment. Don't be afraid. I promise not to hurt you. Do I appear so hideous?"

"My brother got burned making a deal with a demon," Kendra said. "People I love died."

"No deals," Jubaya asserted. "Just a conversation. I wish to help you."

"Why would you want to help me?"

"I will tell you after you take my hand. Don't be afraid. Don't be squeamish."

Kendra didn't like the idea of touching the demon, but she didn't want to be rude, and it was clear the conversation would not progress unless she relented. Bracken would not like it, she felt, but how big of a deal could it be? Was she just being prejudiced? She had the horn and could strike if the demon attacked. If Jubaya wanted, she could lunge at her right now. Instead the demon waited, hand extended.

Kendra stepped forward, bent down, and shook cool fingers that felt like raw hot dogs. The contact gave her shivers. She let go and wiped her hand on her jeans.

"Ah," Jubaya said, her hand disappearing into the pool. "Much better. Why did you not strike me with the unicorn horn? You had my hand. You could have destroyed me."

Kendra felt off balance. "I don't want to destroy you."

"But you could have," Jubaya said. "I am a threat and a problem to your friends. You have personal reasons to mistrust demons. I have caused discord and strife throughout my long years. You made no oath to spare me."

"I don't go around killing people," Kendra said.

"And yet you killed the Demon King."

"He was attacking," Kendra said. "I was protecting my friends."

"You are not ruthless, Kendra," Jubaya said. "It's an endearing weakness. We are fundamentally different, you and I. We do not view the world the same way. We do not employ the same methods. If at any moment in my life I could have killed Gorgrog, I would have done it without hesitation. My approach to life has particular strengths and weaknesses, as does yours. You used Vasilis to slay my king. The Sword of Light and Darkness."

"How do you know?" Kendra wondered.

"When we touched, I saw much that you have seen. Your mind is well protected. I needed voluntary contact for a glimpse. After you killed Gorgrog, you could have claimed his crown. You could have attempted to become the Demon Queen. Why did you abandon the crown to Orogoro?"

"No reason, really. Taking it never crossed my mind."

"We are so profoundly different, Kendra. That was one of the five major crowns. You could have become one of the most powerful women in history."

"I don't really get what you're talking about. Major crowns?"

"The Demon King. The Fairy Queen. The King of Dragons. The Queen of Giants. And the Underking. The five great monarchs. You could have been one of them. Any regrets?"

"Not really," Kendra said. She thought about it. "I wouldn't want to be the Demon Queen."

"But the power."

"Besides, some other demon would have probably killed me."

Jubaya nodded. "Yes. On that point at least we share common ground. Self-preservation. And you're right. My kind would have eaten you alive had you attempted to rule them."

"Orogoro is the new king," Kendra said.

"Indeed. Ruling from a new prison. How very majestic."

"You didn't leave with the other demons," Kendra said.

"And so I am in a position to help tidy up the mess they left behind," Jubaya said. "Rushing forward at every opportunity is not always the wisest tactic. Are any of those who departed talking to the slayer of the Demon King?"

"No."

"You asked why I wanted to take your hand. Demons view the world differently than you do. Let me allow you a glimpse. To a demon, all the world is a chessboard. An elaborate game with so many pieces. A game that can be won. Most of the pieces are virtually irrelevant. But some are important. You, Kendra, are an important piece."

"Me?"

Jubaya gave a slow, rich laugh. "I adore the innocence. Kendra, some would argue that the most valuable pieces in the entire game are the five monarchs. You destroyed one of them. And earned the trust of another. And you befriended the insecure son of a third."

"Raxtus," Kendra said. He had been there at the battle against the demons with his father, Celebrant, King of the Dragons. How much had Jubaya seen?

"Are the monarchs the most essential pieces, Kendra? Or the pieces that alter the destinies of the monarchs?"

"I don't know," Kendra said.

"And yet you bend the world with your will," Jubaya murmured. "We truly are different, Kendra Marie Sorenson. I wish I better understood some of what you don't know."

"Is that what you wanted to tell me?"

"No. Why do you imagine I desired to speak with you?"

"Well, if you think I'm important, I guess to use me somehow?"

Jubaya bobbed her head. "So you do understand something about demons. How do you imagine most demons will view you after you killed their king?"

"I thought they would hate me," Kendra said. "But it sounds like they might also admire me?"

"Right on both counts," Jubaya said. "Would you rather every demon in existence wanted you dead? Or would you prefer to have every demon in existence impressed by you and supporting you?"

"That seems obvious."

"The emotions to drive reactions in either direction are present. Knowing what you know of demons, do you expect they are happy about their defeat? Do you suppose they rejoice that a new age of demonic rule was thwarted?"

"No."

"What do you imagine they want?"

"Revenge."

Jubaya chittered. "Exactly. The question becomes whom they will target. You killed the Demon King. It was a pivotal moment of the battle. But what is the main reason the demons went to the fairy realm instead of spreading across the world?"

"The dragons?"

"That should not be a question. Demons and dragons have an ancient rivalry. If world domination is a game, the battle of Zzyzx created a major shift in the balance of power."

"What can the dragons do?" Kendra asked. "They went back to their sanctuary."

"Yes, they did," Jubaya agreed, "but armed with new power. Heed my words, Kendra Marie Sorenson. I have studied world events for many millennia. A new age of dragons is about to dawn, and there are few who will be ready or willing to stop them."

"How does that affect me?"

"Would you like to see dragons take over the world?"

"No."

"Who else do you suppose would like to see the dragons fail?"

Kendra finally realized where Jubaya was going. "The demons."

"Now you're seeing it."

"You want to help me stop the dragons?"

"Without the backing of the dragons, you would not have stopped the demons. Should you end up fighting the dragons, most demons will see you as an ally and view the fall of Gorgrog through more generous eyes."

"Why would I fight dragons?" Kendra had barely survived her brief stay at Wyrmroost, the dragon sanctuary. Some of the worst experiences of her life had happened there. Dragons were enormous and virtually unstoppable. The last thing she wanted to do was become their most wanted enemy.

"Perhaps you will not," Jubaya said. "But if you do, help

might be found from three demons: Talizar, Batoosa, and Vez Radim. They could be of great service to you . . . and to your brother."

"My brother?"

"You are fairykind. There are some limits to the assistance they could offer you. But Seth is a shadow charmer."

"The last thing Seth needs is new demon friends," Kendra said heatedly.

"He was betrayed by Graulas," Jubaya said. "I wish I could say I was surprised. But interacting with demons can be a more profitable experience when you share common interests. Demons have a score to settle with the dragons. You could receive help from the sources I named. With my mark on you, they will look upon you favorably."

"Your mark?" Kendra asked. She had worried there might be a catch to all of this.

"I shared it when we touched. It will cause you no harm, and only demons can see it. My approval will be a protection and will open doors for you."

"What if I don't want to go through your doors?"

"Then don't," Jubaya said. "I wished to converse with you. We have conversed. If a day comes when you could use help, remember our talk. Or forget it. That choice is yours."

"Okay," Kendra said, once again wiping against her jeans the hand that had touched Jubaya.

"Go tell your unicorn that I will now submit quietly."

"Thanks."

"Your gratitude is premature. Don't thank me yet. The day may come when you actually mean it."

CHAPTER FIVE

Visitors

"I t's good to be back," Doren said as the SUV slowed to a stop in front of a large house with lots of gables and a lone turret.

"Really?" Newel replied. "No more fast-food hamburgers? No more curly fries? No more tacos or milk shakes or gas-station nachos?"

Doren inhaled deeply. "I'll miss the food, and the open road, but you're forgetting something very special."

Newel knocked the heel of his hand against the side of his head. "Forgive me, Doren. Lapse of reason. Maybe those witches Seth visited put me under a spell. How could I forget our brand-new television? Nothing tops it!"

Seth laughed at his friends. Men from the waist up, goats from the waist down, the satyrs had received a big-screen television as a reward for helping Seth find Vasilis and for their contributions during the battle of Zzyzx. It was a major step up from the battery-powered portable TV they had been using.

"I had hoped that after enough television, the novelty would wear off," Grandpa Sorenson said.

"Stan, Stan, Stan," Doren said. "We're not talking about some superficial association. Our relationship with that television only deepens as the months go by."

"Does the novelty wear off when you find true love?" Newel asked. "Or does your devotion increase over a lifetime of commitment and sacrifice?"

"We learned that from television, actually," Doren inserted.

"Right, a talk show," Newel agreed. "That television lets us explore the world! Become infatuated with a million faces! Witness art and music and technological marvels!"

"And watch cartoons," Doren crowed.

Grandpa Sorenson exhaled through pursed lips. "Just be careful. Some humans who watch too much TV turn into couch potatoes. Try not to forget about forests and streams and the thrill of chasing living, breathing nymphs."

Newel winced. "Ouch. I suppose we have been a little off our game lately."

"We'll get back to it as soon as we catch up on the programs we recorded," Doren promised.

The satyrs unbuckled their seat belts and rushed out of the car.

Seth reached for his door.

"One moment, Seth," Grandpa said.

"Sure, what?"

"I didn't want to bring it up in front of the satyrs," Grandpa said, "but we haven't had a chance to discuss your visit with the Sisters."

Seth squirmed in his seat. "I have to be careful. People aren't supposed to know about our arrangement. Bad things can happen if I say too much."

"I understand," Grandpa said. "But it's a long way from Missouri to Connecticut, and you've seemed preoccupied for most of the drive. I expected that having settled your business, you would be relieved."

"Well . . . things are not completely settled," Seth said. "There is another part to the agreement."

Some fire entered Grandpa's gaze. "Have they asked you to do something that makes you uncomfortable?"

"No, it's not the arrangement," Seth replied. "Not that I could tell you if it was. They really will do something drastic if I say too much. They almost came after me just because Bracken mentally spied enough to discover an agreement existed."

"If the upsetting information isn't part of the arrangement, can't you talk about it?"

Seth thought about that. "Yeah, I guess I can. It was just a prediction they leaked. They said a storm is coming. A storm of dragons."

Grandpa's expression grew sober—and a little guarded. "Did they?"

"You know something."

"Just rumors," Grandpa said. "Nothing definitive. But

there has been unrest at the dragon sanctuaries lately. Agad the wizard recently told me to expect a visit. I expect I'll learn more then."

"Really? I'd like to see Agad again."

"I'm sure he'd like to see you, too."

"There isn't much the dragons can do from their sanctuaries, is there?"

"I hope not," Grandpa said. "Dragons embody the greatest threat posed to humans by the magical community. I don't want to worry you, but if there is anything I have learned over the past few years, it is that prisons can fail and magical preserves can fall. We have to stay vigilant. Look, there's your sister."

Kendra emerged from the front door of the house. She waved when she caught Seth's eye.

"I should go see her," Seth said. "She was worried about me."

"Go on."

Seth got out of the SUV and jogged over to his older sister.

"How'd it go?" Kendra asked.

"It's all top secret," Seth replied.

"You have one fewer wraith than when you left."

"At least I still have you."

Kendra gave a patient smile. "Vasilis is gone too?"

Seth scowled. "Yeah."

"It was fun while it lasted."

"Fun for you, hogging all the glory by killing Gorgrog."

"You found the sword. And took out some other demons. It was a team effort."

"I call the next one."

"You can have him," Kendra said. She paused, looking at him closely. "Are you all right?"

"Mostly," Seth said. "It sounds like we might have some trouble from the dragons."

"Says who?"

"I can't really get specific."

"The witches," Kendra said. "A demon just told me something similar."

"Wait, a demon?" Seth asked. "Here at Fablehaven?"

"I went to the fairy realm."

"Bracken finally took you."

"No, I snuck in," Kendra said dryly.

"Were there lollipop forests? And candy-bar roads?"

"There were lots of flowers."

"Rainbows? Sparkles?"

"It was beautiful."

"How did you meet a demon there? Was it made of gumdrops?"

"Some demons never left," Kendra said. "The astrids are working to expel them."

"I knew I got rid of Vasilis too early!"

"Bracken wouldn't want to endanger you."

"I could have been a demon exterminator." Seth's eyes widened. "Is that why he wanted me to settle up with the witches? To protect me from having fun? How much did he know about our deal?"

"I really don't know."

"What did the demon tell you about the dragons?"

"She wanted to warn me there would be trouble," Kendra said.

"It was a lady demon?"

"I think she mostly wants revenge against the dragons. I bet a lot of demons feel that way. Who knows how accurate she is?"

A black minivan was coming up the driveway. Seth stared, baffled. Fablehaven almost never got visitors. The sighting of a strange vehicle was a rare occurrence.

"Who is that?" Seth asked, wondering if it could possibly be Agad.

Kendra started laughing. "Nobody told you?"

"What?"

"You're going to love this. Grandma and Grandpa Larsen invited them."

"Who?"

"Your favorite cousins."

"No," Seth said. He didn't want to speak the name but couldn't stop himself. "Knox?"

Kendra nodded. "And Tess."

The minivan had almost reached the house.

"No," Seth groaned. "This is our place! He'll ruin it!"

"Don't be so dramatic. You usually end up having fun with him. He can't ruin anything. But your attitude might."

"Why would they invite him?"

"Uncle Pete and Aunt Zola wanted to take a trip.

Grandma Sorenson wanted me to remind you that we're not supposed to tell them about any of the magical stuff."

"Of course not. I'm not stupid."

"That's debatable."

The minivan rolled to a stop beside the SUV. A door slid open and a kid hopped out wearing fancy basketball shoes, baggy sport shorts, and a gray T-shirt. His blondish hair was shaved short on the sides but fairly long on top. A pair of military-style dog tags dangled from his neck, and he carried a basketball under one arm. It had been three years since Seth last saw him. Not quite as tall as Seth and a little stocky, Knox looked like an aged-up version of the kid Seth remembered.

"Hey, loser," Knox greeted. "You still have Seth breath?"

Seth held his nose. "It was killed by your Knox socks."

Knox shook his head. "I hear you live here!"

"For now," Seth said.

"Do you have enough trees?"

"It's called a forest," Seth said.

"Hi, Kendra," Knox said. "Did you get shorter?"

"I think you got taller," she replied.

"How old are you now?" Knox asked.

"Fifteen."

"I'm thirteen, like Seth," Knox reminded her.

"I know," Kendra replied. "You were born the same month."

"I came first," Seth said.

"First is the worst," Knox countered. He looked around. "So many trees. Connecticut needs to share the wealth.

They block every view. We couldn't see anything driving here."

"Some people think the trees are part of the view," Seth said.

Over by the minivan, Grandma and Grandpa Sorenson stood talking to Uncle Pete and Aunt Zola. Uncle Pete looked a little heavier than Seth recalled.

"You didn't drive from Texas," Kendra said.

"No way," Knox said. "We flew into Hartford and rented the minivan. Mom and Dad are going to drive around New England with your parents for a week and look at old stuff. And I'm stuck here." He kept looking around. "Do you have a basketball hoop?"

"Nope," Seth said.

"Really? You're not just scared to play me?"

"Truly. Is that basketball signed?"

Knox held it up and pointed out different signatures. "Magic. Kobe. Jordan. LeBron. Curry." Each name looked like it had been written with a real marker.

"Are you serious? That must be worth a ton!"

Knox bounced it on the grass. "Maybe. I didn't buy it. It's all about being in the right place at the right time."

"You met them?" Seth asked.

"Or people I know did," Knox said, bouncing the ball again.

"I wouldn't bounce it," Seth said. "You should keep that one on a shelf."

"I disagree," Knox said. "It'll look cooler all worn out. A ball that gets used."

A petite blonde girl trotted up to them, her shoulder-length hair softly curled. She wore fairy wings and carried a white wand with a star at the tip. Kendra and Seth shot a look at each other.

"Hi, guys," the girl said. "Remember me? I'm your cousin Tess."

"You look so much bigger," Kendra said.

"I am bigger. I turned nine last week."

"You came in fairy gear," Seth observed.

"I love fairies." Tess twirled. "Grandma Larsen told me this is a perfect place for fairies. She called it Fablehaven. Get it? Fable . . . haven. A safe place for storybook creatures."

"I bet she's right," Kendra said sweetly. "Grandma Larsen is pretty smart."

"Looks more like a great place for bugs," Knox said, scanning the area.

Seth could currently see at least ten fairies flitting about the yard. They were so much a part of the scenery that he hardly noticed them anymore. But of course Knox and Tess were blind to them. They saw butterflies and dragonflies instead. Mortals needed to drink milk from the magical milch cow Viola in order to perceive what was really going on at Fablehaven. Seth had eaten walrus butter from a similar creature every morning on his road trip so he could see Newel and Doren as they really were instead of as a couple of goats.

"Butterflies," Tess announced, pointing at a fairy. "I bet they know where I can find the fairies."

Seth and Kendra shared another glance. Tess could have no idea how close she was to getting her wish.

"No hoop," Knox grumbled, bouncing his ball again. "This could be a long week. Do you guys have video games, at least?"

"Grandpa Sorenson isn't big on electronics," Seth said.

Knox looked like he had been shot. "That's right. Your other grandparents are here too. Isn't that kind of crowded?"

"They have different houses," Kendra said. "You'll probably be in the old manor mostly with Grandma and Grandpa Larsen. It looks like a mansion."

"That sounds decent," Knox said. "Is it nearby?"

"It's kind of far," Seth said. "They own a lot of land here. Acres and acres."

"Anything cool?" Knox asked. "Or just trees?"

"There might be a few surprises," Seth said. "You have to be careful. The woods can be hazardous. Grandpa will fill you in."

"Hazardous?" Knox asked. "Like those signs on the way in? *Certain Death Awaits?* Give me a break!"

"The woods can be deadly," Kendra said. "Poisonous snakes. Lots of ticks with Lyme disease."

Knox made a disgusted face. "I hate bugs."

"Old bear traps in the woods too," Seth said. "Some parts are like a minefield."

"That sounds scary," Tess said.

"And fairies too," Kendra said. "So many fairies."

Tessa beamed and waved her wand.

Knox gave a huff. "Right. Fairies and unicorns and leprechauns."

"More or less," Seth said.

"And no basketball hoop," Knox said with a sigh. "I have a feeling this might be the most boring week of my life."

CHAPTER SIX

The Tiny Hero

Seth awoke the next morning to find a mouse squatting on his nightstand. The little creature sat upright, nose twitching, and began to squeak.

Seth continued to use one of the beds in the attic playroom, while Kendra had moved into an empty bedroom on the next floor down. Though the playroom was large, and cluttered with enough toys to hide a hundred mice, Seth had never seen a rodent inside the house.

"You're not a mouse," Seth said.

The furry intruder waved both arms and kept squeaking. The only wild mice Seth ever glimpsed had scurried away at the sight of a human. This one was clearly signaling him.

"Sit tight," Seth said. "I'll be right back."

He hurried down the attic stairs. The mouse was just an illusion. Seth needed some supernatural dairy. Sometimes he envied Kendra's ability to see magical creatures as they really were without drinking Viola's milk.

Grandma Sorenson stood at the stove tending a large pot of oatmeal, her graying hair bound in a large bun. "Good morning, Grandma," Seth said, grabbing milk from the refrigerator.

"Good morning," Grandma said. "Your cousins and the Larsens are coming to breakfast."

Seth poured some milk into a glass. Oatmeal had never been a favorite of his until he had eaten it at Fablehaven. Grandma Sorenson always offered lots of tasty toppings. "We'll have extras to put in it?"

Grandma smiled. "We have honey, brown sugar, cinnamon, almond slivers, sunflower seeds, walnuts, bananas, blueberries, blackberries, raspberries, and boysenberries. Plus homemade bread with my special jam."

"That should keep them from running away," Seth said, then finished the milk in his glass. "You really do spoil us."

"It's one of my fundamental rights as a grandparent," Grandma said. "I'm saving the pancakes and French toast for later in the week."

"Good finale," Seth said. "Don't forget the huevos rancheros."

"Or the heavenly hash," Grandma said.

Seth put the milk bottle back in the fridge. "See you in a bit."

"Is everything all right?" Grandma asked. "You seem in a rush."

"Should have gone to the bathroom first," Seth said,

racing off. He swung by the bathroom on his way to the attic, partly so his statement would be true, and partly because the claim had awakened an urgent need.

When Seth entered the attic playroom, he found a little man waiting on his nightstand where the mouse had been. Proportioned like a normal human, the tiny fellow stood not quite three inches tall. He had black hair and blue eyes, and he wore a dark yellow shirt tucked into brown pants. A little sword hung at his side. His boots looked travel-worn.

Seth knelt down beside the nightstand. "Hi there," he said. "Sorry I rushed off. I had to drink some milk to see your true form."

"Understood," the visitor replied in a squeaky voice. "You are Seth Sorenson, correct?"

"Who's asking?" Seth wondered. "What are you?" The little guy didn't fit the profile of any of the creatures Seth knew—though fairy-sized, he had no wings and was male. He didn't look like a brownie or a leprechaun, either.

The diminutive man bowed. "I'm Calvin of the nipsies."

"You're too big," Seth said. "Nipsies are like . . ." he put his finger and thumb about half an inch apart.

"Good eye," Calvin said. "I wondered whether you would realize I was out of scale with the rest of my kind."

"I've been to the Seven Kingdoms of the nipsies," Seth said.

"I know," Calvin said, "along with the Supreme Gigantic Overlords, Newel and Doren. You three are hard to miss."

"I guess so," Seth said, remembering how easily they could have smashed the elaborate cities full of miniature buildings, bridges, monuments, palaces, ships, and people. "Why are you so big?"

"The elders cast a spell on me," Calvin said. "Among the nipsies, I have a reputation as an adventurer. I hate to toot my own horn. It always sounds hollow. I should have brought letters of recommendation. But anyway—they chose me as their champion and used a spell that turned me into the Giant Hero. Well . . . to them I look like a giant. Seems silly in front of you. Maybe you should call me the Tiny Hero."

"Calvin, the Tiny Hero," Seth said. "That works. Did they send you to fight me?"

Calvin laughed and shook his head. "No! You are Seth?"

"Yeah."

"Slayer of the Lord of Filth?"

"I've killed some gross things."

"You destroyed the Foulest of the Foul? The Curse-bringer?"

"Probably," Seth said. "Does he have a name?"

"We don't enjoy the taste of it," Calvin said. "The demon Graulas."

"Yeah, I killed him," Seth said. "I wish I could have done it more than once."

"We rejoiced at the news," Calvin said. "We had begun to worry nobody would ever slay him."

"He was almost dead for a long time," Seth said, not wanting to mention that he had healed the demon before killing him later.

"Which is why we were concerned," Calvin said. "Because of the curse."

"What curse?"

"The terrible curse of the nipsies," Calvin said. "It was placed on us long ago, before I was born."

"What did it do?" Seth asked.

"The details are obscure," Calvin said. "The elders refuse to elaborate. But we used to be more powerful. And bigger. Maybe even as big as I am now."

"Enormous," Seth teased.

Calvin scowled. "Hey, it makes a difference to us."

"I get it. So did the nipsie elders somehow remove the curse from you?"

"No. But they had ancient magic to create a giant champion. I was chosen."

"What does the curse have to do with Graulas?" Seth asked.

"A deal with Graulas led to the curse," Calvin said.

"I believe that," Seth said. "He pretended to help me, then stabbed me in the back. He overthrew Fablehaven and killed my friend Coulter."

"The curse came with a prophecy," Calvin said.

"Tell me."

"All nipsies can recite it: *The curse arose from the demon's blight; the lord who slays him will set it right.*"

"It rhymes," Seth observed.

"Most of the good ones do," Calvin said. "Some strain more than others. But the basics are clear. Whoever kills the horrible demon will help lift the curse."

"I slayed that horrible demon," Seth said.

"Thank goodness!" Calvin cried. "If the Foulest of the Foul had died from a disease, who would we turn to?"

"I'm supposed to break the curse?"

"With the help of a nipsie champion. There's a second half: *The slayer shall restore our pride, the Giant Hero at his side.*" Calvin drew his sword, dropped to one knee, held out the blade with the point downward, and bowed his head. "I, Calvin son of Brendan, pledge myself to you, Seth Sorenson. From this day forward I am your vassal, keeper of your secrets, protector of your honor, servant to your interests, and defender of your causes."

"Wow, thanks. I'm still not clear on this curse, let alone how to break it."

With his head still bowed, Calvin said, "Nobody is really clear about it. But if you're willing to help, please accept my devotion."

"Aren't you kind of small?" Seth asked.

"You're small compared to a giant," Calvin replied, glancing up at Seth, though his head remained mostly bowed. "And compared to Graulas. You did all right against him! There is more to me than my size."

"But what if you get squished?" Seth exclaimed. "I'd feel awful."

"I'm tougher than I look. It's all part of the champion spell. Stronger than I look, too. Let me worry about the risks. I don't squish easily. You won't regret it. Little people can come in handy. I knew I should have brought some letters of recommendation!"

"Okay," Seth said. "I'll help with the curse."

"Try to be a little more specific. I'm offering my devotion. This is a dramatic moment. Very ceremonial. Something like 'Rise, Tiny Hero, and join your new liege lord.'"

Seth swallowed. "This means I'm responsible for you?"

Still kneeling, Calvin lifted his head a little more. "It just means you accept my service. We're a team, and you're the leader. It'll be fun! I'll help you with anything you need, and we'll also keep an eye out for ways to break the curse on the nipsies."

Seth paused. The little guy seemed eager and fun, but he didn't want this to lead to trouble. "How did you get in here? The house is shielded from intruders."

"Being tiny has advantages. In this case, the brownies helped me out. With brownie permission, anyone smaller than a brownie can gain access to the house using the brownie passageways."

"That's impressive. My sister and I got in that way once. Long story. How do I know you're not an evil spy?"

"I'm a nipsie," Calvin said defensively. "We've never allied with evil! The shadow plague turned some of us dark for a while, but that wasn't our fault. You can count on me. Go check with our elders. Or ask your grandfather. I pledge to serve you faithfully. With an oath and everything!"

"Rise, Tiny Hero," Seth said, doing his best to make the words sound official. "I believe you. I'll be your partner."

Calvin hopped to his feet, swung his sword, then sheathed it. "You won't regret it. Should I call you Supreme Gigantic Overlord?"

"No," Seth said. "The satyrs made up that title. I wasn't part of it."

"Master?"

"How about Seth?"

"Very well, Seth. Want to carry me in a pocket for now?"

"Really?"

"Why not? I'll be fine. That way I'll be with you if you need help."

Seth was currently in shorts and a T-shirt. "Okay. Let me get dressed for the day."

Grandpa and Grandma Larsen brought Knox and Tess to join Grandpa and Grandma Sorenson, Kendra, and Seth for breakfast. They all gathered around the table, a big bowl of oatmeal waiting at each place. Bread, butter, and jam occupied the center of the table, along with the many add-ins for the oatmeal. Knox eyed the bowl of oatmeal with a mix of suspicion and disappointment.

"Thanks for coming over for breakfast," Grandma Sorenson said. "We're happy to have Knox and Tess visiting."

"How was your first night?" Grandpa Sorenson asked.

"Wonderful," Tess enthused. Though she had shed her fairy wings for breakfast, she still wore a tiara. "Fablehaven is a magical place."

Knox snorted. "I don't know about that. But the other house is pretty sweet."

Seth wanted to say that he should have seen it before

the brownies fixed it up. The manor had been abandoned for years before Grandpa Sorenson invited a group of brownies to take up residence there and repair it for the Larsens. But of course Knox didn't know that brownies were real.

"Dig in," Grandma Sorenson invited.

Knox looked down at his oatmeal without excitement.

"Add stuff," Seth prompted, spooning in some sugar. "It can get amazing."

"There's warm bread, too," Grandma invited.

Knox's interest increased as he sweetened up his oatmeal with berries and sugar. Seth snuck little pieces of bread to Calvin, who was hiding in the front pocket of his cargo pants.

"You don't have a basketball hoop anywhere?" Knox asked as he finished his food.

"We could maybe rig one up," Grandpa Sorenson said. "For now, why not let Seth show you around outside. We have a pool here, and a great yard to explore."

"I want to catch some fairies," Tess declared.

"I can help," Kendra offered with a nervous smile.

Seth wondered what would happen if Tess drank the milk. He figured either it would be no surprise at all, or it would completely blow her mind.

"I'm done," Knox announced, blotting his lips with a napkin. "That was the best oatmeal I've ever had. It usually tastes like mud."

"I'll take that as a compliment," Grandma Sorenson said.

"Grandpa Larsen reviewed the rules with you two?" Grandpa Sorenson checked.

"Stay out of the woods because of ticks," Knox said. "No problem. I'm not a big fan of trees. Or bugs."

"I'll stay by the flowers," Tess promised.

"Run along," Grandma Larsen said. "I can see you're ready to go."

The kids left the table. Seth followed Knox out the back door. He might be annoying, but he was still company.

"What are we going to do?" Knox groaned.

"I can show you the yard," Seth offered.

"I can see the yard," Knox said, gesturing at it. "Lots of bushes. Tons of grass. What are you going to do? Tell me the names of all the flowers? This is the most boring place on Earth."

"It's actually not," Seth said.

"Right," Knox said with a huff. "Prove it."

Seth had seldom felt so tempted. He had called Fablehaven boring plenty of times, but hearing it from somebody else made him defensive. What if he gave Knox a sip of Viola's milk, then snuck him down to the dungeon? He could introduce him to the goblins. Maybe release a wraith or two. Wraiths were the opposite of boring.

"Look at your sister," Seth said. Tess was running around a rosebush waving her wand while Kendra tried to keep up with her. "She's having a great time."

"She thinks she's having fun," Knox said. "Tess tries to make everything into a storybook. She believes anything you tell her. Once she got stuck on the idea of fairies being here, she was all set. Tess lives up in the clouds. One of these days she's going to be really disappointed."

"Are you sure?" Seth asked. "What if there really are fairies here?"

Knox stared. "You have to be kidding! That is the lamest thing I've ever heard. Maybe you should go play with Tess."

Seth knew he needed to proceed with caution. Yes, there were fairies at Fablehaven. And so many other amazing things. And yes, Grandma and Grandpa Larsen probably had some interest in sharing those secrets with Knox and Tess or they wouldn't have let them come here. But Seth knew he would be in huge trouble if he showed Knox what was really going on. Grandpa Sorenson had pulled him aside yesterday and insisted Knox and Tess needed to figure out the secrets of Fablehaven on their own.

"What if I told you there were demons here?" Seth asked. "Or monsters? Or treasure?"

"At least that would be interesting," Knox said. "But still dumb. Except the treasure. I wouldn't mind some treasure."

Suddenly Seth had an idea. It would require taking Knox into the woods. But it shouldn't be very dangerous. Not for Knox. Since he didn't know about the magical creatures, the treaty would protect him.

"How about a dare?" Seth challenged.

"I like dares," Knox said hesitantly.

"We'd have to go into the woods."

"What about—"

"I have bug spray. I go into the woods all the time. And I've never seen a snake here. I'll show you cool stuff. And I'll give you ten bucks if you do the dare."

Knox grinned. "You've got a deal."

CHAPTER SEVEN

Steal the Bacon

The cottage where the satyrs spent most of their time had been wired for power. As Seth and Knox approached, Seth could hear the rumble of the television—probably a war show or a superhero movie. It sounded like things were blowing up.

"Could you wait here for a second?" Seth asked Knox.

"Why can't I come in?"

"This house isn't what it looks like. A couple of goats live here."

"Goats? This is way too nice for goats."

"Maybe," Seth said. "But Grandpa Sorenson is using it to hold them. They can be temperamental around visitors. Let me go see what kind of mood they're in. Make sure they've been fed."

"Why?" Knox asked. "Do you have food in that bag?"

Seth patted the leather satchel he was carrying. "Not goat food. Just granola bars and some emergency gear in case of trouble. There's some goat food stored inside the cottage."

"I don't want to wait around all day collecting mosquito bites," Knox said.

Seth took some insect repellent from his emergency kit. Knox closed his eyes and turned his head as Seth sprayed him thoroughly.

"That stuff reeks worse than your breath," Knox complained.

"Let's hope the mosquitos agree," Seth said. "Be right back."

Seth let himself in, closing the door quickly. Newel and Doren sat on a couch watching superheroes do battle.

"Seth!" Doren greeted. "You're just in time for the big showdown!"

"Pause it," Seth said.

Newel took the remote, waited for a moment, then froze the screen with a car in mid-explosion.

"Nice one," Doren said.

"What's up?" Newel asked.

"Remember the duffel bag we lost near the ogre's place?" Seth asked. Of their adventures following the battle of Zzyzx, the bungled ogre robbery had been one of their biggest disappointments.

Newel wiped a hand down his face. "Are you trying to torture me? I think about it all the time! That was way too much treasure to leave behind."

"It was my fault," Doren said. "You made a good throw. I choked."

"It wasn't a perfect throw," Newel said. "It was a little behind you. You needed to slow down a step and turn. But, yeah, you pretty much blew it."

"I would have gone back but she was right behind me," Doren apologized.

"I know, I know," Newel said. "We've gone over this. It was a flawless operation up to that point. Easy money. But you may as well forget it, Seth. The ogres left the bag right where it fell. Which means they're using it as bait, waiting for us to come back so they can nab us. I know it's alluring. Treasure is treasure. But it would be foolish to go back for it."

"Unless the shadow charmer wants to sneak it away in the dark," Doren suggested.

Newel elbowed Doren. "Shadow charmer or not, Seth isn't going to steal a watched prize from an ogre. That's a sure recipe for Shadow Charmer Stew."

"What if I found somebody who would get it for us?" Seth asked.

"Is anybody that foolish?" Doren asked. "Verl, maybe?"

"It's not worth getting Verl killed," Newel said. "We still wouldn't get the treasure."

"Not Verl," Seth said. "What about a kid? A human kid. Somebody who doesn't even know what's going on here at Fablehaven. He has never drunk the milk. Shouldn't the treaty give him a bunch of protection?"

"He would still be trespassing," piped a little voice.

"Who said that?" Doren asked, looking around. "Was it my conscience?"

"I have a new friend," Seth announced, taking Calvin from his pocket. "A nipsie. He's Calvin, the Tiny Hero."

"That's quite a nipsie," Newel said. "What've you been feeding him?"

"I was enlarged by a spell," Calvin replied. "But I'm no Supreme Gigantic Overlord."

Doren blushed a little. "Sorry about all that. I know we used our size to extort some goods from you nipsies. A guy's gotta eat."

"Don't apologize," Newel groused. He looked Seth in the eye. "Why are you carrying around a giant nipsie?"

"He wants me to help him break a curse," Seth said. "He pledged his loyalty to me."

Newel laughed. "What's he going to do? Bring you a peanut? Fend off some butterflies?"

"I might point out that trespassing can forfeit the protection of the treaty," Calvin said.

"Sometimes," Seth said. "But remember, he has never tried the milk. And what if I tell him to go there? Then he would be trespassing with permission. He'd be following orders instead of breaking a rule."

Calvin scowled in thought. "I don't know. That might work."

"Not a bad scheme," Newel seconded, finally sounding interested. "If it goes wrong, worst thing that happens is the kid gets smooshed. How much do you like him?"

"Not a lot," Seth replied. "He's my cousin, though. I can't let him get hurt."

"So you want us along for protection?" Doren said.

"We get away with dangerous stuff all the time," Seth said. "We could still split the treasure three ways."

"Won't the kid get a share?" Newel asked.

"He's doing it for ten dollars."

Newel and Doren tried to hold in their laughter but mostly failed.

"How dumb is this kid?" Doren asked.

"Pretty dumb," Seth replied. "But keep in mind, he doesn't know what Fablehaven is like. He'll just think he's doing a dare."

Newel turned off the television. "This I've got to see. It's hard to beat really good, live entertainment."

"It's a higher fidelity experience," Doren agreed.

"But you have to help me make sure nothing happens to him," Seth reminded them. "That's your end of the deal."

"If the kid dies, we lose our share of the treasure," Newel said.

"But we get an even better show," Doren whispered with a wink.

"He must not die," Seth said. "He's pretty annoying, but technically he's family."

"What kind of treasure is in the bag?" Calvin asked.

"Gold, mostly," Doren said. "Some uncut gemstones. A string of pearls. We lured the ogres away from home and snatched some loot."

"They got back a little too soon," Newel said.

"You robbed their house?" Calvin asked.

"It was all treasure they had stolen," Doren said. "Fair game to take unless they catch us trespassing."

"Which they did," Seth said.

"Once we were off their land, they couldn't follow," Newel said. "We almost got away with the goods. You can see the bag from the border of their territory. At least we could last time we checked."

"They could have moved it," Doren said.

"I don't know," Newel replied. "We only pinched the treasure a few weeks ago. It's hardly been a fortnight since we checked the bag. Once an ogre gets an idea, it tends to linger. Not a lot of competition, if you know what I mean. I bet they're still hoping to spring their trap."

"So you're in?" Seth checked.

"We're in," Newel said.

"But the pip-squeak is out," Doren clarified. "We split the loot three ways."

"Fine by me," Calvin agreed. "I'm here as an observer. And as Seth's champion."

"You get what you pay for," Newel muttered.

"Perfect," Seth said. "Come meet Knox."

"Like Fort Knox?" Doren asked.

"Isn't that full of gold?" Newel wondered.

"That's a good omen," Doren said.

"To him you'll look like goats," Seth said. "I'll have to be careful how I talk to you or I'll look nuts."

"Better hide your pet nipsie, too," Newel said. "What does it look like to blind humans? A ladybug?"

"A mouse," Seth said. "He's right, Calvin. You should duck out of sight."

"No problem," Calvin replied as Seth put him back in his pocket. Doren grabbed his bow, and Newel picked up a coil of rope. Seth went to the door and led the satyrs outside.

Knox stood chucking rocks into the trees. He turned, brushing off his hands. "There really were goats!" Knox said, looking at the satyrs in surprise.

"They're going to come with us into the woods," Seth said.

"Why?" Knox said.

"The kid seems suspicious," Doren said.

"Maybe he's a good judge of character," Newel said.

"Do I need a reason?" Seth asked. "You complained about being bored. I thought bringing some goats would make it less boring."

"I guess," Knox said, eying the satyrs hesitantly. "Are they safe? I'm not sure I trust them."

"He is a good judge of character!" Newel exclaimed.

"Why do they keep baaing?" Knox asked. "Do they bite?"

"Not people," Seth said.

"Don't they need leashes?" Knox wondered.

"They're really smart," Seth assured him. "They'll stay with us."

"Unless you get in trouble," Doren said.

"Then good luck," Newel added.

Knox edged toward them, one tentative hand held out.

"Is he going to pet us?" Newel asked.

"Can I pet one?" Knox asked.

"He better not," Doren said, backing away.

"Why not?" Seth wondered.

"Imagine some kid wanted to pet you," Newel said. "It's creepy."

Knox took the "why not" as permission and reached out. Newel lifted a leg and let Knox rub it. Then the satyr hopped away, and Knox flinched back.

"Feeling jumpy?" Seth asked.

"It jumped first," Knox said. "Think they have fleas?"

"Probably best not to pet them," Seth said. "They can be a little ornery. That one is called Newel. The other is Doren."

"Weird pets," Knox said.

"It's a weird place," Seth said with a shrug. "Come on." He led the way into the woods.

They found the duffel bag right where Doren had dropped it, partly hidden by shin-high grass in a small clearing. The satyrs had shown Seth exactly where the ogre's territory began, and they stood beside a tree just outside the boundary, staring at their reward less than thirty yards away.

"I don't get it," Knox said. "I just go grab the bag? And you give me ten bucks? What's the catch? Are you going to ditch me or something?"

"The goats and I will wait for you here," Seth said. "If I say to run, you should run, but otherwise you can walk."

Knox searched the area suspiciously. "Is the bag full of snakes? Are there booby traps?"

"Your cousin isn't completely stupid," Newel said.

"I don't see any ogres," Doren reported.

"Can you make those goats be quiet?" Knox asked.

"Can I kick him?" Newel asked. "Just a little kick?"

"Or a bite?" Doren proposed. "Goats bite sometimes."

"Focus," Seth said. "I promise I didn't set up any tricks or traps. But there are rumors that this area is haunted."

Knox laughed incredulously. "That's hilarious! You actually believe in ghosts?"

"I don't know about ghosts," Seth said. "Wraiths and zombies, maybe. Or revenants."

"Or ogres," Newel said, stifling a laugh.

Knox shook his head. "You're worse than Tess. If you're trying to scare me, it won't work. I laugh when I watch monster movies. Halloween is one big joke. Your oatmeal breath might be scary, but ghosts? Seriously?"

"You don't ever get creeped out?" Seth asked. "Like at a graveyard? Or in a dark room?"

"Why would I?" Knox scoffed. "How are dead bodies buried in a box underground going to hurt me? What are the headstones going to do? Tell me the date somebody died? And why should darkness bother me, unless I'm trying to find something or walk around. Imaginary stuff isn't scary at all. This will be the easiest ten dollars I ever made."

"This guy is priceless," Newel said. "I've never met anybody with his eyes this closed to our secrets."

"He has no imagination," Doren said. "I get all kinds of freaky thoughts in a dark place."

"Wow," Seth said. "You're pretty brave."

"It's not brave to be realistic," Knox said. "Walking a tightrope is brave. Going to war is brave. This is nothing."

"It's still worth ten dollars," Seth said.

"It better not be booby-trapped," Knox warned, starting toward the bag.

"I didn't sabotage it," Seth said. "I can't guarantee it isn't guarded by ogres or something."

Knox snickered and started toward the bag.

"I still can't sense any ogres," Doren said, sniffing the air.

"There's an ogre around," Newel said. "They're not the brightest bunch, but they wouldn't leave that bag out in the open unguarded."

"Unless they got distracted," Doren suggested.

"It takes imagination to get distracted," Newel said. "Once an ogre gets an idea, he holds on tight. They're mad we trespassed, and they think we'll be back for the loot, so they'll be guarding it. Mark my words."

Doren fitted an arrow to his bowstring. "Doesn't hurt to be ready."

"Could Knox see your bow?" Seth whispered.

"I doubt it," Doren said. "Humans without the milk don't normally see our clothes or what we're holding. They just see a goat."

Seth watched his cousin traipse across the clearing. The area remained quiet. Knox probed the duffel bag with his toe. He obviously was still worried about some kind of prank. Hands on his hips, he looked around, glanced back at Seth, then picked it up.

An ogre charged from cover at the far end of the clearing. The onrushing goliath was nearly twice the height of Knox, with thick limbs and rough, reddish skin. The huge boils on his brutish face looked almost like additional noses. He clutched a bulky club, practically a log, studded with metal flanges and knobs.

"Now, *that* is a Supreme Gigantic Overlord," came a voice from Seth's pocket.

Knox turned and faced the oncoming threat, feet rooted to the ground. The ogre raised his club, closing fast, his face a study in rage.

"Do I shoot?" Doren asked, bow drawn, sighting down the arrow.

"Wait for it," Newel said softly.

The ogre staggered to a stop in front of Knox, club poised to strike, ready to pound the trespasser into the ground like a tent stake, a leer of triumph on his cankered lips. The muscles in his powerful arms tensed and bunched, but the great club remained upraised. His expression shifted from ecstatic fury to bafflement to frustration.

"Knox, run!" Seth called.

The words broke whatever blend of shock and stupor was holding his cousin immobilized. Knox came dashing toward Seth, eyes wide. "Bear!" he shouted. "Bear!"

The ogre sniffed the air, spat, then brandished his club in one hand, bicep swelling like a watermelon. He pointed at Seth, eyes blazing. "You!"

"That's our cue," Newel said.

"This way," Seth called to his cousin, turning and running. Even if the ogre couldn't follow Seth beyond the boundaries of his territory, he could theoretically throw stones. Or boulders.

"That's Mung," Newel panted, racing alongside Seth. "Not the biggest ogre at Fablehaven. But probably the meanest."

Seth glanced over his shoulder. The ogre had already passed Knox and was almost at the border of his territory.

"Hurry, Knox!" Seth called. He jumped over a fallen branch and shoved through a tangle of ferns.

"Uh-oh," Doren said.

"What?" Newel replied.

"Mung just left his territory."

Seth glanced back again. The ogre was beyond the tree where they had watched Knox and still charging hard. Knox trailed behind.

"He can't do that!" Newel shouted.

"And yet he has," Doren replied.

The news prodded Seth to maximum speed. "What do we do?"

"Run for the yard," Newel advised. "He seemed to have his eyes on you. We'll try to slow him."

"What about Knox?" Seth asked.

"I'll stay with him," Doren promised. "Herd him back to the house."

The satyrs slowed, and Seth was running alone. He knew the way back to the yard, but it would take a miracle for him to outrun the ogre.

Stealing another look back, Seth saw Newel and Doren kneeling behind bushes with their rope stretched between them. Mung roared, smashing through the undergrowth like a runaway tank.

Seth caught his foot on a root but managed to stay on his feet. He dodged a tree, leaped over a mossy stone, and then looked back just as the ogre reached the satyrs. Both goatmen had their hooves dug into the ground and strained to keep the rope tight. The tripline caught Mung just above the ankles. The ogre plunged forward, huge body carving a trench in the forest floor, simultaneously slinging Newel and Doren into the air.

Seth kept running. When he peered back again, Mung was already on his feet, stampeding forward. Newel and Doren had bought him some extra seconds, but at the rate the ogre was gaining, Seth knew he had no chance of reaching the yard. "How?" he muttered in frustration.

"You sent in Knox," came a voice from his pocket.

"What?" Seth gasped, still sprinting.

"The ogre couldn't attack Knox because he was innocent," Calvin chirped. "But you sent him in from outside the ogre's domain. That must have freed the ogre to chase you."

"A little late for that info," Seth grumbled as he weaved between tree trunks.

"I'm not sure," Calvin said. "Just a guess. Don't forget that ogres run in straight lines."

"Huh?"

"An angry ogre charges straight for his prey," Calvin said.

Seth remembered Newel and Doren teaching him the same thing. How could it prove useful? The gully!

"You're a genius," Seth panted.

"Common knowledge," Calvin replied.

Seth knew he couldn't reach the yard ahead of the ogre. Not in a fair footrace. But if he temporarily veered away from the house, he could cross the gully. The little bridge wasn't too far.

Branches whipped at Seth as he turned toward the gully. Hopefully his explorations of the area with Newel and Doren would pay off. If the bridge wasn't where he remembered, the ogre would have him pinned up against a steep drop.

As the ogre gained on him, Seth heard the brute's breath coming in slobbery gasps, like a snorting bull. The little footbridge came into view and Seth ran straight at it. He pounded across and then turned, running along the edge of the gully.

If the ogre used the bridge, Seth knew he would soon be mashed into paste. All the ogre needed to do was take the slightly longer way around. But Mung charged straight at him, heedless of the footbridge, eyes promising murder.

Having made it about twenty yards away from the bridge, Seth slowed to wave his arms and stick out his tongue.

The ogre dashed toward the gully, vengeful eyes fixed on Seth. As the oversized brute sprang from the far side, one beefy arm outstretched, the other raising his club to strike, Seth staggered back. Mung was so big and coming so fast that it looked like he might clear the ravine!

The club came whistling down and struck the near side of the gully hard enough for Seth to feel the vibrations. Then Mung fell out of sight.

"Keep going!" Doren called from a distance.

Heart hammering, Seth took off for the yard. The gully was at least thirty feet deep here. Could Mung climb it? It got shallower if the ogre went far enough in either direction, but that could buy Seth enough time to get to the house.

Glancing back, Seth saw hands on the edge of the gully, then a head. Now without his club, Mung heaved himself up. As the ogre started running, an arrow struck Mung in the calf from behind. Seth heard Doren whoop. The ogre stumbled but kept coming.

"Can you make it?" Calvin asked.

"That's the question," Seth replied. He had stretched his lead enough that there was a chance. Seth couldn't think of any other obstacles like the gully that he could use to trip up the ogre. "It'll be close."

CHAPTER EIGHT

Reprimanded

K endra watched as fairies fluttered around Tess, sometimes alighting on her head, shoulders, and arms. To her younger cousin, the tiny winged women looked like common hummingbirds, butterflies, and dragonflies. But Tess seemed elated nonetheless.

"They think I'm a real fairy!" Tess said in an excited whisper. "Look how the butterflies follow me! This never happened to me before."

"She really does worship us," said a lithe, golden fairy.

"Isn't it adorable how she tries to look like us," a scarlet fairy chimed in.

"Pathetic and insulting," accused a white, furry fairy. "She puts on a set of dumpy cosmetic wings and fancies herself one of our sisters."

"Hopeless and flattering," giggled a fairy with dragonfly wings. "She aspires to heights she could never climb."

Several other fairies tittered.

Kendra folded her arms and held back comments. She didn't want to disturb Tess's happy mood with responses that might hint at what the fairies were saying about her. She also didn't want to look like she was scolding hummingbirds.

"I can almost hear them laughing," Tess said with a smile, raising a fairy on her finger to her nose. Judging by the wings, Kendra assumed the tiny woman looked like a butterfly.

The fairy kissed the tip of Tess's nose. "You're a cutie," the fairy said, then dove from her finger in a gliding swoop.

Tess blinked. "Did you hear that? I felt like I heard her talking."

Several of the fairies scattered. Those that remained hovered at a greater distance.

"She couldn't have heard us," the golden fairy said.

"She hasn't had any milk," the scarlet fairy added.

Tess looked around at the fairies. "They seem startled. Did I scare them?"

"It's hard to guess what butterflies are thinking," Kendra hedged.

Tess squinted at them. "I don't think they're normal butterflies."

Part of Kendra wanted to tell her little cousin to follow her instincts. She was perceptive! But Kendra knew it wasn't her place to reveal the big secret of Fablehaven. "Maybe they just—"

Seth came dashing out of the woods, face red and sweaty, eyes wide with alarm. He glanced back over one shoulder before collapsing onto the grass. From the forest came huffing gasps and the splintery crack of branches snapping. Something big was crashing toward the yard.

"What did you do?" Kendra called. Her brother hadn't appeared this flustered in a long time.

"Nothing," Seth said, getting back on his feet, still breathing hard. He wiped sweat from his eyes. "Just having a race."

A massive ogre erupted from the trees and charged onto the lawn, fierce eyes intent on her brother. Tess shrieked. Kendra stared in shock. The founding treaty of Fablehaven prevented creatures like ogres from entering the yard uninvited. How was this happening?

"Oh, no!" Seth cried, darting toward the house. "This isn't fair!"

It shortly became apparent that Seth would not make it. The ogre was closing too quickly. The bloodthirsty brute would overtake her brother within ten steps or so.

Then another giant figure emerged from the woods on the other side of the yard, rocky limbs flailing.

"Hugo!" cried Seth.

Roaring like a landslide, the golem loped across the yard with long, bounding strides, racing to cut off the ogre before he flattened Seth.

The ogre turned to confront the new challenge just

before Hugo sprang at him. Though the ogre was taller than the golem, Hugo was broader through the shoulders, with bigger hands and feet. Plus Hugo was mostly made of stone.

A rocky fist bashed the ogre, knocking him through a neatly trimmed bush. The ogre rolled to his feet and started grappling with the golem. Muscles bulging, the ogre grimaced and snarled as Hugo wrenched him from one position to another.

Before long, the golem had the ogre on his knees, one huge hand clutching the brute's brawny neck, the other poised to punch his face. Hugo stared down at the ogre with empty eye sockets. "Yield," the golem said in a voice that reminded Kendra of boulders grating against one another.

"No," the ogre spat, face contorted with anger. "I will have my prey."

Hugo slapped his free hand down on the ogre's head and began to squeeze. The ogre groaned and tried to struggle, but Hugo just tipped him off balance and kept tightening his grip.

"I yield," the ogre conceded with a grunt.

Hugo stood him up and shoved him toward the woods. "Go."

As the ogre trudged away, Kendra noticed an arrow jutting from his bloody calf. The ogre left the yard without looking back.

"What is that?" Tess asked in a small voice, her eyes on Hugo.

Kendra had almost forgotten her young cousin in the excitement. "What do you see?"

Tess swallowed hard. "It looks like a little tornado filled with dirt. But it went right after the bear. And now it's over by Seth."

"Sorry," Hugo said to Seth. "Late. Came when heard trouble."

"It's not your fault, Hugo," Seth said.

"I have strong suspicions about where the fault lies!" came the voice of Grandpa Sorenson as he hustled across the yard from the house. "Seth Sorenson, what was an ogre doing in the yard?"

"Ogre?" Tess asked.

"Grandpa calls bears ogres," Kendra explained loudly.

"Yes, a bear," Grandpa said. "What have you been up to, young man?"

"Knox is fine," Seth said.

"You involved your cousin?" Grandpa asked, his face turning a shade redder.

"I protected him," Seth assured him.

"Why did he need protecting?" Grandpa asked through gritted teeth.

Seth hesitated. "I had this really good idea."

"Enough," Grandpa said, glancing at Tess. "We'll continue this in my office." He started to lead Seth away.

"Is Knox okay?" Tess asked.

"He's fine," Seth said. "I bet he thinks Fablehaven is a little less boring now."

"Did he call it boring?" Grandpa asked, his angry tone thawing a little.

"What about the whirlwind?" Tess asked Kendra, staring at Hugo.

The golem noticed the attention and started to tiptoe away.

"I'm sure it'll blow someplace else soon," Kendra said.

Tess squinted at it. "It went right for the bear and scared it away. Could it be a bunch of fairies? No. It looks too dusty. Nothing sparkles."

"We sometimes get strange winds here," Kendra said. "It was probably just good luck. Let's go over by the fountain. It usually attracts lots of butterflies."

Kendra caught up with Seth in the upstairs hall. His head was down and he kept banging his fist against the side of his leg. He was heading toward the attic playroom.

"How'd it go with Grandpa?" Kendra asked, approaching her brother.

"What do you think? I'm Grandchild of the Year again. He gave me a medal."

"A medal of shame?"

He gave a token chuckle. "Pretty much."

"How was the ogre able to come into the yard?"

"I was trying to get some treasure back."

"You stole from an ogre? You know better than that!"

"The treasure wasn't the problem," Seth said. "We only took items the satyrs knew the ogres had stolen. They have no claim if we grab stolen property."

"What went wrong?"

"A few weeks ago, while making our escape, we dropped the treasure near the edge of the ogres' domain. We knew the ogres were watching it, so I sent Knox in to get it."

Kendra gasped. "That's what you meant in the yard? About Knox being fine? Where is he? Is he really all right?"

"He's back," Seth said. "Just kind of shaken up. The satyrs led him home."

"You introduced him to Newel and Doren? Grandma told me not to let them in on the secrets of Fablehaven. They have to learn for themselves."

"Calm down. To Knox, the satyrs just seem like really smart goats. Grandma brought Knox into the den while I was talking to Grandpa. Knox thinks he survived a bear attack."

Kendra shook her head. "You could have gotten him killed."

"I was the one in danger," Seth said. "I thought I was home free when I reached the yard. Thank goodness for Hugo."

"I'm more worried about our cousin."

"Knox doesn't have a clue what's going on here," Seth said. "I knew the treaty would protect him. The ogre couldn't touch him."

"The treaty is complicated, Seth. Sometimes innocent people can get attacked for trespassing."

"I brought Newel and Doren, just in case."

"How would they have stopped a rampaging ogre?"

"We always think of something."

"Clearly it was a flawless plan. Good thing nothing went wrong—like an ogre in our yard! You practically scared Tess to death."

"It couldn't have hurt anybody," Seth said. "The ogre could only cross boundaries to come after me."

"Why?"

"Grandpa explained," Seth said. "Since I sent an innocent person someplace I couldn't safely go, the treaty makes me the guilty one. The ogre was free to chase me anywhere inside of Fablehaven unless he yielded the right."

"Even into the yard."

"Obviously."

"Hugo made him yield," Kendra said.

"So now I'm off the hook," Seth said. "I should have brought Hugo in the first place."

"But you were afraid he might tell Grandpa," Kendra said.

"It crossed my mind. He's not great with secrets."

"What's the punishment?" Kendra asked.

Seth lowered his eyes. "Grandpa took away my adventuring rights. I can't leave the yard without an adult human escort."

Kendra knew that would sting. After they had all returned from the battle of Zzyzx, Grandpa Sorenson had granted Seth limited permission to roam certain parts of Fablehaven with the satyrs or Hugo. It was his favorite pastime.

"I'm sorry, Seth," Kendra said. "What was so special about the treasure?"

"Just treasure. Gold and jewels."

"You risked your cousin for some gold?"

"I didn't risk him. I was right that he was safe. I risked myself."

"Why risk anybody?"

Seth tossed up his hands. "If you have to ask, how am I supposed to explain? Because it's treasure, and I figured out a way to get it! What's the point of exploring if you never do anything cool?"

"Except now you can't explore anymore."

"Which is better? Getting grounded from exploring? Or being able to explore but never doing it?"

"I go all over Fablehaven," Kendra pointed out.

"Do you find treasure?"

"This whole place is a treasure."

"I mean actual treasure," Seth said.

"To me, the fairies are much more of a treasure than gold or jewels. And the brownies. And Hugo. Even the satyrs."

Seth shook his head. "I like all of that too. But what about liking those things and also finding gold?"

"Why do I need gold?"

Seth rolled his eyes. "Are you kidding? Have you heard that it's valuable?"

"Our family has plenty of money," Kendra said. "Why would I stir up trouble with the ogres for a little extra gold? Why would I endanger people for it?"

Seth closed his eyes and pounded a fist against his forehead. "Most fun things are risky! You can get hurt playing sports. You can get hurt climbing a mountain. But it's challenging and exciting. People do those kinds of things without getting gold. The gold is a bonus."

"You like running from ogres? You like endangering your cousin?"

"I like exploring. Stuff happens. Sometimes you have to improvise."

Kendra shook her head. "I give up. You're never going to change. You should be banned from Fablehaven."

Seth folded his arms in a huff. "Then Coulter should have been banned. He was a professional relics collector. He spent a lot of time exploring. Patton too. Maddox. These preserves need people like me. You killed the Demon King. Good for you. But who brought the sword?"

Kendra almost asked Seth who got Coulter killed. For the sake of the argument, she wanted to say the words, but it was too true and too painful. In a time of great upheaval, Seth had treated a demon kindly, and the demon had brought down Fablehaven.

"You're sometimes useful," Kendra said, trying her best to be diplomatic. "But we're not talking about finding a magic sword to save the world. We're talking about risking your cousin's life because you're bored."

"He was the bored one," Seth said.

"You always have an excuse," Kendra said. "It doesn't change the fact that you have caused some major disasters."

"And fixed some," Seth said. "It evens out."

Kendra started walking away. Arguing with him was so pointless! But she stopped. "Seth, you matter to me. Please be careful."

"I'm grounded," Seth said. "When I sneak out I'll have to be way more careful."

"You have serious psychological problems."

"I'm logical to psychos?"

"Probably."

"At least somebody gets me."

The next day at the pool behind the house, Kendra watched as Tess splashed in the water, several fairies orbiting her. Despite their many protests about Tess, the tiny winged women couldn't resist that she was fascinated by their favorite subject—themselves.

Kendra had wondered whether Tess would grow tired of pretending fairies inhabited Fablehaven. Instead, her interest in the game seemed to steadily increase. She routinely addressed the bumblebees and dragonflies around her as fairies, and she continued to catch glimpses of their actual natures, humming a melody a fairy had sung or accurately commenting on the color of a dress.

Knox had been in the pool tossing balls at the bin that held some of the pool equipment, but now he was roaming the edge of the patio, whacking rosebuds with a stick. Kendra scowled as she watched blossoms falling to the ground.

"Don't do that to the flowers," Kendra scolded.

Knox turned, eyebrows raised. "There are about a billion flowers here. Nobody is going to miss a few."

"They belong to Grandma and Grandpa Sorenson and they look pretty. Leave them alone."

He swished his stick, knocking off another one. "I finally find a decent game and you want to wreck it. Same old Kendra."

"Are you going to take that?" asked a shimmering silver fairy with wings like mirrors.

"Want us to teach him a lesson?" asked another.

"Not much you can do," Kendra muttered under her breath. "He's protected."

"What was that?" Knox asked, casually chopping off another rosebud.

"I'll have a talk with Grandma Sorenson," she said loudly, as if repeating herself. "She likes her flowers intact."

"I brought lemonade," Seth declared, approaching the pool area holding a tray topped by four glasses, each with a plastic straw. He set the tray on a poolside table.

Kendra was happy for the distraction. Knox tossed the stick aside and hurried over to the table. Kendra strolled that way as well.

"Are they letting you out?" Knox asked.

"I'm not allowed to swim today," Seth said. "And I'm grounded from the woods."

Knox took a sip from the straw. "Not bad. Thanks, Seth."

"Least I could do after almost getting you eaten by a bear. Come get some, Tess. This is a special blend that might help you see the fairies more clearly."

Kendra glared at her brother. She understood he was

trying to be funny, but that was a little too close to the truth.

"How did you know the bear would be there?" Knox asked.

"I wasn't sure," Seth said. "I'm really sorry."

"I'm just lucky you're such a scaredy-cat," Knox said. "You ran away so fast that it went after you."

"You were running too," Seth said. "You were just too slow. Bears like a challenge."

"The bear was scary," Tess said, dripping on the patio as she claimed a glass and took a sip. "Do you get many of them?"

"Hardly ever in the yard," Kendra said.

"You must get some," Knox said. "Didn't you mention bear traps in the woods?"

"We see a few," Seth said vaguely.

"Smart goats, though," Knox said. "They're like dogs. Stayed with me all the way back to the yard."

"Good old Newel and Doren," Seth said. "What happened to the duffel bag?"

"I left it in the woods," Knox said. "The deal was to bring it to you. But you ran off, and it was heavy. Felt like bricks. Was the heaviness supposed to slow me down? You must have known a bear cave was nearby. Did you expect it to chase us?"

"I was just goofing around," Seth said. "I wasn't expecting a bear."

"Whatever," Knox said. "At least it ended up chasing you. The power of karma. You owe me ten bucks."

"A deal is a deal," Seth agreed. "How far did you get with the bag?"

"Just past where you were waiting for me," Knox said. "The goats returned and hurried me along. I was worried the bear might double back."

"Right," Seth said. Kendra could hear the concern behind the word. Her brother was hoping the treasure was safe.

"So when are you going to pay up?" Knox asked.

"Are you planning to take the money in the pool?" Seth replied. "I'll get it to you. But first I need to borrow Kendra."

"I was just about to jump in the water," Kendra said.

"That'll have to wait," her brother answered.

"Since when do you tell me what to do?" Kendra asked.

Seth leaned in close and whispered, "Since Agad showed up. He wants to talk to us."

CHAPTER NINE

Dragonwatch

When Kendra entered Grandpa Sorenson's office, something about the atmosphere made her feel she had interrupted an argument. Perhaps it was the variety of expressions. Grandpa Larsen looked sad. Grandma Larsen seemed angry, though she was trying to cover it up. Grandma and Grandpa Sorenson both looked concerned. Bracken was there, appearing unusually somber. And Agad looked apologetic.

Perhaps it was the absence of conversation after they entered—no greetings, no small talk. Everyone just stared at her and Seth.

Or maybe there really was an intangible tension in the air.

Agad broke the tension first, stepping forward to greet them. Plump and elderly, he had a gray beard that hung almost to his waist. He wore a silky robe of dark blue, topped by a black cloak trimmed with sable. Rings glittered on all his fingers.

"Good to see you, Kendra," the wizard said. "Greetings, Seth."

"Hello," Kendra replied. "Nice to see you, too." She meant it. Agad had given them good advice when they were at Wyrmroost. He had recruited the dragons that had enabled them to win the battle of Zzyzx. And he had helped set things right at Fablehaven after the demons were locked away inside a new prison. Agad was powerful, smart, and on their side.

"Hi," Seth said. "We weren't eavesdropping. Grandpa Sorenson told me to bring Kendra to his office. What's going on?"

"More than you want to know," Bracken muttered.

"I always want to know," Seth insisted.

"Is it bad?" Kendra asked. "Is everyone all right? Warren? Vanessa? Tanu?"

"As far as I know, your friends are well," Agad said. "They all remain on assignment."

It had been months since Kendra had seen any of them. Though she felt certain that Grandpa Sorenson, as Captain of the Knights of the Dawn, knew where they were, he never shared. It was all top secret.

"Then what's up?" Seth asked.

Agad looked at Grandma Larsen. "I'm not sure we've entirely settled on what to tell you."

"Tell us everything," Seth said.

"Careful what you wish for," Bracken warned.

"How bad is it?" Seth asked.

"I don't like it any more than you do, Gloria," Grandma Sorenson said. "But you know the stakes. We should at least have the conversation."

"If we have the conversation, you know what will happen," Grandma Larsen said. "The only way to prevent their involvement is to keep them out of it."

"Out of what?" Seth asked. Then he paled, looking at Agad. "Oh, no. Out of prison? Is this about the ogre? Is Kendra a witness?"

Grandpa Sorenson covered a grin.

"Am I saying too much?" Seth went on. "Are there magical lawyers?"

Agad looked at Seth seriously. "I heard about the incident with the ogre. It was unwise. But reprimanding you is not the purpose of my visit."

Seth looked relieved. "You brought us here to tell us something. Let's do it."

"I agree," Kendra said, her mind flashing back to the robed figure in the driveway of Fablehaven and his dire warning. Was this related to that encounter somehow?

"You know how I feel," Agad announced to the room. "I don't like it, but I would not be here if I had another option. They are remarkable children. They could be of service. However, I am not their guardian."

"Mom and Dad are on a trip," Kendra said.

"We tried to phone them," Grandpa Larsen said.

"They wouldn't understand what is being asked,"

Grandma Larsen said. "Not really. Our world is too new to them. Everything would depend on how we present it. We could make it sound like a holiday. We could make it sound necessary. We could make it sound out of the question."

"What are we talking about?" Seth asked, clearly frustrated. "What do you need us to do?"

"Go ahead," Grandma Larsen said with resignation. "I suppose we know this has to happen or we wouldn't have sent for them."

"They could decline," Bracken said.

"In theory," Grandma Larsen said sadly. "Tell them."

Grandpa Sorenson nodded at Agad.

The wizard cleared his throat. "There has been unrest of late among the dragons."

"Is a storm coming?" Seth asked.

"A new age of dragons?" Kendra added.

Agad furrowed his brow. "What makes you say that?"

"Witches," Seth said.

"A demon," Kendra said.

"I hope those are overstatements," Agad said. "But relations are rapidly deteriorating. We could be heading in that direction."

"Aren't the dragons in sanctuaries?" Seth asked.

"The vast majority, yes, for now," Agad said. "May it ever be so."

"Are the dragon sanctuaries in danger?" Kendra asked.

"We have reason for concern," Agad said carefully. "All at once, across all the sanctuaries, the dragons are suddenly testing their limits. No sanctuaries have fallen, but in some places the situation is turning ugly. I fear we have become too complacent over the years. We're not ready for a coordinated draconic rebellion."

"Give them some history," Grandpa Sorenson said.

Agad nodded. "Have you children ever wondered why we started relocating magical creatures into hidden preserves?"

Seth scrunched his face. "Kind of. But not really."

"To keep them safe?" Kendra guessed.

"That was part of it," Agad said. "But it was just as much to protect humanity. And that started with the dragons."

"Dragons used to run around loose?" Seth asked.

"Essentially, yes," Agad said.

Kendra had met dragons. The thought made her shiver.

"Long ago, magical creatures dwelled alongside mortals," Agad said. "Like tigers in the jungle, bears in the hills, or sharks in the ocean, enchanted beasts wandered the world. There were plenty of wild places back then, and coexistence was not a major problem. The unbelief of mortals helped repel most beings of a magical nature. And there were unwritten laws that generally kept humans and mystical creatures apart."

"Then the dragons got greedy," Bracken said.

Agad held up a finger. "Not without reason. Remember, I was once a dragon, long ago. I remember those times. As mortals spread, the wild places grew smaller. Certain dragons foresaw the day when mortals would claim the entire world. And they started to fight back."

"What happened?" Seth asked.

"The Age of Dragons," Bracken said.

"Dragons got carried away," Agad said. "They started with ships and caravans. Soon it was villages and towns. Even cities."

"Wait," Kendra said. "We would have heard of this."

Agad smiled. "Are you sure? Ancient stories fade or change. Records get destroyed. The magical community has historically done an excellent job at avoiding detection by humankind. Doesn't it seem everyone should know about the preserves for magical creatures dotting the globe? Places like Fablehaven. And the enormous dragon sanctuaries."

"Distracter spells," Seth said. "People can see them but they don't actually notice them."

"That's the idea," Agad said. "History can work much the same way. It helps that people don't want to believe a dragon leveled a city or burned an ancient library. They would rather believe it was a volcano or a war. There was a time when a huge percentage of towns and cities offered tributes to dragons to survive. Some gave treasure. Others provided livestock or even people."

"That's horrible," Kendra said.

Agad raised his eyebrows. "It was dreadful, and getting worse every year. Many realized it had gone too far. I was among the dragons who sided with humankind. Long, long ago, before my time, a mighty dragon named Archadius learned that by permanently taking human shape, he could greatly enhance his magical abilities. Archadius became a wizard, the first of his kind. As you know, all true wizards were once dragons. Magic has never been for mortals—they can only borrow it from magical beings. I made the same choice as Archadius, partly because I had become ashamed of my kind and wanted to stop them."

"It's hard to picture you as a dragon," Seth said.

"It has become difficult for me as well," Agad said. "That was so long ago. Once upon a time I soared the skies and breathed fire. On occasion, I experience echoes of those days in my dreams. It's as close as I get."

"You were one of the founding members of Dragon-watch," Bracken said.

"You know your history," Agad replied.

"I'm not as young as I look," Bracken said.

"Dragonwatch?" Kendra asked.

"The organization we formed to combat the dragon epidemic," Agad said. "A consortium of wizards, enchantresses, dragon slayers, and many others who agreed the tyrannical rule of dragons had to end. We began the practice of confining dragons to sanctuaries. Other magical preserves followed."

"Places like Fablehaven happened because you needed to stop the dragons?" Kendra asked.

"That's right," Agad said.

"When did this start?" Seth asked.

"Almost three thousand years ago," Agad said. "It was a long and bloody process. We were still rounding up renegade dragons all the way into the Dark Ages. There were many casualties on both sides. In the end, the courage of dragon slayers and the ingenuity of wizards overcame the might of our opponents. All the hostile dragons were confined to preserves. Only dragons who had not besieged mortals and who pledged to live according to a certain code of conduct were permitted to remain in the wild."

"The dragons must have been mad," Kendra said.

Agad chuckled. "Furious. Dragons are not accustomed to losing. They did not go quietly. But over time they settled into their new lives."

"And Dragonwatch disbanded," Bracken said.

"Not completely," Agad said. "The organization shrank and the focus changed. Attention was placed on managing the preserves. Later the Knights of the Dawn formed. Eventually Dragonwatch faded away. For a time, one of your ancestors, Patton Burgess, was the sole active member of Dragonwatch."

Kendra perked up. "Patton? Our Patton?"

"I know you idolize him," Agad said.

"Only because he's the coolest guy who ever lived," Seth said.

"Not a poor description," Agad agreed. "I admired him as well. His stewardship was one of the few times a regular mortal took charge of Dragonwatch rather than a wizard."

"Who runs it now?" Kendra asked.

"I do," Agad said. "I'm re-forming it. The need for Dragonwatch has returned. As Seth mentioned, a storm appears to be brewing. I just hope we're not too late to intervene."

Seth brightened. "I get it! You want us to join Dragonwatch! Is that what this is about?"

"Not exactly," Agad said.

Seth wilted.

"But we may need your help with a related matter," Agad went on.

"What?" Kendra asked. Based on the conversation leading up to this, it had to be dangerous.

Agad pressed his fingertips together. "A bit more context first. I was partially involved in stirring up this potential dragon storm."

"The battle of Zzyzx," Kendra said.

Agad gave a nod. "I cut a deal with the dragons because we had to win that battle, and I saw no other strategy that gave us a chance. Celebrant, the Dragon King, would come to our aid only on the condition that governance of Wyrmroost would be passed over to dragons. He became a co-caretaker with my brother, Camarat."

"Who is a dragon," Kendra recalled.

"Correct," Agad said. "As a caretaker, Camarat stays in human form and goes by the name of Marat. Since he is housed at Blackwell Keep, Marat still controls who can go in and out of Wyrmroost. But Celebrant is working to undermine him. In effect, by seeking help from the dragons against the demons, I solved one dire problem by creating a future dilemma."

"This is where the story begins to involve the two of you," Grandpa Sorenson said.

"How?" Seth asked.

"Celebrant has attacked Blackwell Keep three times since my brother took over," Agad said gravely.

"How did Marat stop him?" Kendra asked.

"Blackwell Keep is protected by powerful magic that has been in place since the sanctuary was established," Agad said, scowling in thought. "The arrangement I made granted Celebrant no access to Blackwell Keep, yet he keeps storming the stronghold. Dragons do not attack lightly. They play to win, and they prefer to win decisively. A difficult victory is perceived as weakness. A failed attack is worse. Let alone three failed attacks."

"So Celebrant thinks he can succeed," Seth said.

"It would seem so," Agad said. "The intent could be to intimidate or confuse Marat. But I suspect Celebrant has found a weakness and is trying to exploit it. The Dragon King thinks there is a way to overthrow my brother, but has yet to pinpoint the correct approach. I fear that I know the problem."

"What?" Kendra asked.

Agad scratched his beard. "According to the treaty established when Wyrmroost was founded, the caretaker should be mortal."

"Weren't you the caretaker?" Seth asked.

"That was no problem," Agad said. "Wizards are mortal. We age very slowly, but dragons become wizards by falling to mortality while retaining and enhancing our magic. When I left Wyrmroost to manage the Living Mirage preserve, there was a shortage of candidates for a new caretaker, so I went with my brother. We conferred and decided that as long as he remained in his human form, there should be no problem."

"But there is?" Kendra asked.

"I'm afraid that Celebrant has become aware of this detail and may have found a way to exploit it. I can find no other way to explain his aggression. Perhaps he believes he can make Marat change to dragon shape and lose the claim to his position. Or perhaps Celebrant has found some other vulnerability. But I believe having a human caretaker would resolve the issue."

"What about Celebrant?" Kendra asked. "How can a dragon be a co-caretaker?"

"I had to restructure some aspects of the treaty to grant him that position," Agad said. "Even so, the magical defenses won't protect Celebrant as they would a mortal. Not much of a problem for a dragon with so many powerful underlings. But it could leave Marat exposed."

"What if Marat becomes a wizard?" Seth asked. "Right now he is just temporarily using his human form. Can't he make it permanent? Then he would be mortal."

"Sensible," Agad said. "But the art of turning from dragon to wizard has been lost. I only did it with the help of an older generation of wizards, all of whom have moved on. No dragon has become a wizard for more than a thousand years."

"If Marat can't become a wizard, why don't you take control of Wyrmroost again?" Kendra asked.

"Another sensible solution," Agad said. "Unfortunately, the Soaring Cliffs sanctuary is in an even worse predicament, so I am going to take over that preserve."

Seth looked around the room. "Are you recruiting Grandpa Sorenson? Or Grandpa Larsen?"

"Both capable men," Agad said. "But the caretaker of Wyrmroost must be a true dragon tamer. Not just somebody who can stand in the presence of a dragon and force out a few words—he or she must be able to hold a conversation with a hostile dragon without becoming clouded by fear. Very few dragon tamers remain."

"Oh, no," Kendra said.

"Now you see," Agad said. "With Kendra being fairy-kind and Seth a shadow charmer, when the two of you are in physical contact with each other, you can stand tall in the presence of a dragon. Together you are a dragon tamer. Kendra, Seth, I am here to invite you to become the next caretakers of Wyrmroost."

CHAPTER TEN

Caretakers Wanted

The silence stretched out for a long time. Kendra didn't know how to respond.

"I get it," Seth finally said. "This is a joke. Very funny."

Nobody cracked a smile.

"I think they're serious, Seth," Kendra said, her stomach queasy.

Seth looked around the room. "Us? The official caretakers?"

"Co-caretakers, along with Celebrant," Grandpa Sorenson explained.

Seth failed to resist an enormous smile. "No way. Really?"

"Really," Agad said.

"Take a picture," Seth said. "This is the best moment of my life."

"Are you crazy?" Kendra asked her brother. "Do you get how dangerous this will be?"

"Do you get how in charge we will be?" Seth asked in reply.

"Of one of the most dangerous magical sanctuaries in the world," Kendra said. "At a time when the dragons are attempting an uprising. Right after witches warned you of dragon storms, and a demon warned me about a new age of dragons."

"Life is full of problems," Seth said. "We'll be inside Blackwell Keep. We'll be protected."

"Exactly how protected will they be?" Grandma Larsen asked.

"Blackwell Keep and their status as caretakers should grant all the protection they require," Agad said.

"Until Seth goes adventuring in the mountains," Kendra said. "He'll hear about some treasure and wander off."

"Exercising self-restraint would be critical," Agad said.

"He has none," Kendra said. "Zero. The sanctuary will fall in minutes."

"I get how huge this would be," Seth said. "I'd never do anything to endanger the sanctuary."

"Like how you'd never do anything to endanger your cousin?" Kendra asked.

Seth placed a hand over his heart. "I've made some mistakes and learned my lesson. I promise I'll keep the rules. I'll only go where I'm allowed."

"I don't believe this," Kendra murmured. "Will we have help?"

"Your Grandma and Grandpa Sorenson have offered to come as your assistants," Agad said. "The Larsens would watch over Fablehaven. Blackwell Keep has a skilled, experienced staff, and Marat would remain as an additional assistant caretaker."

Seth dropped to his knees, his expression stunned. "A dragon as my assistant? Yes. The answer is yes. With or without Kendra. Yes. Yes. Yes."

"This works only if both of you come," Agad said.

"Isn't there somebody else?" Kendra asked.

"Nobody I can fully trust," Agad said. "Most of the great old wizards of Dragonwatch have passed on or are actively engaged at other sanctuaries. And wizards have never been plentiful. Remember that all wizards were once dragons. If I send a wizard there whom Celebrant can turn, the sanctuary falls and hundreds of dragons are released. True dragon tamers have become so rare. Few can resist a full measure of dragon fear. You are the only candidates left whom I know I can trust."

"So we're your last choice," Kendra rephrased.

"You're so young," Agad said sadly. "I wish I had another option. We really are in a crisis. I would not be here otherwise. If you can't step in, Marat will hold out as best he can."

"Please, Kendra," Seth said. "We have to do this. The world needs us."

"You just want to be in charge of Wyrmroost," she replied.

"The world needs me in charge of Wyrmroost," Seth declared.

"The world is doomed," Kendra muttered. She looked to Grandpa Sorenson. "You want us to do this?"

"The choice is yours," he said. "I don't want to convey a false sense of security. A preserve like Fablehaven is a perilous place. Being caretaker comes with a host of dangers. Doing the job well can expose you to greater threats. A dragon sanctuary like Wyrmroost is a hundred times more deadly. The preserve is larger. The politics are more complicated. The occupants are more powerful. And with the dragons in a state of unrest, it is not someplace I would let you go if we had any other option."

"But . . ." Kendra prompted.

Grandpa Sorenson shrugged. "If the dragons get free, the world could be destroyed. It could mark the end of life as we know it. If sending you and Seth to Wyrmroost prevents the sanctuary from falling, it would be safer than keeping you here. Safer for you. Safer for everyone. But the choice is yours."

Kendra tried to will the knots in her stomach to loosen. It didn't work. After the battle of Zzyzx, she had found great relief in believing the worst of her troubles were over. She had relished the relatively quiet months at Fablehaven since the demonic crisis had been averted. She had begun to anticipate the path the rest of her life would take.

And here was a new detour. A big one. Maybe a fatal one. She would be in way over her head. She would have to depend on her brother, who had better intentions than ability when it came to coloring inside the lines. And if they messed up, the whole world would pay the price.

But doing nothing might be a more certain path to destruction. Agad needed her help. Her grandparents would not agree to this unless the situation were dire. Kendra had risked her life at Zzyzx to save the world. If she was needed again, and nobody else could do it, what else could she say?

"All right," Kendra said, already wishing she could take it back. "Can any of our other friends come? Bracken, or anyone?"

By the pain in Bracken's gaze, Kendra knew there was a problem.

"In time, yes," Agad said. "As we settle some of the issues elsewhere, we can send some of your friends to aid you. Right now, they are engaged in a variety of critical missions. Warren and Vanessa are working together in one location. Tanu in another. Maddox and Trask in a third. I mustn't be too specific."

"In case we get captured and they try to torture it out of us," Seth said.

"Something like that," Agad admitted.

"And Bracken?" Kendra asked.

"I'm sorry, Kendra," Bracken said. "There is a situation where I'm needed."

"An old enemy," Agad said. "Ronodin."

"That sounds familiar," Kendra said.

"A dark unicorn who willfully corrupted his horns," Bracken said. "My cousin."

"Your cousin?" Kendra exclaimed.

"Ronodin is helping the dragons at Soaring Cliffs," Agad said. "Nobody on site has any idea how to handle him."

"I spoke with Mother about it," Bracken said. "She insists I go after him. There may not be anyone else who can stop him."

Kendra had no words. What was she supposed to say? *Forget the stupid evil unicorn and come protect your . . . what? Your future girlfriend? Assuming no dragons eat her.*

"A dark unicorn," Seth said reverently. "That sounds intense."

"It won't be pleasant," Bracken said. "But it's something I have to do. I'll come to Wyrmroost as soon as I can. If you end up going there."

"Oh, I'm going," Kendra said stiffly, trying not to cry. She couldn't cry. They would be the most embarrassing tears of her life. "I'll be all right."

"At least you'll get to see Raxtus again," Seth said, trying to cheer her up.

The thought was encouraging. The son of the Dragon King was the only nice dragon she had ever met and a real friend. They had been through a lot together. She hadn't seen Raxtus since he had visited Fablehaven shortly after the battle of Zzyx. "True."

"Mother plans to link the new fairy realm to the fairy shrine at Wyrmroost," Bracken said. "I'll make sure she does it immediately. That way I can visit right after I finish at Soaring Cliffs."

Kendra nodded. "You'll be careful?"

Bracken flashed a confident smile. "I'll see you again in no time."

"I will work to send additional help and to find a replacement caretaker," Agad said.

"Once you see us in action, you won't want a replacement," Seth assured him.

"Perhaps," Agad said. "It's not a sure thing you can have the job."

"Wait, you make an offer, then take it back?" Seth complained.

"I lack full power to bestow the position," Agad said. "Even if Marat steps down, Celebrant can veto the new caretaker. The Dragon King would then have a year to nominate a replacement. Marat can veto any replacements Celebrant suggests. If after a year no agreeable candidate is found, Marat can assign anyone and Celebrant cannot block it."

"Does Celebrant know that having us as caretakers could make Blackwell Keep more secure?" Kendra asked.

"He may suspect it," Agad said. "He may not. But he will not casually reject placing two children as caretakers in place of Marat. Even though the two of you have accomplished much in your young lives, he will see your inexperience as an opportunity. And it will be. Talented or not, I would never assign anyone as young as you two to oversee any preserve, let alone a dragon sanctuary, except as a last resort."

"We get it," Seth said. "We're your worst-case scenario. You'd rather have some old guy take over. We'll still do it. What are the chances Celebrant will veto us?"

"If for no other reason, I suspect Celebrant may approve you to save face," Agad said. "Dragons are extraordinarily proud. And not without reason—they are where the food chain stops, the ultimate alpha predator. Celebrant wouldn't wish to seem afraid of anyone, let alone children. But nothing is certain."

"If we become caretakers, could Celebrant keep us from leaving?" Kendra asked.

"Not directly," Agad said. "But remember, he could refuse to instate a new caretaker for up to a year. After you are appointed, if you leave without finding an approved replacement, Celebrant would become the sole caretaker and the sanctuary would fall. He would have authority to free all the inhabitants of Wyrmroost."

"When do we start?" Seth asked.

"Are you both sure you want to do this?" Agad asked, his eyes on Kendra.

"I don't see any other choice," Kendra said.

"Weak," Seth said. "Come on, you killed the Demon King at the most intense battle ever. We can do this."

Kendra felt Bracken's eyes on her. She straightened. "You deserve a firm answer. If taking charge of Wyrmroost will help keep the world safe, I'm in."

"That's more like it!" Seth cheered.

"But is there a place we can keep him tied up?" Kendra asked, jerking a thumb at her brother. "Some sort of spell to prevent him from sneaking out?"

"I'm afraid that, as co-caretakers, you will both have the authority to do as you will," Agad said. "Hopefully you will remember the gravity of the situation and heed the guidance from your grandparents and Marat."

"I won't let you guys down," Seth promised.

"That will have to suffice," Agad said.

"When do we start?" Seth asked again.

"I intend for you to depart immediately," Agad said. "Time is short. I have already been away from Soaring Cliffs for too long. Bracken will accompany you at first to interview the staff. Call it a surprise inspection. Then Bracken will join me at Soaring Cliffs."

"Are we flying there?" Kendra asked, recalling her previous visit to Wyrmroost. "Do you have a helicopter waiting somewhere?"

"No helicopters," Agad said. "But I have a barrel."

"Wait a minute," Seth said. "I know we're your last choice, but come on!"

"A special barrel," Agad clarified. "And a surprise companion. This way."

The wizard opened the doors and led them out of the study. Bracken approached Kendra and placed a hand on her arm, holding her back. The others exited.

"Are you all right?" Bracken asked.

Kendra showed her best impersonation of a smile. "This is all so sudden. I wish you could stay with us."

"Me too," Bracken said. "Ronodin is an old enemy capable of causing a lot of harm. He hasn't surfaced in a long time. I have to go after him."

"I understand," Kendra said.

Bracken placed both hands on her upper arms. "None

of us want this for you. It isn't right. You're so young and you've already been through too much. But your abilities as a dragon tamer are invaluable right now."

He was standing close. Soon he would be so far away. "I'll miss you," she managed to say.

"I'll miss you too," he said, hugging her. "More than you could possibly know."

He felt so good. He was so present. Would he really be gone soon? Would she really be trying to hold off a dragon rebellion without him? "I'd rather stay like this," she said.

Bracken stepped back, his eyes tender. Then he reached behind him for something and held it out to her. It was his first horn. "I want you to take this," he said.

"What if I lose it?"

"We'll find it. Very few enemies would be able to steal it. Do your best to keep it safe. I had all but lost my connection to the horn when the centaurs had it. I've reestablished that connection. Among other things, it will allow us to communicate."

Kendra accepted the pearly horn. It gleamed in her hands. "Thank you."

"We better catch up with the others."

In the living room they found Seth had grabbed his satchel. He stood investigating a man-sized wooden puppet with a smooth, featureless face. The wood looked a bit darker and more polished than Kendra remembered, but the joints of the simple human form were all still connected with brass hooks.

"Look, Kendra!" Seth said. "Mendigo!"

"You fixed him," Kendra said to Agad, breaking into a smile. The automaton had once been a limberjack—a small wooden puppet that danced on a paddleboard. But the witch Muriel Taggert had grown the limberjack and animated him. Mendigo had been through many adventures with Kendra and Seth, finally getting dissolved by dragon poison at Wyrmroost. But they had salvaged his hooks and some splinters of wood, and Agad had apparently remade him.

"Not too difficult," Agad said. "I just needed some time. I thought you might appreciate an extra hand at Wyrmroost."

"What about Hugo?" Seth asked.

"Our golem is so vital to operations here," Grandpa Sorenson said. "Plus he would have to shed a lot of size to squeeze through the barrel."

"This barrel shares space with a barrel at Wyrmroost," Agad said. "If you go inside and crouch down, you will be in both places at once. If you climb out on your own, you'll still be here. But if somebody on the other side helps you out, you'll be there."

"We had a bathtub like that," Seth said. "It connected to the Rio Branco preserve."

"Still does," Grandpa Sorenson said.

"Time to say your good-byes," Agad suggested.

Grandpa Sorenson climbed into the barrel. For a moment he crouched inside. Then he vanished.

Kendra hugged her Grandma and Grandpa Larsen.

"What will you tell Mom and Dad?" she asked.

"A version of the truth," Grandma Larsen said. "We'll explain it was an emergency that only you two could help with. We'll downplay the danger without lying."

Seth hugged Grandma and Grandpa Larsen as well.

"Tell Knox and Tess good-bye," Kendra said.

"We will," Grandpa Larsen said. "Take care. We'll pack some things for you and send them along."

Grandma Sorenson climbed into the barrel.

"Do you want to go next?" Kendra asked Bracken.

"I come last," Bracken said. "Agad wants me to be a surprise. Be ready. If I detect a spy among them, it could get violent."

Seth hopped into the barrel. A moment later Kendra found it empty. She waved one last time to Grandma and Grandpa Larsen and then climbed inside and crouched down.

A strong pair of hands slipped under her arms and lifted her out.

CHAPTER ELEVEN

A New Beginning

Seth watched the brawny minotaur set Kendra on her feet beside the barrel. The bull-headed warrior wore an eye patch and had the silky, chestnut hair of an Irish setter. Seth never tired of seeing monsters; to his delight, most of the individuals who stood in a long line to greet them fit that description.

They were in a courtyard surrounded by gray stone walls. The blocky buildings of the modest castle had small windows and few doors. Under the gloom of an overcast sky, the fortifications looked ancient but sturdy.

The one-eyed minotaur lifted Mendigo from the barrel, and the puppet clattered over to stand near Grandpa and Grandma Sorenson. Bracken was pulled from the barrel last of all.

An Asian man shuffled forward, his long black goatee

streaked with white. He had a shiny bald scalp and calm eyes that seemed to contemplate Seth without looking directly at him. His elaborate scarlet robes were generously embroidered with gold. A circular medallion hung from a golden chain around his neck, set with a single blue gemstone.

"Welcome, Kendra, Seth, and other guests," the man said in a soft, clear voice. "I am Marat, current caretaker of Wyrmroost in partnership with the Dragon King Celebrant." He gestured at Bracken. "I believe you are the unicorn?"

"That's right," Bracken said. "Your brother thought you might like me to meet your staff."

"Indeed," Marat said with a small smile and a slight bow.

"We weren't informed of this," complained a grim being who looked like a centaur, except with the body of a moose instead of a horse. Several scars defaced his brown skin, the most prominent beginning below one ear and curling halfway across his throat. Seth had heard of the alcetaur of Blackwell Keep but had never met him. Most of Seth's previous visit to the keep was spent as a stowaway hiding inside a magical knapsack.

"Informing the staff of a surprise inspection would defeat the purpose," Marat answered.

"What about my years of loyal service?" the alcetaur challenged, heat in his voice. "You would let an outsider judge my value?"

"Those who are loyal have nothing to fear," Marat said. "The crisis confronting us is no secret. We should be grateful for the opportunity to root out traitors."

"It's an insult," growled a minotaur with patchy gray fur and a broken horn. One leg had been replaced by a wooden peg with a silver hoof.

"Now I'm offended," Bracken said. "Most beings find my touch soothing. It cures infections. I bear none of you any malice."

"We don't know this stranger," griped a dwarf. "Why should we trust our fates to his decree?"

"Since when do unicorns lie?" Bracken asked. "Only the disloyal should fear."

"There are many strong, independent spirits on my staff," Marat said. "Most others wouldn't last at Wyrmroost. They perform difficult work in a hostile environment. They do not appreciate being doubted. I volunteer to go first."

"An empty gesture," the peg-legged minotaur said. "Unicorns can search the soul, but since when can they intrude on the thoughts of a dragon?"

"I can't read every mind," Bracken confessed. "But I can usually get a basic sense for intentions. I have no interest in guessing. If I don't get a clear read, I won't make accusations."

"Easy to profess when none of us can verify what you see," the alcetaur said.

"I'm not here to unveil your secrets," Bracken assured him. "Everyone has a history. Everyone makes mistakes. I've been around for a long time. Little would shock me. I'm here to protect your new arrivals. They have suffered the consequences of betrayals before. I'm also here to defend Blackwell Keep against sabotage."

"There are many on my staff whom I do not doubt,"

Marat said, his tone firm. "But I cannot claim to fully trust each individual stationed here. Can any of you? If I have room to doubt one, I must doubt all. I want this inspection. If you would rather resign, now is the time."

Nobody answered.

"I will submit first," Marat said, approaching Bracken with one hand extended. Bracken gripped the offered hand.

"You're Agad's brother?" Bracken asked.

Marat grinned, showing a few golden teeth. "Are we not twins?" The question earned a chuckle from the staff.

"Not exactly," Bracken said.

"We share the same father," Marat explained. "Different mothers."

Bracken stared into his eyes for a long moment, then released his hand. "How should I proceed?" Bracken asked. "Move down the line?"

"Be my guest," Marat said, gesturing toward one end of the lineup.

Bracken walked to the end and stared down at a dwarf. The man was short but broad and muscular. His head was bald on top but the rest of his hair was long, and he had a tidy beard. All eyes regarded the pair.

Bracken held out a hand. "Won't hurt a bit."

The dwarf wiped his nose on his sleeve, stamped a couple of times, glanced down the line at his fellow staffers, then took Bracken's hand.

"Good grip," Bracken said. "You're Obun."

"Better be, or else folks have been getting it wrong all my life," the dwarf said. "Seen enough yet?"

"Yes, thank you." Bracken released his hand and moved to another dwarf.

Seth started counting. The line contained five dwarfs, three minotaurs, a pair of goblins, a troll, a snakelike lady with four arms, the alcetaur, three old women, and Marat. Seventeen in total. Kind of a lot, unless he pictured them staffing the whole castle. Then the number seemed fairly small.

Seth watched with interest as Bracken progressed from person to person. Each handshake held the potential for violence. Seth knew from experience that Bracken was not bluffing. He really could see into minds.

Seth wished he had a sword. No, he wished he had *the* sword. Vasilis. He wondered how many times he would wish that in the days and weeks to come. At least they had Mendigo.

"Get ready," Seth whispered to the wooden figure. "If a fight starts, restrain anyone who attacks Bracken."

Seth held his breath when Bracken reached the minotaur with the peg leg, but Bracken took his hand, exchanged a few words, and moved on without incident. Seth grew tense again when Bracken clasped the hand of the alcetaur, but again there was no confrontation. Creature by creature, Bracken made his way to the end of the line without any wild outbursts.

After finishing his inspection, Bracken returned to stand before Marat. "You have two traitors," Bracken declared.

Angry murmuring broke out among the staff. Some glared suspiciously at one another. Others glowered at Bracken.

Seth felt startled by the pronouncement. After the last handshake he had relaxed with relief. Apparently Bracken had a really good poker face.

Marat held up his hands and the muttering ceased. "Who are they?" Marat asked.

"I invite the guilty parties to step forward," Bracken said.

Nobody moved. Seth guessed the traitors might be hoping Bracken was bluffing. In their defense, it kind of sounded like a bluff.

"Shall I name them?" Bracken asked.

"If you are disloyal, bear in mind that you are currently outnumbered," Marat said. "Let's avoid a scuffle. It is bad enough that we are losing two members of our staff."

Several in the line began drawing weapons, including swords, knives, and axes.

"Put your arms away," Marat ordered. "Do not forget who I am." Things got very quiet. If a dragon couldn't command respect, who could? Marat nodded at Bracken. "Go ahead."

Bracken pointed at a minotaur with brown fur and a battle-ax slung over one shoulder. "Tonak passes information to the dragons monthly."

"Liar!" the minotaur roared. "Fraud!"

"Not always on the same night of the week," Bracken went on. "But he leaves after midnight and returns before dawn. He goes to the old watchtower and meets with a dragon called Baltizar. He is ready and willing to commit sabotage when called upon."

"Brothers!" Tonak called to his fellow minotaurs. "Will

you let these insults stand? Our kind has never been trusted! To arms!" He raised his battle-ax.

The minotaur with the peg leg grabbed the upraised battle-ax, and the reddish minotaur slammed Tonak in the gut with a club. Tonak crumpled, and the peg-legged minotaur tore the weapon from his grasp.

The reddish minotaur seized Tonak by the horns. "We took a chance on you!"

"Lies," Tonak maintained. "All lies."

"I have found your room empty twice in the night," the peg-legged minotaur said. "My eye was already on you."

"I saw him return once in the still hours," the snakelike woman said. "I did not know his errand."

Seth noticed one of the old women scurrying away.

"What about her?" Seth called out.

"She is the other," Bracken said.

"Stop her," Seth whispered to Mendigo. "Don't hurt her."

The limberjack sprang into motion, streaking after the retreating woman. Her eyes widened when she saw the giant puppet racing in her direction. She dropped to the ground, head tucked beneath her hands. When Mendigo arrived, he crouched and placed a wooden hand on her shoulder.

"I will have your horns and hide, Tonak," the reddish minotaur roared. "What are my orders?"

"I will commend Tonak and Myrna to the care of Romnus in the dungeon," Marat said.

"Not Myrna," Obun the dwarf lamented. "She makes the best cinnamon rolls."

"Hear that, Tonak?" the peg-legged minotaur said with

a chuckle. "You're going to spend some time with me down in the dark."

"What harm has Myrna perpetrated?" Marat asked.

"None yet," Bracken said. "She is an assassin awaiting orders. An expert with poison."

"The cinnamon rolls!" Obun exclaimed.

"They weren't poisoned yet," another dwarf said.

"I've committed no crime," Myrna said. "I may have come here with a certain understanding. But I've learned to love and respect you all so much I could never have harmed you."

"Not true," Bracken said firmly.

"Whatever you suspect, I've still done nothing wrong," Myrna cried.

"Coming here as an assassin qualifies as treason," Marat said. He shook hands with Bracken. "Thank you for your assistance. Please excuse me for a moment."

Marat called over the snake lady and the alcetaur. Bracken motioned for Kendra and Seth to come near.

"That was amazing," Kendra said.

"We all have our uses," Bracken replied in a quiet voice. He placed one hand on Kendra's shoulder and the other on Seth's arm. Bracken's next words came directly into Seth's mind. By her intent expression, he assumed his sister could hear them as well.

Listen. I got a good sense of the staff. The snake lady, Simrin, doesn't trust humans. She is loyal to Marat, but watch out for her. She would love to see you fail. Henrick the alcetaur is gruff but extremely honorable. Stay near him. Romnus, the minotaur with the bad leg, is also trustworthy and experienced. The reddish minotaur, Brunwin, is capable and reliable but has a bad temper. The ridge troll is cunning and eager to take advantage of you. The goblin will not betray you, but would steal from you if he could get away with it. The hobgoblin is amusing, but not much use in a fight.

"Hobgoblin?" Seth whispered.

The green-skinned goblin with the froglike features, Bracken supplied. *The dwarfs are generally loyal, but they won't go out of their way for you unless duty demands it. The older women are selfish, none too kindly, and given to gossip. I believe that Marat means well and is concerned for you, but dragons are notoriously difficult to read.*

"Thanks," Kendra whispered.

I wish I could do more, Bracken said. *I'll return as soon as I can. Heed your grandparents. Their presence and advice can save you a lot of trouble.*

Seth looked over at his Grandpa and Grandma Sorenson conversing with a couple of dwarfs. Grandma made some joke and the dwarfs laughed. Seth had seldom felt more grateful for his grandparents. Much of the time, the house at Fablehaven seemed like a normal home with a regular yard. He sometimes forgot he was at a secret wildlife park for magical creatures. That would not happen here. Blackwell Keep was a lonely fortress at the edge of the wilderness. The staff running the place were not kind people who loved him. They seemed almost as foreign as the creatures in their care. Seth remained excited for the opportunity, but he already felt more intimidated.

"I'm glad they're here," Seth said.

Smart sentiment, Bracken communicated.

Marat returned. The two loyal minotaurs and the snake lady had escorted the two traitors into a building and disappeared. Grandpa and Grandma Sorenson drew near.

"Perhaps we could adjourn to my chambers for a private conversation," Marat suggested.

"Great," Seth said.

"I must go," Bracken said. "Make sure your staff understands that these four newcomers are under my personal protection and have found favor with the Fairy Queen."

"Your presence has already sent that message," Marat said. "They will be under my protection as well."

Bracken shook hands with Grandma and Grandpa Sorenson and Seth, and then embraced Kendra. He gave her a quick kiss on the cheek.

Kendra reddened. "Stay safe."

"You too," Bracken said. "See you soon. We'll talk using my horn. Just hold it and reach out with your mind."

"I'll take good care of it," Kendra promised.

"Take better care of yourself." Bracken climbed into the barrel. When Seth peeked inside, he was gone.

Marat brought them to a sitting room sparsely furnished with simple, elegant divans and chairs. Fine carpets softened the stone floor, and folding walls of painted paper showed tranquil scenes of fields, forests, and rivers.

Marat approached Seth as Grandma, Grandpa, and Kendra sat down. "Are you aware that you brought another entity from Fablehaven?" he asked.

For a moment Seth didn't know what he was talking about. "Oh, the nipsie," Seth said, reaching into his pocket.

"I was not informed of his involvement," Marat said politely. "I take it he is not a stowaway?"

"I wasn't aware either," Grandpa Sorenson said, looking at Seth, the reprimand coming across through his expression and tone.

Seth held up the nipsie on his palm. "This is Calvin, the Tiny Hero."

Dropping to one knee, Calvin bowed his head. "Mighty Marat, I hope my intrusion did not disturb you. I meant no insult. I have pledged my services to Seth Sorenson."

"Big for a nipsie," Grandpa said suspiciously.

"You have a keen eye," Calvin said, head still bowed. "My people used a spell to enlarge me when the elders selected me as their champion."

"Rise, little warrior," Marat said. "I have no objection to your presence if the Sorensons are in agreement."

Calvin stood up.

"I meant to tell you," Seth apologized. "It never came up. I sometimes forget he's with me."

Grandpa crossed to Seth and peered closely at Calvin. "He appears to be what he claims."

"Indeed," Marat said. "I sense no darkness in him."

"Bracken could have checked him out," Kendra said.

"I almost volunteered," Calvin said. "But I didn't want

to interrupt. And it might be an advantage that my presence is unknown. You'll have a secret set of eyes and ears."

"That could prove useful," Grandma Sorenson muttered.

"Just you wait," Calvin said. "You'll be glad I came."

"The nipsies don't usually take interest in matters beyond their kingdoms," Grandpa said.

"I'm the exception," Calvin replied. "It's part of my role as champion."

"Why Seth?" Grandpa asked.

"He slew Graulas," Calvin said. "Our ancient enemy."

"Yes," Grandpa said. "I remember hard words from your elders about the demon. They wanted him executed."

"The nipsies chose to settle at Fablehaven because Graulas was there," Calvin said. "His demise was the cause of great celebration."

"Welcome, Calvin," Grandpa said, returning to his seat. "Seth, you should not have brought him without asking me. But I'm glad he's here."

"You will serve Seth as a scout?" Marat asked.

"Scout and bodyguard, yes," Calvin said.

"You have my permission to roam Blackwell Keep," Marat said. "The few hardy brownies here will not trouble you. I recommend you avoid the dungeons. Many unsavory prisoners dwell there. Keep away from the Blackwell if you value your life. And if you stray beyond the walls of the keep, you will be on your own."

"Understood," Calvin said. "Thank you for your courtesy."

"Seth should also avoid the Blackwell," Marat emphasized.

Seth shuddered. During his previous visit to Blackwell Keep, he had snuck out of the knapsack in the night and found his way to the Blackwell. A chain lay coiled beside a circular pit of darkness. Despairing voices had called from the unseen depths, begging for him to lower the chain. Agad had found him there and warned him against visiting the place.

"Of course," Seth said.

"Did you hear him?" Kendra checked.

"Yes, I'll stay away," Seth assured her. He meant it.

"As a shadow charmer you can hear the pleas from the undead contained there," Marat said. "The Blackwell is the greatest danger within the walls of this keep. It could be your downfall."

"Agad warned me too," Seth said. "I already decided to stay away from it."

"Calvin," Kendra said, "make sure he does."

The nipsie looked up at Seth. "Want me to help protect you from yourself in this matter?"

Seth glanced at the others in the room. "Sure." He put Calvin back in his pocket.

"Can he breathe in there?" Kendra asked.

"Just fine, thank you," Calvin called. "I find the pocket quite convenient."

"He has already heard sensitive conversations," Grandma pointed out. "He will hear more."

"You will keep our confidences?" Grandpa asked.

"They could tear my limbs off and I wouldn't tell them what you had for breakfast," came a voice from the pocket. "You can count on me."

"I believe he means well," Marat said.

"So do I," Grandpa agreed.

"It might prove advantageous to hide the nipsie's presence from the rest of the staff," Marat suggested. "The effectiveness of his tiny ears could improve if his presence remains unknown."

"Good point," Seth said.

"Can I offer you any refreshments?" Marat asked.

Everyone declined.

"Inform us about the situation here," Grandpa said.

"Celebrant has attacked the keep three times," Marat said. "He clearly senses a weakness. Since I became caretaker I have retained human form, but we believe that because the caretaker is supposed to be a true mortal, Celebrant may be trying to somehow exploit the discrepancy. So far the magical defenses have held, but I have felt them strain under his assaults. That should not happen when all is in order. If Kendra and Seth remain amenable, I intend to set up a meeting with Celebrant tomorrow for the purpose of transferring the stewardship to them."

"So soon?" Grandma asked.

"I'd rather not give the Dragon King time to contemplate this move," Marat said. "It is possible he will block their instatement. But he will also have tempting reasons to allow it, including their youth and inexperience. Much depends on whether Celebrant is aware that their instatement could stabilize the defenses of Blackwell Keep. Should he refuse them for the position, I will send you back to Fablehaven. If he agrees, you will remain here under my protection and the protection of those who serve us."

"What will you need us to do as caretakers?" Seth asked.

"Your grandparents and I will gradually train you," Marat said. "The first priority will be to keep you safe."

"I want to do the job right," Seth said.

"I admire your determination," Marat acknowledged.

"So do I," Grandpa added. "However, the first order of business will be to survive the interview."

CHAPTER TWELVE

Interview

K endra sat at the vanity in her new room, brushing her
hair. The thick stone walls and small windows made
most of Blackwell Keep feel like the interior of a cave. The
comfortable room was nicely furnished, but cool and drafty.

Mendigo lurked in the corner, a silent sentry, still as a
scarecrow. When Kendra had awakened during the night
to use the bathroom, she had nearly jumped out of her skin
when she found the limberjack posted near her door, though
she had known he was standing guard when she went to
bed. The fur comforter had kept her toasty while she slept,
but the parts of the stone floor not covered by carpeting had
been icy against her bare feet. The bathroom had an archaic
toilet, but at least the sink had both warm and cold running
water.

In addition to the bathroom, her room connected to the

outer hall and to Grandma and Grandpa Sorenson's bedroom, which in turn led to Seth's room. They had their own little wing of the keep to themselves, with an armed dwarf stationed outside at all times. Calvin helped stand watch over Seth's room.

A knock at the door jerked Kendra from her thoughts. It was the door that led out to the hall. She glanced at Mendigo. "Ready for trouble?" she whispered.

Joints jingling, the limberjack gave a brisk salute.

Kendra crossed to the door. "Who is it?"

"Simrin," came the reply.

The snakelike lady had made Kendra uncomfortable even before Bracken had communicated that she didn't like humans. But Simrin wasn't an enemy, and the dwarf on duty had allowed her to pass. Kendra unlocked the door and opened it.

If Kendra ignored the extra set of arms, Simrin looked like a slim, hairless human woman. Except instead of human skin, she had the small, intricately fitted scales of a snake, and her eyes were abnormally dark. The bandolier across her narrow chest held six knives.

"Hello," Kendra said.

"A dragon is waiting to speak to you," Simrin said, her accent more British than American.

Kendra swallowed, trying to keep her composure. "Celebrant?"

Simrin shook her head. "His son."

Kendra brightened. "Raxtus?"

"Quite so. He awaits you beyond the lesser gate."

"I guess he can't come inside the keep," Kendra said.

"Absolutely not," Simrin said, eyes flashing.

"Right," Kendra said, chagrined by the implied scolding.

"I can lead the way," Simrin said.

Kendra glanced at Mendigo. "Come with us."

Simrin escorted Kendra past the dwarf on duty. The snakelike woman moved with liquid grace. Kendra had to trot to keep up with her deceptively quick strides.

They emerged in a courtyard that contained a modest church house and an assortment of gravestones in various states of disrepair. Kendra blinked until her eyes adjusted to the bright sun glaring down from a hard blue sky. Simrin led the way to the outer wall of the keep and opened a heavy iron door. Beyond the door, a straight, narrow passage penetrated the thick wall, interrupted halfway by a gate of iron bars. Simrin unlocked the gate, then stepped through and unlocked the iron door at the far end.

Exiting the keep with Mendigo at her heels, Kendra found a glittering dragon waiting on the rocky ground outside. With a body the size of a large horse, Raxtus was the smallest dragon Kendra had met, though his long neck, tail, and wings augmented his size. His gleaming armor of silvery white scales reflected a rainbow sheen, and his aerodynamic head shone like polished chrome. Unlike other dragons, Raxtus projected no paralyzing aura of fear.

"Kendra!" he said, his voice similar to a confident teenager's, but fuller and richer than a single human voice box could manage. "I can't believe you're here!"

"It's good to see you," Kendra said, reaching up to rub

where his neck met his chest. Her touch increased the luster of his rainbow sheen. She could feel her magical energy flowing into him.

"Whoa, not so bright, the guys might be watching," Raxtus complained.

Kendra backed away. "Since when do you care what other dragons think?"

"Are you kidding?" Raxtus exclaimed. "I've always cared. It just didn't matter because nobody took me seriously."

"They'll take you more seriously if you don't worry about what they think," Kendra said.

"That's true up to a point," Raxtus said. "A respectable dragon wants to maintain a certain persona. Humans are supposed to be frozen with fear around dragons. Letting one pet you wrecks the ferociousness. And lighting up at the touch of a fairykind girl only makes it worse."

"I see," Kendra said.

"I'm sparkly enough already," Raxtus said. "Dragons don't aspire to be glittery."

"Feels good, though?" Kendra checked.

"It really does," Raxtus said with a sigh. "One more little rub."

Kendra stroked his chest for an extra couple of seconds. His scales felt like metal polished to a silky finish.

"Somebody fixed your creepy puppet," Raxtus observed.

"Agad repaired him," Kendra said.

"Are you getting to know Simrin?" Raxtus asked.

Kendra glanced at the four-armed lady standing near the gate, maybe twenty yards away. "A little."

"Twice the hugs when she grabs you," Raxtus whispered.

Kendra couldn't help giggling.

"Can we talk around her?" Raxtus whispered.

"I think so," Kendra said. "She's watching out for me."

"Okay . . . look," Raxtus said, keeping his voice quiet. "I heard a rumor that you and Seth might try to become caretakers here."

"More than a rumor," Kendra said.

Raxtus gave a nervous laugh. "Has anyone mentioned the timing is pretty bad?"

"They say your father is trying to overthrow Wyrmroost," Kendra said.

"Well, he is a caretaker," Raxtus said. "And the Dragon King. Can he overthrow himself? Maybe you could say he wants to establish full control."

"That wasn't the deal with Agad," Kendra said.

"Sometimes deals have more than one interpretation," Raxtus hedged.

"You don't side with Celebrant, do you?" Kendra asked.

Raxtus winced. "Think about it. Your grandparents are caretakers at Fablehaven. Don't they come and go as they please?"

"Pretty much."

"So if my dad is the caretaker of Wyrmroost, why is he stuck here like a prisoner?"

"This is a dragon sanctuary," Kendra replied. "The deal with Agad gave him more control at the sanctuary, not permission to leave it."

"If he can't leave, is it a dragon sanctuary, or a dragon prison? Is Dad a caretaker or an inmate?"

Kendra thought about that. "A little of both, I guess."

"My father has decided the time of holding dragons prisoner needs to end. Are we supposed to be trapped here until the end of time? Because of my unusual upbringing, I was never confined to a particular sanctuary. I can come and go. But what about the rest of the dragons? Why can't they ever leave? How will dragons ever rejoin the world if we never get a chance to practice?"

"What if the practice turns into a catastrophe?" Kendra asked.

"Father will supervise the process," Raxtus said. "Dragons have learned so much during our long captivity. Father doesn't want to destroy the world. But he definitely wants enough freedom to be part of it again."

"The last time dragons were free, they almost took over the earth," Kendra said. "My job as caretaker would be to keep dragons at the sanctuary."

"I know," Raxtus said. "That's why it might be a bad idea to take the job."

"Is that a threat?" Kendra asked.

"I'm just trying to warn you."

"You're telling me to leave Wyrmroost?"

"It isn't safe to stay. It just isn't. I don't want to see you get hurt."

Kendra folded her arms. "So you *do* side with Celebrant on this."

"Weird, right?" Raxtus said. "We were never close. But

not long ago he made me part of his personal guard. For dragons, it's a big honor. The other five are amazing veterans of so many battles. Living legends."

"Weren't you going to keep an eye on some of the other dragon sanctuaries for Agad?" Kendra asked.

"That kind of ended when I got my position with the guards."

"This happened after the battle of Zzyzx?" Kendra asked.

"The battle was the turning point," Raxtus said. "My breath weapon might help vegetation grow, and my magic might only be good for hiding and healing, but my scales are as tough as my dad's, and I'm one of the best aerialists, and my teeth and claws are uncommonly sharp. Those strengths became apparent at Zzyzx, and suddenly the Dragon King took an interest."

After his mother had perished and the other three eggs in his clutch had been devoured by a cockatrice, Raxtus had been protected, hatched, and raised by fairies. Fairy magic had become part of his nature, making him unique.

Kendra knew Raxtus had always wanted the respect of other dragons. Especially his father. But how might earning that respect affect their friendship? Unlike other dragons, he had always been on her side.

"If I become caretaker, would you attack me?" Kendra asked.

"No way. But I might not be able to protect you."

"Would you try?" Kendra pressed.

"It wouldn't matter."

"It would matter to me."

"I owe you so much," Raxtus said. "You know we're friends. I'd try to protect you. I'd do my best. You don't understand my father. He is so powerful, Kendra. And he has so many formidable dragons at his command. My dad is coming to interview you. He'll get here soon. He seems excited. I'm worried he might want you and Seth to have the job. I'm afraid he might be thrilled. That is a terrible sign. You don't understand what you're up against. You don't have to do this. You should go."

"Except I do need to do this," Kendra said. "They're low on dragon tamers. There is unrest all over. They need me."

"Kendra, this is me protecting you. Leave. You don't want to be part of this. If they're short on dragon tamers, let Marat keep filling in. It makes much more sense than a couple of kids."

Kendra wanted to explain that Marat might be part of the reason the defenses at Blackwell Keep were vulnerable. But what if Raxtus shared the info with his father? Plus Simrin was watching. Even if she could trust Raxtus, sharing that information would look like treachery.

"Thank you for the warning," Kendra said.

"Thanks but no thanks?"

"Pretty much."

"Does that mean you're staying?"

"I'm afraid so. It's my duty."

Raxtus gave a snort. "Some duty. You have to make sure my kind can't govern ourselves. You have to ensure we stay prisoners. Even if it endangers your life."

"You know what dragons can do," Kendra said.

"In some ways I don't," Raxtus said. "The dragons I know have been confined to sanctuaries for my entire life. I'm not sure how they might behave if granted some freedom."

"There are some ruthless dragons," Kendra said. "They could destroy the world just as the demons might have."

"Mortals could destroy the world as well," Raxtus argued. "If my father gains the power to let dragons leave the sanctuary, it doesn't mean he'll allow them to run wild. He could leave the most dangerous dragons at the sanctuaries and keep the others on a short leash."

"But if it gets out of hand, the world ends," Kendra said.

Raxtus sighed, then spoke quietly. "I hear you. And to be honest, when I say Dad could leave the most dangerous dragons at the sanctuaries, that would include just about every dragon I have ever met, including him. But it's complicated. I understand their desire for more freedom. And I don't want to be a traitor to my kind."

"I'm sorry you're stuck in such a difficult—"

Raxtus whipped his head around, neck craning high. "He's coming."

"Your father? Do you see him?"

"His wings make an unmistakable whistling sound," Raxtus said. "I knew he'd come soon. He seemed eager. We have a minute at most. You're determined to stay?"

"Sorry," Kendra said. "I'm in a complicated situation too. We have to stay."

"Then stand tall when you talk to him," Raxtus said.

"You'll need all your courage. His presence can sometimes silence other dragons, let alone mortals."

"We'll do our best," Kendra said.

"Go," Raxtus urged. "I'll help all I can."

He disappeared, his presence visible only by a faint ripple in the air. Kendra wished she had the ability to turn invisible too. She felt the wind from his wings as Raxtus took flight.

"Come," Simrin said, leading Kendra back into the keep and locking the iron door behind them, then the gate, then the other door. Mendigo stayed at Kendra's side.

"I can't talk to Celebrant without Seth," Kendra said.

"We'll meet your brother near the Perch," Simrin replied.

"Where?" Kendra asked.

"The platform on the outer wall where caretakers treat with dragons," Simrin said.

"Nobody has told me what to do," Kendra said.

"Show no fear," Simrin said. "Answer his questions. There is little else to discuss."

Following Simrin into a building, Kendra tried to get control of her nerves. How was she supposed to stay calm in front of the Dragon King if she was already scared without him present?

"Do you think Raxtus was right?" Kendra asked.

"On what point?" Simrin asked.

"Should I be here?" Kendra asked. "Should I leave?"

Simrin hissed angrily. "If my opinion makes a difference, you should go."

"I think I should stay."

"Then think it harder," Simrin said. "Either get certain or quit. Your resolve is about to be tested."

They turned a corner and found Seth coming down a hall with Grandma, Grandpa, and Brunwin, the reddish minotaur. "There you are!" Seth called. "Celebrant is here! Did they tell you? Marat is stalling."

"I heard he was coming," Kendra said.

"You don't look so good," Seth said.

"I just talked with Raxtus," Kendra said.

"What?" Seth cried. "You didn't come get me?"

"The dragon asked for your sister," Simrin explained.

"It wasn't fun," Kendra said. "He was warning me. Raxtus thinks we should leave."

Seth shook his head. "Have him get in line. Everyone thinks we're too young. They think it's too dangerous. Maybe we're not the perfect fit. But we're all they've got. We're the last chance to make the defenses secure. Don't talk yourself out of it. We already made up our minds."

Kendra stared at her brother. Running Wyrmroost would be difficult and scary. Trying to contain Celebrant and the other dragons would be a daunting challenge. Raxtus had provided an excuse to back out, and part of her wanted to embrace it. But she and Seth had a duty to perform. Many people were depending on them. "You're right," she said.

"You have to be sure," Brunwin emphasized. "Celebrant will press you."

"We're needed here," Seth said.

Kendra took her brother's hand. "Let's get hired."

"Are both of you sure?" Grandma asked.

"We could go home right now," Grandpa said. "That option is still available. If Celebrant approves you and you become the caretakers of Wyrmroost, walking away gets very complicated."

"I've been sure all along," Seth said.

"The warning flustered me a little," Kendra admitted. "But we need to do this."

"This way," Brunwin said. He led them to a heavy iron door. "I don't interact with dragons. If you go through this door and continue straight, you'll find Marat waiting at the Perch with Celebrant."

Kendra squeezed Seth's hand. "Don't let go."

"Not even if you dared me," Seth replied.

Brunwin opened the door. The walkway atop an interior wall of Blackwell Keep ran straight until it reached a fenced wooden platform that projected beyond the outer wall. Marat stood there waiting.

Beyond him towered Celebrant.

The immense dragon loomed head, neck, and shoulders above the wall of the keep. His flawless armor of platinum scales made him look like a much bigger, bulkier version of his son. Where Raxtus was lean and aerodynamic, Celebrant was heavily muscled, with impressive horns sprouting from his head.

"Now, *that* is a dragon," Seth murmured.

Kendra had seen Celebrant at the battle of Zzyzx, but never up close. Watching him battle demons from a distance was a very different experience from approaching him with his penetrating eyes glaring down, glowing like molten gold. She knew the direct gaze of a dragon could be especially paralyzing, so she did her best to focus on Marat instead.

When Kendra and Seth reached the platform, Marat rested a reassuring hand on Kendra's shoulder. "May I present Kendra and Seth Sorenson, the candidates to replace me as co-caretaker of Wyrmroost and master of this keep."

"So young," Celebrant said in a rumbly bass. "All humans are children to me, but the two of you are children to humans." His articulate words were uncommonly resonant, as if fifty identical recordings of the same voice were being played in unison.

"I'm fifteen," Kendra said.

"Thirteen," Seth added.

"And you can speak in my presence," Celebrant said.

"Yes," Kendra said simply.

His head swooped toward them, jaws gaping large enough to swallow a car, revealing vicious rows of teeth designed to pierce and shred. The great mouth snapped shut almost close enough for Kendra to reach out and touch it.

After initially flinching away, Kendra held her ground. She clenched Seth's hand and he squeezed back. She concentrated on the dragon's nostrils instead of his blazing eyes, trying to stand tall and have courage as Raxtus had advised.

"Can you speak now?" Celebrant roared, the volume hurting her ears, his hot, humid breath washing over them.

Kendra was alarmed, but not frozen. "You're a little close," she said, her voice cracking a bit.

"And you could use a mint," Seth said.

Celebrant reared up again. "Not many mortals can abide my presence," he said calmly, "let alone respond with such insolence. Together you meet the minimum requirements. But what about on your own?"

"They will serve together," Marat said. "All relations with dragons will be handled in tandem."

"Thank you, Marat, but I am more interested in their answers," Celebrant replied.

"Same answer," Seth said. "We're a team."

"And what if you are separated?" Celebrant asked.

"We'll wait to talk to dragons until we're together," Kendra said.

"What about urgent matters?" Celebrant pressed. "What if you're separated during an emergency?"

"We'll stick together," Seth said.

"I hope so," Celebrant said with a dark chuckle. "Inability to perform your most basic duties during a crisis might be considered grounds for removal from your position."

"We'll do our duty," Kendra said.

Celebrant shifted his gaze to Marat. "Am I to be insulted that you wish to instate a pair of human children to function as my equal?"

"Despite their age, Kendra and Seth have proven themselves valiant," Marat said. "She is fairykind and he is a shadow charmer. They are legitimate candidates."

"Yoking me alongside any human caretaker would be an insult," Celebrant said. "Even a wizard." His attention returned to Kendra and Seth. "Are you aware of the dangers involved? Were you told that I have attacked Blackwell Keep three times this past month?"

"Yes," Kendra said.

"I am called Celebrant the Just for good reason," the Dragon King said. "I am powerful but also fair. Consider this your warning. If you accept this position, we will not be on friendly terms unless you share power to control who enters and exits Wyrmroost."

"Those were not the terms you arranged with Agad," Marat protested. "You were to be a co-caretaker, partnering with the caretaker of Blackwell Keep. The caretaker of the keep controls who comes and goes. You were empowered to manage the affairs of the dragons on this preserve. Your authority ends at the gate. You have no power to regulate who passes through it."

Celebrant showed his teeth. "I am not content with this arrangement. I demand the same rights to control access as the caretaker of Blackwell Keep."

"Your contentment is irrelevant," Marat said. "The arrangement cannot be altered."

"Except by mutual agreement between the caretakers," Celebrant said smoothly.

"We won't change the arrangement," Kendra said.

Celebrant glared at her for a long moment. "Then we may find ourselves in conflict. If I were to become the sole caretaker, the power to come and go from Wyrmroost would reside with me. You have been warned."

"Are the applicants acceptable?" Marat asked.

Celebrant drew his head near Kendra and Seth again, sniffing one, then the other. Kendra held still and kept her gaze away from his eyes. Celebrant swung his head over to Marat.

"I will accept the candidates on one condition," Celebrant said. "Make it official right now. Give up your post and instate them as caretakers immediately. Otherwise I will deny them the opportunity."

"Normally we verify our choice with Lord Dalgorel of the Fair Folk," Marat said.

"That is a matter of courtesy, not necessity," Celebrant said. "Dalgorel has no power to veto our selection. It will be as easy to introduce him to the new caretakers as it would be to present them as candidates."

"He will take it as an insult," Marat said.

"Their long-standing position of neutrality makes their reactions irrelevant," Celebrant said. "The endorsement of Dalgorel is a weary custom. This can mark a new tradition. What say you?"

Marat turned to Kendra and Seth. "Are you ready and willing to become the caretakers?"

Kendra hadn't realized it would happen immediately. She looked at Seth.

"Absolutely," her brother said.

Kendra nodded. "Me too."

Marat removed the medallion from around his neck.

"Once the caretaker wielded one of the seven scepters and wore this medallion. As part of the agreement with Agad, the scepter went to Celebrant. This medallion marks the wearer as a caretaker of Wyrmroost and master of Blackwell Keep."

"I better wear it," Seth said.

"It is presented to both of you," Marat said. "You can pass it to another only with permission from Celebrant. The two of you share equal authority no matter who wears the medallion."

"I still better wear it," Seth said.

"It's basically a necklace," Kendra said.

"But it means I'm in charge," Seth said.

Kendra glanced at Celebrant. The last thing she wanted to do in front of the Dragon King was conduct an infantile argument about who got to wear the medallion. "He can have it for now."

Marat approached Kendra and Seth. "Do you, Kendra Sorenson, and you, Seth Sorenson, accept the responsibility of watching over and protecting Wyrmroost, along with the living beings contained herein?" He paused for them to answer.

"I do," Kendra said.

"Yes," Seth said.

Marat nodded and continued. "And do you, Kendra Sorenson, and you, Seth Sorenson, vow to protect the outside world from the living beings at Wyrmroost, and to shelter the living beings at Wyrmroost from any outside threats?"

"I do," Kendra said.

"Sure," Seth said.

Marat stepped nearer to Seth. "Then as a current care-taker of Wyrmroost and as master of Blackwell Keep, of my own free will, I hereby confer my stewardship over Wyrm-roost to Kendra Sorenson and Seth Sorenson, including all rights pertaining to a designated and official caretaker of this sanctuary together with all privileges available to the master of Blackwell Keep."

When Marat placed the medallion around Seth's neck, Kendra couldn't help feeling a little jealous. Marat shook hands with Seth, then with Kendra. Then he turned to Celebrant. "It is done."

Celebrant snarled. "Congratulations, younglings. Enjoy your new status while it lasts." The dragon opened his mouth and a searing blast of blue-white energy erupted forward. Marat raised a golden ax and the energy smeared against an invisible dome covering the platform. The timbers shud-dered beneath Kendra's feet, the temperature increased, and the walls of the keep groaned.

"Back," Marat urged, ax held high.

Kendra and Seth retreated off the Perch to the top of the wall. Marat followed more slowly, shuffling until his feet were on the stone of the wall rather than the wood of the platform.

Celebrant paused, eyes vicious, then breathed out an-other torrent of brilliant energy that spread out along the top of the wall, as if impeded by an unseen barrier. Though dazzling, the attack seemed no more harmful than water against a windshield.

"Get inside," Marat ordered over his shoulder. He placed a mask over his face. It looked ancient, and of Asian design.

Kendra and Seth withdrew along the top of the interior wall toward the metal door from which they had emerged. Marat remained atop the outer wall, his golden ax raised in defiance against the energy smeared across the transparent barrier protecting the keep. He looked so small in contrast to the immensity of Celebrant. Kendra realized that without the magical barrier shielding Blackwell Keep, they would all be extremely dead. Would there even be ashes left?

"Begone, Celebrant," Marat called. "You can do us no harm. By disrespecting these new caretakers you undermine your own authority."

After the deluge of radiant energy stopped, Celebrant leaned his head closer to Marat and exhaled a searing conflagration of fire. Most of the flames flattened against the unseen barrier, but some licked through, only to be repelled by an invisible dome around Marat. Celebrant tipped his head back and shot a geyser of flame into the sky. Then, roaring, the Dragon King seized the Perch with his mighty forelegs and wrenched it from the wall, hurling the entire platform to the ground. After exhaling a final blistering firestorm, Celebrant turned and flew away, wings whistling as his enormity surged skyward.

CHAPTER THIRTEEN

New Job

The next morning, Seth held his first meeting with Calvin since arriving at Wyrmroost. The Tiny Hero had spent the previous day and night exploring Blackwell Keep.

"Tell me you learned some good secrets," Seth said.

"Secrets take time," Calvin replied cheerfully. He pointed at Seth's chest. "Isn't that the pendant Marat was wearing?"

"I'm officially the caretaker now," Seth said.

"Along with Kendra?"

"I guess, technically."

"Don't you want her help?" Calvin asked.

"For talking to dragons, maybe."

"Isn't that a big part of the job?"

"I'm not sure," Seth admitted. "They seem way more interested in eating us."

"I heard about the Perch," Calvin said. "Everybody in the keep is buzzing about it."

"That's one piece of gossip I know plenty about," Seth said. "It made Kendra and me feel very welcome."

Calvin laughed. "You didn't think it would be easy?"

"I thought it would be awesome," Seth replied. "So far, so good, I guess. What else did you learn?"

"I spent some time with a few of the dwarfs. Wish I could get those hours back! Low educational *and* entertainment value."

"Did you find out anything from them?"

"When he's alone, the one called Didger picks his ears a lot. Give the guy a week and he would have enough wax to build a life-sized replica."

"Of you or of him?"

"Of Celebrant, probably."

Seth chuckled. "Are the dwarfs just soldiers?"

"Three work as guards," Calvin reported. "Obun and Didger run the stables."

"Are there horses?"

"Eleven. Plus three mules. And five griffins."

"They keep griffins here?"

"Five," Calvin repeated.

"Since I'm caretaker, that means I have five griffins."

"You and Kendra," Calvin reminded him politely.

"I need more info like that," Seth said. "All the cool stuff I should know about."

Calvin saluted. "I'll do my best."

A knock came at the door that joined Seth's room to

his grandparents'. Without waiting for a response, Kendra opened it and poked her head in. "Good, you're up. Marat wants to talk with us."

"Finally," Seth said. "Where was he last night?"

"Talking with Grandpa and communicating with Agad," Kendra said. "We'll learn more now."

Seth scooped Calvin into his hand. "Want to come?"

"If you don't mind," Calvin said.

Seth pocketed him, then followed Kendra into the next room. Grandma and Grandpa Sorenson sat on the edge of their canopied bed looking solemn. Marat stood in the middle of the room, his face careworn, his eyes tired.

"Have a seat," Marat said.

Kendra chose a chair, but Seth stayed on his feet.

"Celebrant doesn't like us," Seth said.

"That depends on what you mean," Marat said. "He is delighted at the opportunity you provide."

"What about the defenses?" Kendra asked. "Are they stronger?"

Grandpa sighed.

"They remain precarious," Marat said.

Seth had worried this might be the case. After Celebrant had torn down the Perch, Grandma and Grandpa had ushered Kendra and Seth to their rooms. There had been questions about whether the defenses were any better than they had been before. This was the first definitive answer.

"I thought the defenses were supposed to get stronger with us as caretakers," Seth said.

"It was our best guess," Marat said. "Agad and I are baffled that your instatement didn't fix the problem."

"How did Celebrant destroy part of the castle?" Kendra asked.

"The same way he brought his head so near you during the interview," Marat said. "The Perch projected beyond the keep and represented neutral territory."

"He could have killed us," Kendra said.

"Not with me there," Marat said. "Celebrant is fast and strong, but I was ready, and we were only a few paces from a safe refuge."

"Safe for how long?" Seth asked.

"Celebrant gave it all he had, and the defenses held," Marat said. "But I felt them wavering, as they have wavered only recently. Tearing down the Perch was a message. The Dragon King has no respect for you. He doesn't expect to confer with you again."

"I was really looking forward to our next heart-to-heart," Seth said.

"It's discouraging," Grandma said. "You're starting with crippled relations. Celebrant isn't giving you a chance to do your jobs well."

"I accept my share of the responsibility," Marat said. "Celebrant wanted them instated immediately. It meant he was eager. I hoped he was eager for the wrong reasons. I hoped he was focused only on their youth. I hoped he didn't understand that their instatement would secure the defenses."

"But it didn't work," Kendra said.

Marat frowned. "Perhaps he got lucky. Perhaps he knows more than we do. But the defenses are no stronger. And, given Celebrant's eagerness, he won't approve a replacement for you."

"I'm so sorry, kids," Grandpa said. "I've failed you and your parents. This was a gamble, and I'm afraid we lost horribly. You're stuck here as caretakers for at least a year, until you can override Celebrant's vetoes to appoint a replacement. And I have no idea if Blackwell Keep can stand for that long."

Kendra crossed to Grandpa and laid a hand on his arm. "It's okay, Grandpa. We knew the risks. We had to try. And the defenses haven't fallen yet."

"I reached out to Agad," Marat said. "He has no alternate theory for why the defenses became vulnerable in the first place. But we will not rest until we figure it out."

"And we have the barrel," Grandma reminded everyone.

Grandpa nodded. "If Blackwell Keep falls, we can send Kendra and Seth back to Fablehaven. We will move the barrel to a room near ours and keep the children in close proximity."

"Not all the time," Seth said.

"Much of the time," Grandpa said. "Especially if we're attacked."

"But we have to do our jobs," Seth said. "We're the caretakers. It's not a token position. The sanctuary needs us. We'll be safer if we do our jobs well."

"There is some truth to that," Marat allowed. "Although

much of the work should be delegated to your assistants. You should get acquainted with the staff. Your new status as caretakers grants permission to ask questions and expect answers. Much could depend on establishing trust."

"There are some formalities they will need to perform personally," Grandma said.

"Like meeting with the Fair Folk today," Marat said.

"Who are they?" Kendra asked.

"I'd love to hear more about this topic," Grandpa said, extending a hand toward Marat.

"The Fair Folk are a notoriously secretive people," Marat said. "It was not always so, but despite my long years, they kept to themselves even in my childhood."

"Fair Folk," Kendra said. "The name makes them sound nice."

"Nice?" Marat asked as if perplexed. "I suppose they can be nice. It is not how I would describe them. They have long lives. They tend to be very attractive. They wield potent magic. And for thousands of years they have withdrawn from interaction with other magical beings. They maintain a strict position of neutrality, siding with neither demon nor fairy, neither dragon nor giant nor wraith. Is a policy of seclusion nice? Is remaining aloof during emergencies nice?"

"You don't like them," Seth surmised.

"I am slow to dislike anyone," Marat said. "Disliking someone is almost as big a commitment as loving someone, and it carries none of the benefits. I have mixed feelings about the Fair Folk. I find it a challenge to respect capable people who care only for their own interests."

"I have heard vague rumors of the Fair Folk," Grandpa Sorenson said. "Stories about them get entwined with fairy lore."

"They are not fairies," Marat said. "They are roughly the size of humans, and they lack wings."

"Who would know?" Grandpa said. "The Fair Folk are seen less frequently than unicorns. They are true mysteries even to those of the magical community."

"Unless you are the caretaker of a dragon sanctuary," Marat said. "Each of the dragon sanctuaries contains a settlement of Fair Folk. It is not common knowledge. The three biggest settlements are at the three secret sanctuaries—the ones with Dragon Temples, like Wyrmroost. By tradition, any new caretaker of Wyrmroost gets approved by the leader of the Fair Folk before the formal appointment to office. Celebrant compelled me to skip that step. As caretakers, Kendra and Seth must be introduced to Lord Dalgorel, leader of the Fair Folk at this sanctuary."

"Will he come here?" Grandma asked.

Marat shook his head. "The Fair Folk never leave their settlements. They are completely self-sufficient and refuse to take any action that could jeopardize their safety or their neutrality."

"You can get Kendra and Seth there safely?" Grandpa asked.

"Five roads in Wyrmroost share the same protections as Blackwell Keep," Marat said. "The High Road leads directly from Blackwell Keep to Terrabelle, the Fair Folk settlement."

"Where were those roads when we visited last time?" Kendra complained.

"If I recall correctly," Marat said, "last time you were not official guests of the sanctuary. And you made your way to the Dragon Temple, far from any of the roads."

"The defenses of Blackwell Keep show signs of failing," Grandma said. "Is the same true for the roads? This excursion would take Kendra and Seth far from the barrel back to Fablehaven."

"The High Road links two secure locations," Marat said. "It therefore enjoys the same magical protections afforded to Terrabelle as well as the safeguards of Blackwell Keep. The defenses of Terrabelle have shown no sign of faltering. In effect, your grandchildren will be safer on the High Road and in Terrabelle than here at the keep."

"Then why don't they stay at Terrabelle instead?" Grandma asked.

"Neutrality," Grandpa said.

Marat nodded. "The Fair Folk would never grant long-term sanctuary to outsiders. As I mentioned, they could not be more committed to their neutrality."

"How are their defenses better than here at the keep?" Seth asked.

"The Fair Folk possess one of the Seven Scepters of Wyrmroost," Marat said. "Each scepter establishes a protected sovereign territory within Wyrmroost. Even if the sanctuary fell, the territories with scepters could still stand."

"Didn't you say Celebrant got the scepter that used to be at Blackwell Keep?" Kendra asked.

"Yes," Marat said.

"Could that be the problem with our defenses?" Kendra asked.

"One would suppose," Marat said. "But the medallion wields equal power with the scepter. The scepter at the keep was a redundancy."

"Can the medallion leave the keep without messing up the defenses?" Seth asked.

"So long as it remains in the possession of the caretaker," Marat said. "The medallion has some safeguards built in. For example, if you are captured, Seth, simply say, 'medallion, medallion, medallion, return,' and the medallion will teleport back to the vault here inside the keep. The medallion will also teleport to the vault if you are slain."

"So I'll wear the medallion when we visit the Fair Folk?" Seth asked.

"The medallion is meant to be worn always," Marat said. "Send it back to the keep only in the event of a great emergency."

"When should they visit Terrabelle?" Grandma asked.

"I hoped to send them this afternoon," Marat said. "It is already an offense that the Fair Folk were not consulted before the appointment was made. We should introduce Kendra and Seth as soon as possible."

"You won't come?" Seth asked.

"No dragon would be welcome inside Terrabelle unless he was also the caretaker. Henrick will accompany you."

"What about Grandma and Grandpa?" Kendra asked.

"Best if you go alone," Marat said. "The Fair Folk know

Henrick. As gamekeeper of Wyrmroost he is the only person who enjoys the same access as the caretaker. Any extra visitors strain their hospitality, and we've already insulted them."

"Makes sense," Grandpa said.

"Presenting a pair of youngsters as the new caretakers has a chance to arouse pity," Marat said. "Perhaps the Fair Folk will show mercy to them. Kendra, Seth, your first mission is to apologize for getting installed as the new caretakers without their permission. Second is to see if they have ideas as to why the defenses of Blackwell Keep are becoming unstable."

"Wouldn't help with that matter violate their neutrality?" Grandpa asked.

"To a degree," Marat said. "But the Fair Folk have been known to share useful information in the past. It's worth a try."

"We're at a big disadvantage," Seth said. "If these folk are really fair, they'll help us."

"Not that kind of fair," Kendra said.

"Oh," Seth asked. "Are they so-so? Average?"

"Not that either," Kendra said.

"Fair like a carnival?" Seth asked. "With cotton candy?"

Kendra rolled her eyes. "Fair as in beautiful."

"Hopefully at least they will approve of you," Marat said. "Their opinion carries weight across the sanctuary. It could make the inhabitants more accepting of you two as caretakers. Or, conversely, it could influence some of those who dwell here to be unhelpful. With your youth and inexperience, you can use all the help you can get."

"Can Mendigo come?" Kendra asked.

"Mendigo lacks a will," Marat said. "This makes him more of a tool than an additional entity. His presence should not be a problem."

"What about me?" piped up Calvin. "If Kendra has her bodyguard, Seth should have his."

Seth took the Tiny Hero from his pocket.

Marat drew near and stared at Calvin. "You wish to join Kendra and Seth?"

"I've always wanted to meet the Fair Folk," Calvin said. "They are mentioned in some of our oldest tales, but I've never had the pleasure."

Marat stroked his goatee. "The Fair Folk do not appreciate outsiders. But they do enjoy novelties. There are no nipsies at Wyrmroost. Your kind are very rare. And as a matter of fact, Lord Dalgorel's daughter, Eve, has a particular interest in uncommon creatures, and your size lends you a certain innocence. You could probably accompany them."

"They might gawk at you," Seth warned.

"Probably," Marat said.

"Small price to pay," Calvin said with a smile.

"Kendra, Seth, how does this mission sound to you?" Grandpa asked. "You are the caretakers. Ultimately we are just your advisers."

"Seems like we should go," Kendra said.

"Right," Seth agreed.

Marat gave a small bow. "I'll send a message to the Fair

Folk to confirm an audience with Dalgorel. Expect Henrick to come for you shortly after midday."

"What should we do in the meantime?" Seth asked.

"The sooner you get to know the staff, the better," Grandpa said.

"I agree," Marat said. "Your success gaining respect as legitimate caretakers must begin here."

CHAPTER FOURTEEN

Luvians

Kendra and Mendigo met Henrick in the courtyard near the stables. The alcetaur had a huge bow over his shoulder, a quiver of arrows dangling from one side, and a sheathed long knife on the other. He gazed at Kendra without a smile. "Your brother?" he asked.

"Seth went ahead to the stables," Kendra said. "He's excited about the griffins."

Henrick scowled. "Griffins are good for accessing the mountains or the more distant reaches of the sanctuary. But dragons patrol the sky as well. We want the protection of the High Road, which means feet on the ground, which means horses."

"I don't think he was expecting to ride one," Kendra said. "Of course, you never know with Seth."

Henrick started toward the stables. "Your brother is un-predictable?"

Kendra hustled to keep up. Mendigo rattled along beside her. She didn't want to make Seth look bad. First impressions were important. "Curious," she said.

Henrick shook his head. "Wyrmroost is a death trap even for seasoned adventurers. A curious child has no place here."

Kendra felt mildly offended on Seth's behalf. "He *is* the caretaker."

"And I'm the gamekeeper," Henrick said. "As I understand it, my charge today is to keep you two alive. Is that correct?"

"Yes," Kendra said.

"Then curiosity is a problem," Henrick said.

When they entered the large stable, Kendra smelled hay and animals and leather. She saw Seth and a dwarf at the far end of a long row of stalls. At first her eyes passed over the horses, but her gaze returned to the nearest when it used its mouth to turn a page in a book. The book rested on a lectern inside the stall. Several shelves on the inner walls of the stall held a variety of hardcover books. After turning the page the horse kept staring downward.

"Is that horse reading?" Kendra asked.

"All of them read," Henrick said. "They're mute Luvians."

Kendra scanned other stalls, noticing bookshelves in all of them. Several other horses were staring at open books.

"I've never heard of Luvians," Kendra said.

"They were donated by the Zowali Protectorate."

"Is that in Africa?"

"It's one of the protected territories here at Wyrmroost. You'll learn more about it in the days and weeks to come. Have you not looked at a map yet?"

"I haven't," Kendra admitted.

Henrick stared at her grimly. "You are leaving Blackwell Keep as caretaker in a time of unrest without having consulted a map of the sanctuary?"

Kendra gulped, feeling like she had shown up on the day of the test without studying. "I guess I should have taken a look."

"Quite an understatement," Henrick said. "What if a dragon carries me off? What if I drop dead?"

"I guess I would follow the High Road," Kendra said. "We're not supposed to leave it, right?"

Henrick's expression softened a degree. "At least that is a reasonable answer. And the horses know their way around. But you should be more prepared. This is a hostile environment. Proper preparation can reduce the risks."

"I'll remember that," Kendra said earnestly.

Henrick gave a nod. "The Zowali Protectorate is the territory of the talking animals. The Luvians are the illustrious breed of talking horses."

"They can really talk?" Kendra exclaimed, looking at the animals with new interest.

Henrick moved closer, crouching down to whisper. "Not so loud. These are all mute Luvians. Though born from the Luvian line, they have lost the power of speech."

"But they can read," Kendra whispered.

"Their minds are plenty sharp," Henrick said. "The Luvians donate their mute children to the keep as a form of exile. Luvians are very protective of their ability to speak. It's a dwindling trait. They don't allow mutes to mingle with the herd."

"How cruel," Kendra whispered.

"A harsh reality," Henrick said, "but not cruel. The silent ones receive excellent care here. At the age of two years, we give them the option to run free. Few take it."

Kendra approached the nearest horse, chestnut with white splotches. A nameplate on the stall read: *Glory*.

"What are you reading?" Kendra asked.

The horse looked at Kendra, then used her teeth to tip the book on the lectern, making the cover visible.

"*Pride and Prejudice!*" Kendra said. "You have good taste!"

"It's her favorite," said a gravelly voice off to one side. Kendra glanced down at a dwarf.

"Hello," Kendra said. "I'm Kendra."

"Didger," the dwarf said. "Glory is one of our best and brightest. Sweet disposition, still in her physical prime, with plenty of strength and endurance."

"I need a horse for today," Kendra said.

"You're the new caretaker," Didger said. "You can have your pick."

"But I haven't been here long," Kendra said. "I don't know the animals. What horse would you suggest?"

Tapping the side of his nose, Didger glanced at Henrick

with a grin. The dwarf was missing at least two teeth. "This one has some sense."

"I'm not without hope," Henrick said.

Didger looked back at Kendra. "How experienced are you with horses?"

"Not very," Kendra confessed.

"Then Glory could be just the one," Didger said. "She's very considerate of her rider."

"Sounds good to me," Kendra said.

"Why not ask her?" Didger prompted.

Glory had stopped reading and had shifted her head so she could gaze at Kendra with one large eye. The animal seemed politely interested.

"Would you take me to Terrabelle today?" Kendra asked.

The horse stamped once.

"Does that mean yes?" Kendra asked.

Glory bobbed her head and stamped again.

"One for yes, two for no," Didger said.

Kendra stroked the furry cheek of the horse. "You enjoy *Pride and Prejudice*, but you're stuck communicating with yes and no."

Glory stamped once.

"Does that frustrate you?"

Glory gave a very loud stamp and bobbed her head.

"In the play area they have letter tiles," Didger said. "Sometimes they spell out messages. Glory writes poems."

"These horses read books!" Seth announced, coming down the aisle between the stalls. Kendra recognized the dwarf at his heels as Obun.

"I figured that out," Kendra said.

"Have you seen the griffins?" Seth asked.

"Not yet," Kendra said. "I was choosing my horse."

"We get to pick?" Seth asked.

"We're the caretakers," Kendra reminded him.

Seth whacked his forehead with his palm. "How do I keep forgetting?" He fingered the medallion. "How do I choose?"

"Are you an experienced rider?" Didger asked.

"I've ridden a centaur," Seth said.

"Careful how you mock," Henrick warned.

"I did!" Seth said.

"What self-respecting centaur would condescend—"

"Broadhoof, at Fablehaven," Seth said. "It was an emergency."

Didger folded his arms. "Discounting emergency centaur romps, how much experience—"

"Not much," Seth said. "But it's a safe bet that I'm a natural. Do you have any horses like Tempest?"

"Who is Tempest?" Kendra asked.

"Their wildest griffin," Seth said, pointing toward the far end of the stable. The griffin stalls were much larger than the horse stalls, with perches and rocky mounds inside, more like an enclosure at a nice zoo. "The fastest, the fiercest, but not safe for humans yet."

"That griffin may never be rideable," Obun said. "Too much spirit."

"She knows the preserve well," Didger said. "She'll take you where you request. But by her own route, in her own way. She's uncontrollable. Makes even the most seasoned rider sick. But it's hard to give up on that much raw ability. She'll be quite the mount if we can gentle her."

"Do the griffins read?" Kendra asked.

Both of the dwarfs laughed.

"No, lassie," Didger said. "Griffins are a different order of intelligence than the Luvians. Smart for an animal, mind you, but not readers."

"All the horses read?" Seth asked.

"For the most part," Didger said. "Noble can be reluctant."

"Tell me about Noble," Seth said.

"One of our three stallions," Didger said. "On flat ground, probably the fastest."

"Where is he?" Seth asked.

Didger led them down the aisle to the stall of a chocolate brown horse with a black mane. The animal nibbled at hay in a feed box.

Seth picked up the book on the lectern—*The Cat in the Hat*.

"Picture books," Seth said. "Look, Kendra, he mostly has picture books."

Kendra peered into the stall. Slim, brightly colored spines lined the shelves. No novels. The longest book she spotted was *Frog and Toad Are Friends*.

Noble stared at Seth.

"You're a reluctant reader?" Seth asked.

Noble stamped once.

"But you like to run fast?"

Noble stamped again.

"I want this one," Seth said.

"Not a bad pick," Didger said.

"Are you sure?" Henrick challenged. "What about Princess? Her disposition is more—"

"No horses called Princess," Seth interrupted. "Or Fluffy-kins. Or Pony Face. A stallion is a boy horse, right?"

"Yes," Didger said.

"I want Noble," Seth insisted.

"Ask him," Didger suggested.

"Who, Henrick?" Seth wondered.

"No, ask Noble," Didger clarified.

Seth faced the dark brown horse. "Want to get out of here? Take me to the Fair Folk?"

Noble gave a loud stamp.

"Isn't that a lot of horse for a beginner?" Henrick asked.

"It's a Luvian," Obun said. "Sure, they have different dispositions, but don't forget how superior any of them are to a common horse."

"Seth is the new caretaker of Wyrmroost," Didger explained to Noble. "We need him safe and sound."

Noble gave a light stamp.

"It's a deal," Seth said.

"Is that all right?" Kendra quietly asked Henrick.

"I suppose," he grumbled.

"You two head over to the play area while we get them saddled," Obun said.

Seth led the way to an open area where a pair of horses stood at opposite ends of a table with a chess board between them. A white horse with gray dots gripped a bishop in its teeth and took a pawn.

"Now I've seen everything," Kendra said.

"What kind of play area is this?" Seth complained. "It's all board games." He was right. On other tables Kendra saw checkers, backgammon, and Scrabble. "Don't they ever run around?"

"Any horses can run around," Kendra said. "It's incredible that these are playing chess."

"Starshine and Socrates are chess fanatics," Henrick said. "They spend half the day playing the game, and the other half reading books on the subject."

"Do they ever go outside?" Seth asked.

"There's an exercise yard," Henrick said. "And messengers ride them to the different territories."

Seth looked up at Henrick. "Are you sure we shouldn't take griffins?"

"We need the protection of the High Road," the alcetaur said.

"What higher road than the sky?" Seth asked. "Are you sure this isn't because you're too heavy?"

"I'm an alcetaur," Henrick said, straightening. "I don't ever need a griffin to transport me. But the last thing we need is dragons slaughtering our new caretakers in flight."

"Not the goal," Seth agreed.

"Besides, griffin riders need to take the correct precautions," Henrick said. "Although griffins are normally reliable if you express a destination, no intelligent rider takes flight without a map."

"I have a map," Seth said, patting the satchel at his side. "Got it from Brunwin this morning."

"Have you looked at it?" Henrick asked.

"Enough to know Terrabelle is northeast from here," Seth said. "We have to go through a pass to get there. It's in a big valley surrounded by mountains. I have a compass just in case."

"Seth likes to bring an emergency kit," Kendra said.

"I even have some magical stuff in it," Seth said. "The giant Thronis gave me a figurine of a leviathan that can turn into a real one, and a toy-sized tower that can transform into a big one."

"That is . . . sensible," Henrick said warily. "I have some magical items of my own that I use in a pinch. It's wise to be prepared." He scowled. "Unless a compass means you're planning to leave the road."

"Why?" Seth asked innocently. "What's off the road?"

"An agonizing death," Henrick said emphatically.

"The road sounds better," Seth said.

"Don't think for one moment that this is a game," Henrick warned.

"What?" Seth asked. "The horses playing chess?"

Kendra wanted to punch him.

"Leaving the relative safety of Blackwell Keep," Henrick said, his voice alarmingly calm and even. "I admire your courage. I'd rather have jokes over cowardice. But I have no patience for fools. And no interest in bringing corpses home to your grandparents. That is a real possibility at Wyrmroost. Many have died here over the years. Many more will perish in the future. It takes preparation and caution and skill and experience and yes, a little luck, not to be one of them."

"What about an untamable griffin that does lots of loop-the-loops?" Seth asked. "Would that help?"

"This is going to be a long afternoon," Henrick grumbled.

Cantering along the High Road on Glory, the wind in her face, Kendra finally realized how badly she had needed to get out of Blackwell Keep. No gloomy rooms, no whispered conversations, no worried faces—just a long road, a big sky, and rugged wilderness all around her.

Kendra had been to Wyrmroost before, but she had never belonged here. There had been no protected roads on the way to the Dragon Temple. They had scurried around like thieves, vulnerable at every step. She hadn't fully comprehended how hard it was to enjoy the scenery when you were worried about getting devoured.

Today she not only had full permission to be at Wyrmroost—she was a caretaker! And she was being guided to a friendly destination along a secure route by a careful expert who knew the sanctuary well.

While riding a horse that appreciated Jane Austen.

Sometimes life was good.

Not too far into the ride, Henrick came near Kendra, pointing to the north. "We have company."

It took her a moment to spot the pair of dragons heading their way, one with golden scales, the other a bright red.

The dragons circled high above but occasionally swooped near the road. Due to their size and ferocious appearance, Kendra felt extremely exposed. She kept reminding herself that an invisible barrier was protecting them.

"Intimidation," Henrick told Kendra after the red dragon glided particularly close. "Don't let it get to you. We're safe on the road."

"Does it matter that they know where we're going?" Seth asked.

"I don't think so," Henrick said. "This visit to the Fair Folk should be no surprise. Celebrant is just making a statement. He wants you to know he is watching. He wants you to feel like trespassers inside of his sanctuary. That causes real harm only if you believe him."

After a long run, the road began to climb more steeply and the horses slowed to a trot. Mendigo sat behind Kendra, wooden hands on her waist, metal hooks jangling with the bouncy gait. Mountains loomed ahead of them, pockets of snow shining white near the craggy peaks.

"You'll soon see why this is called the High Road," Henrick announced. "We'll rise a good ways before dropping into the valley."

"Hey, Henrick," Seth said, "are you faster than these horses?"

"We don't want to exhaust the mounts," Henrick said. "They need their reserves in case of an emergency."

"That wasn't an answer," Seth observed.

Henrick gave him a pointed look. "The Luvians have

remarkable speed. But not many creatures on four legs run faster than I do."

"How did you end up at Blackwell Keep?" Kendra asked. "The outdoors seems more like your element."

"I'm the gamekeeper," Henrick said. "I spend most of my time roaming the sanctuary."

"Still, how did you get started?" Seth pressed. "Did lots of alcetaurs want the job?"

"It didn't have to be an alcetaur," Henrick said. "And no other alcetaurs wanted the job. We're a solitary breed."

"No families?" Kendra asked.

"Just temporarily," Henrick said. "When we're young. Alcetaurs aren't very numerous to begin with. There is no organized community, like with the other woodland taurans."

"The other what?" Seth asked.

"Rumitaurs," Henrick said. "Men with bodies of elk. And cervitaurs, men with bodies of deer. They move in groups. Alcetaurs spend most of our time on our own."

"How old were you when you left your mother?" Kendra asked.

Henrick gave her a funny look. "My . . . my mother was unusual. She stayed with me for a long time. Much longer than normal."

"How long?" Seth asked.

"Well into adulthood," he said, a small catch in his voice.

"Did you live in her basement?" Seth asked.

Kendra wished for a rock to throw at her brother.

"I don't understand," Henrick said.

"Human reference," Kendra said. "Sounds like your mother meant a lot to you."

"She taught me valuable lessons," Henrick said, his voice more stable. "I sought out Agad years ago at her encouragement."

"Get a job," Seth murmured in an old-lady voice.

"It has given me purpose," Henrick said. "I am not the most sociable person at Blackwell Keep, but you should meet some of the other alcetaurs."

"Jerks?" Seth asked.

"Some of them," Henrick admitted.

"I knew some centaurs," Seth said. "Jerks too."

"Not surprising," Henrick said. "What surprised me is that you rode one."

"They can be all right sometimes," Seth said. "Just don't steal their precious unicorn horn."

"I can see how that would end badly," Henrick said. "They're surly enough without a reason."

"I've given too many creatures those kinds of reasons," Seth said. "I hope it doesn't catch up to me."

"Me too," Henrick said with a laugh. "At least today you're on a fast horse."

CHAPTER FIFTEEN

The Fair Folk

Kendra, Seth, and Henrick paused at the top of the pass to take in the view. The lush valley featured groves of trees, square patches of farmland, expansive fields, a crystal blue lake, several streams, and a few ponds. Farmhouses dotted the valley, along with a few towers and a big mill with a waterwheel beside one of the main streams.

A single town not far from the lake had a wall around it with towers flanking the gate and at the corners. The houses were mostly made of stone or brick. Many had gables, turrets, and swooping rooftops. A few were connected by covered walkways above the cobblestone streets. An impressive castle dominated the center of the town, complete with pinnacled towers.

"It looks like a fairy tale," Kendra said.

"The Fair Folk know how to make an area pleasant," Henrick agreed.

Kendra looked back the other way. The red dragon and the gold one circled in the distance behind them. "Are they losing interest?" Kendra asked.

"Dragons stay away from this valley," Henrick said. "The protections are strong."

"Can we run downhill?" Seth asked.

Henrick glanced at the horses. "What do you say?"

Both mounts stamped once.

"Off we go," Henrick said.

Kendra enjoyed the rush of speed as they descended into the valley, the mountains around them rising as they lost altitude. Despite the speed and the small saddle, Kendra felt secure because Glory ran so smoothly. Mendigo jingled lightly behind her.

Before too long, they were cantering across the valley floor toward the walled town. As they passed the mill, Kendra noticed three large brutes who looked like ogres hauling bulging sacks. They paused to watch Kendra, Seth, and Henrick go by.

"Are those Fair Folk?" Kendra asked, worried the name was false advertising.

"Ogres run the mill under contract with the Fair Folk," Henrick said. "A relatively gentle breed. They grind dragon meal."

"Made from dragons?" Seth asked.

"Made *for* dragons," Henrick said. "A substitute for fresh meat that most dragons enjoy more than they care to admit. It's Terrabelle's biggest export, and it helps promote a gentler sanctuary. Every dragon likes to hunt, but they aren't as eager with full stomachs."

"Oatmeal for dragons?" Kendra asked.

"More or less," Henrick said. "It's a secret recipe derived from grains created by the Fair Folk. I have a hunch more than a little magic is involved. By nature dragons are carnivores."

Kendra watched farms go by until they reached the open gate of the walled settlement. Henrick slowed their progress to a walk. Trumpets let out a flourish as they approached. People lining the road beyond the wall began to cheer.

"Is this for us?" Kendra asked, certain they had blundered onto a parade route.

"You are only the second new caretakers in many decades," Henrick said. "Though Marat became caretaker only a few months ago, your appointment is a major occasion here at Wyrmroost."

"How do they already know?" Kendra asked.

"Marat exchanged messages with Lord Dalgorel about your visit," Henrick said.

The cheering surged and the trumpets blared again as they started up the cobblestone road beyond the gates. Applauding onlookers lined not only the road but also many nearby rooftops and balconies.

"This is more like it," Seth said with relish.

Though Kendra found her brother's comment embarrassing, she couldn't resist a delighted smile. The welcome from the crowd was overwhelming.

Moving up the road, Kendra realized that she had never encountered a comparable setting in all of her adventures on different magical preserves. This wasn't a group of centaurs or satyrs forming a loose community. This wasn't a single cottage or even a castle—it was an entire town, almost a city. It was orderly and detailed. She saw shops and eateries, inns and banks, townhomes and apartments. Thousands of people lived here. The tidy, timeworn buildings had history. It felt like she had crossed into another age, or into the pages of a storybook. The modern world where she had lived and gone to school before coming to Fablehaven had never felt farther away.

People continued to wave and cheer, and Kendra began to wave back. As she became less astounded by the crowd, she began to notice individuals in the throng. Equally balanced between men and women, most of the people appeared to be in the prime of life. Nobody looked extremely old, and she noticed few children and no babies. These Fair Folk looked like regular humans except for one outstanding commonality.

Every face she focused on was incredibly attractive.

The women were gorgeous. The men striking. Not all in the same way—she saw a wide variety of hair colors, facial features, and skin tones, though each person tended to be tall and physically fit.

This was not a town of beauty pageant contestants. It was an impossible collection of beauty pageant winners. These were not the people who showed up to audition; these were the people who got the part. Every countenance shone like that of a bride on her wedding day or a young man entranced by his first love. In fact, the glow of their faces seemed to be literal, as if light fell on them a little more brightly and evenly than on anything else. A panel of judges trying to determine the most beautiful among either the men or the women would have to disband in frustration.

Their physical beauty made the warm reception feel more flattering to Kendra, as if inexplicably all the best-looking and most popular people in the world had decided to celebrate her. Yet there was no condescension in their expressions, no hint that this exuberant welcome was a joke or a mistake.

Could it be genuine? Or was there a catch? The reception seemed too generous to be true.

A single rider came loping down the road on a white horse. For a moment Kendra wondered if the crowds might have gathered for him, but all attention clearly remained on her, Seth, and Henrick.

When the rider drew near, he reined his splendid mount to a stop and raised both hands. The crowd immediately quieted.

The young rider appeared to be around sixteen, his dark hair effortlessly stylish, his golden-brown complexion flawless, his sea-green eyes playful and intelligent. This horseman could be the number-one draw at box offices around the world, regardless of the quality of his movies, or the top pop star in the music industry, no matter what melodies he chose to sing.

Bracken was the best-looking male Kendra had seen in

real life. With a very different look, this rider was his equal. Though none of the men in the crowd were less attractive than this young man, most looked too adult to make Kendra feel as flustered as she did now.

"Welcome to Terrabelle, Kendra and Seth Sorenson," the young rider proclaimed in a clear voice. "I am Garreth, second son of Lord Dalgorel. We only recently learned of your surprise appointment as the new caretakers of Wyrmroost."

"When they were presented as candidates to Celebrant," Henrick explained, "the Dragon King forced Marat to instate them immediately or never."

"So we were informed by Marat," the young man said. "Well met, Henrick."

"Well met, Garreth," the alcetaur replied.

Garreth looked to Kendra, unveiling a smile that made her feel adored and forgiven. "Follow me to the palace. My father awaits our arrival." He winked. "We all look forward to meeting you."

Garreth swept an arm at the crowd, and the applause resumed.

Following him up the road, Kendra could not help feeling undeserving of the jubilant reception. Though the cheers looked and sounded sincere, how could she accept the adulation? These gorgeous people didn't know her. She had done nothing to earn their praise. Was it manipulative? Were the Fair Folk trying to disarm her? The longer she observed the welcome, the more guarded she became inside.

She noticed Seth having a good time. He laughed and

waved and pointed at individuals in the crowd. By contrast, Henrick remained solemn, eyes on the road ahead, enduring the attention without acknowledging it. Kendra hoped she was striking a balance between the two—friendly and grateful but not showboating.

The palace gate stood open. Leaving the masses behind, Kendra rode into a spacious courtyard with glossy tiles that looked better suited for a fancy room indoors. Liveried servants took charge of the horses. After dismounting, Kendra became more aware of how all the people, both males and females, were taller than she was. Kendra had almost caught up to her mother, who seemed to be a pretty average height for a woman, but the typical height among the Fair Folk looked to be a good six inches taller. Though there were many curious, well-dressed Fair Folk in the courtyard, they watched with polite interest rather than applauding.

"Thanks for the procession," Garreth said to Kendra and Seth, his manner more casual. "Sorry for all the formalities. So many people were interested in seeing you, I'm not sure how else we could have managed it."

"No problem," Seth said, still beaming.

Garreth paused, gazing at Kendra. "I'm sorry—you must get this all the time, but you shine so brightly."

Kendra felt warmth rushing to her face. "Thank you?"

He gave a reassuring smile. "It's definitely a compliment. Should we go see the old man?"

Kendra found herself not responding and was unsure how to fix the problem. That smile needed to be registered as a lethal weapon.

"Lead the way," Seth said.

"Your wooden friend is unusual," Garreth commented as they entered a high, broad hall with pale blue walls and white accents embellished by flourishes of crafted silver.

"Mendigo," Kendra said. "Kind of our bodyguard."

"Can he talk?"

"No," Kendra said. "But he's perfectly obedient."

"I want one," Garreth said with lighthearted jealousy.

"We got ours from a witch," Seth said. "Mendigo used to be our enemy."

"I want to hear the story," Garreth said. "I've never had a real enemy. I have some rivals among the Fair Folk, but no foes from outside our society. I was born under our neutrality. Gets pretty boring if you ask me, but I'm not in charge."

Kendra wondered how it would feel to not have an enemy. She had developed so many over the last couple of years.

They passed into a cavernous room where a distinguished-looking man sat on a jeweled throne atop a dais. Though the hair at his temples had hints of white, he remained vigorous and dashing. His chiseled features were enough like Garreth's that Kendra could see they were related, and he possessed an even darker complexion than his son.

But his smile was not nearly as inviting.

"Welcome, Kendra Sorenson," the man on the throne said. "I was not informed that you are fairykind."

Seth leaned nearer to Kendra. "Did you get any of that?"

"Yeah," she whispered back. "You didn't?"

"I only caught your name," Seth said.

Kendra realized the man must be speaking a fairy language. Her fairykind status let her understand fairy languages as effortlessly as English.

"May I present Lord Dalgorel, protector of Terrabelle," Garreth inserted, his tone formal once again.

"Yes, I am fairykind," Kendra finally answered. "And my brother Seth is a shadow charmer."

"So I noticed," Lord Dalgorel said. "An unlikely pairing. Welcome, Seth."

"You're a shadow charmer?" Garreth asked Seth with interest. "I don't have my father's eye."

"An adult is speaking," Dalgorel said in a hard tone.

"Apologies," Garreth said with a small bow.

"I understand him now," Seth whispered quickly.

Kendra realized Dalgorel must have switched to English. She disliked his severity toward his son.

"Please excuse the absence of Lady Dalgorel," the man said. "She is feeling unwell, and this audience comes at short notice. I am given to understand you have already been appointed co-caretakers with Celebrant."

Kendra glanced around the room. Many men and women were assembled, all breathtakingly attractive, dressed like royalty. She felt intimidated to admit they had strayed from tradition.

"Celebrant demanded—" Henrick began.

"Hold your reply," Dalgorel said, raising a hand. "I know what Marat claims. I want to hear from our new friends."

Seth showed the medallion. "Yes. We're already the caretakers."

The room was very quiet.

Dalgorel polished one of his rings with a fingertip. "Were you aware that the Fair Folk normally approve the prospective caretaker before the appointment is made?"

Kendra knew part of their purpose here was to apologize for breaking protocol. Dalgorel might be having this conversation in front of others to make sure the apology was public. She and Seth wanted his support, and hopefully some information. Despite his arrogant attitude, she needed to get this right.

"We had never heard of the Fair Folk before coming here two days ago," Kendra explained. "We only learned how your approval normally works while talking to Celebrant. He told us we had to accept the job and be appointed right then or never."

"Marat tried to get him to wait so we could talk to you first," Seth added.

"You feared the displeasure of Celebrant more than the prospect of offending the Fair Folk," Dalgorel summarized.

"We still got plenty of his displeasure," Kendra said. "He tore down the Perch where the caretakers talk to dragons."

"So I understand," Dalgorel said.

"The Dragon King made it clear we're not friends," Kendra said. "We skipped your approval because otherwise Celebrant would have stopped us from becoming the caretakers. It seemed necessary. We apologize."

"Celebrant does not make idle threats," Dalgorel said. "He would have blocked your instatement had you ignored him. The question remains whether a pair of mortal children have any business becoming the caretakers of Wyrmroost, especially during this uncertain period. Did it occur to you that Celebrant might not have wanted you to talk to me because I would have spoken against this terrible idea?"

"Wait a minute," Seth said. "I'm not sure it was *terrible*."

"Did Celebrant's eagerness send no warning signals to Marat?" Dalgorel asked.

"Marat had other reasons for wanting us to become the caretakers," Kendra said.

"Those reasons are best examined in private," Dalgorel said. "I pity you poor children. I will not add to your woes with displeasure for proceeding without my blessing. You came here promptly to apologize. Apology accepted. But your problems remain. In the darkest hour this sanctuary has seen, Wyrmroost has never been in less capable hands."

"It won't be an easy job," Kendra said, making an effort to stay humble. She noticed Seth glaring at her and hoped he would keep quiet. "We'd appreciate any advice or suggestions."

"I am not heartless," Dalgorel said. "You are young and most likely doomed to failure. Go with Garreth to the green parlor and I will come condole with you about your misfortunes in due time."

"Thank you," Kendra said.

Seth gave no answer but raised his eyebrows at Kendra.

Garreth led the way out of the room.

CHAPTER SIXTEEN

Hints

Seth sat trying to get his temper under control in a fancy room with furniture and walls done in shades of green. He knew this mission was diplomatic. And he knew Kendra wanted him to be polite. But it had been hard to stand there taking insults from Mr. Neutral.

"Are you all right, Seth?" Garreth asked.

Seth realized his expression was probably not very guarded. "Never better."

"My father tends to speak his mind," Garreth apologized.

Seth couldn't hold back. "If he has so many brilliant ideas about how to run the sanctuary, maybe he should get involved."

"Seth!" Kendra scolded.

Garreth held up a hand to stop her. "I hear him. The

complaint makes sense, though you're right to bring it up with me rather than with old Stony Face, especially when he is before an audience. Plenty of the Fair Folk are reluctant about our neutrality, including me."

"Really?" Seth asked. "Then why not join the fight?"

"It's complicated," Garreth said. "The neutrality wasn't imposed by my father. It's a long-standing policy for all the Fair Folk."

"Wouldn't want to mess up a policy," Seth grumbled.

"The ancients set the rules," Garreth said. "Our ancient leaders make the Fairy Queen seem young. The Fair Folk have a long history. Experience has shown that when we get involved in conflicts, the trouble gets worse for everyone."

"So you sit out of every fight," Seth said.

Garreth shrugged. "It isn't easy. There are times I want to get involved. Injustices I want to right. Embattled innocents I want to rescue. But who am I to shatter our truce? We would respond against a direct attack. We keep our defenses ready. But thanks to our neutrality, the Fair Folk have not suffered a major attack in thousands of years."

"What if the sanctuary falls?" Kendra asked. "You'll do nothing?"

"The Fair Folk are not in charge of Wyrmroost," Garreth said. "Terrabelle can stand even if the sanctuary fails. We will look to our own defenses."

"Do you care if it falls?" Seth asked.

"Of course I care," Garreth said. "We all care. We want stability. We don't want mayhem. But we won't break our neutrality."

Seth couldn't help noticing that Garreth sometimes used nicknames for his dad in private but was very polite in public. He doubted whether Garreth would share his dissatisfaction about the neutrality in public either. Were all the Fair Folk like this? Afraid to speak their minds? Afraid to stand up for what they believed?

The door opened and Dalgorel entered with a girl about Seth's age. Seth tried not to pay too much attention to girls as a rule, but this one was stunning—light blue eyes, black hair that fell in twisty curls, and a beautiful face.

"We meet again," Dalgorel said. "May I present my daughter, Eve. I understand you may have brought a small creature for her amusement."

Seth reached into his pocket and pulled out Calvin. The nipsie gave a quick bow. "I'm more a tiny person than a creature," Calvin explained. "No fins or fangs or exotic feathers. Hope I don't disappoint."

Eve hurried over to Seth, peering at the tiny man. "You're so small! But you're not a fairy."

"I'm a nipsie," Calvin proclaimed. "I'm quite big for my kind. Enhanced by a spell. Bit of a giant in nipsie circles, believe it or not."

"I've never met a nipsie," Eve said. Her eager eyes shifted to Seth. "Can I hold him?"

Seth passed Calvin to her.

"I've never met any of the Fair Folk," Calvin said.

Eve held him close to her eyes and prodded his belly.

"Watch it," Calvin said. "That tickles."

"Can we keep him, Father?" Eve asked.

"You know the rules," Dalgorel said. "No outsiders can join us here. Not even brownies."

"He's so small!" Eve complained. "Nobody will notice."

"Enough," Dalgorel said shortly. "Enjoy him as a visitor."

"Can I take him to my room?" Eve asked.

"He's not a doll," Seth told her. "Don't dress him up."

Eve made a face. "Why would I do that? I'd rather find a little ax and see how he does against a mouse."

"Sounds sporting," Calvin said.

Dalgorel rubbed his forehead. "Enough nonsense. Eve, show the nipsie your room if you must, but treat your guest with the utmost respect and civility."

"As you wish, Father," Eve said with a little curtsy.

"Is that okay?" Seth asked the nipsie.

Calvin winked and saluted. "Happy to entertain."

Seth realized Calvin was excited for a chance to snoop around. "See you later."

Eve raced out the door.

"Thank you for accepting our apology," Kendra said.

"Was there another option?" Dalgorel replied. "The damage is done. Celebrant has secured the ideal caretakers for his uprising. It only makes matters worse if I undermine your authority with my displeasure."

"Why do you think we'll be so bad?" Seth challenged.

Dalgorel gave a chuckle. "You're mortal children. Dragon sanctuaries are typically supervised by wizards— mortals of great power who were formerly dragons. I do see that you have power. Nobody has been fairykind for a good while. And a shadow charmer can be useful. I sense you have defeated some powerful foes. Even a dragon, correct?"

"We killed Siletta together," Kendra said.

"No small feat," Dalgorel acknowledged.

"Kendra killed the Demon King," Seth bragged on her behalf.

"So I have heard," Dalgorel said. "You might not want to boast of that feat to every stranger you meet. Acts of aggression can invite retaliation."

"Gorgrog was attacking us," Kendra said.

"Because you put yourselves in his path," Dalgorel said. "I have heard about the battle of Zzyzx. Seeds were planted that day for a major war between demons and dragons."

"But we stopped the demons from taking over the world," Seth said.

Dalgorel gave a small smile. "Is that so? Some might claim you merely postponed them. Others might point out the demons never had a chance to make their intentions clear. Still others could argue you destabilized the dragon sanctuaries and laid the foundation for a worldwide draconic rebellion. With your new positions as caretakers, you will have an excellent view of the consequences."

"We stopped the demons," Seth said. "We'll contain the dragons."

Dalgorel chuckled again. "I understood that the *dragons* redirected the demons. But I respect your resolve. Kendra mentioned that Marat had other reasons for wanting you as the caretakers. I am willing to hear them."

Seth glanced at his sister. She looked uncertain. "The reasons are kind of secret," she said.

"You are welcome to keep your secrets," Dalgorel said. "But if you want my advice, I need to better understand what you two hope to accomplish as caretakers."

"The Fair Folk are reliable at keeping secrets that would give anyone an unfair advantage," Henrick informed them. "You should want any counsel Lord Dalgorel is willing to share."

"The defenses at Blackwell Keep have weakened," Kendra said. "Celebrant keeps attacking because he senses a vulnerability. Marat hoped that having mortal caretakers would repair the magical defenses."

Dalgorel sighed sadly. "This is why Celebrant did not want you talking to me before your instatement. The vulnerability was not related to the caretaker being a dragon. Marat stayed in his human shape. So long as he remained in that form, the qualifications were satisfied."

"Are you sure?" Seth asked.

Dalgorel scowled. "I have been here since Wyrmroost was founded. I know more about this sanctuary than most. My official position is neutral, but I do not want to see Wyrmroost fall. I don't want dragons unleashed on the world. I would have warned you. The caretaker of Wyrmroost was Marat, one of the dragons with the strongest allegiance to the wizards of Dragonwatch. He was a formidable opponent for Celebrant. Now the caretakers are a pair of novices."

"Do you want us to succeed?" Kendra asked.

"What a surprise that would be," Dalgorel said. "But yes,

for the good of the world I would prefer you maintain the integrity of this sanctuary. Balance brings order and peace. History has shown that few circumstances disturb balance more than dragons on the loose. Agad should have considered that before bringing dragons into the fight at Zzyzx."

"Maybe he did consider it," Seth said. "People who actually fix problems sometimes have to take risks."

Dalgorel glared. "This conversation can end immediately if my suggestions are unwanted."

"We want them," Kendra said, elbowing Seth.

"Seth is new to the concept of our neutrality," Garreth explained.

"Then it is one of many issues he does not comprehend," Dalgorel said. "No long-term good has ever come of the Fair Folk going to war. The fewer groups at war, the less strife in the world. We are a voice of reason encouraging other members of the magical community to seek diplomatic solutions. We host peace talks. We counsel against aggression. Our neutrality has brought greater peace than any harm we could have prevented through violence."

"If you say so," Seth mumbled reluctantly. He knew arguing about neutrality wasn't the purpose of this visit. They needed information.

"Do you know how we can fix the defenses?" Kendra asked. "Do you understand what's wrong?"

Dalgorel gave a gloomy smile. "I do."

"Then can you tell us?" Seth asked.

"The information is too vital to come from the Fair Folk," Dalgorel said.

Seth tossed his hands up. "Of course it is."

"Is there *anything* you can tell us?" Kendra begged.

Dalgorel looked from Seth to Kendra. "Your brother is a terrible diplomat. But you have some promise. I understand that his youth, his ignorance, and his inexperience are speaking as much as anything, but even so, he is a caretaker of Wyrmroost, and due to his outbursts I am disinclined to help you."

"I'm sorry," Seth said, not meaning it but trying his best to sound sincere.

"Please, you must be able to give us a hint," Kendra said.

Dalgorel stared at Kendra for a long moment. "Agad should not have let Celebrant take the scepter. He should have given him the medallion instead."

"The medallion doesn't work?" Seth exclaimed.

"The medallion functions," Dalgorel said. "But it is vulnerable in a way the scepter was not."

"Why?" Kendra asked.

"I have already explained too much," Dalgorel said. "You are the caretakers now. You have access to the secrets of Wyrmroost if you learn where to look. And as mortals, you can gain information from a nearby source Agad and Marat may have been hesitant to approach."

"The Dragon Slayer," Henrick said, realization in his voice.

"Who?" Kendra asked.

"Each of the hidden dragon sanctuaries has a designated Dragon Slayer," Henrick said. "Ours is the Somber Knight."

"Is he at Blackwell Keep?" Seth asked. "I didn't see any knights."

"None have seen him for centuries," Henrick said. "If he is still alive, he resides in the catacombs beneath Terrabelle."

"He might be dead?" Seth asked.

"Possibly," Henrick said. "None have communicated with him in a great while. He has a gloomy reputation."

"Isn't this place supposed to be neutral?" Kendra asked.

"Terrabelle is neutral," Dalgorel said. "The Fair Folk did not place the Dragon Slayer here. His lair was created by the founders of Wyrmroost. We have no direct affiliation with the Somber Knight and cannot be held accountable for his presence or his actions. He is a cold-blooded killer known for his stark outlook and unpleasant disposition. His purpose is to wage war against direct physical threats to this sanctuary. But he does have knowledge."

"He's still there?" Kendra asked.

"He should be," Dalgorel said. "The legendary Dragon Slayers are virtually immune to the passage of time."

"We killed a dragon," Seth reminded everyone.

"Any who kill a dragon earn the title of dragon slayer," Henrick said. "It is not easily done. But only a handful have held the designated office of Dragon Slayer. It's an appointed calling, a lifelong responsibility. There are never more than seven in the whole world. The Somber Knight has been at Wyrmroost since the beginning. He might be able to answer the question Lord Dalgorel has raised."

"Why wouldn't Agad or Marat approach him?" Kendra asked.

"The designated Dragon Slayers exist to protect mortals from dragons," Henrick said. "Their enmity with dragons runs deep enough that they have never been too friendly with wizards, either—even the wizards of Dragonwatch who established Wyrmroost. Desperate times can forge unusual partnerships. This particular Dragon Slayer has an especially dark reputation. But the Somber Knight is here as a fail-safe in case of emergency. As caretakers, you have a right to introduce yourselves."

"Perhaps you can learn some of what you want to know," Garreth said.

"Is he safe?" Kendra asked.

"That is not the word I would use," Dalgorel said.

"But you and Seth are indeed the caretakers of Wyrmroost," Henrick said. "You have the medallion. And you are not wizards. You should be able to confer successfully with the Somber Knight."

"I'm sold," Seth said. "How do we find him?"

"The easiest access would be through a portal that connects to the dungeon of this castle," Dalgorel said.

"Can I escort them?" Garreth asked.

"I hold no objection," Dalgorel said.

"What about the nipsie?" Seth asked. "Calvin."

"It might be best to leave him with Eve," Dalgorel said. "The Somber Knight is not fond of visitors. He is fatalistic and slow to improvise. The two of you will place plenty of strain on his hospitality."

"Comforting," Kendra said.

"You may want to leave the limberjack behind as well," Henrick suggested.

"Will you join us?" Kendra asked Henrick.

"I had best not," the alcetaur said. "But I'll accompany you to the edge of his domain and await you there."

"Visit the Dragon Slayer," Dalgorel advised. "Deal carefully and keep your wits about you. Perhaps he can aid you in ways I cannot."

"More like *will* not," Seth mumbled.

Lord Dalgorel gazed at Kendra. "You're about to confront a powerful warrior with a notoriously difficult disposition. If you return without your brother, I may not be surprised."

CHAPTER SEVENTEEN

The Somber Knight

This is the dungeon?" Seth asked with unmistakable disappointment.

Kendra had to agree it was surprising. A brightly lit hall stretched ahead of them, the ceramic tiles of the floor immaculate, bouquets of flowers suspended at intervals along the painted walls. The even light came from plentiful globes rather than torches.

"I know, tidy," Garreth said. "Outstanding food. For a while we had people breaking minor laws just to eat here."

"Really?" Kendra asked.

Garreth raised a hand. "Guilty. I spent a week down here for taking somebody else's horse for a ride. The judge knew I wanted in. He tried to let me off with a warning. I had to haggle."

"Was the food good?" Seth asked.

"Fabulous," Garreth said. "The cooks are real artists. And it was fun to be part of the trend. We'd still have a petty crime problem but they opened up a wing of the dungeon to paying customers."

"What about the actual prisoners?" Seth asked.

Garreth chuckled. "We have plenty of room. There are only three regular prisoners. A giant who attacked Terrabelle like a thousand years ago. We tried to release him but this has become home. There's also a wereboar who comes in voluntarily when the moon gets big. And the rebel Lomo, son of Targon."

"Is he one of the Fair Folk?" Seth asked.

"Yes," Garreth said. "You might like him. He sure wasn't afraid to speak his mind. Lomo fought against our policies of neutrality and eventually became a vigilante. He left Wyrmroost entirely. The Fair Folk are not bound to the sanctuaries. We're here voluntarily. After involving himself in multiple fights out in the world and on other preserves, Lomo was caught and sentenced to the dungeon until he vows to abide by our policies."

"He goes free if he just agrees?" Kendra asked.

"He's far too stubborn for that," Garreth said. "It could end up as a life sentence."

"Do you like him?" Kendra wondered.

"Who doesn't?" Garreth said. "His only crime has been his refusal to abide by our neutrality policy. Many of us share some of his opinions. The difference is, he acts on them. Some of us half admire it, but we have laws for a reason. I helped hunt him down and catch him."

"Was it hard?" Seth asked.

"It took some time," Garreth said. "I wish I could say I played a key role. I was there to support the expert trackers. I was mostly just grateful for the excuse to venture out into the world. The Fair Folk don't join in battles anymore, but we still police our own."

"He's the only criminal from your people?" Seth asked.

Garreth shrugged. "We've been around a long time. The worst of us were weeded out long ago. They left or were exiled. Most of us have learned to get along. When problems arise, we can usually settle them without resorting to the dungeon."

"Why even bother with a dungeon?" Kendra asked.

"Tradition, I guess," Garreth said. "We used to have castles where the dungeons served a real purpose."

"There is much to be admired about the order of your society," Henrick said.

Garreth grinned. "And plenty to dislike about our isolation."

Kendra tried not to melt at how adorable he looked when he smiled. Bracken was definitely her one and only, but wasn't it natural to notice when somebody was attractive? Glaringly, relentlessly attractive.

"Here we are," Garreth said as they turned a corner. Ahead, a bulky iron door awaited. "Beyond here we'll find the catacombs."

"Is that where Fair Folk go for dessert?" Seth asked.

Garreth produced two keys and opened a pair of locks,

one high and one low. "The catacombs should better match what you were expecting. Murky and mysterious."

The door swung inward to reveal a dusty passageway made of stone blocks, lit only by the light spilling in from the dungeon. Kendra could see a long way down the dim corridor. Ever since she had become fairykind, no darkness could completely blind her.

"Dark?" Kendra whispered to Seth.

"Pretty dark," he replied.

Garreth handed Kendra a short silver baton with a light globe at the end. He gave Seth and Henrick similar batons.

"Any monsters?" Seth asked.

"There shouldn't be anything serious," Garreth said. "Our scepter protects Terrabelle from most threats above and beneath. We don't often venture into the catacombs. Nothing worse than giant rats has been reported."

Kendra froze. "Giant rats aren't serious?"

"Nothing bigger than a dog," Garreth assured her.

"Think we'll see any?" Seth asked.

"We could get lucky," Garreth said.

"I'm in the middle," Kendra declared, positioning herself between Garreth and Henrick.

After entering the corridor, Garreth closed and locked the door. "If I die down here, don't forget to take these keys." He dangled them for all to see, then winked as he tucked them into a pocket.

"What if the rats drag you away?" Seth asked.

"Let's all just live," Kendra suggested.

They started down the passage. The way forked more than once.

"You know your way around in here?" Seth asked.

"Not all routes," Garreth said. "The catacombs are one of the few places to find a little adventure without leaving Terrabelle. I come here with friends sometimes when we need a thrill. One of our most typical dares is to touch the door to the Somber Knight's lair. I can get us there no problem."

"I'm memorizing the way back," Henrick said.

The cool, dry air smelled of dust and stone. Everything seemed still and silent, as if they were the first people to walk these halls in centuries. Kendra wondered how long their footprints in the fine dust on the floor would remain undisturbed. Though she stayed alert, she saw nothing more threatening than tattered spiderwebs.

Beyond a crumbling archway, the hall became more like a natural cave, both wider and more rugged, though remnants of masonry still clung to some surfaces. Kendra heard faint chirps and squeaks in the distance that might have been bats or mice.

"This is a cave now," Seth said.

"There are lots of natural caverns down here," Garreth said. "Dead caves, old and dry. We're getting close."

A structure came into view up ahead, projecting from the wall of the cavern, dim at first, then illuminated by their batons. The building seemed like a large tomb, the stonework smoother and in better repair than anything Kendra had seen since leaving the dungeon. Stone stairs led up to a pair of carved bronze doors.

"This is where we part," Garreth announced. "We'll wait for you here."

"Is it unlocked?" Kendra asked.

"Not likely," Henrick said. "But this dwelling was designed to be accessed by the caretaker. Use the medallion. Hold it up and ask for admittance."

"Just ask?" Seth questioned.

"Wizards built this place," Garreth said. "They tend to be practical."

Kendra mounted the steps beside Seth. He lifted the medallion, stretching the chain forward. "Open for the caretakers," he commanded.

The bronze doors immediately began to swing inward, squealing like a pod of dolphins. Kendra took a step back.

"It worked," Seth said, sounding surprised.

Behind the doors, a wide corridor was lit by large globes emitting bluish light. The floor, walls, and ceiling were composed of huge blocks of pale stone, snugly joined. Cold air flooded out, making Kendra shiver.

"We should have brought coats," she said.

A lightweight jacket slid over her shoulders from behind. "Take mine," Garreth said.

Tailored to fit him snugly, the stylish jacket was roomy on Kendra, hanging almost to her knees. A faint smell of him lingered with it. "Thanks," she said, her cheeks flushing.

"Anytime," he replied warmly, then retreated down the stairs to stand beside Henrick.

"Come on," Seth said.

Kendra followed Seth down the hall, their batons adding white light to the blue glow of the globes. No dust or webs polluted the pristine corridor. The cold air smelled pure, if not quite fresh. Didn't truly fresh air require a hint of life? Plants or something?

They descended stairs as wide as the entire hall. Kendra guessed that ten people could go down them at once, shoulder to shoulder. Then the hall ended at another set of bronze doors.

Looking at Kendra, her brother held up the medallion. Before Seth could speak, the doors swung outward, revealing a wider, taller hall. At the far end, a huge knight sat on a throne, clad in a full suit of elaborate black armor that left no skin visible. An enormous sword rested across his knees.

"Who approaches?" asked a very deep voice that carried extremely well despite speaking softly. Kendra wondered if it was being amplified somehow.

"The new caretakers of Wyrmroost," Kendra said. "Kendra and Seth Sorenson."

The knight gestured for them to come forward. The closer they got to the throne, the better Kendra appreciated the scale of the knight. Standing, he would have to be ten feet tall. The armor looked so thick and heavy that part of her wondered whether he could stand at all. What if a little man with a microphone was standing inside the huge chest?

"Who is behind this jest, young ones?" the knight asked, his voice slow and melancholy. "Surely you are not the true caretakers."

"No joke," Seth said. "We were appointed yesterday. Celebrant is the other caretaker."

"I know about the two dragons," the knight said glumly. "Marat and Celebrant. It's a dark hour when dragons govern their own prison. Makes me . . . tired. But children? I see the medallion. I feel the authority. Are there no other humans left to fill the post?"

"No good candidates who are dragon tamers," Kendra said.

"You two are dragon tamers?" the knight asked. "How?"

"We hold hands," Kendra said.

The knight shook his head. "Of course you do. How quaint. And naturally I am the Dragon Slayer who now works for children after the Dragon King has risen to the office of caretaker. Tell me, has a perpetual winter been declared? Is the sun never to rise again?"

"It isn't that bad," Seth said.

"Easy words from the mouth of a child," the knight said morosely. "If you had lived through the horrors and atrocities that plague my waking visions and haunt my dreams, you might not be so quick to underestimate the coming calamity."

"What do you think will happen?" Kendra asked.

"The same as always. Beauty will fade. Prosperity will end. Singing will turn to lamentations. Old age will follow youth, and sickness will replace health. As soon as you are born, death is waiting, inevitable as nightfall. The rising tide of evil will swallow hope and truth and light until only the void remains."

"And I thought Whiner was depressed," Seth muttered to Kendra.

"Who is Whiner?" the knight asked.

"A wraith I borrowed not too long ago," Seth explained.

"We can fight the evil," Kendra said.

"Alas, this is my lot," the knight said. "I wait here in the darkness, not quite dead, not quite living, bleak and useless as a monument to a forgotten kingdom, awaiting the call to arms. I stand watch as the centuries turn to millennia, as the same cycles repeat, pretending that when I am called, I can help by adding to the carnage."

"Have you slain a lot of dragons?" Seth asked.

The knight patted his sword. "That I have done. More than my share. I know my trade. But it is like sending a hydra to a headsman. For every dragon I kill, a new nest is born. We had the dragons in our power. We could have destroyed them. But no, no, no. Why end the threat forever when we can shelter them and give them eons to respawn? And as their numbers grew, those who once opposed them dwindled into obscurity, training no replacements. When the dragons get free this time, there will be no protectors. The world will reel. Crops will burn. Cities will fall. Humanity will scatter and quail as merciless monsters inherit the earth."

"You *are* depressed," Seth said.

"I am called the Somber Knight," he said.

"I think I see why," Kendra said. "Do you still hope to win? The dragons haven't escaped yet. Maybe we can keep them at the sanctuary."

The Somber Knight gave a slow chuckle that sounded like it could turn to sobs. "Hope fled long ago. But I will not surrender." He stroked his sword. "I will walk the weary path of duty until the bitter end."

"We wouldn't mind some help," Seth said.

"Neither would I," the Somber Knight said. "Hours, days, and years have become voids within voids. I stand alone against the impossible. And the universe sends children. How can I serve you? Would you care for some candy? Perhaps a bedtime story?"

"I bet he knows some good ones," Seth muttered to Kendra.

"I have a feeling they would give you nightmares," she mumbled back. Then she raised her voice. "We need to stop Celebrant. He is trying to take over the sanctuary."

"I would gladly be of service," the Somber Knight said. "But I am bound until the dragons stray outside their covenants."

"Celebrant ripped down the Perch," Kendra said.

"Was anyone hurt?" the Somber Knight asked.

"No," Kendra said. "Marat protected us."

"Celebrant is a fellow caretaker," the Somber Knight said. "With that status, I'm not sure I could attack him no matter what rules he violates. Since the Perch was neutral territory, he was within his rights to destroy it."

"He has attacked Blackwell Keep more than once," Seth said.

"To no avail," the Somber Knight replied. "There is no penalty for testing the barrier."

"So, once we're dead, you'll come avenge us," Seth said hotly.

The Somber Knight's voice remained low and calm. "If you die unlawfully, I may be freed to exact retribution."

"Can you fight all the dragons of Wyrmroost at once?" Kendra asked.

"Of course I could," the Somber Knight replied. "But I would perish. I would struggle to best a single dragon in a fair fight. Enchanted armor and ensorcelled blades only get you so far. You don't slay dragons without fighting smart. You engage them on your terms. You rig everything in your favor. Then you might stand a chance."

"We slayed a dragon," Seth said. "Siletta."

"You two raided the Dragon Temple?"

"We had help," Kendra said. "But we killed Siletta. It was an emergency. We were racing against people who wanted to open Zzyzx."

"Siletta had a peculiar set of talents," the Somber Knight said, leaning forward, his voice more interested. "Unusual attacks and defenses centered on her poisonous nature. How did you do it?"

"Unicorn horn," Kendra said.

"Ingenious," the Dragon Slayer said. "That shows promise." He slumped back and sighed. "Too bad you'll both be dead soon. So young."

"We're not going to lose," Seth said.

"Noble attitude, young one," the Somber Knight said. "Hold to your post. Go down fighting."

"We're hoping you can help us," Kendra admitted.

"With the burial? No need. There will be very little left of you. Dragons are thorough."

"We're trying to figure out why Celebrant keeps attacking Blackwell Keep," Kendra explained. "Do you know why the defenses are vulnerable?"

"Will knowing make any difference?" the Somber Knight asked glumly.

"It might help us go down fighting," Seth said. "It might give us a chance."

The Somber Knight tapped his sword. "Have you any suspicions?"

"Is the medallion weak?" Seth asked.

"Blackwell Keep once held the medallion and one of the seven scepters," the Somber Knight said. "Celebrant asked for the keep's scepter when he became a caretaker. Now only the medallion protects Blackwell Keep. Do you know where the medallion gets its power?"

"Magic?" Seth asked.

"The treaty?" Kendra asked.

"Both true in part," the Somber Knight said. "The gem in the medallion is from another of the scepters. The hidden one. The seventh. Only five scepters remain active. One was never recovered when the Roost fell ages ago."

"What's the Roost?" Seth asked.

"Do you truly know so little about the sanctuary you oversee?" the Somber Knight asked.

"We're new," Kendra explained. "Help us learn."

"The Roost is Wyrmroost Castle," the Somber Knight said. "The caretaker used to split time between the castle and the keep. The scepter at the castle was lost. And the seventh scepter was hidden when this sanctuary was founded. It is connected to the medallion."

"Why not keep the scepter with the medallion?" Kendra asked.

"Wizards are always trying to control their environment," the Somber Knight said. "The rest of us attempt to do the same by diverse methods. But the majority lack the power to succeed like wizards can. Wizards appreciate redundancies. The complicated locks they create for their prisons are a good example. With one scepter already at Blackwell Keep, the wizards hid the other elsewhere and magically linked it to the medallion."

"So if somebody stole the scepter at the keep, the other would still be hidden?" Seth asked.

"Yes," the Somber Knight said. "And the magical defenses at the keep would hold. Even if the medallion fell into the wrong hands, it would be difficult to harm the defenses without finding the associated scepter. Celebrant must have sensed that the power source for the medallion is not at Blackwell Keep. Perhaps he thought that meant he could overpower the defenses. I do not believe he can. But if he finds the connected scepter, he could gain easy access."

"So we need to find the scepter," Kendra said.

The Somber Knight inclined his helmeted head. "Now that the previous scepter has been given to Celebrant, Blackwell Keep will be more secure if the scepter connected to the medallion is retrieved."

"Where is it?" Seth asked.

"I am not sure," the Somber Knight said. "I expect the founders concealed it somewhere at Wyrmroost. But even that much is not certain."

"This is a big preserve," Kendra said.

"Enormous," the Somber Knight agreed. "Finding the hidden scepter is a hopeless task. Even without competition from the Dragon King, you could spend the rest of your lives searching and never come close. Or you could be killed by whatever traps or guardians undoubtedly protect it. The hidden scepter is not casually concealed. It is hidden very well."

"Do you have any idea where we could start looking?" Seth asked. "You want Wyrmroost to survive."

"Indeed," the Somber Knight said. "I want Wyrmroost to survive. And I know it will not. And so do you. Beginnings and endings. That is the world we live in. All is temporary. Wyrmroost had a beginning, and so it must have an ending. It's only a matter of time before it all comes crashing down."

"We'd like Wyrmroost to outlast us, at least," Kendra said.

"Your lives are brief," the Somber Knight acknowledged. "With such a limited span of days, some will live through sadder times than others. I'm sorry that you are here now. I am sorry you were tricked into this predicament. You were appointed captains of a sinking vessel. I have a longer life-span than you. I have seen much. Seasons of order degenerate into chaos. Devastation comes and goes. I await the next hour when I am needed. It always comes."

"We need you now," Seth said.

"I can take only limited action," the Somber Knight said. "You want to prolong the inevitable demise of Wyrmroost. You desire help finding the scepter. I have one proposal, by no means a certainty. As a rule, I avoid dragons, except to dispatch them. But there is one dragon at Wyrmroost who might be able to supply the information you need. Dromadus."

"Tell us about Dromadus," Kendra said.

"A former Dragon King."

"There were others?" Seth exclaimed.

"Several, over the millennia," the Somber Knight said. "Former Dragon Kings seldom survive the challenge that takes their crown. Dromadus was an anomaly. He stepped down without a fight. The only Dragon King to abdicate. The dragons considered it unspeakably shameful. Dromadus went from the pinnacle all the way to the bottom. I have never met him. But he was close to the wizards who established Wyrmroost. Dromadus may have knowledge of the hidden scepter."

"Doesn't Agad know?" Seth asked. "Or Marat?"

"No way," Kendra said. "They didn't know why the medallion was weak, or they would already be looking for the scepter."

"Agad became caretaker long after Wyrmroost was founded," the Somber Knight said. "He was the fourth caretaker. Wizards love their secrets. It is possible he never knew the medallion derived power from a hidden scepter. If he did know, then you were set up to become caretakers, and to discover this knowledge on your own, so you would be forced to decide how to proceed without external influence, thereby assuming responsibility for all the associated risks and perils."

"You're good with conspiracy theories," Seth said.

"I don't hide from unpleasant possibilities," the Somber Knight replied. "I embrace them. Some call it pessimism. I see it as an advantage."

"It's somber at least," Kendra said. "How do we find Dromadus?"

"Should you choose to visit him, it will be at your own risk," the Somber Knight said. "I cannot guarantee your safety. An endorsement from me would harm your chances. I have slain too many of their kind for any dragon to trust me."

"Fair enough," Seth said. "Where do we go?"

"Have you a map?" the Somber Knight asked.

After a smug glance at Kendra, Seth removed a map from his satchel and unfolded it. The Somber Knight beckoned them closer. He used a finger to trace a road called the Winding Way away from Terrabelle. His finger left the road, sliding south, and then tapped a spot.

"You will find a grove of giant sequoias here," the Somber Knight said. "Descend through the trapdoor near the center."

"And we'll meet Dromadus?" Seth asked.

"For better or for worse," the Somber Knight said.

"Isn't it dangerous to leave the road?" Kendra asked.

"It is dangerous to visit me," the Somber Knight said. "I have not heard a kind word in many years. Or seen a smile."

"We like you," Seth said, giving a big smile.

"I could slay you where you stand," the Somber Knight said. "I am an executioner, and you have come to my domain. This sword has tasted the blood of thousands."

"I'm trying to stay positive," Seth said, his smile faltering.

"This sanctuary is not a comfortable place for mortals," the Somber Knight said, "let alone for children. But you are burdened by duty. You came here for counsel. If you wish to stand against the Dragon King, finding the hidden scepter would help. You could get killed on the way to Dromadus. Upon arrival, Dromadus could harm or kill you, though of any dragon I know, he seems the least violent. Should you survive, you may not learn what you hope to know. If you do, you could perish searching for the scepter. You could also lose the scepter to the Dragon King and hasten the fall of Blackwell Keep."

"I think that covers all the terrible things that could happen," Seth said.

"Speaking broadly," the Somber Knight said. "It would be difficult to number every horrific way you could die."

"Cheerful," Seth said, using a pencil to mark the spot the Somber Knight had shown them on the map. "Thanks for the tip."

"Anything else we should remember?" Kendra asked.

The Somber Knight stood, towering over them, and raised his sword in front of his helmet. "In spite of your youth and the near certainty of failure, I salute your efforts to fulfill your responsibility to protect Wyrmroost."

Bringing a hand to his brow, Seth saluted back. "And

we salute you for sitting here in the dark all these years waiting to help."

The Somber Knight gave a small bow, then sat back down on his throne. "Do not trouble yourselves about my plight. Mine has ever been a thankless post. Go, young ones. Travel well. Live as long as fortune permits."

CHAPTER EIGHTEEN

Off the Road

Henrick stood in a private room with Seth and Kendra, muscular arms folded across his broad chest, scowling in thought. "I don't know," the alcetaur said. "I have orders to bring you kids directly back to Blackwell Keep."

"But you see why we might need to change the plan," Seth said. "If we have a chance to find the scepter, we have to go after it."

"Technically, we are the caretakers," Kendra reminded the alcetaur. "And technically, the orders you receive from others are advice. Seth and I give the real orders."

Henrick uncrossed his arms, then refolded them. He looked stumped.

They were in a small, fancy room Dalgorel had loaned them. The smaller the room, the less Henrick looked like he belonged. The moose portions of his body made him so big that he had to maneuver carefully to avoid toppling the furniture.

"I admit you are the caretakers," Henrick said after a pause. "But the job of your advisers and staff is to keep you alive. Sometimes that fundamental duty might even supersede your orders. The Somber Knight is sending you into precarious territory. To get to the grove, I'll have to lead you off the road and into the wild. Your safety will be in jeopardy."

"We know," Seth said, exasperated. "The Somber Knight explained every horrible possibility."

"And you still want to move forward?" Henrick asked, looking from Seth to Kendra. "You're united in this decision?"

"I think so," Kendra said. "I mean, if we go back to Blackwell Keep to discuss it with everyone, we just lose time. And what if Grandma and Grandpa try to stop us from going to Dromadus? It needs to happen. We have to find that scepter."

Henrick furrowed his brow. "If Dromadus would reveal the location to anyone, it would be the caretakers. Also, your youth might play on his sympathies. I'm not sure anyone else could approach him with a realistic chance of success. But you two have been placed in my care. My area of expertise is traveling this sanctuary, and in these tumultuous times I must strongly advise against leaving the roads or protected areas."

"But . . ." Seth prompted him.

Henrick sighed. "But this is an emergency. I can see the sense in your argument. The gamble may be justified. It would also be risky not to pursue the scepter. I respect you for wanting to protect the sanctuary. If you are united in this decision, I will respect your authority to make it. I will guide you to the sequoia grove and do my best to keep you alive."

"Yes," Seth said, pumping a fist. "That's all we wanted to hear."

Kendra produced the unicorn horn. "Is it all right if I talk to Bracken first? Since we can't reach anybody else, I want to get his opinion before moving forward."

"Come on!" Seth complained. "What good is that going to do? He can't be objective! You're his favorite! He won't want you in danger."

"He's seen me in danger before," Kendra said. "Coming here in the first place was dangerous. I just want his input."

"Bad idea," Seth said. "We know what needs to happen. We should go do it."

"Maybe I'd also just like to talk to him," Kendra said. "You know, in case something bad happens."

"Wow, you really want to jinx us, don't you?" Seth exclaimed. "Want me to reserve a couple of coffins just in case?"

"Can I have some privacy?" Kendra demanded.

"Tell him hi for me," Seth said. "I'll go find my Tiny Hero."

Seth left the room. Henrick followed him to the door, stepping carefully to pass between a chair and a sofa.

"Please apologize to Bracken for me," the alcetaur said. "I spoke against him when he visited, but he uncovered a pair of traitors for us. Tell him that I wish him well."

Henrick ducked through the door and closed it.

Kendra held the horn tightly.

Bracken, she projected with her mind. *Can you hear me?*

Sure, Kendra, came the reply. *I wondered when you would reach out. I tried to contact you before I went to bed but I couldn't get an answer.*

I've kept the horn with me, Kendra assured him. *You must have tried when we were riding horses.*

Are you exploring the sanctuary? Bracken asked with alarm. *That might not be a great idea. The rebellion is heating up. It's happening at all seven sanctuaries. The unrest seems co-ordinated, and it keeps getting uglier. Truces are breaking. People are dying.*

We need something to stabilize the defenses at Wyrmroost, Kendra said. *Nobody can hear us, right?*

I'm shielding our thoughts, Bracken said.

Celebrant ripped off part of Blackwell Keep. The defenses held, but they're vulnerable. We need a scepter. One of seven that create safe places at the sanctuary. Seth and I have a lead. It looks like we're the only good guys who can retrieve it. If Celebrant got to it first we'd be doomed. I think we need to go after it.

Is your grandfather in agreement?

We haven't had a chance to ask him. We're with the Fair Folk. As the new caretakers, we had to pay them a visit.

Not bad-looking, are they? Bracken commented know-ingly.

Kendra felt her cheeks grow warm. Why was she sud-denly feeling guilty? She hadn't done anything wrong. Could he sense her emotions from the other side of the world? Probably not. He was only supposed to sense what she deliberately sent to him. *I guess so,* she finally replied.

Can you check with your grandfather first?

Not without going back to Blackwell Keep. I think this needs to happen. Seth does too. Henrick confirmed that he'll take us if we both agree. He sends greetings, by the way.

Henrick is smart, Bracken expressed. *So are you. Do what you think is right. But don't take a single unnecessary risk. Things are getting messy at the sanctuaries. I'm sorry you got drawn into this.*

You got pulled into stuff too, Kendra replied. *Are you all right?*

I've been better. I'm in a cave for the night, high on a mountainside. I'm trying to track Ronodin. Soaring Cliffs is in a sorry state. Several dragons are rampaging. Only locations protected by magic are secure.

Celebrant seems ready to wage war.

Those defenses might be your only hope, Bracken thought to her. *If finding the scepter will make those defenses hold, it is probably worth the trouble. But don't press your luck. Get the scepter and then get back to the keep. I have a feeling this is just the beginning.*

Thanks for the advice, Kendra replied. *Stay safe.*

You too. My mother has connected the new fairy realm to the fairy shrine at Wyrmroost, so when I finish here I can come to you that way.

Good news!

Hope to see you soon. I want to help.

I know, Kendra assured him. *I wish I could help you too.*

Help me by surviving. Be smart. Don't underestimate your-self. Tell Seth not to overestimate himself. And say hello to Henrick. He has integrity. Trust the good people helping you. I'll come as soon as I can.

Good-bye, Bracken.

'Bye.

The communication ended. She had felt as if she were right next to Bracken, their thoughts flowing easily to one another, and suddenly she was alone in a room holding a pearly horn. Putting away the horn, Kendra went in search of Henrick and her brother.

With help from a servant, Seth found Eve in her room. She turned from where she sat at a small table, her expression guilty, a smear of yellow pudding at the corner of her lips.

"What are you up to?" Seth asked.

She wiped the pudding away with the back of her hand. "Hi, Seth. I was just introducing Calvin to my favorite dessert."

Seth approached the table and found Calvin stripped down to a pair of shorts, wading in a bowl of pudding. He smiled up at Seth and waved. "Look what I found!"

"I see you've been hard at work," Seth said.

"Oh, come on!" Calvin exclaimed. "Are you telling me you would pass up the chance to swim in a pond of delicious vanilla custard?"

"Probably not," Seth admitted.

"Taste it!" Calvin suggested. "I'm serious, it's in a class by itself."

Eve handed Seth a spoon. "You really should."

"Your feet are in it," Seth said.

"I washed up before entering," Calvin said. "I didn't want to taste my feet either. Scoop from over there." He pointed. "I haven't spent any time on that side of the bowl."

Seth tried a bite of custard. It was really good! Sweet and cool and creamy.

"If I could shrink down I would join you," Seth said. "Where is Tanu when I need him?"

"Tanu?" Eve asked.

"My friend," Seth said. "A potion master. He can make a shrinking potion."

Eve clapped. "Bring him sometime! That would be spectacular."

"Take one last taste," Seth told Calvin. "We have to go save the sanctuary."

"Aren't we returning to Blackwell Keep?" Calvin asked. He scrambled up the side of the bowl—no small feat at his size. Without pause he dangled from the rim and dropped to the table.

"Nope," Seth said. "We're going to go find a dragon called Dromadus."

"No you're not," Eve said jealously. "The oldest dragon at Wyrmroost? Are you serious?"

"He might have info that will help us," Seth explained,

her amazement increasing his pride about the whole endeavor.

Eve stomped a foot. "That is unfair. I've lived at a dragon sanctuary my whole life and I've never even seen a dragon."

"Never?" Calvin asked as he got dressed.

"Don't they fly over sometimes?" Seth wondered.

"They steer away from this valley," Eve said. "And I'm not allowed to leave it."

"You have time," Seth said. "You're only, what, twelve?"

"So?" Eve said. "That's a long time. And there are hardly any other kids my age."

"How come?" Seth asked.

"Almost no babies are being born anymore," she said. "Nobody is sure why."

"If nobody is having babies, won't the Fair Folk eventually become extinct?" Seth wondered.

Eve laughed. "No. The Fair Folk age more slowly when we reach adulthood. Much more slowly. We'll be around for a long time. But I probably still won't get to see a dragon. Imagine being a kid stuck at a dragon sanctuary with a bunch of adults and never seeing a dragon!"

"That would be torture," Seth had to admit. If he were in her situation, he was pretty sure he would find a way to sneak a peek.

"And then some mortal kid comes along who gets to talk to a dragon his third day here!"

"On the second day I was attacked by the Dragon King," Seth said. "And I've seen dragons before. And a hydra. A bunch of demons, too."

Eve grabbed the front of his shirt. "I want your life! Take me with you."

Seth glanced at Calvin, who sheepishly shrugged.

"I can't," Seth apologized. "Your dad would be furious. What about your neutrality?"

Eve released his shirt. "The neutrality is stupid. Lots of us think so, but nobody admits it. Only Lomo had the guts to do something about it, and we locked him up."

"You agree with Lomo?" Seth asked.

"Of course," Eve said. "We're not part of the world. It's so boring here. I want to do something. See something. Smuggle me out. I'll be a big help!"

"Is she serious?" Seth asked Calvin.

"I think so," the nipsie said.

"Everyone will watch us leave," Seth said. "It won't work."

"Wait for me outside of town," Eve said. "I'll catch up. I'll bring a horse and everything."

Seth appreciated what she wanted. He saw her genuine eagerness. He could relate to how she felt. "I just can't, Eve. Your dad helped us. We want him on our side. Henrick would never allow it."

"You're the caretaker," Eve said. "Tell Henrick to obey. My dad can't do anything to you. He's neutral. He'll just send people to get me. Hopefully they won't catch up before I meet a dragon—and maybe see some other wonders. I'm still a kid. I won't get a big punishment. The dungeon for a while at worst, if Dad decides to make an example of me, but the dungeon is nice. If I apologize I may not even get that."

"Your dad could stop helping us," Seth said. "He's the reason we went to the Somber Knight and found out about Dromadus in the first place. You're right that I'm the caretaker. And I have to be a good one. Kendra and I need to visit Dromadus as part of our job. You'd just be coming for fun. What if I get you killed? I can't risk that."

Eve pouted. "You have reasons to go. Good for you. But don't pretend you aren't excited to meet Dromadus. I can tell."

"I'm excited," Seth admitted.

"I wish I was caretaker," Eve said. "I wish I had an excuse to have adventures."

"Careful what you wish for," Seth said. "This might get us killed."

"At least you will have lived," Eve replied sulkily.

"I wish I could bring you," Seth said. "Maybe someday."

"Really?" Eve asked.

"I hope so," Seth said. "As long as there is still a sanctuary to see."

🐉 🐉 🐉

Having bid farewell to Lord Dalgorel, Kendra, Seth, and Henrick cantered away from Terrabelle. Mendigo rode behind Kendra, and Calvin was safely stowed in Seth's pocket. They left the valley by a different road than they had used to enter. The sun had already fallen below the mountains, and the light was fading from the sky. Seth kept looking back at the city. Part of him wondered if Eve would appear on a horse.

"The Winding Way would eventually bring us to the Zowali Protectorate," Henrick said. "Perhaps someday you can visit the realm of the talking animals. But we'll leave the road well before arriving there."

"Will the darkness help cover us?" Kendra asked.

"From some creatures and some dragons," Henrick said. "Others will see us better than we can see them. We have to move fast. I have ranged far and wide on this preserve. I will use all my experience to protect us."

"Do we have any protections as caretakers?" Seth asked.

"Some inherent protections come with the office," Henrick said. "But you have also killed a dragon at this sanctuary. You entered her lair and initiated the conflict. That act forfeited much of your protection. You do have one other important advantage: Celebrant appears to want you as caretakers when he stages his rebellion. If you died, a new caretaker would be selected. He might hesitate to kill you."

"Marat told me Celebrant can't get the medallion by killing me," Seth said.

"Correct," Henrick said. "Upon your demise the medallion will teleport back to Blackwell Keep. Same if you command it to return. Celebrant knows this. That feature may not save your life, but it could give the Dragon King less reason to capture or kill you."

As they rode up to a pass out of the valley, Seth kept looking back.

"I don't think she's coming," Calvin said. The words

surprised Seth because they came from near his ear. The nipsie had apparently climbed from his pocket to his shoulder.

"Are you going to fall?" Seth asked.

"I know my limits," Calvin said. "This is easy."

"Do you think Eve really would have tried to meet us if I had agreed?" Seth asked.

"I don't think she was bluffing," Calvin said.

"She seemed adventurous," Seth said.

"Pretty girl," Calvin added offhandedly.

"Don't be gross," Seth said.

"You didn't notice?" Calvin asked.

"Maybe a little," Seth said. "But that isn't why I liked her."

"That may change in a year or two," Calvin said. "Trust me on this."

"Isn't she a little big for you?" Seth asked.

"I already found my true love," Calvin said. "Serena. Besides, Eve is too young. I'm tiny but fully grown."

"Serena is with the other nipsies?" Seth asked.

"No," Calvin said. "I wish. She left with a group trying to research the nipsie curse several years ago. Never came back."

"Several years ago?" Seth asked. "How old is she?"

"I'm older than I look," Calvin said. "Nipsies age like the Fair Folk—everything slows down in our late teens. Many magical beings age more slowly than mortals."

"I've noticed," Seth said. "Do you think Serena is all right?"

"I worry," Calvin said. "She has to be in trouble or she

would have returned. In my heart I believe she is alive. We share a special connection. I would feel it if she perished."

"Do you know where she went?" Seth asked.

"All I know is she left Fablehaven," Calvin said.

"Can she do that without permission?" Seth asked.

"I did," Calvin said. "The wizards who designed these preserves didn't really plan on people smaller than fairies. We tend to escape notice."

"Do you want to find her?" Seth asked.

"I would like that very much," Calvin said. "I'm always paying attention. I hope that breaking the curse will help."

"I hope so too," Seth said.

They rode through the pass, leaving the valley behind. Stars appeared as the light expired. The night became colder as they rode on. A moon rose, silvering the edges of clouds and occasionally peeking through. The surrounding wilderness remained mostly obscured in shadow. No artificial light brightened the forests and slopes around them. Bulky shapes loomed in the dimness, recognizable only as trees or boulders from just the right angle or in close proximity. Seth wished he could see what creatures were hiding in the darkness. At least Kendra had really good night vision. Hopefully she would provide an early warning if trouble showed up.

The Winding Way stayed true to its name, curving around obstacles in the rough terrain and climbing or descending steep slopes in serpentine switchbacks. The horses alternated between a swift trot and a gentle, loping pace. Once, in the distance, Seth heard a low, tremendous roaring.

Another time he heard an otherworldly screech, echoing down from high in the night sky.

At a point where trees lined both sides of the road, some of the branches interlocking overhead, Henrick came to a stop. "We can leave the road here," he said. "The trees will provide cover."

"Great," Seth said. He patted his horse's neck. "How are you holding up, Noble?"

The horse gave a single stamp.

"Luvians are tireless as long as you don't push too long at a full gallop," Henrick said. "One thing disturbs me: no dragons."

"Is that a problem?" Kendra asked.

"Dragons openly watched us much of the way here," Henrick said. "I assume it was mostly a form of intimidation. But I haven't sensed a dragon high or low since leaving Terrabelle. Either they are no longer watching us or else they want us to *think* they are no longer watching us."

"Uh-oh," Seth said.

"They were expecting us to go to Terrabelle," Henrick said. "Maybe they assumed we would return to Blackwell Keep and stopped watching. Or maybe they saw us depart along an unexpected route and started watching stealthily."

"Dragon ambush," Seth said.

"Or simple reconnaissance," Henrick replied. "Who knows? Our visit to Dalgorel was expected. But Celebrant would be very interested in our present movements. An ambush could be catastrophic. We have not yet left the road. We can still turn back and head directly to the keep."

"If we saw dragons, that would be a problem too," Kendra said. "We already made this choice. Let's go."

"Did you notice the dome on the ridge as we left Blackwell Keep?" Henrick asked.

"Yes," Seth said.

"I missed it," Kendra admitted.

"It's a safe hut," Henrick said. "The protections of Blackwell Keep extend to more than fifty such enclosures around Wyrmroost. They can even stand against dragons. They are marked on your map, Seth. I have been saved by a safe hut more than once. If you lose me somehow, get back on a road or find a safe hut and wait for rescue. The horses can guide you."

"We have safe huts at Fablehaven," Seth said. "I've used them."

"I'm glad you're familiar with the idea," Henrick said. "Noble, Glory, you remember the maps we looked at back at Terrabelle?"

Both horses gave a single stamp.

"You understand our destination?" Henrick checked.

The horses stamped again.

"And the locations of the nearest safe huts along the route?"

Again the horses stamped.

"Then with both caretakers in agreement, we should get moving," Henrick said. He led the way off the road into the trees. Kendra showed no hesitation. Seth had seldom felt prouder of his sister.

Bridges and Bears

K endra, Seth, and Henrick trotted under the trees, a vague shadowland of contorted shapes. Underbrush rustled as the horses plunged forward in single file. Kendra knew she could see better than Seth and probably better than Henrick, and still the shapes sliding past remained confusing. She kept her head down to avoid the grasping limbs. Vegetation swished against her legs. Henrick maintained a quick pace for a long while, finally slowing to a walk.

"We're being watched," Kendra whispered. She could see eyes at the edge of the dimness.

"Perceptive," Henrick said. "Nothing to fret about. Just moss people. Shy folk. Hiders, not fighters. We're about to lose the cover of trees for a time. Stay with me."

They emerged from the woods on a wide, grassy slope. The horses cantered downhill. After the gloom under the trees, the moonlit panorama looked bright. Kendra scanned the sky. Patches of clouds obscured many of the stars. She saw no dragons.

Up ahead, the slope fell away into a ravine. A bridge spanned the gap, and another slope rose on the far side. As they approached the bridge, a lean form sprang up from underneath, blocking the way. The creature had a narrow chest and abdomen, but broad shoulders and long limbs. The heavy jaw and upturned tusks emphasized a pronounced underbite, and thorny spines covered the scaly scalp. The lanky figure stood nearly as tall as Henrick.

"Slow the pace, travelers," the figure announced. "This bridge has been claimed."

Henrick came to a stop, holding out a hand for Kendra and Seth to halt as well. Glory obeyed him before Kendra could react.

"Stand down," Henrick ordered. "This bridge is property of the sanctuary, accessible to all."

"Don't get lost in the past when we're standing in the present," the creature said. "I'm no historian. This bridge might have been common property long ago. Today it has been claimed. Today it is mine."

"I am Henrick, son of—"

The creature waved away his words. "I know who you are! I'm not new."

"Then you know I'm the gamekeeper of Wyrmroost," Henrick said.

The creature chuckled. "Are you? Or *were* you?"

"I am," Henrick said firmly, taking a single step forward.

"You know who I am?" the creature asked.

"I know your kind," Henrick said. "Stand down before this escalates."

"And what kind is that?"

"Gate troll," Henrick replied. "Sometimes called a bully troll."

"And here you come, subtle as a brick, threatening me on my bridge," the troll said. "Price just went up. Way up."

"I'm in no mood for play," Henrick said, his hand a blur as he pulled an arrow from his quiver and set it to the string of his bow.

An ax appeared in the hand of the troll, and he lunged to the side of the bridge, where the railing provided some cover. "But you're the gamekeeper! Surely you like games!"

"Stand down and wait for easier prey," Henrick said. "You're out of order."

"Whose order?" the troll asked. "I heard the Dragon King is the new chief around here. Tore up Blackwell Keep. Not long now before he drives off the mortals. What rules will you enforce then? What status will you enjoy? Way I see it, the time of listening to you give orders has come to an end."

"You stand before me armed, troll, impeding my way," Henrick said. "I'll ask you a third time; then I let arrows fly."

"That so?" the troll replied. "Looking for a fight tonight, are you? Even with the precious cargo watching?" He looked past Henrick to Kendra and Seth.

"I'm warning you, Grimp," Henrick said, pulling the arrow back, ready to fire.

Grimp crouched low, now mostly hidden behind the railing, his ax still visible, glinting in the moonlight. "You know my name! Is that supposed to impress me? Here you are, skulking about in the night. Two kids in tow. Sanctuary on the brink of anarchy. You really want to fight? How fast can you kill me, mooseman? Before any kids get hurt? Before we raise a commotion? Don't you want to hear my terms?"

"Speak," Henrick said, arrow still ready.

Grimp licked his lips. "After you cross, the bridge belongs to me. Officially. Not squatter's rights. Not a claim. Mine. Final word from the illustrious gamekeeper."

"Unacceptable," Henrick said with a growl.

"It costs you nothing," Grimp replied. "I already claimed it. This bridge is almost never used by the Blackwell staff. And you won't be pretending to have a say over it much longer."

"Unacceptable," Henrick repeated.

"I'll throw in lifetime privileges," the troll said. "You ever come back this way, cross as often as you like, with whoever accompanies you."

"Not a chance," Henrick said.

"One last offer," Grimp said. "Tell me who is with you and your business tonight. On your honor. And you're free to pass."

"I'm glad that was the last offer," Henrick said.

"Are you sure you want a brawl rather than a negotiation?" Grimp asked. "Are you sure you can take me before they get hurt? Are you even sure you can take me?"

"Let's find out," Henrick said.

"No counterproposal?" Grimp asked.

"Sure. Move out of the way. Three. Two."

The troll lifted a tube to his lips. Kendra flinched, fearing it was a blowgun, but the troll ducked under the railing and slipped beneath the bridge. A long, low note sounded. A moaning call.

"Ride!" Henrick yelled, bow still ready.

Glory surged forward and Kendra hung on tight. Mendigo sat behind her, clattering and tinkling. "Protect us as needed, Mendigo!" she called.

Galloping beside her brother, Kendra raced across the bridge. Henrick followed, bow still ready. Looking back, Kendra saw no sign of the troll. But the moaning call kept sounding.

"Dire bears," Henrick said as he caught up. "The scoundrel is calling dire bears. He knew he couldn't stand up against me in a fair fight. Trolls and their traps."

They started racing up the slope at the far side of the bridge. The way ahead was clear except for brush and bushes, with trees off to either side.

"Dire bears sound bad," Seth said.

"Bigger and more aggressive than any bear you know," Henrick said. "Magically enhanced. Huge and fierce. Several roam this area of the sanctuary."

"Will they come?" Kendra shouted.

"Depends," Henrick said. "If Grimp prepared correctly, he conditioned them by blowing the call and having fresh meat at the bridge."

A huge roar bellowed from off to one side.

"Not good?" Seth asked.

"Glory, Noble, keep going toward the grove," Henrick said. "I'll rejoin you later."

With an arrow still held ready, Henrick veered to the right, toward the sound of the roar. Kendra watched in fear as a pair of bears the size of elephants stormed out of the forest. Grotesque spines bristled on their heads, backs, and shoulders, and vicious teeth showed when they roared again.

Henrick ran straight at them, an arrow nocked and ready. He swerved as the nearest sprang at him, launching an arrow into the immense, shaggy beast. The attacking bear just missed the alcetaur, who circled around and released a second arrow into the hindquarters of the other dire bear.

Glory continued to pound up the slope beside Noble. The weedy ground streaked by in a blur. Kendra realized that she could get really hurt just by falling. Glancing to the side and back, she saw that Henrick had succeeded in getting the hulking bears to chase him.

"Should we help him?" Seth called.

"He wants us to get away," Kendra replied. "He told us he's fast. If we go back we might endanger him more. Once we're clear he can run."

"What about Mendigo?" Seth asked.

"Against the bears?" Kendra shouted. "I don't think he's big enough. He wouldn't even slow them."

Seth seemed satisfied.

Kendra looked back again. Henrick was leading the dire

bears toward the bridge. The bears were very fast, but his zigzagging path seemed to give them trouble. Turning was not their forte.

Noble and Glory plunged into woodlands again, and Kendra could no longer see Henrick or the colossal bears. The deeper they fled into the trees, the more Kendra hoped the horses knew where they were going. She had no idea.

After some time they emerged from the woods. The horses ran along ridges and over hills. Racing through the night without Henrick kept Kendra on edge. The night sounds made her anxious—ominous hoots and chilling howls. What if they met more dire bears? Or a dragon?

As they cantered across a moonlit meadow, Kendra heard hoofbeats from behind. Turning, she was relieved to see Henrick catching up. Noble and Glory slowed without being told.

"We can pause here," Henrick said, coming to a stop. Sweat glossed his torso, and he was panting. There were no-ticeably fewer arrows in his quiver.

The horses halted as well.

"Are you all right?" Kendra asked.

"I got some exercise," Henrick said. "There were a few close calls."

"Those bears were enormous," Seth said.

"Dangerous beasts," Henrick agreed. "Savage. Strong. My arrows were minor annoyances. But the dire bears lost interest in me after I outdistanced them."

"Should you have bargained with the troll?" Kendra asked.

"I wish I could have," Henrick said. "I didn't want to provoke violence, especially with you two present. But Grimp was testing his limits. As you witnessed, our authority is in question right now. If I had yielded to his demands, word would have spread quickly that we are on our way out and can be bought. That we back down under duress. It would have spawned much bigger problems in the future."

"Good thinking," Seth approved.

"Necessary thinking, if we want Wyrmroost to survive," Henrick said. "This sanctuary is a wild place under the best conditions. We already have enough enemies. We can't afford to lose our credibility."

"Are we getting close to Dromadus?" Kendra asked.

"Almost there," Henrick said. "This way."

Kendra and Seth followed Henrick to the edge of the meadow. They rode through some small trees and came out into a field. At the far side of the field, Kendra saw a grove of sequoias towering in the moonlight.

"That has to be it," Kendra said.

"I believe so," Henrick replied, eyes on the sky.

Kendra looked up too, scanning for dragons. She saw only stars. The moon was slowly disappearing behind another cloud.

They hurried to the redwoods. The grove included perhaps fifty trees, spaced widely apart, with little undergrowth between them. Deep, jagged grooves marred the rough bark of the thick trunks.

At the center of the grove they found a clearing. Toward the center of the clearing a pair of what looked like cellar doors were flanked by large stones. The upright stones had flat surfaces that carried several inscriptions. Kendra could not read some of them. The rest repeated a single word: WELCOME.

"I see a lot of 'welcome,'" Seth said. "What does the rest say?"

"Probably the same invitation in various languages," Henrick said. "I can't read them all. But enough to guess."

Kendra dismounted and approached the stones. "I can read these." She touched the legible words. Each "welcome" looked like English to her, though she knew several were being translated by her fairykind abilities.

"'Welcome,'" Seth said, touching one that Kendra could read. "And this. And this. This too. And this."

Some of the inscriptions Seth indicated looked like gibberish to Kendra. As a shadow charmer, he could read some languages that remained foreign to her. But she knew that some of the languages she understood were illegible for him.

"Impressive," Henrick said. "Between the two of you, you can decipher most of the languages of the magical races. Highly unusual for mortals."

"What if the stuff we can't read is the fine print?" Seth asked. "*Welcome . . . to dinner. You are the main course.*"

"The simple welcome message is ominous enough," Henrick said. "One of the first rules of Wyrmroost is to let sleeping dragons lie. Don't stir up trouble with the most powerful predators in the magical world. Dragon lairs are never inviting. And yet this one has a clear invitation."

"Like a spiderweb welcoming the flies," Kendra said.

"You get the idea," Henrick replied, looking around. "You two came to see Dromadus. We appear to be unobserved."

"Are you coming with us?" Kendra asked.

"My presence would reduce your chances for help," Henrick said. "Your vulnerability makes you more appealing. And inside the lair of a dragon, if he decided to kill you, there would be nothing I could do to stop him."

"Would the dragon freeze you up?" Seth wondered.

"I can hold my own against a dragon," Henrick said. "I can still move and speak. Otherwise I would be an unfit gamekeeper. But the presence of a dragon is not comfortable. My preference is to run."

Kendra took Seth's hand. "I guess it's just us."

"And me," Calvin chirped from Seth's pocket. "I've never met a dragon."

"Don't be surprised if you get frozen with fear," Seth said.

"That's never happened to me before," Calvin said. "Either I'll find out I'm as brave as I suspect, or I'll have a new experience. Good either way."

"It might help if the dragon doesn't notice you, Calvin," Henrick said. "They can concentrate their intimidation on a target."

The alcetaur crouched, grabbed one of the heavy, wooden cellar doors, and heaved it open. A dim stairway yawned before them.

"Nothing creepy about that," Seth said, peering down. "Just an old basement in the middle of a forest. Where a dragon lives."

"What about Mendigo?" Kendra asked.

"I don't think the puppet can help you or harm you in this matter," Henrick said.

"Mendigo, stand guard with Henrick," Kendra said. She smiled at her brother. "Shall we?"

"Ready to fly into the spiderweb?" Seth asked.

"Let's not think of it like that," Kendra said.

"Jump into the cooking pot?" Calvin tried.

"Not that way either," Kendra said. "I'm not sure we need a comparison. Walking into a dragon's lair is bad enough."

"Amen," Henrick said. "Keep your wits about you. Be polite but show no weakness."

"Did you hear the polite part, Seth?" Calvin asked.

"I know," Seth snapped.

"You're the boss," Calvin said brightly.

Kendra looked back at the horses. "Thanks, Glory. Thanks, Noble. Good job back there."

The horses bobbed their heads.

"Stop saying good-bye," Seth said. "You're jinxing us. We'll see them in a minute."

"Henrick, do you have any paper?" Kendra asked. "Maybe we should write a quick will."

"Come on," Seth growled, pulling his sister forward as she laughed at her own joke.

CHAPTER TWENTY

Dromadus

Kendra and Seth walked down, down, down. Soon all Seth could see was blackness. Glancing back, he could barely make out the moonlit door. Then even that disappeared. Another step. Another. With one hand sliding along the wall, he blindly trusted that the stairs continued.

"Can you see?" Seth asked.

"Yeah," Kendra said, her hand giving his a reassuring squeeze. "Dim, though."

"Should I get out a flashlight?" Seth asked. "Or does that make us too obvious?"

"It would make us pretty obvious," Kendra said.

"You have amazing eyesight," Calvin said. "I see pretty well at night. But this looks like the darkness in the middle of darkness, where, from the highest mountain, under a starless sky, all horizons are black, and light has never touched.

But we're beneath the mountain, in the deepest cave, where—"

"We get it," Seth interrupted. "It's really dark."

"You can almost take a bite out of it," Calvin said.

"What do you see?" Seth asked.

"It's so black that I'm kind of imagining faint shimmers of color," Calvin said. "Like when you close your eyes too tight for too long. Oh, wait, my eyes were closed. It doesn't make a difference!"

"I was asking Kendra," Seth clarified.

"Just more stairs," Kendra said. "They go as far as I can see. A long, straight staircase. Rough steps, carved out of the rock."

"Is it narrow?" Seth asked.

"Pretty narrow. Not much bigger than the entrance. Hugo could touch the ceiling."

"There must be another entrance," Seth said. "A dragon wouldn't fit."

"Unless he goes in and out in human form," Calvin said.

"Good point," Seth agreed. "Kendra, tell us if you see anything interesting."

"Are more stairs interesting?" she asked.

"Barely," Seth replied.

They descended without speaking for a time. Seth was quietly glad to have Kendra's hand to hold.

"I see the bottom," Kendra reported.

"Tell me when we get to the last step," Seth said.

About forty steps later she started warning him. "Five more, four, three, two, last one."

"What does it look like now?" Seth asked.

"A roundish tunnel cut through the rock," Kendra said.

"Not like a natural cave?" Seth asked.

"No," Kendra said. "Like it was drilled. Or burrowed. It looks too even."

They walked forward in darkness. Seth kind of shuffled in the hope that his toes would bump against any unseen obstacle.

"The ground is smooth," Kendra told him. "I see a door! The tunnel ends at a door. Old, thick wood, like the doors at the entrance."

Eventually they stopped. Seth heard Kendra pull the door open.

"More darkness," Calvin said. "With the door closed, do you think it is even darker in there?"

"I think we've reached the limit," Seth said.

"This is big," Kendra said. "Huge. Not a tunnel anymore. I can't see the far side. A big cavern. High ceiling."

"Could a dragon fit?" Seth asked.

"Yes," Kendra said, leading them through the doorway.

"Do you see a dragon?" Calvin asked.

"It looks empty," Kendra said.

"I'm getting out my flashlight," Seth said. Keeping hold of Kendra's hand, he used his other hand to open his satchel and root around. He took out a flashlight and switched it on. The light seemed extra bright after the prolonged darkness. It was a good flashlight with a strong beam, but even so, it barely illuminated the far side of the vast cavern. A large rock pile littered most of the room, a jumble of dusty stone, perhaps the remnants of a cave-in. There was no dragon in view.

Seth swung the flashlight beam around the cavern. There was no other apparent exit. No doors or caves.

"Is he even here?" Seth asked.

"Maybe he's gone," Kendra said. "It looks abandoned. Maybe there's another room."

"Can he walk through walls?" Seth asked.

"A secret passage?" Kendra wondered. "Hello?" she called. "Dromadus? We need your help!"

They listened to the silence.

"This is a bust," Seth said. "That's what we get for listening to a dusty old knight who sat in the same room for a thousand years. Should we be surprised he's not up to date?"

The rock pile shifted, boulders scraping and rolling. Startled, Kendra and Seth both skipped away from the disturbance. The huge head of a dragon craned up from the rubble, nostrils flaring. The head looked cunningly hewn from rock, the top all knobby, a few tendrils dangling like whiskers from the stony mouth. Seth spotlighted the head with his flashlight. The sudden dust in the air made the beam of light look almost tangible.

This head was bigger than Celebrant's head. Seth tried to imagine the size of the body attached to such a head. It had to fill much of the room, entirely buried in rocks.

"Why would the Somber Knight send you to me?" the dragon asked in a gentle, resonant baritone, dark eyes blinking.

"You almost gave me a heart attack!" Seth shouted. "Are you Dromadus?"

"Such is my fate," the dragon responded. "I did not mean to alarm you. Lying quietly can be a useful way to discover the intent of intruders. I believe you mentioned the Somber Knight. At least he fits your description. What is his interest in me?"

"We're the new caretakers of Wyrmroost," Kendra explained. "He thought you could help us."

"The Somber Knight has never taken much interest in dragons except to kill us," Dromadus said. "Why would he want me to advise caretakers?"

"Celebrant is a caretaker now too," Seth said. "He has been attacking Blackwell Keep. The Somber Knight wants to save the sanctuary."

"As do you, I suppose," Dromadus said. "I removed myself from the affairs of wizards and dragons long ago. I will not raise fang or claw against a dragon, least of all the Dragon King."

"We just need information," Kendra said. "Celebrant has the scepter from Blackwell Keep. We need to find the other one. It won't harm the dragons. It will just protect us."

"And the Somber Knight believes that I know the location?" Dromadus asked. "Why would a defeated old dragon know such a precious secret?"

"You were friends with the wizard who founded Wyrmroost," Seth said. "He might have told you."

"Archadius established Wyrmroost," Dromadus said. "The first and greatest wizard. Others helped him. Archadius and I had a friendship of sorts, though in the end he despised me. I am a popular dragon to hate."

"Why?" Kendra asked.

"That is a long story," Dromadus said.

"We came a long way," Seth said.

"You are young," Dromadus said. "It will exhaust you."

"Give us the basics," Seth said.

Kendra elbowed her brother. "We'd love to hear anything you're willing to share."

"How much do you younglings know about me?" Dromadus asked.

"You used to be the Dragon King," Seth said. "We didn't know you were made of rock."

Dromadus gave a soft laugh. "Though I have an unusual form, I am not entirely made of rock. In my prime it was said I had the toughest hide of any dragon. And I was certainly among the most powerful. Many dragons challenged me for my kingship, as happens over the centuries. And many dragons died."

"How many?" Seth asked.

"More than I care to remember," Dromadus said. "But one mattered more than the rest. My nephew, Ezarod. He was my very favorite in the family. A very interesting dragon with great potential. I helped mentor him. I will confess that I liked him better than my own children, who tended to be fierce but dull. But Ezarod did something my children did not. He attempted to take my crown."

"Oh, no," Kendra said. "How terrible."

"I fought him," Dromadus said. "I bested him. He would

not yield. And so I slew my favorite nephew to maintain my status. I have never been the same."

"The Somber Knight told us you gave up the crown," Seth said.

"I did," Dromadus acknowledged. "I was already disengaging with my position before the fight with Ezarod, but I had a tradition to uphold, and Ezarod had wounded my pride. I won the fight, but it finished me. Not long after my victory, I effortlessly did the unthinkable. I abandoned my crown. I offered it to a dragon who I thought would make a good leader. He accepted, then was killed for the crown ten years later."

"What happened to you after giving up the crown?" Kendra asked.

"I became an outcast," Dromadus said. "My wife forsook me. My children renounced me. My supposed friends rejected me. It came as no shock. I had done the unpardonable for a dragon: I had become a pacifist."

"You won't fight?" Seth asked. "Does that mean you won't eat us?"

"Probably not," Dromadus said. "After slaying my nephew, I decided to stop ending lives. Originally I had decided never to kill another dragon. Over the years my conviction has grown. I do not believe in harming other thinking creatures."

"Why doesn't a dragon just come and kill you?" Seth asked.

"Not worth the risk," Dromadus said. "Unlike most Dragon Kings, I was never defeated. Why go up against a shunned, undefeated dragon? There is little glory in slaying an outcast. I never stated that I would not defend myself. Whether I actually would or not remains untested. I live quietly. I cause no trouble. I am disliked, but it is easy to forget me."

"Well, I like you," Kendra said.

"You have to like me," Dromadus said. "You want my help. And you know that I could kill you very easily."

"You just hide down here in the dark?" Seth asked.

"Like your Somber Knight in some ways," Dromadus said. "Except I am not waiting to commit violence. Dragons spend a good deal of time inactive. We are large. It requires great energy to move. Even more so as we age."

"Don't you get hungry?" Seth asked.

"Is that a wise question, from a tiny bite of food?" Dromadus asked. "Don't be alarmed. I am not hungry. My dinners are delivered by ogres."

"Dragon meal from Terrabelle," Kendra surmised.

"A filling substitute for villagers," Dromadus said. "Quite tasty. Many dragons partake, some more quietly than others. Who needs to consume people, sheep, cattle, walruses, elephants, whales, or giants? My ogres bring me more food than I can consume. An inactive dragon needs less than you would think. We hibernate efficiently."

"Do you even know where we can find the scepter?" Seth asked. "You weren't clear about that."

The dragon shifted, rocks and boulders rumbling. "Are you truly the caretakers? It seems ludicrous. As if Celebrant made a wish and Marat gave up his post for two mortal children."

"It's complicated," Kendra said. "There weren't many options. And Agad was hoping human caretakers would strengthen the magical defenses at Blackwell Keep."

"Have the resources of Dragonwatch grown so thin?" Dromadus asked.

"We're not so bad," Seth complained.

Kendra squeezed his hand.

"I suppose you're better than nothing," Dromadus said. "Which is a small compliment indeed. I do know the location of the hidden scepter. Since the sanctuary was founded, you are the first to ask me."

"Will you tell us?" Kendra asked.

"Explain why exactly you want the scepter," Dromadus said.

"To protect Blackwell Keep and keep Wyrmroost from falling," Kendra said.

"To what end?" Dromadus asked.

"To keep the peace," Kendra said. "So the dragons won't run wild."

"Celebrant is a powerful king," Dromadus said. "Don't you think he deserves to rule his own sanctuary?"

"He helps rule," Kendra said. "But look at the history of dragons. If they get free, they will try to take over the world."

"Likely true," Dromadus said.

"Likely?" Seth exclaimed. "Have you met a dragon?"

"Are you sure this boy is one of the caretakers as well?" Dromadus asked Kendra.

"We're a package deal," Kendra said.

"I believe your motives are correct," Dromadus said. "I believe your intent is sincere. But only a fool gives up something for nothing. What can you offer me?"

"I thought you were a pacifist," Seth said.

"A pacifist need not be a fool," Dromadus said heavily. "Sometimes pacifists have greater need for strategy than those willing to fight."

"Do we have anything that you want?" Kendra asked.

"Not that you can rightfully give," Dromadus said. "So it must be promises or services. Promise me this. The next time you have the opportunity to kill a dragon, show as much mercy as possible. Work to save the dragon, not to kill the dragon. Can you make that vow?"

"You think we'll have a chance to kill a dragon?" Seth asked.

"You already killed Siletta," Dromadus said.

Seth stared at the ground. "You know about that?"

"Dragons can recognize a dragon slayer," Dromadus said. "I better than most. If you promise to show as much mercy as possible the next time a dragon falls into your power, and if you promise that each of you owes me an additional favor of my choosing, I will reveal the location of the hidden scepter."

"I'm going to be running errands for the rest of my life," Seth muttered.

"Excuse me?" Dromadus asked.

"I just owe some other people a favor too," Seth said. "They're piling up."

"Not a favor that makes us betray our duties as care-takers," Kendra clarified.

"Nothing that betrays your fundamental morals or duties," Dromadus said. "But it might be difficult and uncomfortable."

"Can I talk about it with Seth?" Kendra asked.

"Be my guest," Dromadus said. "If it aids in your deliberations, be aware that this is my only offer."

"All right," Kendra said.

Seth huddled close to his sister.

"You have to do it," came a voice from his pocket. "You need the scepter. It's not a bad deal."

"You can still talk?" Seth asked.

"Told you I was brave," Calvin said. "The dragon is impressive. Like a talking mountain."

"Calvin is probably right," Kendra said. "We just *have* to find the scepter."

"Quieter," Seth said. "He can probably hear us."

"Every word," Dromadus said. "Who is the third party?"

"My secret ally," Seth said. "A hero of great renown."

"Have you reached a decision?" Dromadus asked tiredly.

Seth looked at his sister. "You're right. We have to do it."

"We have a deal," Kendra said to the dragon.

"Very well," Dromadus replied. "I will hold you to it. I am not beyond exacting revenge for broken oaths."

"Message received," Seth said. "Where do we go?"

"You must walk the Path of Dreams," Dromadus said.

"Is that an actual place?" Seth asked.

"The scepter lies at the end of the path," Dromadus said.

"And where does the path start?" Seth asked. "At Wyrm-roost, I hope?"

"In this chamber," Dromadus said, shifting again. Boulders ground against one another.

"Really?" Kendra asked. "Right here?"

"Archadius built this lair to house me and to hide the start of the Path of Dreams," Dromadus said. "The path will not be easy to walk. You could lose your lives."

"We figured," Seth said. "Can we go get a friend? Maybe two? Some people to walk the path with us?"

"No," Dromadus said. "The path is meant for caretakers."

"What about me?" Calvin asked from Seth's pocket.

"I suppose the invisible hero can join you," Dromadus said. "But only because I am in an indulgent mood. His size amuses me."

"We have a servant," Kendra said. "Not a person. A limberjack. Like a living puppet. Can we—"

"Only you two and the invisible hero," Dromadus said. "I control access to the Path of Dreams. Do you wish to try for the scepter or not?"

"We want to try," Seth said. He glanced at Kendra. "Right?"

She took a deep breath. "Yes."

"Then back away," Dromadus said. "I haven't moved this much in centuries. It would be a shame if I accidentally crushed you."

CHAPTER TWENTY-ONE

Path of Dreams

Kendra and Seth retreated through the doorway into the tunnel to give Dromadus plenty of space. From the cavern came all the tumult of an earthquake, accompanied by a gritty dust plume. Seth hurriedly closed the door before the dust became unbearable. The tremendous rumble continued as if the entire cavern were caving in. The ground vibrated beneath their feet.

Kendra watched her brother. He looked so young and uncertain, his eyes wide, his hair dusty, the flashlight crammed against one ear, his hand covering the other, trying to mute the thunder of colliding rocks.

How had they ended up here? What if this got them killed? Couldn't somebody else handle this crisis?

It finally got quiet.

"All right," Dromadus invited. "You may return, young mortals."

With Seth's hand in hers, Kendra pushed through the door. Globes of light now illuminated the cavern. Dust hung in the air. A deep depression in the floor led down to a square hole with a staircase going deeper. It was impressive to think that Dromadus had filled much of that void. The rocky rubble had mostly been shoved to one side of the room, sloping high against the cavern wall.

Dromadus loomed on the other side.

The way he was curled up, the ancient dragon almost looked like a great heap of stone himself, although the rock patterns of his stony scales were too regular, and the head at the top disrupted the illusion. Dromadus was immense—at least twice the size of Celebrant, and so bulky. Each claw looked big enough to crush a truck.

"You're huge!" Seth exclaimed in awe.

"Our kind tend to grow as we age," Dromadus said. "You mortals shrivel up. Very demeaning."

"Can I walk the Path of Dreams alone?" Kendra asked.

"Excuse me?" Dromadus asked.

"Why risk both our lives?" Kendra asked.

"No way!" Seth shouted. "If one can go, it's me. You have like zero practice surviving."

"I've survived a lot," Kendra said.

"I appreciate the strategizing," Dromadus said. "But I take it you must be in contact with one another to function as dragon tamers?"

"He's good," Seth muttered.

"Then you will need to stay together to walk the Path of Dreams," Dromadus said. "And you're welcome. That advice give you a chance."

"Thank you," Kendra said. "Is there anything else we should know?"

"Alas, I do not know the mechanics of the path," Dromadus said. "Archadius kept the specifics hidden, as wizards do. The unworthy will not survive. Death is likely. Off you go."

Hand in hand, Kendra and Seth climbed down into the depression until they reached the opening where the stairs began. Globes lit the way to the bottom, perhaps a hundred steps away, one long flight.

"The Path of Dreams doesn't sound too bad," Calvin said. "I can sometimes fly in my dreams. And breathe underwater."

"We explored a place called the Dreamstone in Australia," Seth said. "It was pretty terrible. Not happy dreams."

"We can do this," Kendra said. "I want to see Mom and Dad again. I want to see Grandma and Grandpa. They're depending on us. We have to do this."

They walked down the stairs. At the bottom, a short hall led to an archway. Engraved runes embellished the walls of the hallway.

"Seth, can you read any of that?" Kendra asked.

"No. Can you?"

"None of it," Kendra said.

"Don't ask the nipsie," Calvin piped up. "He's probably illiterate."

"Can you read it, Calvin?" Seth asked.

"No," he replied.

Kendra paused at the archway. "We need to keep hold of each other," she reminded her brother.

"I've held on so far," Seth said.

"Just don't let go," Kendra said. "I don't want to die frozen by fear."

"Stop thinking so much," Seth said, towing her through the archway.

The smallish room was mostly empty. Dimmer globes softly illuminated polished walls of copper embossed with runes and images of fanciful animals. Against one wall stood a long, narrow table with three corked bottles on top.

"No other doors," Seth said.

"What's with the bottles?" Kendra wondered.

They crossed to the table. All three bottles were made of smoky blue glass and looked old. None had labels.

"Should we drink one?" Seth guessed.

"That seems trusting," Kendra said. "What if they're poison?"

"Maybe one is poison," Seth said. "Or two of them. And the other lets us go forward."

"At least one of us should make it," Calvin said.

Seth removed Calvin from his pocket. The nipsie looked up at Seth curiously.

"Maybe you should wait outside," Seth said. "No need for you to risk your life too."

"Wait, are you joking?" Calvin asked. "The main reason lords call their vassals is to go to battle. This is why

I'm here! To stand by you when things get bleak. I'm not going to help break any curses if I hide at the first sign of trouble. I'm the Tiny Hero, right? Not the Tiny Bystander." He pointed at the bottles. "Let me drink first. The one on the left. I have a good feeling about that one. The middle one is an obvious pick, so we should stay away. The right? Most people are right-handed. Wizards would expect folks to reach for the one on the right."

"I'm not sure we should plan on drinking them," Kendra said. "At least not at first. Maybe we could open all three and smell them."

"I think she's onto something!" Calvin exclaimed. "We test if some smell sweeter than others. Because the sweet one is probably a trap. Especially if it's the middle one."

"I'll open the left one first," Seth said, putting Calvin back in his pocket, then picking up the bottle. "Kendra, hold my shoulder instead of my hand so I can give it a good pull." Kendra slid her hand from his grasp and up his arm to the back of his neck, maintaining contact the whole way. Seth grabbed the cork and pulled. Then he changed his grip and pulled again. "It's stuck."

"Let me try," Kendra said.

"It doesn't need cooties," Seth protested.

"You're going to get punched," Kendra threatened, giving his neck a squeeze.

"Settle down," Seth said. He handed her the bottle. "I'm pretty sure I loosened it. Good luck."

Seth kept a hand on Kendra's shoulder as she tried to

unstop the bottle. There was no give. It was tricky to get a good grip. The cork felt cemented in place.

With his free hand, Seth rummaged in his satchel and came out with a pocketknife, then used his teeth to unfold a corkscrew. "I've never used this."

"You have a corkscrew?" Kendra asked, handing over the bottle and returning her hand to the back of his neck.

"It took me a second to think of it," Seth said. "I wasn't sure the knife had one." He twisted the corkscrew into the cork, then started to pull. His arm trembled.

"Let me try," Kendra said.

"It's coming," Seth said through gritted teeth. A moment later the cork popped off and greenish smoke began to geyser from the bottle's mouth at an alarming rate. After momentarily fumbling with the bottle, Seth aimed the mouth so the smoke gushed away from them.

"Put it down!" Kendra shrieked, letting go of Seth. "Hold your breath!" He hurriedly replaced the bottle on the table. Kendra grabbed his hand and yanked him back toward the archway. Green smoke continued to fountain upward, spreading across the ceiling in flowing ripples.

Kendra and Seth ran out of the archway and turned to watch. Soon the smoke clouding the air made it impossible to see the bottle, but they could still hear it hissing out. The smoke stopped at the archway, as if encountering an unseen barrier. Before long the archway held back a swirling wall of green fog from top to bottom. Kendra could see no more than a couple of inches into the room.

"Now what?" she asked.

"When the gas first started, I thought it might be a message," Seth said. "Patton once left one that way."

"Looks more like a trap," Kendra said.

"Maybe it will clear out," Seth said. "Let's give it some time."

They waited.

"I don't hear the bottle hissing anymore," Seth observed.

"The smoke looks just as thick," Kendra said.

"Maybe we should hold our breath and try to get the other two bottles," Seth suggested.

"It won't be easy," Kendra said. "We won't be able to see in there."

"Usually smoke is thinner near the ground," Calvin said, his little head poking out of Seth's pocket. "But this looks thick all the way down."

"What if we open another bottle and it's more smoke?" Kendra asked.

"We retreat up the stairs," Seth said.

"Let me test it out," Calvin offered. "I don't trust those fumes. Let me hold my breath and run in there a little ways, then come back out."

"No, I'll do it," Seth said. "I didn't see any dragons in there. When Kendra let go of me I didn't freeze up. I'll make a run for the bottles alone."

"Not alone," Kendra said. "If you're going, I'm going too."

"How does that make sense?" Seth asked. "Why risk both of us?"

"Because Dromadus warned that we'd die if we didn't

stay together," Kendra reminded him. "What if you run in there alone and then we can't find each other?"

"Hey!" Seth shouted, pointing.

Kendra followed his finger to where Calvin was dashing across the floor toward the archway. "How'd he get down?" Kendra asked.

Seth let go of Kendra and ran after the nipsie, but Calvin had too much of a head start and raced into the green haze before Seth arrived. Kneeling at the archway, Seth reached blindly into the smoke, feeling around, but soon withdrew his arm.

"He's gone," Seth said. "He's sneaky and fast! He must have climbed down my leg from my pocket."

"Hopefully he'll be right back," Kendra said.

"He better be," Seth said. "He just disobeyed an order from his leader."

Kendra rolled her eyes. "You'd never dream of disobeying an order. Especially when you think you're right."

"Calvin!" Seth called. "That's long enough! Can you hear me? Come back!"

They stared at the green smoke and listened to the silence.

"Oh, no," Kendra said.

"Calvin?" Seth tried again. "Can you hear me? Are you lost? Follow my voice! Answer if you can."

They waited.

"He's not coming back," Kendra said. "He said he was just going in a few steps and right back out."

"And what have we learned?" Seth complained. "Nothing. Did he accidentally take a breath? Is he dead?"

"All we know is the smoke is dangerous," Kendra said.

Seth stared at the archway, hands on his hips. "We have to try for another bottle. What else can we do?"

"I guess we could leave," Kendra said.

"Can we really?" Seth asked. "Can we leave behind the scepter? Leave behind Calvin? Just go back to Blackwell Keep with nothing? What if Celebrant knows we're here? What if he figures out what we're after? What if he sends somebody to get the scepter tomorrow? Or tonight? What if someone is on their way right now? I wonder if anyone has lost a preserve just two days after becoming caretaker?"

"Those are good points," Kendra said. "But if Celebrant knows we're here, what if we get the scepter and he steals it from us on the way back?"

"We can worry about that once we have the scepter," Seth said. "We'll talk to Henrick and be as sneaky as we can. But first we need to get it. We can't lead Celebrant to the hidden scepter and then leave it behind."

"Maybe he didn't have us followed," Kendra said. "We never saw any dragons after Terrabelle. Maybe we're about to die from a poison cloud for no reason."

"We hold our breath," Seth said, taking Kendra's hand. "In and out. Run to the table, we each grab a bottle, and we run out. No breathing."

"I guess," Kendra said uncertainly. "Seth, are you sure?"

"I'm not sure we'll make it," Seth said. "But I'm sure we have to try."

Kendra sighed in resignation. "Okay. I'm in. Are you ready?"

"Breathe slowly, then take a deep breath and hold it," Seth advised. "Three." He breathed in and out. "Two." Kendra breathed in and out with him. "One." They breathed in. Seth gave a nod.

Holding his hand tightly, Kendra let him lead her into the smoky room. The dense fumes irritated her eyes, so she closed them. All she saw with them open was green.

Kendra had not traveled many steps before she began to feel light-headed. She stumbled and barely caught herself. She felt Seth stumble as well. The floor seemed to tilt. She became dizzy. This wasn't going to work. She tugged Seth back toward the door. He yanked her in a different direction, almost making her fall.

Still clutching Seth's hand, Kendra remained still. She had lost her orientation. Maybe they could find a wall and work their way back to the door. How long could she keep holding her breath? It was already becoming a struggle.

The floor seemed to swing out from under her. Kendra felt like she was floating. It was peaceful. She opened her eyes. The green smoke no longer irritated them. She realized she was breathing. The smoke didn't bother her lungs. It smelled kind of good. Once again the soles of her feet pressed against a floor.

And then the smoke dissolved. It didn't blow away. It just rapidly dissipated to nothing.

She stood in a long room paneled with dark wood and full of coffins. Melting candles provided gentle light. The disturbing containers rested on tables and stood up against the walls. All were closed.

Kendra could still feel Seth's hand in hers.

But he was gone.

Or invisible?

She reached for him with her free hand. She couldn't feel him, not his body, not his arm. But she could still feel his hand in hers. Kendra squeezed tightly. He squeezed back.

"Seth?" Kendra asked quietly, not daring to yell. "Can you hear me?"

There came no reply.

But his hand remained in hers. That was something.

What had happened? Was this a dream? It looked and felt very real. She felt extra alert rather than asleep.

But how did she get here?

What if the coffins started to open? Kendra wasn't sure if she could handle it.

The room had no windows or doors, unless perhaps they were hidden behind coffins. The walls and furniture were clean, but the coffins looked old, and the air smelled vaguely of perfume. Something about the scent made her suspect it was barely masking unpleasant odors.

The coffins remained shut.

"Hello?" Kendra asked. "Is anyone here?"

There came no answer.

What was she supposed to do?

Her eyes were drawn to the nearest coffin resting on a table. Dare she look inside? What if it contained a monster?

What if she started a chain reaction, and zombies attacked from every side?

She glanced at an empty corner of the room. Maybe she should go sit down. Did she have to peek inside a coffin? Was that necessary? But she needed to find the scepter. And Seth. And Calvin. Would sitting still do any good? Probably not. She had chosen to walk the Path of Dreams. This was probably all part of it.

Kendra approached the nearest coffin and rested her free hand on the lid. She surveyed the room. How many coffins in total? Fifty? Maybe sixty. Lots of them stood upright against the walls, like sarcophagi. Would bodies tumble out if she opened those?

At least this coffin was lying flat. She wanted to lift the lid but couldn't quite bring herself to do it. What if there was a skeleton inside? Or a putrid corpse? Or a vampire? She supposed that if the coffins were full of enemies, they would attack sooner or later. She might as well find out.

Squeezing Seth's hand tighter with one hand, Kendra pushed up the lid all the way, then gasped and stepped back, tears filling her eyes.

It wasn't fair.

Inside the coffin rested her Grandpa Larsen, eyes closed, looking just as he had when she had attended his funeral, down to the clothes and the hairstyle. At the time Kendra had not known she was viewing a duplicate body created by a stingbulb. The sight brought an unwelcome wave of emotion.

Kendra closed the lid.

She stood motionless for a moment, trying to recover from the sight. Squeezing Seth's unseen hand, she took a steadying breath.

Now she knew this was at least partially a dream. She had left Grandpa Larsen back at Fablehaven, safe and sound. Right? That could not really be him in the coffin.

But it had looked exactly like him.

Kendra approached another coffin, lifted the lid, and found Grandma Larsen inside. It was less surprising this time, but not much less disturbing.

What was the point of this place? To torture her?

Where was Seth right now? She assumed he could feel her hand. Was he experiencing his own twisted nightmare?

She went to the next coffin, lifted the lid, and stared at the corpse of Grandpa Sorenson. She had never seen him dead before, but this was exactly how he would look. She told herself he was safe at Blackwell Keep. He was fine. But the sight was still horrible.

Kendra poked his side. She didn't like the feel. Too rigid. Unnatural. She wasn't sure how a dead body was supposed to feel. She had never poked one before.

The next coffin held Grandma Sorenson. She knew by now to expect dead people she loved, but there was no way to really get used to it.

The next lid she opened revealed Seth. Her stomach clenched. He looked so authentic. And dead. But she was still holding his invisible, disembodied hand, so she trusted that he was alive.

Lifting another lid revealed Coulter Dixon, their old

friend whom Graulas the demon had killed. This created a different horror inside Kendra because he was actually dead.

Clenching her teeth, Kendra closed the lid and began to speed through coffins. She opened each one, glanced at the person, then moved on. She tried not to feel shock. She tried to pretend she was at a wax museum looking at fakes. Because it was fake. It had to be! But it looked perfectly real. And she felt completely awake.

Mom. Dad. Warren. Tanu. Lena. Patton.

No matter what she told herself, each new corpse made an impact. She considered stopping, but what if one of the coffins held the scepter? She had to make sure.

She had finished the coffins on the tables. The majority of the grim containers stood upright. Kendra decided to systematically make her way around the room.

The first upright coffin she carefully opened held Vanessa. Her body did not tumble forward. She looked just as dead as everyone else, except she stood with no problem. Maybe they used hidden straps?

Kendra made her way along the wall. Dale. Trask. Agad. Maddox. Her friend Alyssa from school. Her friend Brittany. Mara from Lost Mesa. Berrigan from Obsidian Waste.

After closing each upright coffin, Kendra peeked around the back to make sure it wasn't covering a door or window. So far all she had seen was more wall.

As Kendra progressed, the corpses remained familiar, but they were people she knew less well. Former teachers. Acquaintances. People she had met while adventuring. She tried to brace herself to find Bracken, but he kept not appearing.

When Kendra came to a full-length mirror between two upright coffins, she was startled by her reflection. It was definitely her, but she looked older, more adult. She was taller and somewhat curvier, with more adult features. She looked gorgeous.

Glancing down at herself, Kendra saw that her body didn't match the maturity of the reflection. Not even the clothes were right.

Kendra contemplated the coffins. Was this supposed to represent her future? Was she going to outlive everybody?

A sudden thought jolted her. She had considered becoming an Eternal. The enchantment given to mortals would grant her long life, and, in return, the new demon prison would not be able to be unlocked while she and the other Eternals remained alive.

Chills tingled down her back and spread across her shoulders. Was this room demonstrating her fate if she became an Eternal? To watch her loved ones die? Or were they all going to die before her for other reasons?

Kendra shook her head. She was giving this horrible place too much credibility. It was just scary nonsense. None of this meant anything.

Leaving the mirror behind, Kendra opened more coffins and discovered more dead acquaintances. Soon she was down to the last unexplored side of the room. As she worked her way along the row, Kendra noticed her feet squishing in mud.

She paused.

Hadn't it been a wooden floor, similar to the walls?

She felt sure it had been.

But now the entire floor was covered in dark brown mud.

Stepping forward to the next coffin, Kendra sank beyond her ankles. By the next coffin the mud was at her shins.

Five left.

The nearest coffin contained Aunt Zola, who had dropped off Knox and Tess before going on vacation with Kendra's parents.

Four left.

Kendra slogged to the next coffin, the mud feeling softer as she sank deeper, almost to her knees. She opened the lid to reveal Uncle Pete, Zola's husband.

Three left.

Every step was a chore as the mud overtopped her knees. Kendra pulled open the next coffin to reveal Knox.

Two left.

Kendra plunged deeper with each step, pushing forward through the increasingly soupy mud. When she reached the second-to-last coffin, Kendra had sunk to her waist, making the coffin seem much taller. She continued to slowly sink, as if standing in quicksand. She pulled open the coffin to view Tess, her young features pale in death. Tess was the youngest corpse Kendra had seen, and even after being somewhat numbed by viewing so many familiar cadavers in rapid succession, the sight of her dead little cousin stabbed Kendra with new pain. Tess was supposed to be running around the yard chasing fairies. What sicko had created this horrible place?

One left.

After closing the coffin, Kendra waded forward. She sank quickly to her shoulders, and her movements felt more like treading water than wading. Her feet no longer encountered any firmness beneath them, so she kicked instead of stepped, and stroked with her arms. It was like swimming in glue. Kendra made sure to keep hold of the invisible hand, but she was beginning to really flounder. She could barely keep her head above the mud.

With a desperate lunge, Kendra grabbed the bottom of the final upright coffin. For a moment she clung to it, catching her breath. Then she pulled it open to reveal . . . nothing. No body. No shape to the inside of the container. Just darkness.

Kendra was no longer used to the impenetrable blackness she was seeing. Nothing was completely dark to her anymore unless she closed her eyes.

One thing was certain. She needed to get out of this mud before she drowned. Despite the mushy surroundings, none of the coffins or other furniture in the room were sinking at all. It seemed the mud specifically wanted her.

Kendra boosted herself up into the empty coffin, her body slurping out of the muck. Reaching into the darkness, Kendra felt no back to the coffin. Was this what she had been looking for? Some kind of secret passage? A way out? Why was it so perfectly dark? She could still see nothing.

Rising, still clinging to Seth's invisible hand, Kendra stepped into the blackness. She could not feel the ground beneath her feet, but she wasn't falling, just sort of floating along. It was so dark she felt blind. From behind she seemed to hear the voices of her friends and family calling to her.

But that didn't seem very likely. Not in this place. She had just seen them.

And they were all dead.

CHAPTER TWENTY-TWO

Banquet

Seth saw only green fog. He couldn't glimpse his own hand until it nearly touched his face. The room seemed to be spinning. He felt woozy. All sense of direction was gone. But he had to find the other two bottles! He had to grab them and get out!

Kendra hauled him in one direction. He tugged the other way, but he was no longer sure if he was heading toward the table with the bottles, back toward the archway, or toward an empty corner.

Seth tried to keep walking, but his feet no longer seemed to touch the ground. He pedaled in the air, floating along inside a green haze, gripping Kendra's hand tightly.

And then he felt the floor again. The green smoke disintegrated.

Seth stood in the middle of a banquet hall with a parquet

floor and a coffered ceiling, dimly lit by candles in huge chandeliers. A pair of incredibly long tables stretched the length of the room, one on each side of him. Dozens of shadowy diners ate and murmured. Liveried servants whisked away empty plates and platters as quickly as they replenished food and tableware. Nobody seemed to pay Seth any mind.

He still held Kendra's hand, but she wasn't visible. He found he could move his arm freely, as if her hand were no longer connected to her. He tested the air around her invisible hand but could feel no other part of her body. The grip of the hand temporarily tightened, and he squeezed back.

"Kendra?" he whispered.

She did not reply. All he had was the feel of her hand.

The odd scene produced more questions than answers. Had he teleported here? Was it really happening? Could it be a dream? Why could he feel Kendra's hand but not the rest of her?

And then Seth knew something. There was someone behind him. Since the banquet hall had materialized out of the mist, he hadn't turned around. And he felt certain somebody was there. Somebody besides the oblivious diners and servants. Somebody bad.

Part of him didn't want to look. Part of him wondered if he could walk over to one of the tables and blend in with the guests. But he turned around.

A demon stood at the far end of the room. He was the only other person in the hall not serving or eating the feast. He stared directly at Seth.

The demon had a head vaguely like a wolf, but with

darker, oilier fur and glowing red eyes. The height of a man, he wore a cloak that hid most of his body except for his rat-like hands and feet.

Seth had never met this demon before. But there was a strange familiarity. He knew his kind. The demon did not look away.

Steeling himself against showing any fear, Seth approached the demon. He stopped just out of reach.

"Seth Sorenson," the demon said, revealing an alarming array of sharp, twisted teeth. Seth wondered if there were orthodontists for wolves. "We finally meet."

"You know me?" Seth asked.

"We all know you," the demon said.

"All the wolf people who lurk around at parties?" Seth asked.

"I am Talizar," the demon said. "I suspect we can form a mutually beneficial relationship."

"Let me guess," Seth said. "Demon?"

"Indeed," Talizar said.

"I'm done with demons," Seth said.

"How can that be?" Talizar asked calmly. "You are a shadow charmer. You are part of the family."

"I'm no demon," Seth said.

"You need a mentor," Talizar said.

"Do you know what I did to my last one?" Seth asked.

"Graulas was on his way out," Talizar said. "You helped him along. Any mentor who falls to his protégé deserves what he gets. The elite among us have all destroyed some of our teachers."

"You want to help me even though I killed the last demon who helped me?" Seth asked.

"Graulas betrayed you," Talizar said.

"You won't betray me?" Seth asked.

"Only if you let me," Talizar replied.

"What if I kill you?" Seth asked.

"Try if you must," Talizar said. "But don't fail. You won't like what follows."

Seth tried not to let the threat chill him. "Might be smarter to stay away from each other."

"Not if you want the scepter," Talizar said casually.

"What do you know about it?" Seth asked.

"Enough," Talizar said. "And I know you're wandering blind in regard to your abilities. So much lies dormant. You could do so much more. Be so much more."

"I've made deals with demons before," Seth said. "Never again. I'm serious."

"You might be serious," Talizar said. "But are you right? The dragons are a major threat. You can't stand against them alone. You're hopelessly overmatched. Demons and dragons are not friends. I could help you."

"No way," Seth said. "You'll help until you betray me."

"Don't let betrayal become advantageous to me," Talizar said. "Follow a few simple principles and we could both greatly benefit from a partnership."

"Graulus killed my friend," Seth said, trying not to tear up. The anger and grief were overpowering. It took a moment before he could speak again. "I won't risk that happening again."

"Your emotions are tangled," Talizar said. "Did your dealings with Graulus contribute to the death of a friend? Perhaps. But how many people would have died without that partnership? Would you still be alive? What about your sister?"

Seth thought about it. Without Graulus he might never have recovered the unicorn horn from the centaurs, which could have meant Kendra and many of their friends would have died the last time they came to Wyrmroost. Could they have possibly defeated the dragon Siletta without the horn? No Graulus also might have meant no Vasilis, which could have meant the demons might have won the battle of Zzyzx.

Gritting his teeth, Seth growled. "You demons always turn things around."

"We see clearly and speak accurately," Talizar said. "Most people find it very disorienting."

"Meanwhile you try to take over the world," Seth said. "You kill and lie and betray."

"When it suits our aims, I suppose," Talizar acknowledged.

"I don't need or want your help," Seth said. He looked around the busy banquet hall. "How do I get out of here?"

"That would be helping," Talizar said.

"I'll take a hint just this once," Seth offered.

"I can do more than hint," Talizar said. "How would you like to know what else you can do as a shadow charmer? I can help you activate new abilities right now. How would you like to walk out of here holding the hidden scepter?"

"I guess that would be nice," Seth said hesitantly.

"Easy," Talizar said. "Enter into an agreement with me. Your former sponsor is dead. Accept me as your new sponsor, and the scepter is yours."

"What exactly would that mean?" Seth asked.

"It would mean you and your sister will survive the Path of Dreams," Talizar said. "Then I'll help you devise a strategy to return the scepter back to Blackwell Keep."

"But what would I have to do if you were my sponsor?" Seth asked.

"You would come visit me in the flesh," Talizar said. "And you would be ready to answer when I call. I'll do favors for you, and you'll do some for me."

"Isn't this already a visit?" Seth asked.

"This is a dreamspace," Talizar said. "We're not physically together at the moment. We're inside a powerful construct produced by extremely talented wizards. What you say and do is binding. Sustain an injury here, and you'll actually be hurt. Die here and you're dead."

"How did you get here?" Seth asked.

"Once you came here, your mind provided access to me," Talizar said. "This dreamspace forms scenarios in connection with those who visit."

"Do you have the scepter?" Seth asked.

"I know how to get it," Talizar said. "I can guide you."

Seth hesitated for a moment. It would be nice to have help finding the scepter. It would be useful to learn new shadow charmer abilities. Much of what Talizar was proposing sounded reasonable.

But Graulas had sounded reasonable too. Demons could be very convincing. That didn't mean they were trustworthy. Seth had learned that the hard way.

"I'd rather find it on my own," Seth said.

"As you wish," Talizar said, drawing his cloak more snugly around himself.

"Are you going to attack me?" Seth asked.

"If I wanted you dead, we would not be talking," Talizar said. "I am not in the habit of repeating offers. However, if you decide you could use help, please feel at liberty to seek me in the real world. Assuming you survive this dreamspace." Talizar glanced beyond Seth. "Keep an eye on this lot. Always eating, never satisfied."

For a moment all went dark. When Seth could see again, Talizar was gone.

And the banquet hall was silent.

No more mumbled conversations. No more silverware clinking against china. No more hurried footsteps of servants.

Talizar had conversed with him at the end of the great hall, so Seth had his back to the two long tables. He reluctantly turned around.

Nobody was eating. No servants were in motion. Everyone had frozen in their positions, some sitting, others standing. And every pair of eyes was on Seth.

He was unsure whether the people had transformed or whether it was just that he had never taken a close look. Now he could see that they were all undead, though not as shadowy as wraiths or as mindless as zombies. All of the corpses looked dried out, with a hint of intelligence in their gazes.

As one, the undead revelers and servants began slowly moving in his direction. Chairs slid back. Figures stood and turned. The entire assemblage inched deliberately toward Seth.

Waves of fear began to wash over Seth, a troubling iciness that slithered across the surface of his skin but failed to penetrate inside. Seth recalled experiences when undead beings had utterly paralyzed him with fright. But since he had become a shadow charmer, none had succeeded, though he was sure he had never felt this raw volume of fear projected in his direction. Each figure in the room seemed to generate as much fear as the revenant he once faced.

He clung to Kendra's hand.

He needed a way out.

The undead assembly advanced so slowly that it felt like weird performance art. Still, even without speeding up, they would eventually corner him. There had to be at least a hundred of them. If they increased their pace, he would fall prey to them in a matter of moments.

Scanning the walls, Seth saw no windows or doors. But nearby, right behind where Talizar had stood, hung some velvet drapery.

Racing to the curtain, Seth heaved it aside to reveal a door. He seized the handle and found it locked. Desperate, Seth jiggled and pulled with all he had, but the door refused to budge. He fingered a large keyhole.

Did Talizar have the key? Or was it someplace else?

The undead continued to approach in slow motion. From where he stood, Seth searched the area. His eyes felt drawn to a large key dangling from the neck of a withered, aristocratic-looking woman toward the center of the banquet hall.

Seth surveyed the rest of the undead but noticed no other keys. His eyes kept returning to the desiccated noblewoman. That key looked about the right size. Seth decided he had to get it. If the undead party guests started moving at a normal speed, this would not end well. But if he didn't unlock the door, it would end badly for sure. He had to try.

Seth raced forward. The undead crowd continued to move with uncanny slowness. Seth weaved through the group, ducking and dodging to avoid grasping hands. He had experienced dreams in which he moved with syrupy slowness while an enemy chased him at a normal speed. This felt like the reverse.

The people looked horrifying, with sunken cheeks, leathery skin, and wispy hair. Seth had dealt with the undead many times, but something about dehydrated corpses dressed in fancy clothes was particularly unnerving. Despite their ponderous pace, all of them changed course toward him in response to his movements. All gazes tracked him, and outstretched arms reached in his direction.

As Seth reached the woman with the key, he ducked around behind her. The undead mob continued to converge on him one prolonged step at a time. As the undead noblewoman gradually turned, mouth gaping, Seth grabbed the slender cord attached to the key and pulled it over her head.

Seth found that the way back to the door was a lot less open now that so many of the undead crowd had converged toward him. He was almost out of room to maneuver. A hand brushed his arm, causing searing pain.

Diving sideways, Seth rolled under a table and scrambled along between the chairs, the key in one hand, the other still clinging to Kendra. Instead of moving to block his path, the undead mob came directly at him, which allowed him to reach the end of the table without much trouble.

The undead diners continued to follow, but Seth made it back to the door well ahead of them. He jammed in the key, twisted it, turned the knob, and pushed the door open.

Impenetrable darkness awaited beyond the threshold.

Hardly comforting.

But the blackness was more appealing than becoming the main course at the banquet.

Seth stepped through the doorway and closed the door. Then he ran blindly into the darkness. Before he had taken too many steps, his feet no longer touched the ground. He was floating, and perhaps slowly rotating, but without any perceptible gravity or visual cues, it was difficult to be sure.

He clung to the unembodied hand in the darkness.

CHAPTER TWENTY-THREE

Scepter

When the darkness lifted, Kendra found herself standing beside Seth, his hand in hers. He returned her stare, looking as surprised and relieved as she felt.

"Seth!" Kendra exclaimed, fighting back hysterical tears. "Are you all right?"

"Sort of," he replied, looking shaken. "How about you? Any sign of the scepter?"

"Just a lot of dead bodies," Kendra said.

"I saw dead people too," Seth said. "They attacked me."

"Were they people you knew?"

"No, dried-up zombies. Really slow ones."

"I saw you, Mom and Dad, our grandparents—pretty much everyone we know. Dead. In coffins."

"That's no fun," Seth said.

"I'm glad you're all right," Kendra said. "Hopefully that means the others are okay too."

"I could feel your hand the whole time."

"Me too."

Seth looked around. "Where are we now?"

They stood in a cave that widened up ahead into a massive cavern lit by flaming cauldrons. Glittering deposits of crystals adorned the walls, most white, others clear.

"I'm not sure," Kendra said. "Look at all the crystals."

From up ahead came a loud crunch.

"What was that?" Seth whispered.

"I'm afraid to find out," Kendra said. "It's been a nightmare so far."

"I spoke to a demon back where the zombies were," Seth said. "He called this a dreamspace. He told me we can still get hurt and die."

"What demon?" Kendra asked.

"He was called Talizar," Seth said. "I've never seen him before. Head like a wolf."

Kendra remembered the name. It was one of the three Jubaya had mentioned. "What did he want?" she asked casually.

"He wanted to help," Seth said. "He promised to help me learn new abilities and to help us find the scepter. Don't worry—I turned him down. I may mess up sometimes, but I eventually learn."

They heard another crunch.

Kendra pulled Seth forward. "We better go see."

Though the rugged walls of the cavern bristled with

crystals, the ground was surprisingly flat and smooth, almost polished. Off to one side of the cavern, in a circular depression, they found four eggs, each the size of a watermelon. Two were covered in scales, almost like a pineapple, but purplish in color. A third was glossy smooth with swirling hues, like marble. Fine grooves crisscrossed the last one. It appeared to be made of pure gold.

With another crunch, it became apparent that the swirly one was hatching. The egg rolled over, revealing a pair of scaly legs poking out and a network of cracks.

"Dragon eggs," Seth said, looking around. "That means there might be a mother nearby."

"So cute," Kendra said. "Look at those little claws trying to get free."

"Cute until they take over the world," Seth said.

"You can't blame this little guy for that," Kendra said. "He's just starting out. Maybe he'll be like Raxtus."

With another crunch, the gap between some of the cracks widened.

"Should we help him?" Kendra asked.

"Oh, no!" Seth said.

"What?" Kendra asked, worried he had seen the mother. Instead, following his gaze, she beheld a huge scorpion approaching, firelight shining off its black carapace. It was gigantic, the tail curling up higher than their heads, the claws large enough to snip off a leg.

Seth tugged Kendra away, backtracking toward the narrower part of the cavern where they had entered. The scorpion followed at first, claws scissoring. Then it paused and turned toward the depression where the eggs rested.

"It's going after the eggs!" Kendra cried.

"Better the eggs than us," Seth said.

"But the dragons," Kendra said. "They're little and help-less. Raxtus almost got killed when he was a baby. We're caretakers here. We have to help them."

"It's just a dream," Seth said.

"A dream where real things are happening," Kendra said staunchly. She picked up a loose rock and flung it at the scorpion. The stone skipped off the ground nearby, but the scorpion turned toward them, tail raised to strike, the tip quivering.

After a tense moment, the scorpion swiveled back toward the eggs. Seth flung a rock that hit the base of the tail.

This time the scorpion rushed at them. It was fast! Kendra and Seth retreated, but the creature gained quickly.

A bone-quaking roar interrupted the chase. Kendra and Seth ducked reflexively. The scorpion changed course, scuttling off to one side. A second roar shook the cavern. The scorpion darted toward a large crack in the rock wall. Just before it reached the opening, a huge claw fell on it, smashing the scorpion flat with a meaty crunch.

Holding Seth's hand tightly, Kendra looked up the furry leg to the dragon gazing down at her. Kendra had never seen a dragon like this one. Instead of scales, it had thick, coarse hair, chocolate brown. The head looked like something between an African buffalo and a crocodile, with two sets of horns that flared out wide before curving back in.

"I see I have visitors," spoke an impossibly rich female voice. "Has no one ever instructed you not to come between a mother dragon and her young?"

"We were trying to protect your eggs from a scorpion," Kendra said.

"So I witnessed, or you would not be alive," the dragon said. "Can both of you speak in my presence? What are your names?"

"Kendra."

"Seth."

"What folly brings you here, young ones? The lair of a dragon is no place for mortals."

"We didn't mean to come here," Kendra said. "We're looking for something."

The huge dragon brought her head closer. "Explain yourself. Looking for what, exactly?"

Kendra glanced at Seth. He shrugged.

"Your lives depend upon a truthful answer," the dragon said. "I possess little patience."

"The hidden scepter," Seth said. "We are the caretakers of Wyrmroost. We're looking for the scepter that helps protect Blackwell Keep."

"So I presumed," the dragon said. "I am Burelli, guardian of the labyrinth that leads to the scepter. And I have a problem."

"What?" Kendra asked.

"I should kill you," Burelli said. "But you just protected my offspring. At least one of them would have perished without your intervention."

"So you won't kill us?" Seth asked.

The dragon considered them for a long moment. "I will give you a sporting chance. Five minutes. Enter my labyrinth and I will wait five minutes before giving chase. Find the scepter and you are free to go. Otherwise, I will do my duty and devour you."

"But we're the caretakers," Kendra said. "It belongs to us. Why not just give us the scepter?"

"I guard the scepter," Burelli said. "My orders come from the founders of Wyrmroost. You have my offer. The time starts now."

"Which way?" Seth cried.

Burelli turned, looking back the way she had come, where the cavern continued to widen. "Hurry," she said. "I'm fast."

Hand in hand, Kendra and Seth started running. "How about a little more time?" Seth called out. "We're tired from fighting the scorpion."

"Your time is counting down," Burelli warned.

As Kendra and Seth raced across the smooth ground, the cavern continued to expand—the ceiling soaring higher, the walls growing farther apart. Up ahead, a twenty-foot wall made of stone blocks spanned the width of the cavern. The wall had a single gap.

"That's the labyrinth?" Seth complained. "The dragon can fly above it! How is that fair?"

Seth was right. The ceiling of the cavern only continued to rise beyond the apparent start of the maze.

"At least we're not dead yet," Kendra replied. "We better be quick."

Beyond the breach in the wall, the way branched to the right and to the left. Periodic cauldrons of fire provided light. "I wish we could get up top," Seth complained, looking up.

"The walls are too high," Kendra said. "And much too steep. Which way?"

"We should split up," Seth said.

"We'll get paralyzed when the dragon comes," Kendra said.

"How many extra steps do we get by not freezing?" Seth said. "Like ten? And she can't attack both of us at once. Splitting up turns four minutes into eight."

Kendra didn't want to do this alone. But the argument made sense. "Okay," she said, letting go of his hand. "Hurry!" She took off to the left. Seth ran to the right.

Strangely, Kendra still felt like she was holding his hand. After she let go of Seth, the invisible hand inexplicably returned.

"I still feel you!" Kendra called.

"Me too!" Seth replied.

Kendra ran as fast as she could. There was no time to methodically explore the maze. She had to rely on instincts and luck.

With each intersection she passed, Kendra lost hope. There were too many alternatives. She rounded corner after corner, choosing without pause at every junction.

Kendra clung to Seth's unseen hand. Maybe it meant the dragon would not be able to paralyze her. She tried to think positive. If she was fast and lucky, she might find her way to the scepter. It could be around the next corner. It might appear at any moment.

The first dead end disappointed her. By the third she was starting to feel disoriented. After hitting the fifth dead end, for all Kendra knew, she might be heading back to the start.

She began to regret not being more methodical. She should have turned right every time, or taken some measure to reduce the chances of backtracking. Too late now. She was sweating, but she kept her legs pumping. How much time remained? Five minutes might have already gone by.

She had an ache in her side. Her legs were getting rubbery. Out of necessity, she eased down from a full sprint.

And then the dragon roared.

Seth raced around a corner, found an intersection, turned left, then right at the next fork, and rounded a corner to face a blank wall. He ran back to the previous juncture and went the other way.

This was going to be bad. They didn't have enough time.

"Seth!" piped a little voice. "Down here! Seth!"

Seth skidded to a halt. Sure enough, looking down, he found Calvin running toward him, waving both arms above his head.

"Calvin!" Seth exclaimed with relief. "You're all right!"

He scooped up the Tiny Hero. "There's a dragon coming." Seth started running again.

"I found the scepter!" Calvin cried. "It was just too high up! I couldn't reach it. Turn around!"

Seth stumbled to a stop. "You know where to go?"

"That way," Calvin said, pointing.

Seth ran as directed. "Can you really get us back there?"

"Left!" Calvin shouted. "I wouldn't be very useful if I forgot. Keep going straight."

"There are lots of turns," Seth said, hesitant to hope.

"Twelve more turns," Calvin said. "Go right. Eleven now."

"Kendra!" Seth called. "If you can hear me, follow my voice! I found Calvin! He knows the way."

"Straight," Calvin said. "Did you see the dragon with the big horns? Left!"

"You saw her too!" Seth exclaimed. "She gave us a five-minute head start."

"Go right. Really? At least she gave you a chance. Straight, then left."

"Not much of one until I found you. How long have you been here?"

"Keep going. Not too long. My legs feel like rubber. Lots of running. Up ahead turn left."

"This labyrinth is enormous for somebody your size," Seth said.

"You're telling me! Go right. I had some help getting to the scepter. Now left. Sprinting back to the entrance was exhausting."

"You made it to where I found you?"

"Left," Calvin said. "This will double back on itself. First this corner. Now that corner. It keeps winding for a bit. I'm so glad you found me! I was trying to get to the entrance so we wouldn't miss each other in the maze. Okay, now right."

"Who helped you get the scepter?"

"Now go left," Calvin said. "It's a long story. We're almost there. I'll tell you if we make it. Now right."

A gargantuan roar reverberated through the cavern. Seth's legs and lungs burned, but the mighty bellow helped inspire him back to a full sprint.

"This will be close," Calvin said. "I see her!"

"How?" Burelli exclaimed incredulously. "Impossible!"

"Left," Calvin urged. "Run hard! That's it!"

Up ahead Seth beheld a covered dead end—the only roofed portion of the labyrinth he had seen. Two cauldrons burned within. And between them, mounted horizontally on the wall, hung a golden scepter sparkling with jewels.

Not risking a glance back, Seth sprinted with everything he had. He could hear enormous wings flapping and the ominous whistle of air rushing over a tremendous body.

Fifteen more yards.

"Halt!" Burelli called.

Ten yards.

"Here she comes!" Calvin warned.

Seth dashed into the roofed portion of the corridor.

Five yards.

He heard a whoosh of dragon breath and felt a wave of blistering heat flooding his way. The light of the oncoming

fire brightened the end of the maze, glaring brilliantly off the scepter.

Seth jumped.

His fingers closed around the scepter just as the heat became unbearable.

Race to the Keep

Kendra heard Burelli exhale and saw the volatile glow of her flames brighten the cavern overhead, and then everything went momentarily dark. When she opened her eyes, Kendra was on the floor in the room where they had started. The green smoke was gone. Three bottles still sat on the table at one end of the room, two corked, one unstopped.

Seth lay beside her, his shirt and hair a little singed, smelling faintly of smoke. They were still holding hands. With a smile, he held up his other hand to display a golden scepter roughly three feet long. The top bulged into a knob crusted with jewels.

"You got it!" Kendra said, sitting up. "Were we really there? Was it a dream?"

"I'm not sure," Seth said. "It seemed real. I felt your hand the whole time."

"Maybe because we were really just lying here," Kendra said, giving his hand a squeeze.

"Wherever we were, it left marks," Seth said, showing her some circular bruises on his arm. "Those were from zombie fingertips. They barely touched me. Those creeps were worse than zombies. I'm not sure what they really were."

"Probably liches, if their touches bruised," Calvin said. "Zombies wouldn't leave a mark from a touch, and a revenant would have withered the area more."

"Calvin!" Kendra said happily. "You're back! We were worried about you!"

"He saved the day," Seth said. "He really is the Tiny Hero! He had already found the scepter and led me straight to it."

"I was about to tell Seth the story," Calvin said.

"Let's hear it," Kendra invited.

Calvin looked pleased to have an audience. He used his hands a lot as he spoke. "So, running into the smoke didn't turn out so well. I got dizzy really fast, and suddenly I was in a room with big people clomping around. Wizards never design places like this with tiny adventurers in mind. Since when do fairies hunt treasure? Or brownies? Or leprechauns? Doesn't happen."

"Leprechauns have treasure," Seth interrupted.

"Having and hunting are two different things," Calvin said. "Leprechauns get their gold through magic, inheritance, or trickery. Not adventuring. Anyhow, I ran for the door, squirmed underneath, and ended up in a really dark place. Then I was in the glittery dragon cave. That huge dragon with the big horns was in there, sitting on her nest. Climbing the dragon took some time."

"You climbed the dragon?" Seth exclaimed.

"No problem," Calvin said. "Very furry. Lots to grab onto. I was too small for her to notice."

"Why climb her?" Kendra asked.

"So I could get close to her ear," Calvin said. "I was following a hunch, because the cavern looked enormous. I kind of covered my mouth and tried to make a faraway voice. I'm sure my size helped."

"What did you say?" Seth asked.

Calvin covered his mouth and demonstrated how he spoke. "Hurry, grab the scepter. Let's go."

"What happened?" Kendra asked.

"The dragon's head jerked so fast I nearly fell off," Calvin said. "And I was holding on tight! What do you suppose the dragon did next?"

"Went to check!" Seth exclaimed.

"She flew up over the maze," Calvin said with a wink. "I made a mental map. I'm good with spatial thinking. Kind of a specialty. The dragon swooped down by the covered portion of the labyrinth and stuck her head inside. I slid down her head, hung from her lowest whiskers, and dropped. Amazing how well you can take a fall when you're tiny and fortified by magic. I didn't even twist an ankle."

"She took you right to the scepter?" Kendra asked.

"Straight to the main prize," Calvin agreed, barely

containing a laugh. "Then she flew around investigating the maze, making sure there were no intruders."

"That must have been when we came in," Seth said. "The nest was unprotected."

"Probably," Calvin said. "The scepter was too high for me to reach. So I used the map in my head to run back toward the entrance. I went as fast as I could and was getting close when Seth found me."

"Then Calvin directed me back to the scepter," Seth said. "When I snagged it, I woke up here."

"It brought me back too," Kendra said. "Right after I saw fire brighten up the cavern."

"It was close," Seth said. "I got a little singed."

"At least we made it," Kendra said, standing.

Seth got up too. "Well, I wouldn't go that far. We got the scepter. I'll feel like we've made it when we get it back to Blackwell Keep."

"A correct sentiment," came the voice of Dromadus from well beyond the room.

"Do you hear everything we say?" Seth asked.

"If your voice carries, I'm going to listen," Dromadus said.

"He has good ears," Kendra whispered.

"No visible ears really," Dromadus replied from afar. "Unsightly things, if you ask me. But excellent hearing, yes."

Kendra gave Seth's hand a squeeze. "Let's go."

"Are you sure you don't want to try another bottle?" Seth asked.

She pulled him out of the room, though he pretended to be reluctant. They went up the long flight of stairs, then climbed out of the depression to find Dromadus waiting where they had left him.

"Impressive," Dromadus said. "I did not realistically expect to see you again. Perhaps Agad and Marat have better judgment than your ages suggest. I believe I underestimated your Tiny Hero as well."

"We still have to get the scepter back to Blackwell Keep," Seth said.

"A vulnerable predicament," Dromadus said. "You will either hasten your destruction by losing the scepter or else postpone it by succeeding. Either way, congratulations on taking decisive action. I wish you well in your efforts to promote peace."

"Thanks for your help," Kendra said.

She and Seth exited the cavern into the long tunnel. At the far end Henrick awaited with Mendigo and the two horses. A glowing stone held by Henrick provided illumination.

Kendra and Seth rushed to him.

"Is that what I think it might be?" Henrick asked, indicating the scepter.

"The scepter was hidden here," Seth said. "We got it!"

"That is . . . incredible," Henrick said. "To tell you the truth, I believed it was a long shot that we would ever find the scepter. Of course, now we have a new problem."

"I guess you brought the horses down those stairs for a reason," Kendra said. "Hi, Glory. Hi, Noble."

The horses stamped and tossed their heads.

"I confirmed that a dragon has been spying on us," Henrick said. "Mobando. A member of Celebrant's personal guard, and one of the most dangerous dragons in the sanctuary. He is strong, fast, stealthy, and intelligent. You were inside this lair for a long time. Eventually Mobando got curious and came too close. When I became aware of him, I led the horses down the stairs. Otherwise he may have tried to kill us or run us off. Though I do not believe Celebrant wants you dead yet, he would not hesitate to make your journey back to Blackwell Keep as miserable as possible."

"But now we have the scepter," Seth said.

"Which changes everything," Henrick said. "The Dragon King would gleefully kill us all for that scepter. He doesn't have to endure a co-caretaker anymore if Blackwell Keep falls."

"We're pinned down," Kendra said.

"Perhaps not as badly as it appears," Henrick said. "Nobody knows what you found here yet. Not for sure. I expect that Mobando will sense the scepter's powerful magic. It will be too potent for him to miss. But he may not know what it is at first."

"So what do we do?" Seth asked.

"They probably assume you wanted to counsel with Dromadus," Henrick said. "I'm not sure if they will guess why. They could presume you just came for general advice. So we leave together as if our mission is accomplished. We don't rush. We head back toward the Winding Way. I'll carry the scepter."

"You?" Seth asked.

"I'll do my best to hide it," Henrick said. "Whoever carries the scepter is in great peril. I'm fast, and I have some evasive tricks. I know this sanctuary like nobody else. I have eluded dragons before, though I have never been hunted as I will be hunted if they figure out exactly what I have in my possession. If Mobando strikes before we get back to the Winding Way, you continue to the road and then return to Blackwell Keep through Terrabelle and along the High Road. Maybe I can make it to a road too. If not, I'll invent a route through the wild. If I have the scepter, Mobando will chase me and you'll have a reasonable chance of surviving."

"What if we let Mendigo transport the scepter?" Seth asked. "We could leave Mendigo behind. Leave without him. Then, after we leave, maybe he could sneak the scepter back to Blackwell Keep."

"Not a bad stratagem," Henrick said. "But Mobando is subtle and smart. He will probably notice if your wooden puppet suddenly disappears. It will raise suspicions. And if Mendigo is discovered by the dragons, he won't have a chance of evading them. I realistically could."

"I wish we could shrink it," Calvin said from Seth's pocket. "Dragons have a hard time tracking me. Burelli didn't even notice I was there."

"We're a long way from Blackwell Keep on fast horses," Henrick said. "That distance is a lot greater when your legs are an inch long."

"I've gone much farther," Calvin said. "Tiny people

learn to travel in a variety of ways. Not just on foot. But wishing I could make the scepter smaller won't make it so."

"Your plan sounds good, Henrick," Kendra said.

"Should we go?" Seth proposed.

"How are you horses?" Henrick asked. "Was this enough of a rest? There could be a lot of running before you get back to your stalls."

Both horses reared up slightly, then gave single stamps.

Kendra and Seth followed Henrick and the horses up the long stairway. Even having already descended the stairway, Kendra was amazed how long it was. Her legs burned by the time they reached the cellar doors that led out to the sequoia grove.

"Remember," Henrick whispered, "stay calm until I run. There is always a chance the dragons will just watch us. If we make it to the Winding Way, we should reach Blackwell Keep with no problem. If I have to run off, ignore me and get to the Winding Way as soon as you can."

"Got it," Seth whispered.

Henrick held out a hand, and Seth passed him the scepter. The alcetaur wrapped the scepter in some material he took from one of the pouches he wore like saddlebags. Then he opened the doors and led the horses out into the grove. Dawn warmed the horizon. The stars were fading. A light wind ruffled the sequoias.

"Let's all hope for more wind," Henrick muttered. "Dragons find high winds inconvenient."

"I didn't know we pulled an all-nighter," Seth said.

"Time flies when you're running for your life," Kendra replied.

Kendra swung onto Glory and patted the horse. They trotted out of the grove and into a field.

And then a huge green dragon swooped down and landed in front of them, blocking their path. The spines on its neck and back looked almost like fins, and it had a narrower build than most dragons Kendra had seen, with a more serpentine neck and head. Yellow eyes glared with malevolent interest, and a long, purple tongue tested the air.

"What errand takes you so far from the road?" the dragon inquired in a whispery but penetrating voice.

Kendra found that she could not move. Seth was too far away on Noble for her to try to take his hand. Her thoughts remained clear, but she was paralyzed, as if she had almost stepped on a rattlesnake and somehow become trapped in that first instant of frozen surprise.

"Greetings, Mobando," Henrick answered. "We consulted with Dromadus. I am with the new caretakers. I am Henrick the gamekeeper. We have a right to be here."

"I see," Mobando replied. "I am interested in what our illustrious new caretakers have to say. What news from Dromadus?"

Kendra wanted to speak. She had words ready. But her lips would not function. It was so easy when holding Seth's hand, she had almost forgotten how impossible it was without him.

"Do not trouble the children," Henrick said. "They were up all night and are weary."

The head swung closer to the alcetaur. "One last query. It appears Dromadus may have entrusted a valuable object to your care. That dragon is a known scoundrel and craven. Show me what he gave you."

"Ride!" Henrick cried, splitting into five different identical versions of himself and racing off in five different directions.

Kendra had no time to contemplate the bizarre sight before Glory was off and running. Noble came alongside, hooves hammering the ground. Her paralysis ebbing, Kendra craned to look back and saw the five identical Henricks each divide into five more identical Henricks, for a total of twenty-five.

Mobando gave a hiss that grew into a roar. Snakelike head swaying, the dragon expelled a dark mist at the fleeing Henricks. The cloud enveloped some, but they kept running, heads down, hands protecting their mouths. The mist couldn't reach all of them—too many were bolting in too many directions.

"Poison gas!" Calvin cried.

Mobando looked their way, then returned his attention to the alcetaurs. Each Henrick held an identical bundle. The dragon took flight, chasing one of the nearest Henrick duplicates.

"I don't think he's going to chase us," Kendra called.

Seth glanced back. "He might if he gets you know what."

Kendra realized her brother had a point. They might

not presently be at the top of the priority list, but that could change.

Glory and Noble raced back the way they had come last night as the sky brightened and the sun came up. Kendra kept an eye out for dragons but saw none. She wondered how Henrick was doing. She had no idea how his replication magic worked, but she hoped it had provided enough distraction for him to get away. If he managed to return the scepter to Blackwell Keep, the mission would be a success and they might have a realistic chance of saving Wyrmroost. If not, there might not be a Blackwell Keep by the time they returned.

The horses stayed under the cover of trees as much as possible, sometimes skirting open fields to stay beneath leaves and branches. It slowed their pace a little, but Kendra figured the cover was worthwhile if a dragon might be looking for them. Whether thanks to the skill of the horses or simply due to good luck, they not only avoided dragons but didn't see any other threats for a long time. As far as Kendra could tell, the sanctuary might be deserted.

At length they reached the slope that descended to the bridge over the ravine where the troll had summoned the dire bears. Before the horses could fully emerge from the trees, Kendra asked them to stop. They immediately complied.

"That troll is probably still down there," Kendra reminded everyone. "And we don't have Henrick this time."

"We can't bargain," Seth said. "And we can't waste time. Let's rush him. Maybe throw Mendigo at him."

Kendra glanced at the limberjack. "Mendigo, if that troll tries to stop us, attack him. Don't let him call for bears. Keep him busy. Then follow us once we're clear."

"Good enough," Seth said. "Let's go."

Glory and Noble charged out into the open, hooves thumping against the turf. The area looked so different and innocent bathed in the golden light of the rising sun. Kendra enjoyed the rush of the speed, and hoped that perhaps Grimp would stay out of sight.

As they approached the bridge, the troll came out from underneath, ax in hand, leering confidently. The horses slowed, allowing Mendigo to leap down and run ahead. The limberjack seemed faster than Kendra remembered. Had Agad upgraded him?

Grimp glared at the oncoming puppet and readied his ax. He swung as Mendigo arrived, but the limberjack dove low, pulling the troll's ankles together and yanking his feet into the air. Grimp fell hard.

Glory and Noble sped up, pounding past the troll as he struggled to rise. Mendigo wrestled vigorously, his wooden body in constant motion. As she crossed the bridge, Kendra glanced back and saw Grimp flat on the ground a second time.

The horses charged hard up the slope. Kendra never heard a call for bears. Just before going back under the trees, Kendra looked back and saw Grimp and Mendigo still grappling.

The pace slowed again under the trees, but they still saw no other signs of life, including dragons. Kendra could hardly believe it when the horses trotted onto the Winding Way with no interference.

"We made it!" Kendra exclaimed.

"The dragons don't care about us," Seth said. "They want what Henrick has."

"Right, but I'm still glad we didn't get eaten," Kendra said.

Seth leaned down and patted Noble. "We have to get back to Blackwell Keep and make sure Henrick is all right. You've gone a long way. If you want, you can take us to Terrabelle and maybe we can borrow fresh horses."

Noble shook his head and stamped twice. Glory stamped twice as well.

"They don't like that idea," Kendra said. "Think you can run back to Blackwell Keep?"

In response, the horses took off, quickly accelerating to a gallop. The speed made Kendra momentarily breathless.

"Go at a speed you can maintain," Kendra said.

Glory answered with a single toss of her head.

As the ground rose and fell, the horses never slowed to less than a canter. They spent a lot of time at a full gallop. Kendra watched the sky but observed no dragons. Were they being watched secretly? Or were they irrelevant compared to the importance of getting the scepter?

Her desire to get home in a hurry made the road to Terrabelle seem to last forever. Kendra knew from looking at Seth's maps that the roads did not represent the most direct route back to Blackwell Keep, but of course cutting through the wilderness was unthinkable with dragons on the prowl.

They rushed across the valley without nearing the town, and exited on the High Road.

On the way down from the pass, the horses kicked into an even higher gear. Kendra held on tight. She watched for dragons but saw none. The pace slowed a little as the ground levelled out, but less than Kendra expected. These mounts had remarkable endurance.

When Blackwell Keep finally came into view, so did the dragons. Lots of them. Soaring in the sky beyond the walls of the keep. Flanking the High Road near the gate. And roughly a dozen clustered around the dome of the safe hut visible on a nearby ridge, Celebrant among them.

There must have been at least fifty dragons of different shades, sizes, and textures. Some had smooth, small scales. Others had scales so rough and weathered they looked like shingles on an old roof. Some were metallic. A few were furry. Most of the heads looked reptilian, but a minority bore more resemblance to wolves or oxen or lions.

"I don't think Henrick made it yet," Seth shouted. "I hoped that a more direct path through the wilderness might get him here ahead of us. It looks like they're here to head him off."

"He might be in the safe hut," Kendra said, indicating the dome atop a ridge within view of the keep. "A bunch of dragons are gathered there, including Celebrant."

"Or they're blocking it off," Seth said. "We'll find out soon."

The gate opened as they approached. Kendra and Seth rode through to find Grandpa and Grandma Sorenson waiting in the courtyard with Marat. Kendra dismounted and Grandpa engulfed her in a big hug. Grandma came next. Then Kendra turned and patted Glory, thanking her. The horse bobbed her head in reply.

"We were so worried," Grandpa said. "Are you all right?"

"We found the scepter," Seth reported.

"What?" Grandpa asked.

"The medallion works because it's connected to a hidden scepter," Kendra said. "We found it."

"Amazing," Marat said. "That unravels the mystery. Henrick has the scepter?"

"Yeah," Seth said.

"He is trapped in the nearest safe hut," Marat said. "We heard roaring in the distance, then watched as Henrick barely made it there ahead of several dragons. He must have led them on a mighty chase. A host of others arrived soon thereafter. I could not fathom what need would drive Celebrant to trap him there. Now it makes perfect sense."

"Can we free him?" Kendra asked.

Marat smiled sadly. "With this many dragons standing guard? My dear, it would take a miracle."

CHAPTER TWENTY-FIVE

Recruits

Seth stared out from the battlements atop the outer wall of Blackwell Keep at the dragons wheeling in the sky, their shadows fluttering across the ground. Enormous and fierce, any one of them would have sent the population of a village running for their lives. It was a sight he had hoped to enjoy ever since learning that dragons were real. At the battle of Zzyzx he had been too busy fighting demons to properly observe the colossal predators, and the dragons had departed soon after the combat ended.

Today he could stare as long as he wanted. Eve would be so jealous.

But he couldn't really enjoy the experience.

Henrick was trapped in the safe hut with the scepter. Nobody had a plan to get him out.

Almost nobody.

Seth had a really good idea.

Even just thinking about the plan that was forming in his mind made Seth glance around guiltily. Grandpa and Grandma were not in sight. Neither was Kendra. Seth had deliberately separated himself from them.

Placing his hands against the rough stone wall, he sighed.

Grandpa wouldn't like this plan. Neither would Grandma. Neither would Kendra. They would stop him if they knew what he wanted to do.

Should he stop himself? Was he being reckless? Kendra seemed to think he followed any crazy thought that crossed his mind. But he was supposed to protect Wyrmroost. He was the caretaker. Doing that job wouldn't always be safe. Getting the scepter in the first place had been extremely dangerous.

The more Seth pondered his strategy, the more certain he became that his family would be wrong. They wouldn't like it, but it should work.

The plan would not put Kendra, Grandma, or Grandpa at risk. Not at all. And it might protect them. Seth would suffer the greatest risk by far. If anybody died, it would be him. Only one other person would really be exposed to danger.

Seth wished he could pull this off alone. But there was no way to do it without one other person. And he would need a little extra help.

He turned and looked down into the courtyard. Who could he trust? If somebody blabbed to Grandpa, he suspected his plan would never get implemented. He needed an accomplice who would carry out his orders quietly. Ideally, it would also be somebody who could confirm his strategy.

Simrin was walking across the courtyard. Seth had noticed that she seemed very close to Marat. If Marat learned the plan, he could go to Grandpa. And that would be the end of the plan.

Seth descended a staircase to the courtyard. As he reached the bottom, Brunwin, the reddish minotaur, exited a door on the far side.

Bracken had described Brunwin as reliable but with a bad temper. Seth seldom saw him talking with others. Maybe the bad temper would help encourage the minotaur to take matters into his own hands to get the scepter.

Unable to think of a better candidate, Seth hurried across the courtyard to Brunwin. "Can I ask you something?"

The minotaur stopped and looked down at him. "You're the boss. What is it?"

"I know a way to help Henrick," Seth said.

"We're trying to formulate a strategy," Brunwin said. "I'm not sure there is any realistic way to succeed. Not with ten times our resources."

"If I figured out a way, would you keep it secret?" Seth asked.

"Depends why you want it kept secret," the minotaur replied.

"Grandpa won't like it," Seth said. "Neither will Grandma or Kendra. They'd try to stop me. But I know it will work."

Brunwin snorted. "You think you can get to the safe hut and back?"

"No," Seth said. "But I think I know somebody who can."

"Really? Who?"

"Will you keep it a secret?"

"You're the caretaker," Brunwin said. "You can order me to keep it a secret."

"If I do, you can't say anything?"

"I could. But I'm supposed to follow orders, and I probably would do so. Who is it?"

"A person who wouldn't suspect he is at a dragon sanctuary," Seth said. "If I sent someone like that, wouldn't the treaty protect him?"

"You're talking about a mortal?"

"Yes. A boy who has no idea that magical creatures are real."

Brunwin's nostrils flared. "Well, if he had no suspicion there were dragons here, and he was only acting under your orders, yes, I suppose he would be protected. But if he caught on to what was really happening, he could be ripped to shreds."

"I don't think he would catch on," Seth said. "His imagination doesn't work that way. What if he had the scepter?"

"It's neutral ground," Brunwin said. "If he is oblivious to where he really is, following instructions in good faith, the boy should be protected, even with the scepter in hand, even against scores of dragons. Of course, that is all theory. Nobody has ever tested the treaty against so much power. And there is nobody here like the boy you describe."

"But there is back at Fablehaven."

Brunwin stared at him. Then he gave a nod. "If you give the boy his orders, the dragons could come after you across any boundary at Wyrmroost. Including into Blackwell Keep."

"I know," Seth said. "I would have to run. Or fly, actually. Can you have one of the dwarfs ready Tempest?"

Brunwin stared at him again. "Where could you hide?"

"Let me worry about that," Seth said. "I don't want to say it out loud until the last minute. If the dragons cut me off, I'll be a goner."

"Tempest is fast and skillful," Brunwin said. "But dozens of dragons watch the keep. Chances are you won't make it no matter where you go."

"I know," Seth said. "I'm willing to risk it to save Henrick and protect the keep. If the keep falls, we all die. If the dragons get free, the whole world is in trouble. Even if the dragons get me, this should work. I have to try."

Brunwin rubbed his hands together. "Seth, this is by far the best solution I've heard. Ingenious, really. It could work. But the price could be steep. Are you sure?"

"It's my job to protect the sanctuary," Seth said. "Help me do this."

Brunwin extended a hand. Seth shook it. "I admire your courage," the minotaur said.

"To somebody who hasn't had any milk, do you look like a guy or a cow?" Seth asked.

Brunwin glared.

"I mean bull," Seth amended. "A guy or a bull."

"Eyes closed to magic normally recognize me as a man."

"Perfect," Seth said. "Go tell whatever dwarf you most trust what we need. Then meet me at the barrel."

Seth found the sole goblin at Blackwell Keep guarding the door to the room where the barrel was kept. The creature was shaggier and more apelike than most goblins Seth had seen, with big hands and black fingernails. Seth could not recall his name, so he just gave the goblin a nod and proceeded down the hall and around a corner to wait for Brunwin. Hopefully the minotaur could help him gain access to the barrel.

"You're going after Knox?" came a sneaky voice from his pocket.

"I wish I could think of another way," Seth said.

"It's a clever plan," Calvin assured him. "Exciting! But if things go wrong . . ."

"I'll be dead," Seth said. "They can scold me at my funeral."

"What if Knox gets hurt?"

"He should be safe. When we tried this with the ogre, it was kind of a mess for me, but not for him. I have to trust that, or I couldn't do it."

"How are you going to convince him to come?" Calvin wondered.

"I'm working on it," Seth said. "All I know for sure is I can't tell him the truth. Not knowing about the dragons is part of his protection."

They waited until Seth heard Brunwin addressing the goblin guard. Then Seth came around the corner.

"Tell nobody of this," Brunwin was saying. "This is a secret mission for the good of the sanctuary."

The goblin gave a salute. "As you wish." He took out a key and opened the door. Brunwin ushered Seth inside and closed it.

Seth peeked into the empty barrel, then turned to Brunwin. "The boy is named Knox. When he comes through, he'll think we're playing a game. Treat it like the game is important. Take him to the door Kendra used to visit Raxtus. When I fly over the wall, send him to the safe hut."

"Understood," Brunwin said.

"What about the dwarfs?" Seth asked.

"Obun will help. He and Didger are preparing Tempest as we speak."

Seth climbed into the barrel and squatted down. "I need to get to Fablehaven," he said. Inside the barrel, he was at both places at once. He knew that if anyone at Fablehaven was near the barrel, they would hear his voice. All he needed was for somebody at Fablehaven to reach inside and touch him, and he could exit there.

A pair of hands helped him out of the barrel. The hands belonged to Doren! Suddenly he was in the living room at Fablehaven. Newel was there too.

"So good to see you!" Doren said. "It gets dull around here without you."

"What a surprise," Newel said. "Is everything all right?"

"Should we get old man Larsen?" Doren wondered.

"No, please," Seth said. "I'm glad you guys are guarding the barrel. I'm here on a secret mission."

Doren pumped a fist. "Helping with a secret mission tops watching an empty barrel any day."

"Good," Seth said. "I have to borrow Knox."

"By *borrow*, you mean . . . ?" Newel asked.

"I need to bring him to Wyrmroost for a few minutes," Seth said.

Newel folded his arms. "We're supposed to get permission from old man Larsen before letting anyone go from Fablehaven to Wyrmroost."

"What's this old man Larsen business?" Seth asked. "His name is Hank."

Doren shrugged. "We like the ring of it."

"Don't change the subject," Newel said. "You're asking us to ignore our duty."

"We can't explain this to Grandpa Larsen," Seth said. "I'm the new caretaker of Wyrmroost. Do it under my authority. I'll take any blame."

"You're what?" Doren asked. "The what-taker of what, now?"

"Caretaker of Wyrmroost," Seth said, showing them the medallion.

"Looks fancy," Doren conceded.

"Did Stan and Ruth disappear or something?" Newel asked. "And every other possible candidate?"

"They needed dragon tamers," Seth said. "Kendra and I qualified."

"You're serious," Newel said.

"Dead serious," Seth said. "And we really have an emergency."

Newel nudged Doren. "Hear that? We know the caretaker of Wyrmroost."

"We could rule that place now," Doren said. "Can you imagine? A caretaker on our side? One who doesn't care at all about the rules?"

"Hey," Seth said. "I care about the rules."

Newel and Doren both laughed. Doren slapped his woolly thighs.

"Nobody is watching," Newel finally said. "You can deal straight with us."

"I want to be a really good caretaker," Seth said. "But first I have to save the sanctuary."

"With Knox?" Doren asked. "Come on. What's the real story? Need to snatch some more treasure?"

"Kind of," Seth said. "That's not important. Listen, unless you let me take Knox, Wyrmroost will fall."

Newel and Doren grew serious. "We're at Fablehaven, Seth," Newel said. "The caretaker of Wyrmroost doesn't call the shots here. Why not run it by Hank?"

"He won't want me to do it," Seth said. "But it has to happen!"

Doren gasped and covered his mouth. "Are you sacrificing Knox to the dragons?"

Newel placed a hand on Seth's shoulder. "There are other ways to deal with annoying cousins."

"Knox will be fine," Seth said through gritted teeth. "If

anybody dies it will be me. Are you two going to trust me or not? You're supposed to be my friends."

Newel placed his hands behind his back and avoided eye contact. "See, Seth, the thing is, old man Larsen, er, Hank, trusted us with this post so we can earn television time."

"Said he'd block our cable signal if we didn't stand watch," Doren said. "Stan promised us a television, but there were no guarantees about the signal. Old man Larsen got us on a technicality."

"You won't help me because it might interrupt your shows?" Seth asked.

"We promised to be good guardians," Newel said. "It's a sacred trust. And, yeah, if Hank gets mad, what will become of us? I can't go back to an antenna, Seth. It isn't civilized."

"I'll tie you up," Seth offered. "You can say you had no choice."

"But we'll look like wimps," Doren said.

"Wait a minute," Newel said. "Hank won't want wimps watching the barrel."

Doren smiled. "Good point."

"I promise you won't get busted," Seth said. "I'll take all the blame. You can say I had permission from Grandpa Sorenson."

"Do you?" Newel asked.

"Um, sure," Seth said.

"You have to lie better than that," Doren said. "Everyone will see right through it."

"I mean, yes, Grandpa Sorenson sent me to get Knox," Seth said. "Grandma too. Absolutely. Happy now?"

Newel sighed. "Seth, are you sure you know what you're doing?"

Seth took a deep breath. "I'm sure."

"It's a good plan," Calvin called from his pocket.

"Are you still toting that little guy around?" Doren asked. "I was sure a sparrow would have eaten him by now."

"Don't tease him," Seth said. "Calvin has already helped save the day."

"Must have been a short day," Newel muttered.

"This really is an emergency," the nipsie asserted.

"My new friend Calvin is on my side," Seth said. "Are my old friends big enough to help?"

"We'll help," Newel said.

"We aren't the Supreme Gigantic Overlords for nothing," Doren maintained.

"Are Grandma and Grandpa Larsen nearby?" Seth asked.

"With Stan and Ruth gone, the Larsens moved in here with Knox and Tess," Newel said. "I think it was partly to be near the barrel. And partly to be near the yard and the front gate and the cow out in the barn."

"Are they around?" Seth asked.

"Gloria is on a shopping trip," Newel said. "Hank is out inspecting something with Hugo."

"What about Knox and Tess?" Seth asked.

"Out by the pool," Newel said.

"Have you seen a basketball with writing on it?" Seth asked.

"I know right where it is," Doren exclaimed. "In the hall by the front door."

"Could you hide the ball for me?" Seth asked. "Someplace where Knox won't find it."

"No problem," Doren said.

"I'm going to go get Knox," Seth said. "I'll be right back."

Seth ran to the kitchen and out the back door. Dale was working in the garden. He stopped pushing his wheelbarrow and waved at Seth. "Everything all right?"

"I'm good," Seth called. "I just have a question for Knox. Then I'll be gone again."

"Okay," Dale said, returning to his task. "Good to see you."

Seth hustled to the pool. Tess splashed in the shallow end, giggling at the flock of fairies attending her. Knox sat on the patio, using a magnifying glass to make a wood chip smoke.

"Hey," Seth said. "That's my magnifying glass."

Knox looked up. "Seth breath? I thought you were at camp."

"I'm not back for long," Seth said. "Just a quick visit."

Knox held up the magnifying glass. "I found this in the attic."

"You can keep it," Seth said. "My better one is in my emergency kit."

"I have a big one at home that can cut through stone," Knox bragged.

"I bet," Seth said. "Look, I need your help with something."

"I can recommend some extra-strength mouthwashes," Knox said.

"I'm serious," Seth replied. "I'm playing a game at camp. And you can help me win."

"Oh, no," Knox said, shaking his head. "I'm not going to summer camp. Being bored is bad enough. I don't want to be told how I have to be bored by a bunch of counselors."

"You'll just help our team win a game," Seth said. "No counselors."

"Why would I want to help *your* team?" Knox said. "Can I be on the other team?"

"I thought you might want to win your basketball back," Seth said casually.

"My basketball?"

"The one signed by Jordan and LeBron and everybody? What's it worth to you?"

Knox threw his head back and laughed. "What? Are you holding it hostage?"

"It's in a safe place," Seth said. "For now."

Knox laughed again. "You're so dumb! Do you actually think all those players really signed it?"

Seth just stared. There was nothing to say.

Knox kept chuckling. "I wrote those names myself. I didn't even check what their real signatures look like. Do you think I would actually play with a ball like that? It would be in a vault."

Seth tried to reformulate his strategy. "Just come. This camp will blow your mind. I'll give you an awesome prize if you help our team win."

"What awesome prize?"

"I don't know," Seth said. "Gold or something. Maybe jewels."

Knox laughed again. "How dumb do you think I am? You don't have gold. How far away is this camp?"

"Have you heard about VR?" Seth asked.

Knox gave a huff. "Virtual reality? I probably know a hundred times more about it than you do."

"It's a virtual reality camp," Seth said. "We can get there from the living room."

"You're such a liar," Knox said.

"Prove me wrong," Seth replied.

Knox twirled the magnifying glass in his hand. "Only because I'm bored."

"Hey, Seth!" Tess cried from the pool. "I thought you were gone!"

"Just a quick visit," he replied.

"Aren't the fairies beautiful?" Tess asked.

"They look like bugs to me," Seth said.

"If you say so," she said with a wink.

"Those bugs really do follow her around," Knox said. "It's weird."

"Is she okay if we leave her here?" Seth asked quietly.

"Dale is keeping an eye on us," Knox said. "No unsupervised swimming is a big rule for Grandpa and Grandma Larsen."

"Follow me," Seth said.

He led Knox into the house, through the kitchen, and into the living room. Newel and Doren stood near the barrel.

"What is with Grandpa letting these goats roam the house?" Knox said. "I can't believe they haven't eaten the furniture."

"Maybe you *should* sacrifice him," Newel suggested.

Seth pinched the back of Knox's neck.

"Ow!" Knox cried. He punched Seth on the shoulder hard enough to make it ache. "What was that for?"

Seth rubbed his shoulder. "I was giving you a VR implant."

"You make up the worst lies ever," Knox said, looking around. "Do you have a headset?"

"Headsets are old school," Seth said. "The newest tech goes right into your nerves."

"Nice try," Knox said. "They don't have anything like that yet."

"Really?" Seth asked. "Climb in that barrel and say, 'Wyrmroost.'"

Knox glanced at the barrel and snorted. "Yeah, right. It looks pretty high tech."

"Prove me wrong," Seth challenged again.

"Want to make a bet?" Knox asked.

"Sure," Seth said. "Anything."

Knox stared at him. "Let's just see." He climbed into the barrel and stood there. "What do I say again?"

"Squat down and say, 'Wyrmroost.'"

"I'm not squatting," Knox said. "You're going to tip me over or something."

"I could tip you over now," Seth said. "You have to get

the implant closer to the sensors. Squat and say it. If nothing happens, you're right, I'm wrong."

Knox squatted out of sight. "Wyrmroost."

Seth moved forward and peeked into the barrel. It was empty.

"Want me to tie you up?" Seth asked the satyrs.

"We'll settle for ratting on you as soon as we're asked," Newel said. "Go save Wyrmroost."

"And, seriously," Doren said. "Don't get your cousin killed."

"I'll do my best," Seth said, climbing into the barrel.

CHAPTER TWENTY-SIX

Gambit

"Brunwin?" Seth called.

The minotaur lifted him out of the barrel.

Knox was looking around the room in astonishment. "How are you doing this?" he asked.

"I told you, virtual reality," Seth said. "Cool tech, right? You've met Brunwin?"

"Just barely," Knox said. "But this can't be happening."

"And yet it is," Seth said. "Hard to argue with that. Now, we really do need to win this game. Are you listening?"

"Okay, yeah," Knox said.

"This is a big environment," Seth said. "It's called Blackwell Keep. Looks totally real. The game is like capture the flag. This fort is our base. Brunwin will take you to a door. When he gives you a signal, you'll go to a dome on a ridge and get a golden scepter guarded by a moose."

"A moose?" Knox asked.

"It's a weird game," Seth explained. "The programmers are kind of insane. Anyhow, tell the moose you were sent by Seth to get the scepter and then bring it back to the fort."

"Won't the other team try to get me?" Knox asked.

Seth shook his head. "You're not officially part of the game. They can't get you. You may see weird stuff. Animals. People. Just hurry back to the fort. They shouldn't be able to mess with you."

"They may try to tell you things to trick you," Brunwin said. "They might make offers. Don't listen. Bring the scepter to the fort."

"Doing this right is a big deal," Seth said. "This is the championship. I saved this loophole for when we really needed it. The other team is full of complete jerks. Worst of the worst. Whatever they offer, they're lying. And whatever they offer, tell us and we'll triple it. This game is the whole point of the camp. I'm serious. You'll be a hero."

"Okay," Knox said. "You're sure the other team can't tag me?"

"Try to avoid them," Seth said. "But yeah, I'm sure. I'm going to go cause a distraction. Brunwin will take you to the starting point. Are you good?"

"I guess," Knox said. He looked around the room. "I still don't get how this works."

"Maybe we'll show you the technology after the game," Seth said. "It's really incredible. Brunwin, we need to disguise him somehow."

"I'm well ahead of you," the minotaur said. "We don't

want him recognized before we send him on his mission. I have a robe for him."

"Then we're ready?" Seth asked.

"Go to the stables," Brunwin said. "I'll await your signal."

They exited the room. Brunwin thanked the goblin and reminded him to keep quiet about their visit to the barrel.

"Who is this?" the goblin asked, indicating Knox. "I'm supposed to inform Marat and Stan if anyone comes through."

"I approve it," Seth said.

"I'm supposed to be told in advance," the goblin complained.

"You weren't informed because this newcomer is a secret of the highest priority," Brunwin said. "This is happening on Seth's authority and mine. We'll make sure all who need to know are informed."

The goblin growled softly. "I don't like it. I was given specific orders. I'm not taking the fall for this."

"No authority at Blackwell Keep can overrule Seth," Brunwin said harshly. "And I'm your superior too. You risk trouble only if you divulge our secret. Understood?"

Mumbling unintelligibly, the goblin waved them away.

After parting from Brunwin and Knox, Seth walked briskly to the stables. He wanted to run but was worried it would draw too much attention.

"This is so exciting," Calvin said from his pocket. "I thought the ogre was good. And the Path of Dreams. But sixty dragons? That wins easily."

"You can't come with me," Seth said.

"Oh, no," Calvin said. "Don't even try. We've been over this. If you go down, I go down."

"Not this time," Seth said. "My only chance to get away is going to a certain place. I don't want to say where that is until the last minute. If you come, it could mess up my chances."

"Are you making this up to protect me?" Calvin asked suspiciously.

"No," Seth said. "I'll explain afterward. You'll understand."

"Explain now," Calvin challenged.

"I don't want to say it out loud," Seth said. "Just in case the dragons are somehow spying. But there is something you can do for me."

"I'm listening," Calvin said.

"Think you can make it to the safe hut ahead of Knox?" Seth asked. "It would be nice if somebody could tell Henrick about our plan to make sure he'll hand over the scepter."

"Consider it done," Calvin said.

As Seth crossed the yard outside the stables, he heard a voice call out his name. Turning, he found Simrin hurrying to catch up to him.

"Your grandfather is looking for you," the snakelike woman informed him. "As is your sister."

"Okay," Seth said. "I just want to check on Noble. That horse did an amazing job getting me back here."

"Perhaps it can wait until later?" Simrin asked. "Stan is anxious to speak with you."

"Tell him I'll be right there," Seth said. "We're in a

stalemate with the dragons. I'm already at the stables. He can wait an extra minute."

Simrin paused. "Stan noticed you were missing. There has been some concern you might take rash action to help Henrick."

Seth forced his best imitation of an incredulous laugh. "Against all those dragons? Are you kidding? What am I going to do, try to get the scepter on horseback?"

Simrin's eyes narrowed. "There are griffins in the stables."

Seth huffed and shook his head. "I would never risk the scepter by trying to steal it with a griffin. I promise."

"Let me accompany you to visit Noble," Simrin said. "Then I will escort you to your grandfather."

Seth frowned. "Listen, I'm the caretaker here. I'm going to the stable and I don't need a babysitter. Tell Grandpa I'll be there soon."

Simrin gave a nod, then turned and ran. She was fast!

Seth realized she was going to tell on him.

He dashed into the stables and ran down the aisle. "Hi, Glory," he said as he sprinted past the mare. "Hey, Noble!" he said when he reached his mount. "Great job today! You're the best."

Farther down the aisle, Seth saw the two dwarfs. They held tethers connected to Tempest.

"Are you ready?" Seth called.

"We put the training saddle on Tempest," Obun announced.

"Training saddle?" Seth asked, skidding to a stop as

he reached the dwarfs, wondering how long he had before Simrin returned with Grandpa.

"It's a tad bulkier than a standard saddle or a racing saddle," Didger said. "But it provides the rider more support. A griffin in training might turn too sharply and break your back or send you flying from the saddle."

"Okay," Seth said. "I do want sharp turns. How do I mount up?"

"Haven't you ever ridden a griffin?" Obun asked.

"I flew with one before," Seth said. "Never in a training saddle."

Seth reached into his pocket and took out Calvin. Then he crouched, pretending to check his shoelace as he set the nipsie on the ground. Calvin gave a thumbs-up and rushed to hide in some straw.

"Do you know your destination?" Didger asked. "We should make sure Tempest knows where to go before she takes off. It could prove important with so many dragons out there."

"Let's tell her last minute," Seth said. "We should hurry. I'm running out of time."

Obun and Didger helped Seth into a saddle with a high back, then secured straps around his legs and waist. "This isn't super comfortable," Seth said.

"The back of the saddle is less rigid than it seems," Didger said. "Under enough pressure it will bend. It could save your spine today."

"How do I get out of the saddle?" Seth asked.

"Ingenious, really," Obun said. "Just tug these two

releases at the same time." He showed Seth the straps he meant. "Tug hard, lad, and you'll be free."

"Brunwin told us you were sure about this," Didger said. "But are you really? There are so many dragons out there."

"We'll outrun them," Seth said. "Right, Tempest?"

The griffin gave a screech.

"She's fast," Obun said. "And inventive. And still half wild. Normally I would say riding her on a clear day with no enemies would be a significant risk. But I don't think any of our other griffins would have as good a chance against these terrible odds."

"I should go," Seth said.

"The destination?" Didger reminded him.

"The Fairy Queen's shrine," Seth whispered.

"The shrine?" Obun exclaimed. "Doesn't matter if you're caretaker. You'll be obliterated for setting foot there."

"Maybe," Seth acknowledged. "But my sister is becoming friends with the Fairy Queen. The Queen has helped her before in emergencies. I'm hoping she'll help me. I can't think of any other options. I better go."

"Fairy Queen's shrine," Didger repeated loudly. "Do you understand?"

Tempest bobbed her head and screeched.

Obun and Didger untethered the griffin. Tempest flexed her wings.

The door at the far end of the stable opened. Simrin stood there. Seth could see Grandpa, Grandma, Kendra, and Marat following behind.

"Stop that boy!" Simrin ordered.

"Seth!" Grandpa called from behind her.

"Go, Tempest," Seth urged. "Now! Fly!"

Apparently *fly* was the magic word.

Tempest raced down the aisle to the nearest door. It burst open, and the griffin sprang into the air, rising in a spiral, wings flapping aggressively. The protests from the ground quickly faded out of earshot. Looking down, Seth saw Blackwell Keep shrinking below him. He realized that the spiraling climb enabled Tempest to gain altitude without passing beyond the barriers protecting the keep.

After some time, the griffin swung to one side, tucked her wings, and entered a steep dive. Seth felt like his insides rose to his shoulders, and he couldn't help laughing as tingles coursed through him.

Still diving, Tempest passed beyond the barrier.

And then the real ride began.

Several dragons came at them, but Seth could only barely track what was happening. It was like riding a roller coaster designed by a mad genius. And the train kept jumping off the tracks, only to land back on them again.

Seth squinted against the wind roaring over him. They looped and dove and swerved and climbed and spiraled. Often Seth had no sense of direction, not even up and down. Dragons flashed in and out of view. He could hear their bellows over the wind in his ears.

He tried to see if he could spot Knox moving beyond the wall, but when he tried to look at the ground, he was lucky to catch sight of a greenish grayish blur. Otherwise he saw sky.

They darted in and out of danger so quickly that Seth had no time to fear specific threats. Almost every dip and roll came as a jarring surprise. Their erratic movements were like hang gliding in a hurricane, whipping from one direction to another without warning. Some of the turns made the edges of Seth's vision darken. A dragon wing brushed by close enough to touch. Scales of different colors blurred around him. Tempest dove, falling faster than seemed possible, only to swoop up again and bank in a spiraling curve.

Enormous teeth snapped, and wicked claws slashed, but the griffin bobbed and weaved and plunged, remaining unscathed. Tempest shrieked. Seth yelled. The wind of their speed tore away the sound.

As if they had reached the eye of the hurricane, the flight suddenly evened out. They climbed steadily. Seth was so dizzy that it took a moment for him to realize they weren't turning or corkscrewing anymore.

Looking around, he found all the dragons behind and below him. None seemed able to keep up. Blackwell Keep was shrinking in the distance. There was no chance of seeing Knox. Seth hoped his cousin was all right.

Kendra reached the walls of the keep in time to watch Seth and his griffin weaving through the host of dragons. As dragons pursued, converging from all directions, the griffin looked trapped several times, only to narrowly avoid destruction with its unpredictable maneuvers. Her eyes had difficulty following the acrobatics, as a bank to the left became a dive to the right interrupted by a tight loop and then a corkscrewing plunge. No toddler could have scribbled a wilder route.

The adroit griffin used the quantity of dragons as an advantage, cutting between them to create congestion, often almost causing collisions. As the dragons corrected to avoid one another, Seth and his griffin knifed through the openings.

Kendra kept waiting for the griffin to try to make it to the safe hut. A multitude of dragons had gathered around the dome on the ridge, apparently anticipating the same eventuality. But the griffin never attempted to get close. Seth and his winged mount were disappearing into the distance. Against all odds, they were getting away.

Kendra became aware of Grandpa Sorenson at her side. "What is he doing?" she asked.

"Oh, no!" Grandpa exclaimed in alarm. "He wouldn't. What am I saying? Of course he would!"

"What?" Kendra asked.

Grandpa pointed at the ground beyond the wall, and Kendra saw a figure jogging away from the keep. "Is that . . . ?" she asked hesitantly.

"Your cousin Knox," Grandpa said.

A huge white dragon with smooth, pearlescent scales swooped at Knox, only to draw up short. Other dragons followed suit, closing as if to attack, then veering away, either gaining altitude or landing off to one side. A big red dragon planted itself directly in front of Knox, blocking his way forward, only to shift out of his path as the boy drew near.

"He's going to the safe hut," Kendra said. "Why aren't the dragons stopping him?"

"That little rogue," Grandpa muttered. "He's pulling the same trick they used on the ogre."

Understanding dawned for Kendra. "Knox doesn't know."

"Somehow Seth brought him here and talked him into fetching the scepter," Grandpa said.

Kendra watched her cousin trotting forward. What did he see instead of dragons? Did he have any inkling how near he was to death? "Will it work?" she asked.

"I would never have tried it," Grandpa said. "The theory is sound. But to risk an innocent child? Without his knowledge? I would have let Blackwell Keep burn. I would have let the dragons lay siege to the safe hut. Henrick would have starved or made a run for it. Running would have failed. If the alcetaur perished from hunger, the dragons could have accessed the hut; its magic operates only if there is a living being to protect within its walls. Wyrmroost would have fallen." Grandpa became silent for a moment. "I would have never let Seth do this, Kendra. I would have stopped him. But it might work."

"If Knox is protected, wouldn't other people be protected if the dragons eventually got loose?" Kendra asked.

"There are specific rules at this sanctuary to protect ignorant mortals," Grandpa replied. "The unbelief of mortals can help repel magical creatures out in the world at large, but it carries no specific protections beyond that. If the dragons get loose, all of humanity will be in danger, as they were long ago."

A gasp announced that Grandma Sorenson had arrived and seen Knox on his way to the safe hut. Marat stood with her.

"That can't be Knox," Grandma said.

"It's him," Kendra said.

Grandma's hand covered her mouth. "The poor boy!"

"The founding treaty of Wyrmroost appears to be protecting him," Grandpa said. "That and his ignorance." He looked to the sky. "Save your worry for Seth."

"The ogre trick," Grandma said. "Seth gave the order. Now the dragons can follow him anywhere."

Grandpa turned to Marat. "If Seth ordered an innocent to retrieve the scepter, could the dragons follow Seth outside the borders of the sanctuary?"

"Absolutely," Marat said. "They could and they would. And once outside, they would be under no mandate to return."

Grandpa teared up. A sob escaped him. "That foolish, brave boy. He knew exactly what he was doing. He sacrificed himself to save the sanctuary."

"Marat could have stopped him," Grandma said, "when Seth fled on the griffin. Before he passed beyond the protective barrier. Marat could have taken dragon shape and stopped him."

"Perhaps," Marat said. "Tempest is extremely fast. If she saw me in pursuit, she may have fled beyond the barrier at a less advantageous altitude. And do not forget, your grandson is the caretaker. None of us have the right to override his decisions."

"We have a duty to protect him," Grandma said.

"From foolishness, perhaps," Marat said. "This plan is not foolishness."

"How long could that griffin elude the dragons?" Grandpa asked.

Marat squinted into the distance. "Celebrant would clearly prefer to take Seth alive. None of the dragons used their breath weapons. Tempest is our fastest, wildest, most skillful griffin. She could probably last another twenty minutes if she makes good use of the available space."

"Can the dragons hunt Seth indefinitely?" Grandma asked.

"No," Marat said. "Once his innocent pawn is back behind safe barriers, the dragons have until sunrise the following day to exact their revenge. After that, all barriers at Wyrmroost will guard Seth as they did before."

"Is there any chance of him lasting that long?" Kendra asked.

Marat gave a small smile. "There are perhaps three places at Wyrmroost where Seth could successfully hide, assuming he could get access. All of them would take him to a place beyond the regular parameters of the preserve. Tempest appeared to be heading toward one of them."

"Where?" Grandma asked.

"The Fairy Queen's shrine," Marat said.

"That clever boy," Grandpa muttered.

"Would the Queen admit him?" Grandma asked Kendra.

"I can't say for sure," Kendra said. "They met at Zzyzx. I hope so."

Everything went white as Tempest soared into a cloud. The cold, onrushing vapor quickly dampened Seth. He tucked his head to breathe easier.

They swooped down out of the cloud but soon darted into another. And a third. Tempest climbed up into the blue sky as if heading for outer space, then began to plunge. The air rushing over Seth became a howling gale as they gained velocity, sacrificing altitude for speed.

The dragons from Blackwell Keep were even farther back, but others were converging from different parts of the sanctuary, coming from the left and the right. The dive steepened, arrowing toward a mountainside. Seth saw a high waterfall that split in two around an outcrop.

Of the several dragons coming toward them, none were close yet, so Seth assumed Tempest was streaking toward their destination. His eyes scoured the mountainside for signs of a shrine. He had never visited a Fairy Queen shrine, but by Kendra's description, he knew it involved a spring and a bowl and a little fairy statue.

As the mountainside drew nearer, Seth tightened his grip on the saddle. Once they landed, the dragons would not be far behind. His life might be almost over. Trespassing at the shrine could kill him. If it didn't, the dragons could still get him unless the Fairy Queen answered his pleas.

Tempest zoomed toward a projection of dark gray stone. The griffin's wings spread, slowing them at the last moment. They landed at the base of the gray stone. Seth fumbled with the release straps, panicking as nothing happened. He did not want to get roasted by dragons because he couldn't get out of his saddle.

After a few tugs, he got it right, and the straps binding him to the saddle went slack. Tempest bobbed her head toward a wide shelf of rock ahead of them. Water trickled from the shelf. It had to be the shrine.

"Go, Tempest," Seth said. "Get away. Escape the dragons."

The griffin took two steps back and screeched, looking hesitant.

Seth waved his arms. "Go!"

He turned and ran to the shelf. When he glanced back, Tempest was flying away. At least five dragons were closing in. He didn't take time to give a good look.

"I'm sorry!" Seth cried, running across the shelf to the spring. "Sorry, Fairy Queen! Don't kill me! This is an emergency!"

He saw a little golden bowl beside a tiny statue of a fairy. He dropped to his knees in front of the statue. The fact that he was still alive seemed like an encouraging sign.

"This is Seth Sorenson," he said, speaking quickly, unsure if anybody was listening. "You know my sister? Kendra? I'm friends with Bracken? I met you at Zzyzx. I gave Kendra the sword that killed the Demon King?"

A light breeze wafted over him, smelling like fresh snow and ripe fruit. Then he caught the scent of evergreen sap, and a salt-tinged hint of the sea.

"I need a huge favor," Seth continued. "Dragons are coming. I need to enter the fairy realm. The dragons can follow me anywhere. But I bet they can't go there. You let Kendra visit. Please hide me!"

Seth heard mighty roars above and behind him. Glancing up, he saw several dragons closing in, moments away, jewel-bright scales gleaming, teeth flashing.

"Please!" Seth shouted. "They'll kill me! Please!"

Shimmering whiteness temporarily filled his vision. Still on his knees, Seth felt like he was sliding and turning. Then the whiteness vanished and Seth knelt in a green field under a clear sky streaked with warm colors, as if a sunset had leaked and filled the entire expanse. No mountainside. No dragons. No spring. No little statue.

Just a man.

He was extraordinarily pale but not sickly. His ageless features held a serene expression with a slight smile. His hooded robe shimmered between silver and gray.

His eyes were kind, with a hint of sadness. He stared at Seth with interest.

"You're not the Fairy Queen," Seth said.

"I am not," the man replied, his calm voice matching the emotions in his gaze.

"Did she bring me here?" Seth asked.

"I brought you here," the man said.

Seth stood up. He had knelt so hurriedly at the shrine that both knees were bleeding. He hadn't felt the scrapes at the time. He was still unwinding from the near-death experience. Part of him had not expected to survive. But now he was evidently safe. "Thank you so much."

"It was the least I could do, Seth Sorenson."

"Do I know you?"

The man's smile increased a fraction. "You brought your sister the sword that ended my bondage."

Seth's eyebrows went up. "You're him! The Fairy King!"

"I am," he said.

"I thought you didn't talk anymore," Seth said. "I mean, I heard . . ."

"I haven't had much to say," the Fairy King said slowly. "It has been a difficult transition."

"You saved my life," Seth said.

The Fairy King stepped forward and embraced Seth. "It was nothing. I can never repay you, Seth. Not in a thousand lifetimes."

The embrace ended and the Fairy King stepped back. Seth felt a little woozy. Pure love and appreciation had seemed to flow into him during the hug.

"How did you know I would be here?" Seth asked.

"I didn't," the Fairy King said simply. "I seldom leave the palace, but today I went for a stroll. I ended up here. And I heard your cry." The Fairy King placed a hand on Seth's shoulder. "This is a realm of purity. Those who have been touched by darkness do not belong here. We share a peculiar bond, Seth. I have been touched by darkness. As have you."

"I'm a shadow charmer," Seth said.

"And I wallowed in darkness through ages of relentless torment," the Fairy King said. His eyes became faraway, his voice nearly emotionless. "I did not believe there would be an end. I had lost myself in ways I could never explain. Through the haze of my limited faculties I assumed I must have joined the undead." His eyes returned to Seth. "And then it ended. And now I am free. No more chains. My prison, my hell, is becoming a paradise. And I hardly know how I fit in. But I know I am grateful to you and your sister. I will never forget."

The Fairy King stepped back.

"I need one more favor," Seth said.

"Not one," the Fairy King admonished. "Endless favors. I can never repay you."

"Can you send me to Fablehaven?" Seth asked. "To the shrine there? I need to get back to Blackwell Keep at Wyrmroost. I have a way there from the house at Fablehaven. My family needs me. I have to help my sister. And I need to make sure my cousin is all right."

"As you wish," the Fairy King said with a small nod. "Follow me."

CHAPTER TWENTY-SEVEN

Alone

K endra watched from the top of the outer wall of Blackwell Keep with Grandma, Grandpa, and Marat as Knox ran back from the safe hut, the golden scepter in his hand. All around him, dragons hissed and growled, bellowed and roared. They gouged the earth with their claws and shattered boulders with their tails. They exhaled fire into the sky, and icy blasts of frost, and various shades of lightning, and mysterious gasses.

But none of the dragons burned up Knox. Or froze him, shocked him, poisoned him, devoured him, or flattened him. Celebrant tried to attack him. The Dragon King got closer than the others but still stopped short. Eyes fierce, Celebrant opened his great jaws, but nothing came out. The Dragon King moved to block Knox's path but then slid out of the way at the last second.

As Knox neared the keep, several dragons took on human shapes. They chased him, but he ran from them as if playing tag. Though a few of the dragons in human form got close enough to touch him, none did. They didn't tackle him, or trip him, or restrain him. It became plain that they simply couldn't.

The humanoid dragons called out to Knox, urging him to stop or wait. They promised riches if he dropped the scepter. Knox ignored them and kept running.

"He's going to do it," Kendra said.

"It looks that way," Grandpa said carefully, clearly not ready to believe until Knox made it within the walls of the keep.

Then Knox reached the postern door and passed out of sight.

The dragons wailed in frustration. Several shot lightning or fire at the keep, only to have it blocked by the invisible barrier.

"Impressive," Marat said. "The barrier seems as strong as ever. I believe the problem with our defenses is solved."

"Let's go see your cousin," Grandma said to Kendra.

They found Knox in the courtyard, not far from the door through the wall. He still held the scepter. Brunwin stood with him.

"Good job, my boy," Grandpa Sorenson called.

Knox looked their way. "You guys are here too? Why was I the last to hear about this?"

"How much did Seth tell you about this place?" Grandpa asked as they approached.

"He said it's virtual reality," Knox explained. "I didn't know tech like this existed. No headset? Everything looks so real! How did you get hold of it?"

Grandma Sorenson reached Knox and gave him a hug. Kendra hugged him as well.

"Everyone has secrets," Grandpa Sorenson said. "Thanks for being a good sport and helping us win."

"It wasn't very hard," Knox said. "I got worried when those people started chasing me at the end. But when they got close they sort of stopped trying. Seth said nobody would be able to get me. I guess he was right."

"What else did you see?" Kendra asked.

"Same as you," he said.

"People sometimes see the same things differently here," Kendra explained.

"The weather was bizarre," Knox said. "Clouds of dust and light. Whirlwinds. Mist. It looked bad, but the mists and whirlwinds drifted away when I got near. The moose guarding the scepter was probably the scariest part. Those antlers were humongous."

"But the moose let you have it?" Kendra asked.

"Just like Seth told me," Knox said. "He was right about everything."

"I demand audience with the caretaker!" Celebrant boomed.

"Hear that thunder?" Knox asked. "No storm clouds! Such random weather!"

"I feared this was coming," Marat said. "I will try to placate him." He hurried toward the nearest stairs up the wall.

"This is an emergency," Celebrant roared. "I demand an immediate audience!"

"Ruth, would you take Knox back home?" Grandpa asked. "Then stand guard. If Seth reached the fairy realm, he might make his way back to Fablehaven through the shrine. He mustn't come back to Blackwell Keep until sunrise tomorrow or the dragons will be able to enter to get him."

"This game sounds complicated," Knox said. "I want to see the dragons. How are the graphics?"

"Amazing," Kendra said. "But for now you should go."

Grandma led Knox away.

"I will not be ignored," Celebrant threatened. "Show yourself, caretaker. Counsel with me!"

"Do you want to go underground?" Grandpa asked. "There may be depths below the keep where we can't hear him."

"Won't it be a bad move if I hide during an emergency?" Kendra asked.

"It isn't ideal," Grandpa admitted.

"Ah, Marat," Celebrant shouted. "I believe you are no longer the caretaker. Bring me the masters of this keep! Unless they have fled?"

"I want to listen," Kendra said. "If Celebrant needs proof a caretaker is here, I may need to show myself. Maybe Marat can stand by me."

"If Celebrant sees you are paralyzed by dragon fear, he can claim you're unfit for duty," Grandpa said. "It might be safer to keep you completely out of sight."

"We should listen," Kendra insisted.

Grandpa led Kendra into the tower nearest to where Marat stood on the wall. From within the tower, Kendra listened to Marat and Celebrant argue back and forth.

"I reiterate, there is a caretaker here," Marat insisted. "But it is not her responsibility to be at your disposal every moment. I would be delighted to set up a meeting for tomorrow."

"Not tomorrow, not tonight, not in an hour," Celebrant demanded. "I know she is in there. This is an emergency."

"You are causing the emergency," Marat placated.

"They caused the emergency when they moved a scepter without permission!" Celebrant blustered. "I am a caretaker equal to them in authority and deserve to be consulted about the movement of scepters."

"It was the scepter that pertains to their medallion," Marat soothed. "None of your affair. You have your own scepter."

"All seven scepters on this preserve are my affair!" Celebrant ranted. "I saw Kendra enter the keep. She has not exited. I have reason to believe her brother has fled the sanctuary. If Kendra will not talk to me, I am going to declare her incompetent and take over her duties."

"You can't do that!" Marat protested.

"Are you sure?" Celebrant asked. The Dragon King raised his voice even more. "Kendra? I know you can hear me, Kendra! Come face me or I must assume you are incompetent. This is an urgent matter. A real caretaker is required at Blackwell Keep. Not a pretender."

"Come back tomorrow," Marat ordered.

"We'll let the barrier decide if she is competent," Celebrant said. "As a caretaker of Wyrmroost, I renounce the incompetent caretaker of Blackwell Keep and demand to take over all responsibilities pertaining to that office!"

"You have no such right!" Marat declared.

"Don't I?" Celebrant asked. "The barrier is feeling mushy all of a sudden. If the caretaker is going to quail behind walls of stone instead of treat with her colleague, I'm not sure my claim can be denied."

Kendra heard the roar of fire and saw a red glare. She peeked through a window to see Celebrant blowing fire directly onto Marat from above. An invisible dome protected Marat, but Celebrant was clearly stretching beyond the unseen barrier protecting the wall to rain fire down on him.

Was the barrier bending? Would it break? Was she being an unfit caretaker?

Kendra gritted her teeth.

From what Celebrant had said, it sounded like Seth might have escaped. But even if her brother had made it to the fairy realm, he couldn't return to Wyrmroost until tomorrow morning.

Should she try to talk to Celebrant? Was there a chance she could resist his power? Calvin could stand alone against dragons. Trask could do it. Patton could do it.

Maybe it was time she figured it out.

What if she froze? Would it be worse than hiding? Probably. It would be proof that she was not a true dragon tamer. Celebrant might denounce her, break through the magical barrier, gobble her up, and destroy the keep.

But what if she succeeded?

In the Path of Dreams, Kendra had felt Seth's hand even without his presence. Sure, they may have been touching while they both dreamed, but in the dream they were separate. And Seth had kept running even when the dragon was about to catch him.

Could that be a sign? Was there a way for Seth to be present even though he was absent? He had risked his life to save Wyrmroost. He had risked his cousin, too, but that was a conversation for another day.

If Seth could risk his life riding through a host of dragons on a griffin, couldn't she do this? Couldn't she look to the example of his courage? Couldn't that make him sort of present?

Or was she kidding herself?

"Kendra!" Celebrant called. "Come to me or forfeit your stewardship! Dragons, attack! This barrier cannot hold! She is a fraud!"

Kendra heard more fire being expelled.

She gripped the unicorn horn. Seth had retrieved it. Didn't that make him kind of present? It also connected her to Bracken.

Bracken, can you hear me? Kendra asked.

In a situation, came the hasty reply. She could feel his panic. Something was wrong.

Me too, Kendra communicated. *I have to talk to a dragon alone.*

Then do it, Bracken urged. *Be strong. The power is—*

His voice in her mind cut off abruptly.

Bracken? Kendra thought with all her effort. *What happened? Bracken? Are you all right?*

She felt no answer.

Something had to be really wrong. Apparently there was trouble all over. A quick peek revealed Celebrant blasting Marat with flame again.

"Attack!" Celebrant thundered.

"I have to," Kendra apologized to Grandpa. He looked pained but didn't move to stop her.

Squeezing the horn tightly, Kendra stepped out from the tower and onto the top of the wall. Lightning and fire crackled and roared against the unseen barrier from multiple directions.

"I'm here," Kendra called.

Celebrant was flung back. After a moment the other dragons stopped attacking.

Leaving Marat behind, the Dragon King moved along the wall to where Kendra stood. If a dragon could smile, Celebrant was doing it. He showed flagrantly carnivorous teeth, and his eyes glowed brightly.

"There you are!" Celebrant said. "Taking a nap, were you?"

He was close now, just beyond the wall from where she stood. If she leaned forward, she could touch his snout. Kendra concentrated on the nostrils. Not the eyes.

She wanted to answer. She had words to say. But her body was betraying her.

"You're not petrified, are you?" Celebrant asked smugly. "That would hardly befit your office. Speak up, Kendra. You're making the wrong impression."

How did they do it? How did Patton make his body work when it was involuntarily frozen? Was it just a matter of willpower? Again she had words to say. Again they would not come.

Celebrant chuckled theatrically. "Is this the caretaker of Blackwell Keep? This stupefied mute? This is an insult to the office of caretaker. She appears unfit for service."

"The girl is weary!" Marat called, rushing along the wall to where Kendra stood. "She has hardly slept. Try again in the morning."

Kendra knew she was not unfit. She and Seth had just retrieved the scepter! She had killed the Demon King! She could remember the feel of Vasilis in her hand, the power humming through her.

In that dark moment, with the demons bearing down on them, her family had needed her. All of fairydom had needed her.

And now her family needed her again.

Kendra felt something shift inside of her.

"No," she said. "We'll talk now."

Celebrant flinched as if she had struck him.

Then the Dragon King leaned as close as he could to the unseen barrier, teeth bared in a snarl, eyes glaring.

"You are an inadequate caretaker," he accused.

Kendra tightened her grip on the horn. Which meant she could move.

Seth had risked his life. He couldn't be here because he had done his job well. He had figured out a way to get the scepter to the keep.

She couldn't let Celebrant win. Not like this.

She looked into his eyes. Her whole body trembled. She needed to end this and get away.

"I feel the same way about you!" she shouted. "You tore down the Perch like a vandal! You keep attacking your fellow caretakers! I denounce you! You are a fake! You are a joke! You can't even stop two children from taking what you want! I demand you return your scepter! If any of your subjects had the courage of a little girl, they would take your crown! Slink back to your hole, worm! We're trying to relax!"

For just a moment, one perfect, silent moment, Celebrant stared not in rage, but in horror.

And Kendra turned her back on him.

"Come back here!" Celebrant bellowed. "How dare you!"

She did not turn. She refused to glance back. Her legs felt unsteady, but she kept walking.

"Nobody turns their back on me!" Celebrant thundered.

Kendra kept walking.

She could hear him breathing fire. Or energy. Or something.

It didn't matter. The barrier would hold.

Celebrant was making a lot of noise.

But underneath it, as she entered the tower, Kendra heard a comforting sound.

Marat was laughing.

CHAPTER TWENTY-EIGHT

Acceptance

Seth was still trying to believe that he was not in trouble. At Fablehaven, he had met Newel and Doren on his way back to the house. They had been coming in his direction. Grandma Sorenson had sent the satyrs to get a boat and rescue him from the island at the center of the fairy pond. It spoke to their friendship that Newel and Doren had been willing to paddle anywhere near that deadly island. But the naiads had already brought Seth a boat and shuttled him across the water, as the Fairy King had promised they would do before bidding Seth farewell.

Seth learned from the satyrs that Knox had returned from Wyrmroost. Despite his confidence that his cousin would be fine, the news was still a huge relief.

Grandma Sorenson had hugged Seth fiercely and smothered him with kisses when he found her guarding the barrel. That was to be expected if she had thought he was dead. It was so great to hear that the plan had worked. The scepter was secure at Blackwell Keep. The barrier was at full strength again. Seth was still convinced the scolding would come eventually.

Instead, Grandma put together a nice meal and sent him to bed. He was so tired, having stayed up the previous night adventuring and riding horses. Not to mention outrunning a dragon horde on a half-trained griffin.

After awakening before sunrise, Grandma Sorenson and the Larsens had shared a delicious breakfast with him. Knox had pestered Seth for another virtual reality experience. Seth had explained how expensive it was to formally enroll in the camp, and how the administrators now viewed Knox as an outlaw for interfering in the game as an unregistered user.

Grandma had the barrel moved to the dungeon to prevent Knox from trying to sneak through. When she brought Seth back to Wyrmroost not long after sunrise there, he received a hero's welcome. Before returning, he had accepted the possibility that he would be stripped of his position as caretaker. Or, if he was irreplaceable for a time, perhaps they would just lock him up?

When he arrived, Marat and the staff were assembled, along with Kendra and Grandpa. Mendigo was there as well, having made his way back to the keep along the roads. Brunwin had given him a wink and a nod while the others cheered.

The opposite of a scolding.

Seth discovered that Tempest had returned on her own. The dragons hadn't even chased her. They had withdrawn from the keep shortly after Kendra had spoken with Celebrant alone. Henrick was back too.

The plan had worked.

Now Seth stood in Grandma and Grandpa Sorenson's room with Kendra, Henrick, and Marat. Surely he would finally be told how reckless he had been. Seth couldn't endure the tension any longer. He knew it was a rookie mistake to draw attention to his crime, but he had to end the suspense.

"Aren't you guys going to scold me?" Seth blurted.

Everyone looked to Grandpa.

"Well, Seth, that depends," Grandpa said. "Do you deserve a scolding?"

Seth paused. He could almost feel the thin ice beneath his feet beginning to crack. He needed to tread carefully. "Not really," he said, as casually as he could manage.

"No?" Grandpa asked, curious.

"I thought of a way to save the sanctuary," Seth said. "I was the only one at risk."

"What about your cousin?" Grandma asked.

"I knew he would be safe," Seth said.

"I've lived and worked on enchanted preserves for over fifty years," Grandpa said. "I wasn't sure Knox was safe. Were you, Marat?"

"I wasn't sure," Marat said.

"Nobody was sure," Grandpa said. "Except you. What

about Kendra? If you had died, she would have been vulnerable to Celebrant."

"I knew she would have the scepter," Seth said.

"But if I couldn't talk to Celebrant, he could denounce me as caretaker and take over," Kendra said.

"I didn't really think that through," Seth admitted. "Sorry."

"It so happens that even though you lived, your sister had to speak to Celebrant alone," Grandpa said.

"You did?" Seth exclaimed. "Really? Solo?"

"And she performed admirably," Marat said. "Though I fear relations may be irreparable. Celebrant was never your friend. But he was willing to pretend in some ways. I believe all pretenses are over. The caretakers of Wyrmroost are at war."

"We were already heading that way," Seth said.

"We have now arrived," Henrick confirmed.

"Any other thoughts?" Grandpa asked Seth.

"I did my best," he said.

Grandpa Sorenson crossed to him and gave him a big hug. "I know you did, my boy. You were placed in an impossible situation, Seth. You assumed the mantle of caretaker for one of the most dangerous sanctuaries on the planet. You had a plan that you believed in. You did your best. How can I scold that?"

The hug ended. Seth stared at his grandpa. "Should I have told you the plan? I wanted to tell you. Would you have helped me improve it?"

"Honestly, I'm afraid I would have stopped you," Grandpa said. "And Wyrmroost would have fallen."

"It would have fallen without Henrick, too," Kendra said. "I can't believe he made it so far with the scepter."

"I used all of my tricks," Henrick said. "All of my knowledge and equipment. It was almost enough to get me back to the keep. But by the time I arrived, too many dragons were standing guard. I was relieved to access the safe hut."

"How did you split into so many people?" Seth asked.

"I have a lot of tools," Henrick said. "Equipment that distracts or attacks or grants limited invisibility. But the crowning jewel of all my gear is the Prism of Reflections. It creates four duplicates, for a total of five, then four more of each, for a total of twenty-five. Some duplicates had heavy distracter spells on them, some light. Mine was right in the middle. The Prism of Reflections even duplicated my gear, including the magical signature given off by the scepter. It gave me a good head start."

"The duplicates looked real," Kendra said.

Henrick shook his head. "All but me were illusions. But the illusions were strong enough that you would think you had felt something if you brushed up against one of them. The Prism creates illusions capable of confusing all five senses. Six senses, really, if you count the distracter spells and replication of magical signatures."

"Your combined actions saved Wyrmroost," Marat said. "I wish that all sanctuaries had been so fortunate. I wanted to wait until you were assembled to share this information. I'm sorry to report that Soaring Cliffs has fallen."

Kendra looked pale. "Bracken," she said numbly.

"And Agad," Marat said. "And many others. We do not know their fates. We lost communication when the dragons took over."

Kendra's jaw was clenched. Tears shimmered in her eyes. She squeezed the unicorn horn in her hands. "I've been trying to contact him. No answer."

Marat went to Kendra and ran a finger along the horn. "Bracken is alive. The nature of the horn would change if he expired."

Kendra broke down into sobs. Seth heard a blend of relief and worry in her weeping. He drew near and rubbed her shoulder.

"Does that mean we have dragons on the loose?" Grandpa said.

"It means there could be many dragons on the prowl," Marat said. "Former captives free to roam the wide world for the first time in centuries. Only time will tell what they do next."

Kendra was slowly regaining control. "Can we help Bracken and Agad?"

"We'll do all we can," Marat said. "The remaining members of Dragonwatch are already organizing a scouting mission, which can hopefully lead to a rescue."

"We can't go," Seth guessed.

"You are bound to Wyrmroost for at least a year," Grandpa said.

"Unless Celebrant lets us appoint a new caretaker," Kendra said.

Marat chuckled. "Which will not happen. Celebrant has learned that you are much stronger adversaries than he first supposed. But you shamed him, Kendra. Deeper than he has ever been shamed. You humiliated him in word and deed."

"I wish I could have heard that," Seth said with a groan. "I miss all the good stuff."

"You weakened his position as Dragon King," Marat continued. "I know Celebrant. He will do everything in his power to block your escape. Only defeating you will satisfy him."

"We have a lot to consider," Grandma said.

"We need more help here," Grandpa said. "I will put out a call to the Knights of the Dawn. The scepter will protect Blackwell Keep from a direct assault. But there are other ways to wage a war. We must try to prepare against every eventuality."

"Reach out to your people," Marat said. "I will reach out to mine. We'll meet tonight to discuss how to go forward."

Marat and Henrick left the room.

Grandma sat beside Kendra, comforting her. Grandpa patted Seth on the arm.

"You two children continue to astound me," Grandpa said. "In only a few days, you have stabilized the defenses of Blackwell Keep, exposed the intentions of the Dragon King, and gained acceptance as the caretakers of Wyrmroost."

"Do they really accept us?" Kendra asked.

"You should hear the chatter around the castle," Grandma said. "The tune has changed since you were first appointed."

"What were they saying before?" Seth wondered.

"There may have been a lack of enthusiasm about your potential to do the job well," Grandpa said diplomatically.

"Will you send someone to help Bracken?" Kendra asked Grandpa. "Some Knights of the Dawn? I don't know the Dragonwatch members."

"It's my top priority," Grandpa said. "We have to find Bracken and Agad, and hopefully we can regain control of Soaring Cliffs. It won't be easy, and our resources are stretched. Other sanctuaries are dealing with rebellion as well."

Kendra sighed. "I'm glad you'll try. Does the Fairy Queen know?"

Grandpa shook his head.

"We have to tell her," Kendra said. "Bracken is her son. She may have ways to help."

"We'll get a message to her somehow," Grandpa said. He patted Seth's arm. "I think someone in your room will be eager to greet you."

"The Tiny Hero!" Seth said.

He went and opened his door in time to see a miniature figure scuttling away toward the nightstand. Seth closed the door.

"Were you spying on us?" Seth asked.

Calvin stopped and looked up at Seth. "It's what I do! I think your grandfather spotted me. Sharp eyes."

"You could have just come in," Seth said.

"It seemed like a family conversation," Calvin said. "I wanted you to think you had your privacy."

Seth walked over and scooped him up. "Did you make it to Henrick before Knox?"

"I sure did," Calvin stated proudly.

"There wasn't a lot of time," Seth said.

"I whistled up a bird," Calvin said. "A thrush. Not as impressive as a dragon, but serviceable. The trick is learning how to steer them."

"Whistled it up?" Seth asked.

"I call them with my pipes," Calvin said. "It's really convenient when it works."

"You have lots of hidden talents."

"So do you."

"Good job finding the scepter," Seth said. "You really did save the day. Kendra and I are getting a lot of credit, but we'd be toast without you."

Calvin beamed up at him. "Just doing my duty. It's not every day you get to ride a dragon."

"Kendra was able to talk to a dragon alone," Seth said. "You can too. I'm the only loser who can't."

"You're the *loser* who really saved the day," Calvin said. "I can't believe you went to the fairy realm. You were right not to bring me. I doubt they would have let me in."

"I met somebody there," Seth said. "He asked me not to tell anyone."

"Must have been a unicorn," Calvin said. "Or an astrid. Not a lot of males in the fairy realm."

"You know a lot," Seth said.

"I keep my eyes open," Calvin said. "I'm always learning."

"I'm learning too," Seth said.

"Learning what?"

"If you're going to take a huge risk, and you want to stay out of trouble, it really helps if your plan actually works." Seth started rummaging in his emergency kit.

"What are you looking for?" Calvin asked.

Seth pulled out an onyx model of a tower and a slip of paper. "Let's go get Kendra. I think we need to send the dragons a message."

Kendra and Seth stood on the wall near where the Perch had been destroyed. A few jagged pieces of lumber still projected from the stonework. Behind them huddled Grandma and Grandpa Sorenson, Marat, and several members of the Blackwell Keep staff.

Seth leaned over the brink so he could see Brunwin crouching down below on the bare ground just beyond the castle wall. The minotaur looked up and waved an arm. Then he turned and trotted back toward the gate.

Seth held up the paper from his emergency kit. The words were written in gibberish, followed by a phonetical translation in English. Agad had suggested he simply needed to utter the phrase to activate the magic.

Seth spoke the nonsensical syllables, then watched as the tiny tower Brunwin had placed down below began to expand and ascend. The stone of the tower was a little darker than the gray blocks of Blackwell Keep, but lightened to match the stone of the keep as it grew. The flat top of the square tower stopped rising as it drew even to the height of the wall, and complementary battlements sprouted up. As the transformation ended, the tower fused to the keep as if part of the original design. The area atop the tower was at least twice the size the wooden Perch had been.

Seth breathed a sigh of relief. The tower had conformed to the keep better than he had hoped. Part of him had worried the new tower might damage the wall.

Kendra hugged him from behind. "It's perfect," she gushed.

A cheer went up from the assembled staff.

Marat peered down at the new tower. "That was highly adaptable magic," he said. "A first-rate enchantment. It's a strong statement, Seth. Well done."

For a moment all was still. Then, in the distance, faint enough that it might have come from his imagination, Seth thought he heard a dragon roar.

THE ADVENTURE CONTINUES IN
DRAGONWATCH, BOOK TWO

COMING IN 2018

Acknowledgments

Publishing my stories is a team effort, and I enjoy thanking the individuals involved. I'm excited to work once again with some of my favorite people at Shadow Mountain Publishing and Simon & Schuster (Aladdin imprint) to bring *Dragonwatch* to readers!

I must thank Emily Watts, Chris Schoebinger, and Liesa Abrams for their remarkable editorial skills. Each of them helped improve and clarify the story. I also got useful feedback from my brilliant agent, Simon Lipskar.

Many others provided valuable reactions as well. Thanks to Mary Mull, Sadie Mull, Jason and Natalie Conforto, Cherie Mull, Bryson Mull, Tucker Davis, and Pam Mull for finding opportunities to improve the story and for catching mistakes.

Numerous people combined their talents to produce and market *Dragonwatch*. I must share my deep appreciation for Brandon Dorman, who once again created an awesome cover image and other outstanding illustrations to help bring the book to life. Thanks also to the production team at Shadow Mountain, including editor Emily Watts, art director Richard Erickson, and typographer Rachael Ward, and to the marketing and sales team at Shadow Mountain, including Dave Brown, Julia McCracken, John Rose, Ilise

Levine, Sarah Cobabe, and, of course, Chris Schoebinger. In addition, special thanks to the team at Aladdin for their constant support, including Mara Anastas, Liesa Abrams, Catherine Hayden, Carolyn Swerdloff, and Mary Marotta.

As always, I owe so much to my family for their love and patience. My kids light up my life, and their mom continues to be a huge support in my writing. My parents and siblings have also helped me in numerous ways.

And finally, thank you, dear reader, for giving *Dragonwatch* a try. Without you, my stories would serve no purpose. I'll share more thoughts with you in the following note.

Note to Readers

I have pondered for years how to bring the characters of Fablehaven back to life in a new series. In 2006, *Fablehaven* was my first published novel. I finished the series by completing the fifth book in 2010, and mentioned at the back of the book that I would not write a sixth volume. I did, however, express hope I would one day create a sequel series.

That day has arrived!

The idea for Dragonwatch evolved over the past few years, and it eventually became a story I had to share. This story is the first installment of a five-book series. I will do my best to write a new book each year until I am done.

If you enjoyed *Dragonwatch* and haven't read the previous Fablehaven books, I encourage you to dive into them. You'll learn a lot more about Kendra and Seth, their friends and family, and the enchanted preserves they protect, and you'll get to experience a bunch of fun adventures.

If you are up to date with Fablehaven but haven't tried my other novels, consider Five Kingdoms, the story of a group of friends who are kidnapped into another world. It is fast-paced and is written for the kind of reader who enjoys Fablehaven. I'm currently working on the fifth and final book in the Five Kingdoms series. It's going to have a big, cool finale. You might also consider trying Beyonders or The Candy Shop War.

I can't wait to bring readers more books in the Dragon-watch series. If you think the books are fun, spread the word to others who might enjoy them! Your book purchases and recommendations enable me to keep writing these stories, so thank you for your support.

If you would like to connect with me, search for my author page on Facebook, try @brandonmull on Twitter, find @writerbrandon on Instagram, or check brandonmull.com.

Reading Guide

1. Why was Bracken worried to let Kendra talk to the demon Jubaya? Why did Kendra decide to speak to her? Do you feel she made a good choice? Why or why not?

2. Seth sometimes gets bothered by his cousin Knox. In what ways are the two boys different? In what ways are they similar? How could their similarities and differences lead to trouble between them?

3. What similarities does Kendra share with her cousin Tess? What differences exist between them? Why do you think they seem to get along better than Seth and Knox do?

4. Why did Agad and Marat want Kendra and Seth to take over as the caretakers of Wyrmroost? In what ways were Agad and Marat correct? In what ways were they mistaken?

5. Did you agree with Seth's decision to return Vasilis early to the Singing Sisters? How might Vasilis have come in handy at Wyrmroost? How might it have made things worse?

6. Name some reasons the satyrs are good friends and companions for Seth. In what ways are they negative influences?

7. Calvin describes himself as a hero. In what ways did Calvin display heroic actions and attributes?

8. At the start of this story, Raxtus is the only dragon Kendra would consider a friend. Give some reasons Raxtus

was unhappy to have Kendra at Wyrmroost. How could his relationship with his father complicate his friendship with Kendra? Did Raxtus feel like a friend to Kendra in this story? Why or why not?

9. If you could have a guided tour of Wyrmroost hosted by three staff members of Blackwell Keep, would you take the opportunity? Why or why not? Which staff members would you choose as escorts? Why?

10. Why did Kendra and Seth decide to leave the safety of the magical barriers protecting Blackwell Keep, Terrabelle, and the five main roads? How could that decision have ended badly? Do you agree with their choice? Why or why not?

11. Seth argues that to have fun and pursue interests we sometimes need to take risks. What are some risks you take in your life? What are some risky activities you choose to avoid?

12. Marat said, "Disliking someone is almost as big a commitment as loving someone, and carries none of the benefits." How does hating someone require effort? How can it harm the person being hated? How can it harm the person doing the hating? What are the benefits of the effort that goes into loving somebody?

13. Seth tricked Knox into retrieving the hidden scepter. In what ways was that unfair to Knox? Why did Seth feel it was worth the risk?

14. Why did Kendra risk speaking to the Dragon King alone? What new ability did she develop as a result? When has doing something uncomfortable helped you develop a new talent or ability?